SPINNING JENNY

A Novel

Sylvia Ann McLain

ISBN: 1539890287
ISBN 13: 9781539890287

CHAPTER ONE

A line of slaves, coffled together, comes down a shady street. Cornelius watches them approach. He counts thirteen of them, bound together by iron collars, skins glistening in the Natchez heat. A trader rides behind them.

Cornelius hates dealing with slave-traders, the same way he knows not to touch any slime. But he needs to buy another field-hand, and this trader has a coffle. He's already been to the slave exchange of Franklin and Armfield's; he knows the prices there.

The slaves shuffle toward the corner where he waits. Most of them keep their eyes down, fixed on the hot road; but the last in line, a young girl, looks around at the busy town as she trots along.

The trader shouts for them to move into the shade of some trees beside the road. They sink onto the grass, their arms thrown out. He dismounts and props his gun against a tree.

Cornelius walks over. "You selling any of those?" he asks.

"They all for sale." The trader's eyes are slits in a leathery face. "All it takes is money."

"How much for one of the field-hands?"

"Six hundred easy. And the women, five-fifty up to six."

Cornelius fingers the four hundred dollars rolled in his pocket. "I can't go that high."

"How high kin you go?" The trader spits a stream of tobacco onto the ground.

Cornelius steps back. He knows he's rushing things, trying to buy another hand with the little money he's saved. But Malachi, his only slave, is old and can't do the hard work the cotton takes. And by summer's end Cornelius hopes to be a married man. He'll be meeting with Stephanie's father soon, and he needs to present himself as a man with a future. A two-slave man.

"I won't pay more than I need to," he says.

The trader looks around at the slaves. "That girl over there I could let go cheap," he says. He points to the little girl Cornelius noticed earlier; she sits with her knees pulled up under her chin, watching the two men. "She's strong. I can testify to that. She just walked clear from New Orleans. If you're short of means, she could be a field hand."

Flies hum. Sweat sticks his shirt to his back. Cornelius waits.

"She ain't got no fambly if that's what you're wonderin'," the trader says.

"Orphan?"

The trader shrugs. "I reckon."

Cornelius walks over to the girl. She straightens her legs and props herself back on her arms to look up at him.

"How old are you?" he asks.

No answer.

"How old, girl?"

"She's 'bout ten," the trader says. "And she don't speak English. That's why I'm lettin' her go so cheap. Whoever gets her'll have to teach her."

"She speak French?"

"Not that I've noticed. Actually, she's a Africky." He lowers his voice. "'Course, I'm telling you that in confidence, it being illegal to bring 'em in to the country and all, but I bought her off a boat that docked at night, down by New Orleans, with a hundred wild Africkies on board. They come by way of Cuba. This girl don't seem wild, though, bein' so young. She'd work out good as a field hand. She could be trained." He spits. "This coffle's been more trouble than most I've had. I even had to buy 'em some clothes in Baton Rouge so they wouldn't be travelling stark naked. They was wearing rags when I bought 'em. And that girl don't belong to any of the women, so they don't look out for her. But then I had to give 'em a little extra time at the rest-breaks, and go up on the rations a little, all because of her, so she could keep up." Another stream of tobacco splatters the grass. "I shouldn' a took her, I guess, but a short coffle's just like money wasted, 'cause you're gonna make the trip anyway."

Cornelius turns around to watch a driver passing with a wagon-load of men, en route to the slave market. "How much for that young 'un?"

"Oh, I could let her go for five."

"Five's too much for a young 'un that don't even speak the language."

"Well, four then."

"I'll take her for three-seventy-five, and not one picayune more." Cornelius looks away.

"Done." The trader motions for the girl to stand up. He fishes in his pocket for a pencil and a scrap of paper. "Here's your bill of sale," he says, scribbling. He holds out his hand. "And my three-seventy-five?"

Cornelius pulls out his roll of dollars and counts the money into the other man's palm. He looks at the bill of sale. "I can't make this out. What's her name?"

"Name her what you like," the trader says, folding the money away. "She ain't got no name but a Africky one anyway, I reckon. That's why I left that part blank. You fill it in." He unlocks the collar from around the girl's neck. "You better grab her. You got something to hold her?"

"I'll just hold her hand."

"Better tie her. She might run faster'n you think, and there goes your three-seventy-five."

Cornelius takes her hand. He sees with a sinking feeling how little she is, her head barely reaching his chest.

He walks with her out of the grove. They cross Commerce Street, a bustle of wagons and horses and cattle. He watches the traffic, wishing he could visit Stephanie. She's only three miles away from him at this very moment, at home in a red-brick mansion just east of town. But he'd wasted a good part of the day at Franklin and Armfield's, watching full hands go for more than he had in his pocket.

Buying this girl was a mistake, he thinks. She won't be able to be a half-hand, or even a quarter-hand, until she gets bigger. But now he can claim to be a two-slave man; that's the price he'll pay for Stephanie's hand in marriage. He's a slave owner for sure now, something his mammy told him never to be in his whole life. And his mammy only five years dead. She would've hated to see what he's become. She'd twist in her grave.

He leads the girl down the long slope of Silver Street to Natchez-Under-the-Hill, where the ferry docks. As they walk past the ramshackle buildings there, Cornelius catches the eye of a smiling woman in an open doorway. She sticks her tongue out at him. A little farther down the street he hears a shout and a woman's laughter coming from an upstairs window.

If he had money he could pass a day or two here. Life's quiet on the Bayou Cocodrie, too quiet when he's not working in the fields. And after all, when will he have a chance to spend time here again? Maybe never. But he has to think about Stephanie, about his future.

As they wait for the ferry, Cornelius studies the girl beside him. He can see that her hair, now tangled, was once braided against her scalp. And her skin's caked and crusty. The profile is handsome, though -- she has high cheekbones and almond-shaped eyes.

She watches the ferry glide across the river.

After it docks and the boatman gives the signal, passengers jostle onto the deck. They bring on crates of chickens and pigs, and one even drives a haltered yearling right onto the deck. Cornelius leads the girl to the front railing, away from the other passengers. When the boat moves out, she stands behind him, close to the middle of the deck. She watches the animals warily and steps behind Cornelius when a calf noses her.

As the ferry pulls away from the dock, Cornelius gazes glumly at the low Louisiana shoreline. "Well, you'll need a name," he muses. "I guess I'll call you Jenny, something I can say easy. That was my mammy's name, anyway. You be Jenny from now on." She stares at him. "Jenny," he repeats. "Malachi'll have to teach you the rest of the words you need."

When they get to the other side, Cornelius leads her up the low bank and points to where his horse is tied. "We've got twelve miles to go, Jenny," he says. "You can ride with me. I reckon you've walked enough if you came all the way from New Orleans. Lord, you do need a bath, though, girl." He mounts the horse and reaches down to pull her up, but she stands still. "Come on," he snaps.

He grabs her hand and pulls, swinging her up behind him. She grips the back of his saddle.

"You ever been on a horse before?" he asks. Probably not, he figures. "Nothing to be afraid of, Jenny girl."

He nudges the horse's sides and they canter over the rise into a flat region of woods and yawning fields. Her bare feet bob beside the saddle. "It'll be late when we get home," he says as they trot down a road where blackberry bushes hug the roadside; the sun's an orange ball sinking behind a line of trees.

The horse slows to a walk, and as twilight comes Cornelius's mood goes black too. The day's turned sour. Now he owns two slaves, and he needs both of them to work his fields. But one's an old man past his prime and the other's a skinny kid who can't speak the language. She'll have to be trained. But she was all he could afford.

Slumped in the saddle, he guides the horse west into the night. The air's grown sticky, even though a warm wind is blowing. After an hour the moon comes up behind them, lighting the road. By the time they reach the cabin on the banks of the Bayou Cocodrie, it's a few minutes past midnight, seventh of June, 1833.

CHAPTER TWO

In the morning Malachi wakes to a wet white fog blanketing the Cocodrie.

Going to the out-house in the half-light, he sees a lamp flicker at the window of the cabin, so he knows Cornelius is already up. A few minutes later, at the back door, Cornelius says, "Mornin', Mal," and hands him a plate of johnny-cakes. Mal holds the plate while Cornelius pours molasses over the pancakes, and then he sits on the porch steps and eats with his plate balanced on his knees.

As he does every morning, he looks out across the yard, but this morning there's no view; everything disappears into a wall of fog this side of the barn. Somewhere out there are the flat green fields that butt up against the swamp, and the shiny Bayou Cocodrie that slices the woods. The things he can make out -- the shed, the out-house, the rail fence -- look dark and shrunken. It's as if the world ends, right there at the fence.

He's been here three years, but this place isn't much like the other places he's lived, on the plantation south of New Orleans where he worked in the cane fields, or the big cotton plantation in Alabama where he married Lula. This territory west of Vidalia seems like a wild frontier. Somewhere out to the west is the Nolan's Trace, a road that runs clear over to Texas; and there's a river that's said to be the prettiest in Louisiana, called the Black River. It even has a ferry that'll take you to the other side. And right nearby here is the Bayou Cocodrie.

The big plantations here aren't like the ones he knew in Alabama. There, the plantation houses looked settled, as if they grew out of the ground a long time ago and were slowly sinking back into it. But here the big houses spring up tall out of the new-cut woods, and the hands have to clear the fields before they can plant them. Cabins and little farms sprout between the plantations. Everybody plants cotton and by nighttime everybody knows they've put in a day's work.

Master Cornelius's place isn't much, less than a hundred acres. But the work's easier here than in Alabama. And Cornelius is no hard task-master. He works about as hard as Malachi does most days. No, this ain't a bad place for his old bones, Malachi thinks, except for lonesomeness, which can't be helped on a place with only two men to run it.

But this girl, now. Malachi won't look at the bed on the porch where the girl sleeps. The old cornhusk bed is where he and Cornelius sit outside on cool evenings. But then last night Cornelius came back with this girl, and he pointed her to the nearest resting place, which happened to be the bed on the porch. She flopped down there and fell asleep without a word.

Malachi won't say a word about what looks to him like a foolish buy -- a puny girl instead of the strong field-hand they need. So he eats the hotcakes and then goes into the kitchen.

"When that girl wakes up let's show her how to chop cotton," Cornelius says, getting up from the table. He hands Malachi his empty cup. "We may as well get her started on the work. Meanwhile, I want to tramp that swamp by the bayou to see if it can be drained.

We might be able to ditch it. Let the girl eat something, and then we'll hand her a hoe. There's still some hotcakes left."

"Yessir."

The two men walk out to the porch. The girl is asleep on her stomach, her legs thrown out like two black sticks from under her shift.

"She won't eat much," Malachi says. "I bet she won't eat one whole hotcake."

Cornelius shrugs and turns to walk away. "Well, you see. You might have to use Indian signs with her. She don't speak English."

"Well, I sure as hell cain't use Indian signs," Malachi mutters after Cornelius has disappeared into the fog. He pours water from a bucket into a bowl and rinses the plates and cups and sets them upside down on a towel.

Maybe that girl can help in the cabin, Malachi thinks. He'd like to have somebody else doing this woman's work. The way it is now, Cornelius cooks and Malachi cleans up. And Cornelius is a fair cook; he said he learned it when his mammy was sick in Georgia and he had to take over the kitchen duties. The men eat what Malachi raises in the garden -- corn, beans, sweet potatoes, greens -- and drink what little milk the cow gives. Cornelius buys biddies at the store now and then, and the chickens have two choices: turn into good layers, or end up in the stewpot. Sometimes both. And their neighbor Missus Margaret McKee never comes to visit without bringing them some food.

But most of their meals come from what Malachi fishes and Cornelius hunts. Mal pulls fat catfish from the bayou, and Cornelius rolls the fillets in corn meal and fries them in butter. If Mal hooks a snapping garfish they eat that too, glad to have it even though it's full of bones and the eggs are poison.

And the venison Cornelius shoots -- dark steaks he soaks in milk and simmers in a pan -- the men eat those in silence with sharp jabs of their knives. In the winter Cornelius hunts woods hogs with his dog Leopard, and they eat the pork smoked or salted. And squirrels, rabbits, wild turkeys, birds -- all everyday meals. Malachi wishes Cornelius would bag possums and raccoons, but Cornelius won't eat them for some reason, so Mal goes without two of his favorite meats. Once Cornelius shot a bear and they ate that greasy thing, too.

But Cornelius can't cook the kind of roux-based food Mal got used to when he worked in the cane fields. Cornelius said he ate the Creole food in New Orleans before he came to the Cocodrie, but he can't cook it. Malachi knows that's so; when Cornelius makes a gumbo, it comes out bad, not spiced enough, or something. What Cornelius learned to make in his mammy's kitchen was plain country fare. Still, Malachi admires Cornelius for being able to cook.

It'd be good to have the girl do some of the kitchen work, Mal thinks, but not if it means he'll have to work harder in the fields. No, maybe it's better to keep her out of the kitchen altogether.

He sets hotcakes on a plate for her, breaking off a piece of one golden cake for himself. He pours himself the rest of the coffee and sits down at the table, rubbing his stubbled chin. "Law, I'm hoping we don't try to ditch that field," he mumbles. "I ain't up to that hard work." He finishes his coffee and rinses his cup.

He wanders out to the back porch. The bed where the girl slept is empty.

He walks to the end of the porch and looks over to the outhouse. Has she gone there? Most likely. When she comes out, he'll see if she wants a hotcake. The sun's a white halo in the early morning haze. When the fog lifts, it'll be a fine day, cool for June: a day he'd rather spend fishing than ditching.

First he has to see that she eats something. The privy door's ajar.

"Girl?"

He goes over to the privy and looks inside, but it's empty. Then he walks back through the cabin. He'd have seen her if she'd gone through the cabin. She's not out in the yard, at least not for the twenty feet or so he can see before the fog walls everything in.

He looks across the yard at his cabin. Cornelius built the one-room house for himself when he first came to the Cocodrie. But by the time Malachi got here, Cornelius had already built himself the bigger house with two rooms. It has a floor of wide pine boards and a porch on the front and back. But the names stayed backward: the men call Malachi's quarters the "little house," while Cornelius's respectable house is "the cabin."

The little house is way better than some quarters he's had. At the cotton plantation in Alabama, the roof of his cabin was so bad that him and Lula sat soaked and miserable whenever the heavens opened. But here the roof only leaks in two places, little drips but not over the bed, and the walls are chinked tight. Malachi is suddenly worried about the place where he sleeps. What he feared most about Cornelius buying another field-hand was that the new hand would be put in with him. From here the little house looks just the way he left it. But the girl might've gone there to find herself a better bed.

Well, he won't take to the idea of having anybody but himself in his bed. The girl would probably get the husks all shifted into some new shape, and, being a kid, she might even wet the bed. He stomps across the yard. But when he opens the door, he sees that his place looks just as he left it, the bed angled into one corner with a quilt pulled over it, his jacket and hat hanging from a rack of antlers on the wall.

He walks back across the yard and around to the back of the cabin. In the fog he can't see even the trees along the bayou where Cornelius is, so he shouts, "Master Cornelius!" No answer. He climbs over the rail fence and hurries toward the trees. "Master Cornelius!"

"What is it?"

"I can't find the girl," Malachi says. "She's nowhere 'round. Maybe you better come help me look."

"You over by the gate?" Cornelius comes out of the fog like a ghost. "Can't find her? She was right there asleep on the bed."

"Well, she ain't there now," Malachi says. "I was inside cleaning up, and when I come out, the bed was empty."

"All right. Let's go look."

Cornelius calls out as they near the house. "Where are you, Jenny?"

"Jenny. So that's her name," Malachi mutters as he tramps along behind. "Nice of you to finally tell me."

"Jenny!" Cornelius yells.

"She ain't around here nowheres," Malachi says. "I looked all around, even looked in the little house. Looked in the privy. That girl's run away."

"She can't run away. She don't know where she is."

"Well, she ain't here."

Cornelius walks through the cabin and stands on the porch for a moment. "All right, you saddle Tearose and I'll go looking. Maybe she took off down the road."

"Yessir."

Malachi sits on the steps and watches Cornelius go back into ghost-land. "Don't know how you gonna find her in this fog," he says. "She could be hiding in the woods, or anywhere else. Mebbe she ain't down the road a-t'all. She might a gone the other way. How much trouble'd you get when you brung that young'un here?"

Cornelius shouts for her at the next turn in the road, pulling Tearose to a skittering halt. Maybe she's squatting down in the fields so she can't be seen, or hiding in the woods, afraid to come out. He curses under his breath; he should have waked her up earlier so she could learn the place. But he didn't, and maybe she didn't like Malachi's looks. So she ran away.

Where the road turns to the right, a stream runs across a low place. Would she go that way?

On an impulse Cornelius rides into the woods, where vines and moss hang like ribbons from the oaks. The horse steps gingerly over bare roots that snake outward from the old trees. When he calls out the girl's name, his voice echoes back. He knees the horse around a turn, and there she is, standing by a tree, her arms straight down to her sides and her shoulders slumping. The color of her shift is the color of the tree-trunk.

"Jenny?"

She turns around. Her wild hair sticks out, and her face is teary and crumpled.

He reaches down and grabs her wrist.

"What do you mean running off like that? You can't wander around out here in the woods! You want some wild bear to eat you up?"

He realizes he's wasting his breath, since she can't understand a word he says. But the tone of his voice will make an impact, he figures. She glances up at him and then looks down at the ground, swallowing ragged sobs.

He pulls her up to ride behind him as he'd done yesterday.

But he's flustered about her running away; he'll lose his profit from the cotton last year if she disappears.

"You just forget about running off, you hear me? I'm not letting you go. You *are* going to stay at the cabin, and you *are* going to hoe cotton. So you can just forget about running off." But he knows she probably suffered at the hands of the slave-mongerer he bought her from, and since she can't speak his language and he can't speak hers, she'll have to learn things slowly. As they ride back to the cabin, he feels ragged sobs shaking her.

"Oh, shit, Jenny, I'm sorry," he mutters, kicking the horse's side to goad it into a trot.

Malachi is sitting on the steps when they ride up.

"Found her in the woods, Mal," Cornelius says. He still feels rattled. Jenny slides off the horse, still sniffling.

"That girl ain't big as a minute," Malachi says. "Seem to me you might as well have let her run on off."

"She's big enough to hoe cotton," Cornelius snaps. "And I'm not letting her run off. She was just scared, that's all. You get her some hotcakes like I told you to. I'm going back down to the swamp to figure out where we can put that ditch." He stalks away.

Malachi studies Jenny. "Where'd he get you, anyways, girl?" he asks. "I bet you didn't come from Franklin and Armfield's, not with you dressed like that. When I was there they was most interested that we put on a good appearance for the buyers. No, I bet he got you from some old trader somewheres." He snorts. "You come on in the kitchen with me. I don't want you lightin' out again. He'd figure it was my fault for sure if you run off again." He motions to the girl to come into the cabin with him, but she stands still.

"Get on in here, girl!" he snaps, but she doesn't move. "You come here!" He reaches over and grabs her arm to pull her toward the porch. But she digs in her heels. The pain in Malachi's bad back flares sharply. He can't pull her. He turns her loose suddenly and she falls backward. Then she hops to her feet and sprints away, across the yard toward the woods.

Malachi throws his hat to the ground. "You come back here, girl! This minute! You gonna get a beatin' sure enough this time!" But she's already run into the woods.

He raises his fist. "God a-mighty, now I gotta go tell Cornelius she's gone again!" He storms through the cabin and out across the back porch, pushing past the bed where the girl slept last night. He kicks the rickety frame, sending it a few inches down the porch. Then he hurries toward the swamp, his back burning at every step. He sees Cornelius striding toward him.

"She's gone again!" Mal shouts.

Cornelius didn't hear, so Mal shouts again, "She's run off!"

"Run off again?" Cornelius lopes toward him.

"Run off quicker'n lightnin'," Malachi pants. "And me without even my back turned. Run so fast, there wasn't nothin' I could do but watch her go, and then come get you. You'll have to get the horse again."

Cornelius glares. "What is wrong with you, Mal? Can't you even hang onto a stupid young 'un?" He storms out of the field, Malachi following an angry distance behind.

CHAPTER THREE

"Which way did she head?" Cornelius asks when they get back to the cabin.

Malachi points. "Out that way, and she didn't even look back. Just left like she sure didn't plan to stay here."

"Well, she's stayin', whether she likes it or not," Cornelius snaps. "If she went in the woods over there, she'll probably end up at Randall's place. I'll try to head her off where the road comes out of the woods."

He looks first in the woods, but she's not where he found her before. And she's not at Randall's, a place about a mile to the west, where the land is higher. And she hasn't been seen at the shack belonging to Hallorans, poor whites who live in the scraggly woods along the bayou. That leaves only Cedar Breaks, the plantation of Jake Turley. Cornelius spurs the tired horse to a gallop.

Cedar Breaks, of all places. The largest plantation in the Cocodrie, and the most profitable. Most planters make eight bales of cotton for every field-hand they work, but the Turley place makes far more than that on its nine hundred arpents. But how?

Because Turley leaves it all -- cotton row and cabin row, as the saying goes -- to his overseer Dubrenne for weeks at a time while he and his wife go off to Natchez. Dubrenne knows how to use the whip, gossips say, and he's stingy handing out the meat and molasses.

But overseers are hard-bitten men, so most people don't blame Turley and his batty wife for what goes on at Cedar Breaks. It's Dubrenne that people avoid, in town. And they whisper about him after he passes. He takes mistresses among the slave women and fights with the men, and it's said he goes after young girls -- slave girls as young as twelve. Cornelius spurs his horse to a gallop.

An hour later the fog lifts, as Cornelius rides up to the main house at Cedar Breaks. Beyond the trees, cotton fields stretch toward a blue line of woods.

Off to the left a lane passes in front of a row of slave cabins and ends at a whitewashed cottage that Cornelius figures must be the overseer's house. The cabins look deserted except for the last cabin where an old woman sits outside, watching over some toddlers.

He rides to the overseer's house and knocks on the door. When no one answers, he turns back toward the main house.

As he passes the cabins, the woman minding the babies calls out, "Sir, if you lookin' for Master Dubrenne, he ain't there."

"Is he down in the field?"

"Well, he might be in the field, or he might be up at the big house."

Cornelius hears the accent in the woman's words. What is it – Jamaican? Is this how Jenny would sound if she talked?

"I'm looking for my girl Jenny," Cornelius calls, but she seems not to hear. She picks up one of the toddlers and goes inside the cabin.

At the main house, Jake Turley himself opens the door. Turley's white hair stands up in wisps above his yellowy face.

"Mister Turley, good afternoon. I'm looking for my girl that's run away. She's about this high," he holds his hand at chest level, "and she don't talk. She come this way?"

"Ain't seen her." Turley starts to close the door.

Cornelius steps forward. "She could've come into your fields, over by the road. She run away from my place through the woods, and that would've taken her out by the road. It leads this way."

"It leads other places too. She come here, I'll let you know." He closes the door.

Cornelius turns back to his horse, passing some field hands. He can't ask them for information; Turley might be watching right now from behind one of those dark windows, and Cornelius knows better than to ask slaves for information a master won't give. If he did, the slaves would pay. So he mounts Tearose and gallops off the place.

Alice Turley has been good as childless for a long time. Her last boy Andre, angry and sullen, left home ten years ago, and since then she's lived a lonely life. Neither of her sons ever visit or send a letter, and she doesn't know where they're living. And Jake, married to her for half a century, seems a stranger now. He sleeps in Andre's old bedroom at the other end of the house, saying he needs a whole bed to himself and can't stand the way Alice thrashes about in the hot nights.

This morning Alice hears the sound of hooves on the drive outside, and she peers through the bedroom window. "Eula, who's that out there?" she says to her maid.

Eula walks to the window. "Well, it look like Master Cornelius Carson. I don't know what he'd want."

"Probably come to see Dubrenne." Alice watches the visitor ride away. Without turning around she says, "You gettin' all my dresses ready for Natchez? *All* of 'em, not just the street dresses? The party dresses, too?"

"Yes'm. Me and Lydia gettin' them ready. They be ready when you go to leave."

And you can't hardly wait 'til I'm gone, can you, worthless? Alice thinks. She starts to say something else, but when she turns around Eula's already gone, taking the coffee cup she wants refilled.

She walks across the room and stands in front of the mirror, patting down her hair and smoothing her skirt. Maybe the gentleman caller will come back. An hour ago she'd put her on her old black frock with a red silk rose pinned to the shoulder, something she wore to a party in Natchez last winter. Now she sees that dust from the floor has drawn a light-colored ring around the bottom of her skirt. The dress is too old to be worn in Natchez this year, but that silly Eula ought to notice it needs washing. Or Lydia, who's supposed to be the laundress.

The bedroom smells musty; Eula needs to empty the pot. So Alice goes downstairs; looking through the parlor windows, she sees Jake riding away. So he's gone off without her and not bothered to say where he's going. She twists her mouth to hide the hurt. A dark hole of abandonment yawns in front of her, but she forces it away. She goes out to the back porch and sits on the rickety chair there.

"You bring over that bucket! I'm tellin' you to do it, girl!" Inside the house Eula is screeching at -- who? Lydia? Tamsy? Alice doesn't turn around to look. Eula's always squawking about something, trying to get the other girls to do their share of the housework.

Alice will just sit here in the silvery light, her hands folded in her lap. She can ignore the house-girls' squabbling. She doesn't care about women's work -- gardening, cooking, sewing, knitting, darning; it's pointless to her. And Jake pays it no mind. Only the cotton matters to Jake.

He said they're going to Natchez next week, so she'll just bide her time, living for her visit to Natchez. Today is just a fog-wrapped country afternoon of no particular interest.

Cornelius rides slowly, looking into the woods. If the girl's gone for good, there goes his whole profit from the cotton last year. He can put up posters like those he sometimes sees tacked to trees along the roads, advertising runaways. And there'll have to be a cash reward for her return. But paid with what?

He spurs the horse to a gallop as he nears the cabin. Malachi is sitting on the porch.

"She come back?" Cornelius asks.

"No sir. I took the mule and looked all through the fields, but she ain't there. You tried the Turley place?"

"I tried there, and Hallorans', and Randall's. She's not anywhere unless she's hiding out in some deep swamp, and I don't guess I'd ever find her in there."

"That girl's brung us some big trouble, I'd say," Malachi says. "I'll fetch you some food." He brings out a plate of beans and cornbread and hands it to Cornelius. "This is what you made yesterday morning."

Cornelius sits on the top step and eats. The sun hangs low.

"Well, we know she can't go that way," Malachi said, pointing toward the east, "'cause she'd come to the bayou, and I doubt she'd want to swim it."

"Not likely."

Malachi scratches his head. "The last time I seen her she was headin' down that path over there. That's where I seen her go. And where it forks, one fork leads over by the Hallorans', and the other goes by Master Turley's place. I don't know what that leaves, if Master Halloran ain't seen her."

Cornelius stares at the place where the path curves past some palmettos around the base of a pine tree and into the woods.

"Mal, I still think she's at Turley's."

Alice would like to go for a drive, but Jake's always too busy to take her. And she can't drive out in the countryside alone, it wouldn't be proper, and she doesn't want to drive with one of the slaves. The only way she's found to break the monotony of this dreary country life is to take long walks down the roads and side-paths of the plantation, but today she doesn't feel like walking.

From the porch Alice can see out across the fields where the field hands are working. They look an inch high above the carpet of green cotton. She wonders if Toussaint and Patsy are out there in the field. They're two of the ordinariest, sweatiest, tiredest-looking hands on the place. They'd be hard to pick out from this distance.

But just a few days ago, on one of her long walks, she'd seen Toussaint and Patsy -- it makes her heart pound even now to remember it -- lying naked on the ground at an open place in the woods, not far from the bayou. And Toussaint was on top of Patsy, their shiny bodies moving in unison, their limbs entangled. She'd watched from behind a tree, fascinated. This furtive thing in her own life, something Jake gave up long ago, was being done right out in the open, in the sunlight. Patsy and Toussaint must've slipped away from the cotton field for it when Dubrenne went up to the house for something.

She'd watched, open-mouthed, until Toussaint shuddered and rolled away from Patsy and they both lay panting, naked as the day they were born and both of them looking pleased as if they'd done something that took intelligence.

Then they'd jumped up like they heard a shot and grabbed their clothes. Toussaint tried to grab Patsy again but she pushed him away with a slap and a giggle before he chased her back through the woods toward the cottonfield.

That was a week ago. Now Alice hopes she'll see two of the ant-like figures slip away from the others and head for the woods. But they all seem to be working steadily. She squints and shades her eyes with her hand, trying to make out which is Patsy, and which is Toussaint.

A shout coming up from the barn startles her. It's a commotion; two figures are coming to the house. As they get closer Alice sees that it's the field-hand Lathan and a much smaller person, and there's a struggle between them.

Lathan's face is sweat-sheened. "Miz Turley, I foun' this girl down by the fence hidin'," he says. "What you want me to do with her?"

Alice stands up. "Who is she?"

"I dunno, ma'am. I asked her, but she wouldn't say." The girl looks down at the ground; Lathan holds her arm.

"Well, leave her here, I guess. Who does she belong to?"

"Ain't no tellin', ma'am." He turns loose of the girl's arm but keeps one hand on the back of her shift. "Uh, Miz Turley, I a little bit afraid this girl might bolt."

"Did you ask her who she is? Bring her on over here to me. I'll hold her."

"She won't talk." Lathan pulls the girl over to the porch. Alice takes the girl's arm.

"Whose girl could you be?" Alice looks into the girl's face. "Well, I bet they'd like to know where you are. You run away, I reckon. You come inside with me."

A fly drones in from outside and follows them down the hall. Alice calls, "Eula? Tamsy?" No answer.

She takes the girl into the parlor and closes the door behind her, in case what Lathan said is true, the girl might bolt. The room is dark after the glare of the outdoors. Alice turns up the lamp; its flame glows through the smudged chimney-glass that Eula forgets to clean.

"You smell the worst of anybody I ever smelt," Alice mutters, sitting down on the sofa and staring at the girl. "But you know, you could be a foundling. Wouldn't Mister Turley be surprised if you just turned up here, and we got you without a penny's cost." She runs her hands up and down the girl's thin arms.

"Cat got your tongue? Maybe you're deaf and dumb." The girl's hair hasn't been brushed in a long time, and her skin's caked with dirt; but she's little and scared-looking and she looks like an ebony doll in a ragged shift. Alice saw a doll like that once, in a shop in New Orleans. "You don't talk? If you a mute, you could be my pet," Alice says. "It's been a long time since I had a pet. I had Tamsy, and Patsy before that, but those girls just grew up so quick. You could be my new pet. I'll just get you cleaned up, and give you a dress, and brush this hair. You really ain't a bad-looking girl."

CHAPTER FOUR

Cornelius holds Tearose to a steady canter the entire ride, stopping only once to let the horse drink from a stream. By the time he gets back to Cedar Breaks, the sun is behind the trees and blue shadows stretch across the cotton fields. Slaves are walking to the cabins.

Cornelius rides to the big house and ties Tearose in front of the gallery. He knocks on the door. The house-girl who answers has a round young face, a white tignon on her head.

"Master Turley here?" he asks.

"No sir." Her voice is a quavering soprano whisper.

"Is Master Dubrenne here?"

"He down in the fields."

"I'll go find him." Cornelius walks around the side of the house, past sheds, cribs, and privies, and then down a path between the barn and the cotton-house. Beyond a rail fence he can see field-hands lining up at a shed; the small figure supervising them is Dubrenne. The overseer has a well-polished pistol stuck in his belt. The field-hands form a ragged line, keeping their eyes down. One by one they step inside the shed to lay their hoes down, then step back out.

"Mr. Dubrenne, I need to speak to you," Cornelius calls.

The overseer looks around and motions the line of slaves to stop. "Yeah?"

Cornelius hops the fence. "I lost a girl, about this high. She ran off, and I think she must've come by this way."

"Well, I ain't seen her. If I do, I'll send one of the boys to tell you." He turns his back to Cornelius and motions for the slaves to move the line along.

Cornelius hesitates. He has no evidence that Jenny's here, just a hunch, but he figures if Dubrenne has her, he won't want to say so. And she could be hiding most anywhere on this big plantation.

"She won't talk, and she's wearing a shift," Cornelius says.

"I told you, I ain't seen 'er," Dubrenne says without looking around.

Cornelius looks at the men and women in line, their coal-black faces shiny with sweat, unreadable. He can't ask them. But if Jenny's here, some of them might know it. "She's about this high," he says again. "She's very dark, and she don't speak English." He wants the slaves to hear him.

Dubrenne motions the line to stop. He turns around to face Cornelius. "I told you she ain't here," he mutters.

"She must've come this way," Cornelius says. "She's just this tall--"

"Are you hard a hearin'?" Dubrenne steps toward him. But as he did, Cornelius sees two men waiting in line look over at the corn-crib beyond the fence.

"I think we oughta look around here," Cornelius says. "She's a runaway. She's probably around here somewhere." He points. "Let's check that crib."

"I'm telling you she ain't here."

"Oh, I believe you, but you never know with a girl like Jenny. She could be hiding most anywhere." He walks toward the corn-crib and scales the fence.

Dubrenne curses and stalks after him. "She ain't here, I say. Hell, you think she's shut herself up in a crib? Look at the size of that lock. You know we gotta keep it locked to keep the hands from stealing. Now how's your girl gonna get herself in there and then lock it from the outside?"

"Why don't we take a look?"

"Because I ain't got the key, that's why." Dubrenne touches his pistol.

"Well, you better find it, because I aim to open that door one way or another." This little man thinks his pistol makes him a foot taller. Still, Cornelius hadn't thought, when he rode away from his cabin, to bring his own weapon. He folds his arms and plants his feet apart, staring at the overseer. "I just been up at the main house, and Mister Turley said I should look around. He said a girl like Jenny could be hiding most anywhere here. You just get the key."

Dubrenne glances toward the big house. "You're wasting my time." He turns to a man walking along the fence. "Toussaint, go get me the key for this crib." He faces Cornelius again. "I'm tellin' you, your girl ain't on this place."

Toussaint comes back with a ring of keys. Dubrenne flips the keys in his palm and then jams one into the lock, which falls open with a clank.

Cornelius pulls the door open. The crib is pitch-black inside, but after a moment he can just make out the pile of unhusked corn filling half the crib. He ducks through the low door, inhaling the cool musty air. Jenny's not there.

"Satisfied?" Dubrenne asks.

Cornelius walks away. But as he strides past Toussaint, he sees the field-hand point toward the main house.

Cornelius stops. Would Jenny be hidden in the house? She could be in a closet or downstairs in the cellar.

He walks over to the house and climbs the steps to the small back porch, which is cluttered with buckets and milk-cans and a rickety-looking chair. The same startled-looking girl who'd greeted him earlier answers his knock on the back door.

"I'm looking for a runaway girl," Cornelius says. "Is she in this house?"

The girl backs away, nodding. "Yessir. A girl come here this evenin'. She upstairs with Miz Alice."

"I'm here to get her." He follows the girl down a short hallway that leads to the front of the house. At that moment Alice Turley comes down the stairs.

"Why, Mister Carson, whatever brings you back here today?" She half-smiles.

"Mrs. Turley," he says, holding his hat in his hand, "I'm looking for my girl Jenny, a runaway about this high. Your housegirl said she was here."

Alice draws in a short breath. "Oh, she's *your* girl," she says, glancing toward the top of the stairs. "I didn't know whose she was. And Lydia told you--"

"Yes, ma'am."

Alice looks as if she wants to say something else. But then she says, "I'll get your girl." She goes upstairs, leaving Cornelius in the dark hall.

A moment later Jenny creeps down the stairs. She wears a different dress now, a faded blue dress with a patched skirt. Alice comes down right behind her.

"I was gonna clean her up," Alice says, "but I only got as far as the dress. And I couldn't coax a word out of her all afternoon."

"I'll get the dress back to you," Cornelius says as he reaches out to take Jenny's hand.

"Oh, no. It's an old one of Patsy's. Let her keep it, her being a mute and all."

"Thank you, ma'am," Cornelius says. "Sorry she troubled you."

"Oh, no trouble..." Alice follows them to the front door.

Outside, Dubrenne walks toward him. "Sir --" he starts to say, but Cornelius looks away. He leads Jenny over to where Tearose is tied.

Dubrenne follows. "Mister Carson--"

"I believe slave-stealing's still a crime in this parish," Cornelius says. He swings into the saddle and yanks Jenny up in front of him.

They gallop away from Cedar Breaks and onto the road that leads back to his cabin. Jenny's head bobs with the horse's gait, her matted hair just under Cornelius's chin.

A mute, Alice Turley said. That hadn't occurred to him.

I never should've bought this girl, Cornelius thinks as Tearose slows to a canter. The road is dark under glittering stars. She's been nothing but trouble all day long. Maybe he can sell her, and use the money to buy a real field-hand. But who'd buy a mute for any decent price? He's bound to lose money. No, he's stuck with her now. And he has only himself to thank.

Now and then a shadowy animal streaks across the road. As they ride up to the cabin, Malachi comes out holding up a lantern.

"I got her back," Cornelius says as he sets Jenny down in front of the porch and then dismounts. "They had her in the house at Turley's place."

"Oh Lord, I've heard about what goes on over there," Malachi says. "I'm scared to look at 'er, for fear she'll light out again."

"Then don't look at her. Put the horse away." He takes Jenny's hand and leads her into the cabin.

She stands in the middle of the room as Cornelius lights the lamp. He sits on the straight chair and pulls off his high boots and sets them against the wall. Then he points Jenny to the rocking chair. She sits on the edge of the seat, her hands resting lightly on the sides of the chair.

"Question is now, how we gonna keep her from running off again?" Malachi asks when he comes back in.

"Damned if I know. It's possible she's a mute. But she's gotta start understanding things. And she better start tonight, because I been chasing her all day, and I'm too tired to run after her if she lights out again."

Cornelius pulls his chair up in front of the girl. Malachi leans against the wall next to the rack of antlers where Cornelius's buckskin jacket hangs.

"Now, look, Jenny," Cornelius says, "you're gonna have to stay right here. And you're gonna have to learn some things. For your own good, and mine too. And I know you don't understand a word I'm saying." He glances at Malachi, who shrugs.

"Tell you what, Mal, this girl's bound to be hungry," Cornelius says. "There any biscuit left, or any cornbread?"

"There's cornbread. I ate the last of the biscuit."

"Well, bring the cornbread over here, will you, and some milk, too. She's probably not eaten anything all day."

Cornelius continues, "We'll start with your name again. Jenny. Jeh-nee. That's you." He points at the girl and says "Jeh-nee." She stares at him grimly.

Malachi hands Cornelius a cup of milk. "Here," Cornelius says, handing it to her. She drinks in big gulps. Then he hands her a plate of cornbread, and she breaks off big chunks and stuffs them into her mouth. She sits with crumbs sticking to her chin and a white milk mustache lining her upper lip.

"You can't run off anymore," Cornelius says. "It's not safe. You've gotta stay right here on this place. Are you listening to me?"

The girl begins to test the rocker, leaning back and letting the chair rock forward, her dusty feet landing flat on the bearskin rug. But her expression is haggard.

Cornelius leans forward with his arms resting on his knees and stares at her. "All right, you don't understand me anyway. But you've got to understand that you have to stay here. There's no other choice, because there's no place else for you to go. You can't go back where you came from. You better be right here in the morning. You can sleep on the floor in the little house with Malachi."

Malachi comes away from the wall as if a wasp has gotten into his pants. "Uh, Master Cornelius, sir, I don't think that's such a good idea."

"Why not?"

"Well, they's just not space enough for anybody else to sleep in the little house. Nossir. They's just barely enough space for my bed. I believe we better find some other place for this girl."

"Then where we gonna put her?"

"Same place she was last night, I'd say. If it was good enough for last night, it'll still do."

"How we gonna keep her there? She might run off if she sleeps out in the open like that."

"Well, she can't sleep in with me. No. I don't believe that'd work."

"All right, then *you* sleep out on the porch with her tonight. Bring up your mattress and make a pallet there on the floor by her."

"I gotta sleep on the porch?"

"Unless you want to put her in the little house."

"Well, what if she slips away in the night while I'm sleepin'?"

"You don't let her slip away, that's all."

Malachi sighs. "I'll go bring my mattress up."

As the old man goes out the door, Cornelius sits with his shoulders hunched, his hands clasped loosely between his knees as he studies the girl who rocks back and forth. She might never learn the first thing, much less ever be a proper field-hand. Maybe there'd be a buyer for her somewhere; the Cocodrie was hungry for hands. Maybe some woman would take her on for a housegirl, where she could learn how to do things and not run off. He might even make money on the deal. He'd never sell her to Jake Turley, no matter what the profit. But if an offer came from someone else ... But she'd be hard to sell, with her frank eyes and her defeated look. And being a mute. Who'd want her?

Jenny rocks back and forth, watching him. Malachi comes back with his mattress across his shoulder. He carries it to the back porch and slings it down beside the sofa.

"Come on, Jenny, I've got to show you some things," Cornelius says, motioning her to follow him out to the back. He leads her across the yard to the privy, but she hangs back when he opens the door to the dark little building.

"All right, the smell'll tell you what it's for, so it's here when you need it." He takes her to the back porch again and motions for her to get up on the high bed. "This is your bed," he said, patting the corn-husk mattress. "Bed," he repeats.

She climbs up on the bed and lies with her arms straight down at her sides. "You'd better be here when the sun comes up," Cornelius says, shaking his finger at her, "because I can't chase you any more, girl."

Weariness washes over him and he sits down on the top step. "Mal, break out the jug. I need some whiskey."

"I expect you do," Malachi says, getting up to get the jug from the cabin. Then for an hour the two men sit on the steps and drink, passing the jug back and forth and not bothering with a glass for either of them. Malachi grows drowsy while Cornelius tries to think of a way he can sell the girl for a profit.

CHAPTER FIVE

From where Jenny lies on the bed, she can see the silhouettes of the two men who sit on the step, their backs to her. Beyond them, a million stars twinkle against the black sky. Far off, a dark line of trees rises.

She's just numb now. She can't run away. She understands that now. The tall man brought her back here again and again, talking to her all the while.

"Jeh-nee." That was what she heard most. "Jeh-nee."

All day she ran, only to find herself in a strange house where an old woman took her out of her shift and put her in this patched blue dress. She fingers the soft sides of the skirt.

But the tall man came for her again.

Where on earth is she? Where is Mother? Or Kofi? Will she ever find them again?

All at once she sees her mother -- an image clearer than the silhouettes of the men. For an instant, it's bright sunlight -- sun on the Accra plain, trees in the distance, and her mother, smiling, her head high and the baby tied on her back. And Kofi walking up ahead. She blinks as the vision shines clear as daylight. Then the vision crumbles, cracks into a million pieces and winks out.

The men turn around to look at her as she sits up on the bed, staring into the darkness. But the vision is gone.

She lies down again.

There's a scuffling of boots as the men get up. The tall man goes into the house and the old man walks over and lowers himself onto the mattress by her bed. He flails around for a minute, muttering. Then silence.

She sits up again and looks down the dark length of the porch, at the glittering sky, at the dark woods. Now her mother is a memory of a vision. She saw her so plainly.

I am Abena, Esi's child. I am the prettiest girl in the village.

"Jeh-nee," she says. "Jeh-nee." That's what the men say to her so often, and the word sounds strange. The man on the floor snores.

She'll keep the vision of her mother in her mind. It will comfort her.

She yawns. Then, for the first time in many weeks, she sleeps in the same place she slept the night before.

"That Jenny seem more reasonable today," Malachi says. "I believe she might work out all right."

The girl watches the men. She's eaten a plate of Cornelius's hotcakes and molasses and now stands with her arms encircling one of the porch-supports, one bare foot propped atop the other.

"I guess today's as good as any to get her working in the cotton," Cornelius says. "The grass'll take it if we don't get after it. I'll take her out to the field. You come on down when you finish here." He hands Malachi his coffee cup and beckons for the girl to follow him. He leads her out to the lean-to shed next to the stable where he keeps his tools.

"This'll about fit you," he says, handing her a hoe and taking a different one for himself. He leads her across the open yard behind the stable and over the fence.

Then they're in the field, in long rows of cotton stretching straight to the woods along the bayou. A thin layer of ground fog lies above the cotton plants, lifting in wisps as the sun burns it off. The field, wet with dew, has a rich rank smell.

"Now, you see these weeds," Cornelius says, pointing to the green shoots which poke through the earth between the cotton plants. "If we don't chop 'em out, they'll choke the cotton and it won't make a stand. So here's how we hoe it." He bends his long back into the work. He slices the corner of his hoe into the earth and pulls toward each cotton plant. Then he hacks away the grass that's sprouted since he hoed this row two weeks ago. The chopped weeds lie uprooted and wilting in the furrow. He works all around the plant, careful not to bring his hoe too close to the precious stalk of the cotton plant itself, until finally the bush stands by itself in the rich Delta soil.

"Now you try it," he says to Jenny, pointing to the next plant. She stands still, resting the heel of her hoe on the ground. So Cornelius reaches over and chops the hoe into the ground for her. Then he points at the ground again.

She copies his motions, hacking clumsily. Cornelius moves her hands down on the handle, left hand under right, so she can use more force. Then he steps across to the next row.

"Now I'll do this row and you do that row, and see if you can keep up with me," he says. But she steps over to the next row too.

Cornelius sighs. "All right, we'll both chop the same row. You work behind me." He walks around her and begins to chop again. She copies what he does, watching him out of the corner of her eyes. When he stops and stands upright to rest his back, she stops too.

"Now look, I don't know what good it's going to do to have us both working the same plants. I've got 'em done before you get to 'em. You can't do anything but cause damage. Let's hopscotch 'em." So he chops one plant and leaves the next, letting her work the odd plants. She hacks at the ground. "Malachi ought to be getting out here soon," he says after a few minutes, as sweat runs down his face.

Finally, after what seems to Cornelius far too long a time, Malachi walks out to the field, his hoe resting on his shoulder. Cornelius is struck by the older man's gimping walk. Little wonder the fields take so long to hoe, what with Malachi's bad back. But slow and steady would do the job, if the girl could learn the work.

Malachi carries a water-jug which he hands to Cornelius, who swings it to his shoulder and takes a long swallow. Then he hands the jug to Jenny.

"Mal, you take over here for a while. I need to go up to the cabin," Cornelius says. "I've got a letter to write. And tomorrow I'm going to Natchez."

Malachi fans his face with his straw hat. "Yessir. This girl learning to work a cotton field?"

"Maybe. Jenny, go sit under that tree over there and cool off." He points to an oak tree some yards away. The girl looks over at the tree and then back at Cornelius, but she doesn't move.

"Let's go, Jenny." Cornelius motions her to follow him.

Under the tree, roots splay out in knobby fingers. Moss from its curving branches sweeps almost to the ground. Jenny sits where he points, between the horns of two roots with her back against the trunk and her legs straight out in front of her. "Now I'm going up to the house," he says. "You rest a few minutes, then go work some more with Malachi."

He walks back down the furrow to where Malachi is. "You watch her that she doesn't run off. See if you can do a better job at it than you did yesterday, all right? Get her back out here to chop before too long."

"Yes sir. I don't believe she'll run off no more. I'll see to it she don't."

Malachi hoes as Cornelius walks away. "You gonna write a letter, huh?" he says when Cornelius is too far away to hear. "Never knowed you to scribble too many letters before. No sir. And you makin' all these trips to Natchez. Bet there's somepin' you ain't tellin' me. Somepin' big up your sleeve."

A few minutes later he calls out to the girl, "Get on over here, Jenny. We got work to do." She's pulled some strands of moss down from low-hanging branches and spread the strands on the ground.

"Get over here, girl!"

He walks over to where she sits and pulls her up by her arm. She scrambles to her feet.

"Look, miss, you got to work this here field. Cornelius didn't get you so you could sit around playing, you hear? He brought you here to make things easier on me. My back hurts and I ain't about to chop this field by myself. So you just get over there."

He points to the field. Jenny rubs her arm where he grabbed it, and glares at him. Then she grabs her hoe and tramps back into the field, where she begins to chop.

"That's better. Just go a little faster," Malachi says, and picks up his own hoe. Together they slowly work their way down the row and back again. Malachi sees that her plants aren't as clean as they should be, but at least they're half-hoed.

He mops his face with his bandanna. "You got to get better at it than this," he says, "but I guess for the first time that ain't bad.

How 'bout we go sit under that tree for a spell?" Jenny follows him to the tree and they both plop down, Malachi with his back against the trunk, his straw hat pulled down over his eyes, and Jenny sitting a little distance away, playing with the moss again.

"Don't you run off, girl," Malachi mumbles drowsily.

Winding the moss around her fingers, she looks up through the branches at the translucent blue sky.

"T - ee," she says quietly as she weaves some of the strands of moss together. "Tuh-wee." She shakes her head as she tried to form the word. "Twee." She glances at Malachi. His breath is a slow whistle under his hat; he's asleep.

It's hard, this loud, staccato language they speak here. To her ears it sounds flat, not at all like the musical notes of her own language. She lays the long strands of moss on the grass and hops to her feet to pull another strand down.

"Chah co'nnh," she says. That's what they call the work they do here, but she can't say it right.

"C'nee yuh." That's the white man's name, but she's not saying it right either. She looks back at the house. From here she can just make out the roof of the little cabin where she's slept for two nights on the back porch. "Mee-sa C'nee yuh." No. Not right.

But she sees how it is here between the men and herself. She's watched to see which jobs Cornelius has Malachi do and which he keeps for himself, and how much Malachi talks, or talks back. Malachi plainly is not in charge, but he's more in charge than she is.

She's beginning to see her own place here, too – she's important enough to be chased after when she runs away, and the men watch to see that she eats. But then she has to work, too, even in this sticky hot field. Cornelius made that plain this morning, when he showed her how to use the hoe.

Beside her, Malachi begins to snore. She looks at him with her head cocked to one side. "Mah lu kye'."

She takes some of the strands of moss and ties the ends together, making a necklace. Then she lifts the circle of moss and lowers it over her head. It rests on her flat chest against the grimy dress. She pats it with satisfaction. There, now she has something pretty to wear, an adornment of her own making. She leans back and stares out at the field.

"Jeh - nee," she says. "Jeh - nee." That's starting to sound almost right.

CHAPTER SIX

Cornelius sits with Stephanie on the bluff south of Natchez, eating sweets from a basket and looking west. Louisiana stretches out before them in a low blue haze.

"Do you think people always hunger for something?" Stephanie asks, nibbling daintily at a jelly cake.

Cornelius smiles, too polite to say what he's hungering for. "Well, I expect they do," he says. "Men do, anyway. That's where their ambition comes from."

Stephanie touches her lips with her handkerchief. "Women have ambitions too." She looks pretty in her blue dress, her feet tucked under her wide skirt, her chestnut hair shining. "They want to build something, to make a life. That's what I yearn for." She gazes at the horizon. "Can you see your house on the Cocodrie from here?"

"Nope, I can't make it out," he says with mock seriousness as he looks out at the horizon. "I just can't understand it, either. It's only twelve miles. I should be able to see the place from here, shouldn't I?"

They both laugh. "Maybe we'll see a steamboat," he says.

A few yards in front of them, the cliff drops straight down to the Mississippi River far below. They look up and down the river.

"No steamer yet," she says, "but here comes the ferry." She points. Cornelius cranes his neck to watch as the ferry docks at the foot of Silver Street. "You better not look down there," Stephanie says. "There's things down there that'll make you blush."

"As if you knew that for yourself," he says. From where they sit on the bluff they can't see much of Natchez-Under-the-Hill. "I bet you never go down there."

"I certainly don't," Stephanie says. "I stay up here in Natchez proper."

"And you never go under the hill to Natchez improper," Cornelius says. It's an old joke. They both laugh. "Every time I come into Natchez to see you I have to come through Under-the-Hill, you know."

"Don't tell me about it."

"I certainly won't," Cornelius says, grinning. "Remember when you dropped your parcel in the street in front of the King's Tavern?"

"Sure I do. Some handsome farmer picked it up for me."

"That's right. And it could have been some grizzled old man who picked it up. You don't know how lucky you are."

"Oh, yes, I do." Her eyes twinkle.

Cornelius looks away. "When's your father coming back from the Bayou Boeuf?"

"He'll be here by the end of the week. That's what his letter says. It depends on when he can get away from his cane."

"Can I see you when he's in town?"

Stephanie smooths her skirt. "He'll leave that up to Esther, like he always does. She's raised me since I was five, so whatever she says, Papa goes along with."

But maybe not about this, Cornelius thinks. He takes a plum from the basket. "What's his plantation like, over on the Boeuf?"

Stephanie shrugs. "I don't know. But I know it's several thousand arpents. I've never seen it."

"He's never taken you there?"

"He says it's no place for a lady." She pouts. "I never get to go anywhere. Other girls go to New Orleans or even to Europe. But I'm always stuck here in Natchez with old Aunt Sophronia. And she hardly ever comes out of her room. Just stays in there with her bottle of Cherry Bounce. How boring!"

"I've been a few places. Up and down the river. And before that, six years ago, I came all the way from Atlanta to New Orleans. I wasn't but sixteen years old."

"Why'd you leave Georgia?"

Cornelius looks away. "Well, my mammy died and it seemed like the soil on our farm was worn out anyway. I couldn't see staying there to starve. I kept hearing about the Southwest, so I decided I'd give it a try. I figured there'd be more chances down here than there was up there."

"Weren't you scared, coming to New Orleans all by yourself?"

"No, I wasn't scared. I knew there'd be work."

"What kind of work?"

"Boilerman on a steamer is what I was. For more than three years. The dock-bosses liked to hire us Scotch-Irish boys instead of using slaves because you never knew when the boiler might blow up. Slaves cost too much to risk it. None of the boilers ever blew on my boats, though."

Stephanie frowns. "I hate slavery. I think it's shameful to put a price on a human being. Like Esther. She's been as much of a mother to me as my own mother could've been. I couldn't put a price on her."

"Well, when I was a boilerman, the price on slaves was higher than the price on us." He laughs. "And then I kept seeing the boats going down the river loaded to the rafters with cotton bales, so I figured there must be money in cotton. So I saved my wages for a whole year and moved up here to the Bayou Cocodrie. I knew the girls were prettier up here anyway."

"And you bought a hundred arpents."

He realizes he's told her all this before. "I guess it doesn't sound like much to you, but it was all the land I could afford. And I haven't taken in more than half of what I've bought. But I want to buy more."

"I bet you'll be a planter someday. You'll build one of these big houses and have a thousand arpents in cotton."

He moves closer to her. "Do your predictions always come true?"

"Sometimes they do."

"Would you have a prediction if I told you I'm writing to your father, telling him I want to speak to him? About us."

"Um, I might have a prediction. But I won't tell you what it is." Suddenly serious, she looks up and down the river. "You know what I'd like best of all?"

"What?"

"I'd like to see a steamboat coming in at night, with all the windows lit up and the sparks flying out of the stacks. I've heard that's a beautiful sight."

"I'll bring you up here and show you that sometime."

"You think Esther would let us come up here at night?"

"We won't tell her," he says, moving still closer to her. He leans over and kisses her on her forehead where bright beads of perspiration stand like tiny crystals. She raises her face and he kisses her lips. She puts her arms around his neck and lets him repeat the experiment. A steamboat called *Cherokee* is headed downriver, late from Vicksburg, white smoke billowing from its twin stacks and the steam whistle hooting three sharp blasts -- one long and two short. But up on the bluff, neither of the young people notice.

The next day, Cornelius mails the letter he'd written to Emile Coqterre. Then twice a week for a month after he mailed it, he rides to the settlement to check with the woman who runs the hotel about any letter that's come for him. Finally, one comes.

He goes outside and stands on the sidewalk in the sunlight, knowing his whole future is contained in that folded paper. He studies the scribble of his name on the outside of the letter. Well, Emile Coqterre hasn't forgotten his roots. This letter is written on the cheapest kind of paper.

Then he opens it, careful not to tear:

At Carefree
Natchez, Mississippi
Sunday, June 30th
My Dear Sir:
Come ahead.
/s/Emile Coqterre
Esquire.

He's surprised at its abruptness. His own letter was courteous, even courtly: a request to meet with Mister Coqterre to discuss "a matter of great importance to both you and me." He'd written it in his best hand on the best paper sold at the store, and signed it "Your most obedient humble servant." But now this curt reply comes: what can it mean?

Well, he's not entirely surprised. Any man might not want to lose a beautiful stepdaughter. But Stephanie will be marrying a man with two slaves, whose future looks bright, and who can always care for her -- maybe not in the style she's accustomed to, but someday, surely, she'll live in a planter's mansion Cornelius will build for her, and have dozens of servants. She'll live as fine a life as any matron in Natchez. Cornelius will have to convince Emile of that.

He forms an image in his mind of this man he's never met. He's seen the formal portrait of Emile that hangs in the parlor at Carefree, a dark-haired man with black eyes, a sly Gallic face. Emile is probably stern, cold, and haughty -- just the opposite of his lively, friendly, generous stepdaughter.

If only he could tell Stephanie about his visit -- but Emile would probably see any letter he writes. No, Stephanie knows he's going to see her stepfather; best just to let the visit be on its own terms. Tomorrow he'll go, before Emile decides to leave Natchez to go back to the Bayou Boeuf. Tomorrow.

He folds the letter and puts it in his pocket. Then he rides to a small house a half-mile down the road where a widow named Rosie Martin is waiting to be paid for a new white shirt she's made for him. A man needs to be well-dressed to make the visit he now plans to make, to Mister Emile Coqterre of Carefree.

At dawn the next day Cornelius leaves the cabin early after telling Malachi to finish hoeing the garden. Jenny still sleeps on the porch bed. Well, the two would get to the garden at some point. At mid-morning he sees Natchez rising on its hill above the Louisiana lowlands. Natchez with its steeples and mansions. Natchez-on-the-Hill.

At Vidalia some farmers have set up a market near the ferry-landing, with wagons of watermelons and bushels of tomatoes and beans and potatoes. While he waits for the ferry, Cornelius buys a piece of taffy candy from a ragged kid who has a tray of the sweets. He slips it into his pocket.

By noon he's riding through the wooded hills east of Natchez. As Tearose trots along the drive that curves up to Carefree, Cornelius drinks in the beauty of the place, the red-brick exterior and tall shuttered windows, the grounds planted with rosebushes and magnolia trees, the columns that look almost dainty on the big house. Two people trying to touch fingertips can't reach around one of them, Cornelius knows; he and Stephanie once tried that.

Behind the house is the kitchen, and behind that a plain two-story building where the slaves of Carefree sleep.

Carefree. Even the name is splendid. And Stephanie might be looking out from behind one of the upstairs windows right now, watching him ride up. He straightens in the saddle.

CHAPTER SEVEN

A shaft of sunlight breaks through the heavy clouds that have blanketed Natchez all day and finds the narrow opening where Emile hasn't pulled the parlor draperies quite closed. A bright beam falls across his chair and shoots an amber reflection through his whiskey glass, then touches the folded letter lying on the table. Emile is sitting alone, thinking, and his hand is moving slowly along the inside of his thigh.

He wants it dark. Each afternoon for the past two weeks since he's been home from the Boeuf, he's pulled the curtains closed and plunged the room into gloom. He hears the sounds of his household, the floor creaking as someone walks about upstairs, or someone hurrying down the wide stairs in the main hall, but as long as the door is closed, no one disturbs him. Carefree's a quiet house, anyway, a house of soft-spoken women. Sophronia and Stephanie and Esther.

There, he feels it. And there, again. His hand rests still on his thigh and he picks up his whiskey.

With probing fingers he examines his leg again. Then he runs his tongue across his lower lip. Both places. Hard masses under the skin. Growing.

He stares into the cold fireplace. Above the marble mantel, a portrait of a young woman looks down. Emile pours himself another drink.

How long has it been since he first found the masses? A month or more. But he pushed them out of his thoughts during the busy days on the Boeuf. It's only during his idle days here in Natchez that they trouble him. Another reason to work, he thinks. Too much idleness is poison itself.

The sound of a horse's hoofs on the drive outside breaks his thoughts. When he hears Esther answering the front door, he goes to the window and opens the draperies.

In a moment, as he expects, Esther's light tap at the door tells him his guest has arrived. He swings the door open, looking past her.

"Master Cornelius Carson's come to see you, sir," Esther says. Emile nods and shakes his guest's hand. Esther bustles away.

Emile gestures the young man into the parlor and motions toward a chair. He takes in Cornelius's long stride, his spare frame, the plain jeans trousers, the fine-featured face above the proud shirt. He sees his guest return his appraising glance.

"A drink, Mister Carson?"

"Yes, thank you, sir." Cornelius sits forward on the chair.

Emile sits in the chair opposite and studies his guest. "I have your letter," he says, gesturing toward the letter on the table. "And from what my daughter tells me, I know why you've come to see me."

"Yes sir." Cornelius clears his throat. "I've come to ask for Miss Stephanie's hand in marriage, sir."

Emile lets Cornelius endure a long cold stare. "Marriage," he repeats. He touches his thigh, then drinks another swallow of whiskey.

"I can provide for Miss Stephanie, sir, if you'll consent."

Emile raises his glass to his lips and then feels the welcome burn as the whiskey rolls down his throat. "I understand you have a place on the Bayou Cocodrie."

"Yes sir. I have a hundred arpents, bought free and clear with my own money, and I have two slaves. Field-hands. I bought the second one just a few days ago."

Emile can hear the hall-clock count the seconds through the open door. "Stephanie's seventeen. Do you think that's old enough to be married?"

"Sir, I think it's perfect."

Emile sees that the younger man meets his gaze, comfortable with the silence that follows.

Cornelius says, "Stephanie's told me her mother was just seventeen when she married her father."

Emile tries to read the younger man's motives -- is it greed or simply ambition that brings him here? "Well, that's true." He lifts his glass toward the portrait over the fireplace. "Has Stephanie told you much about her mother?"

"No sir."

"No. Well. That's her portrait there. I don't suppose Stephanie remembers much about her." Emile gazes at the portrait. The artist had painted Josephine in a stiff, old-style pose, but anyone could see she'd been pretty. Her brown hair was pulled straight back and she wore a lace cap. "Josephine was a widow when I married her, you know," Emile says. "And she had the littlest, prettiest baby. That was Stephanie. Stephanie's father was a horse trader, killed not far from the Chickasaw council house, before she was born."

"Yes sir. She's told me that much."

"You can still see where he's buried. A mound of stones with a fence around it, if you know where to look. It's probably been taken by the forest by now, though." He studies the portrait. "Do you think she looks like Stephanie? That was painted right after our wedding."

"Well, the hair's the same color. Same shape to the face."

"Actually only a passing resemblance, I'd say, having seen them both. Stephanie must've gotten her looks from her father's side."

Emile gets up and walks to the window. The green lawn looks cool and inviting under the trees. The clouds have scudded away to the east.

"A marriage in the church?" he asks without turning around.

"Certainly."

Emile begins to reflect, almost as if talking to himself, "You know, from here you can almost see the hill where Josephine lived, atop that rise. She had a house on Franklin Street before I married her. Just a little bungalow. And after I'd courted her for a few weeks, I asked her to marry me. But she put me off, put me off. That's when I decided to build this house. The grandest house in Natchez, I thought. If that wouldn't persuade her, nothing would. So I started the foundation, had the cornerstones laid and the walls begun, all without saying a word to her. Then I went to ask her to marry me one last time."

"Quite a wedding present."

Emile turns around. "If you marry Stephanie, it'll be yours someday."

"That's not why I want to marry her."

"I might believe that if I chose to, Mister Carson. I think I understand motives. Well." He looks up at the portrait again. "Josephine and I had a child of our own, you know. A son. Born deformed. Killed along with his mother out on the Trace." He gazes out the window again. "Josephine was going to see her people, up at Washington, Mississippi. To show them the baby. Stephanie had the chickenpox, so she stayed here. And all the hands were sick, so I let Josephine go alone. I thought, a daytime trip by buggy. Only seven miles. No danger, I thought. But I didn't foresee a broken axletree. I didn't foresee Josephine and the baby waiting by the side of the road for help to come. Waiting until dark." He clears his throat. "What came by wasn't help."

He walks to his chair and stands behind it. "There's danger in the countryside, Mister Carson," he says. "Bigger dangers than you realize. And that's why my daughter can't leave Natchez."

Cornelius stares at him. "Not leaving Natchez, sir? Why not?"

"Because she's safe here. Why do you think I've never taken her to my place on the Boeuf? Because it's not safe. All the rest of my family's gone, except for my sister Sophronia. Died of cholera or corn whiskey, every one of them. Now Sophronia's taken to her bed and Stephanie's all I've got left. I'd never let her marry anyone outside of Natchez. And that includes you."

"Sir, my place on the Cocodrie is safe--"

Emile raises his hand in a gesture of dismissal. "It's too far. I'll never let her move out there. And after all, why would I allow Stephanie to live like she'd live with you? I don't want her to be a country woman, with a passel of kids and rough hands. I don't want her old at thirty and dead at forty."

"Oh, no sir. She wouldn't --"

"So you stay away from here. Away from Stephanie and away from Carefree. I don't want you to ever come back here."

Cornelius's face drains white. "Sir, you can't mean that! I love Stephanie!"

Emile sighs. "Love's such a thin emotion, Master Carson. It's as passing as the seasons. If you don't think so, look around at all the people love couldn't hold together. Stephanie'll marry someone of her own rank in life. Someone here in Natchez, who can give her the life she deserves. You can't. And you'll leave this house now."

"You can't keep me from Stephanie, sir. I'm prepared to fight for her!"

Emile smiles. "You're a Louisiana man, sir, but here in Mississippi our new state constitution has wisely outlawed dueling. So I don't believe you'll fight me." *No matter how many Natchez men still cross the river to the dueling grounds at Vidalia, laws or no,* he thinks. He has no intention of settling this dispute that way. "This is my house, and I'm ordering you away. Can you find your own way out?"

For a moment Cornelius doesn't move. Then he strides over to the door. With his hand on the doorknob he turns to face Emile. "This can't be the end of it, sir."

"It is, Mister Carson. You go on back out where you came from. Your business here is finished." He walks to the window, his back to his visitor. In a moment he hears the sound of Cornelius's boots clumping on the marble floor of the hallway, and the front door slams.

He watches as Cornelius swings up onto his horse and gallops away down the long drive. The nag kicks up a small cloud of dust as it disappears around the turn in the road.

"Goodbye, Mister Carson," Emile says to the empty room as he pulls the curtains closed. Then he walks into the hall, ignoring Esther's questioning expression, and goes down a side hall that leads to a small bedroom. For only the second time since he's been back at Carefree he feels a need to talk to his sister Sophronia. If she hasn't already drunk herself unconscious today, he'll try to talk to her.

Cornelius stops Tearose at the bend in the road and looks back where the gabled roof of Carefree rises above the tree-tops. He feels frozen.

How could a day begun with such high hopes end so badly? To Emile Coqterre he didn't amount to enough, even with his hundred free-and-clear arpents and his two slaves. Why should that impress a man with a thousand arpents in cane and a hundred slaves, and a house built to be the grandest place in Natchez?

He rides through the town toward Natchez-Under-the-Hill and the ferry landing beyond. He crosses the river, hardly noticing the breeze on his face or the other passengers. Vidalia passes in a blur.

He should be a gentleman, he thinks, and accept Emile's refusal with dignity. And then what happens to Stephanie? She'll be pushed toward some other man more to Emile's liking, a Natchez man, no doubt. Cornelius grimaces as he pictures Stephanie in the arms of some spoiled dandy, in the grand rooms at Carefree, its chandeliers ablaze with candles and Emile beaming in the background. God! Does the man even know how to smile?

Or he can fight Emile's decree, prove himself again as he'd proven himself once before when he came from Georgia to make a new life in the Southwest. People are still pouring into the Natchez, fortunes still being made. But can he scramble up the ladder? Maybe if he takes in all his arpents, and uses the money from his cotton to buy more land. Eight bales per hand is the standard, but his crop probably won't be that high with his two field-hands. Counting himself, he might make six bales per hand, eighteen in all – that's the best he can hope for. Maybe if he saves and reinvests he can yet win Emile over. In the meantime will he ever see Stephanie again?

His head begins to throb. He stops to water Tearose at a stream, but after that he keeps the horse plodding along. It's dusk when he turns onto his own land, splashing across the low stream that runs across the road and then rounding the curve that leads up to his cabin.

When he gets to the cabin, Malachi is sitting on the porch. "Put Tearose in the stable," Cornelius says.

He walks through the cabin and out to the back porch. His throat feels dry and dusty from his long ride. He dips the gourd into the water-bucket on the shelf, irritated that Malachi's let the bucket go nearly dry. Then he stands on the porch looking out toward the fields. The cotton plants look silvery in the twilight. Money in the fields.

But he feels poor. Coqterre humiliated him with his cold stare and evaluating eye. Stephanie will marry someone of her own rank in life, Emile said. Thank God Jennie Carson wasn't alive to hear that, she who devoted her life to raising her son proper and proud. And it's so much worse that the insult came from black-eyed Emile Coqterre, arrogant with his new money. One generation and you're rich. One generation and you forget where you came from.

Jenny comes around the side of the house lugging a bucket of water. Cornelius realizes with a sudden surge of anger that Malachi sent her for the water only when he saw Tearose coming up the road. It was probably her only chore all day.

She sets the pail down and gets the water bucket down from the ledge with a clatter. She pours the water into the bucket and then tugs at it but can't lift it up to the high shelf. "Put it down. I'll set it up there," Cornelius snaps.

She walks over to her bed and sits on it, her feet not touching the floor.

"What did you do today, Jenny?"

She says nothing, of course. Cornelius studies her. The girl looks awful, really, with her hair sticking out in all directions, her skin covered with the dirt of half the state -- dirt from as far away as New Orleans, no doubt. The once-clean dress Alice Turley gave her is grimy. She tucks her hands under her knees and stares with him at the field.

He reaches into his pocket and takes out the taffy and hands it to her. She licks it and then pops the whole thing into her mouth.

"You ever gonna talk?" he asks, not expecting an answer. He feels depressed again, and poor. How does a man get from a cabin to a plantation house? Emile would accept him if he were a planter, with a hundred slaves and a Natchez house, but no planter is he.

His mouth tastes dry again; his eyes feel like sandpaper, and his head throbs. And useless little Jenny is sitting there watching him.

He sets the water bucket on the shelf and goes back inside his house.

CHAPTER EIGHT

The next day Amos and Margaret McKee drive over to Cornelius's cabin. He's already working in the field with his two slaves, even though long shadows are still drawn across the cotton plants and the leaves are brushing dew on the three workers. When Amos calls "Hello!" from the road, Cornelius walks over to greet his old friends. Margaret, her dimpled face shaded under a large sunbonnet, sits in the buggy and beams at him.

"There's a frolic at Dayson Thompson's cabin tonight," Amos says, hunching forward, his elbows resting on his knees, the reins loose in his hands. "We're on our way to the store, so we thought we'd swing by and invite you."

"Dayson's?"

"He's got a clearing in the woods next to his house, and we'll have lots of whiskey and a barbecue. Dayson's supplying the meat. You coming? Margaret's been worried about you, since she ain't seen much of you down at the store or at these get-togethers."

Cornelius looks back toward his fields. The cotton needs hoeing, but maybe work like he has in mind can wait for a frolic. It'll be a chance to hear some music, talk some politics, dance with some girls. All that's rare enough in the Cocodrie.

"Start about dark?"

"Yessir. Jay'll banjo and Martin's Tom'll fiddle."

"Now, who's that you got there?" Margaret asks. "Besides Malachi, I mean?" She gestures toward the field.

Cornelius glances over his shoulder. He feels a little ashamed in front of his neighbors. "Oh, that's my new girl. Jenny."

Cornelius sees Margaret's expression change. Yes, that's Jenny sure enough, standing there in her filthy dress. He sees how awful she looks, her face dust-streaked, her hair a bushy tangle.

"I tell you what, I have a dress might fit her," Margaret says. "Used to be Mildred's, but you know that girl's grown so big she can't wear it any longer. Why don't I send Euphonia over with it? You can use it for your girl there."

"That's mighty kind, Miss Margaret."

"We'll see you tonight, then," Amos says, clicking the reins.

As the McKees ride away, Cornelius turns back toward the fields, toward the endless work that awaits him. A frolic would do him good, after his long and disheartening trip yesterday. It'll raise his spirits.

He ignores the slaves as he hoes the cotton. He has some memories of other frolics.

Ruetta Halloran. Well.

An hour later Euphonia rides over to the cabin. McKees' oldest daughter is a tall, long-faced woman, not pretty, but she has a forward, plain manner that Cornelius rather likes. He imagines that Phony was a tomboy when she was a kid; she's in her mid-twenties now, older than he is, and it's no secret that Margaret wants to see Phony married.

She gets down from the horse and stands at the fence swinging the dress over her head like a flag. Cornelius waves back at her. She hangs the dress on the fencepost and rides away.

In the late afternoon Cornelius stops working and motions to Mal and Jenny. As the three of them trudge toward the cabin, Cornelius says, "I'm going to a frolic tonight, Mal. You go ahead and make supper."

"Yessir." Malachi glances back at Jenny, who's behind them.

"I'm taking Jenny," Cornelius says.

Hesitating only a moment, Malachi says again, "Yessir."

Malachi fixes their supper, as he usually does. Supper is the light meal of the day; tonight it's just leftover crumbled cornbread with milk. As he carries a pail of milk across the yard to the cabin, Malachi thinks again of something that's occurred to him before; he can let Jenny have the chore of milking the cow. Even though the cow is gentle, it's hard for him to sit on a bucket to coax a little milk out of her. Jenny would have to be shown how to do it, of course, but she can learn. The girl watches everything, and she learns fast.

He's already given her some jobs he doesn't care for: drawing the water, throwing scraps to Leopard and the cat, hoeing beans and peas in the garden. He might teach her to wash clothes someday, but he doubts she's big enough to handle that job yet.

This evening she's sitting on the porch cradling a kitten. The stray cat at the stable had a litter, and Jenny's made pets of them. As he walks across the porch he's impressed by how thin her limbs look. No, she can't handle the laundry just yet.

But as he sets the pail of milk on the table, the thought comes to him that she might not be here when she gets big enough to do laundry or milk a cow. Cornelius is taking her to the frolic. He could sell her there.

The certainty of his thought gives him a shiver. He should warn her! *Watch out! A slave sale's coming!* But she can't talk, so what words would he use? And even if she understands, there's no escaping a slave sale, once a white man's decided on it. Lula couldn't escape it, and neither could he.

It's going to happen to Jenny, if he's reading the signs right. And he feels bad for the girl, so bad. Three times in his life, he's known what it is to be sold. A few minutes later, as he pours the warm milk over the cornbread, and Jenny takes the tin bowl from him, he has to turn away; he can't look at her face.

Cornelius washes himself at the edge of the field. Before he got Jenny he could wash himself right out in the open, but since she's been here he's tried to bathe half-hidden, and he changes his clothes in the cabin. After he gets clean enough, he goes back to the cabin and adjusts the lamp brighter, then pulls off his work-clothes and dresses for the frolic.

First he puts on the white shirt he'd worn to see Emile Coqterre, but on second thought he takes it off and puts on one of his clean country shirts. There's no reason to put on airs; all the other men will be wearing everyday shirts like this one, plain cotton shirts with gathered sleeves and a tie at the neck. The widow Martin made him two of the shirts last spring. Besides, his recollections are too raw. Emile Coqterre had wounded him. Well, tonight he won't think about Stephanie. He pulls on his clean jeans and wipes dust off his boots and puts on a black broadcloth coat.

It's only when he walks out onto the porch and sees Jenny sitting there with her bowl of cornbread that he remembers the dress Euphonia brought over. It must still be hanging on the fence. He walks down to the field and takes the dress off the fencepost and brings it to the girl.

"Here's a new dress for you," he says.

She sets the bowl down and goes around the side of the cabin and puts the dress on. A few minutes later, bashfully holding the sides of the skirt, she walks back to where the men are sitting on the porch.

She looks much better. The dress hangs not quite down to her ankles, and it's too big. But it's clean, and her coal-black skin's a contrast to the green and white checks. And she's obviously tried to tame her wild hair, tying it into three pigtails with pieces of twine. She'd managed to catch about half of the flying strands.

Malachi watches them drive away in the wagon.

Cornelius drives down a road that's just a narrow path through the woods; the wagon rocks over tree-roots and sags into holes. Since Jenny's been here, she's gone to the store twice with Cornelius, and she's gotten used to the look of the little settlement, with its buildings and a few houses. The store is the building she knows best, because both times he'd gotten her a sweet there. She knows Cornelius's fields, of course. They're just as flat as those around the settlement, but not as big; even when they hoe at the far corners of the fields they're never out of sight of the sloping roof of the cabin. And she knows the bayou, because Cornelius and Malachi take her fishing there. The first time she fished she pulled a wriggling catfish out and then threw the whole thing, pole and line and fish, high up on the bank while the men laughed. And tonight, this is a new place to go to, a frolic.

She knows some words now, but she keeps them to herself. A lot of what the men say is nonsense to her.

Before she sees the frolic she hears it, the tinny thrum of banjos jumping on the night air. Then a fiddle takes up the tune, and they come out of the woods at a cabin in a clearing.

Cornelius unhitches Tearose to graze in a patch of untrampled grass. Then he goes over to where the dancing is. Jenny follows, looking around.

"Sit over there," he says, motioning her toward a quilt that someone spread on the ground near some older women. Then he goes over to greet some of his friends. Jenny sits down, her legs crossed in front of her.

In the clearing dozens of people are milling about, laughing, talking, and calling out to each other over the music. Some perspiring black men are barbecuing pork over a smoking pit. Bonfires send puffs of white smoke to the sky. When the musicians start a new tune, the women clap and sway, and the men choose their partners. The women's skirts are wheels of color as they spin around.

What a sight this place is! It's more people in one place than she's seen since she came here, even more than when Cornelius takes her to the settlement. Where did they come from? Did the woods cough up all these laughing, dancing people, just spit them out for the frolic?

The whites pass a jug around. Jenny watches as Cornelius circulates among the women. He goes from one group to another, a fine figure in his broadcloth coat. As they've worked in the fields the past few weeks, he's gotten browner; Jenny's seen it.

It isn't long before a lady is standing next to Cornelius. When the music starts he twirls her through the reel. An older woman beams on the sidelines and claps to the rhythm of the music, her big hips swinging her skirt from side to side.

A few minutes later, a black girl about Jenny's age sits down on the quilt beside her. "What's your name?" the girl asks.

Name. That's a word she knows.

"My name's Mildred. Who you come with?"

Jenny looks over at Master Cornelius, who's still dancing with the tall lady. She points.

"That man over there? Dancin' with Miss Phony? Now, how about that? How come you don't talk?"

Jenny picks at the stitches of the quilt. Mildred shrugs and says, "Well, it don't matter to me if you talk or not. You want to dance like them?" She hops up and holds out her hand to Jenny, who gets up slowly.

"Your master won't mind if you dance a li'l bit, I bet," Mildred says, taking Jenny's hands. "I like to dance! I like to dance! Dance! Dance!"

The girls skitter sideways. Jenny's not at all sure she should be dancing, but Mildred's taller and stronger than she is. Their galloping feet keep time with the music. Suddenly Mildred releases Jenny's hands and then they both collapse squealing with laughter onto the quilt.

Cornelius glances over at Jenny once in a while. Then he forgets about her as he finishes dancing the reel with Euphonia McKee. He goes to talk politics with some of the men. All the talk is Andy Jackson and the Indians, Andy Jackson and the Bank, which pleases him – he's an ardent Democrat himself. And there's talk about how the crops look this year -- good, generally -- and what the price of cotton might be. Twenty cents a pound, if things turn out well, most of the men think. Oh, it isn't like the glory days, back in 1800, when it was selling for 28 cents a pound -- some of the old-timers remember it -- but even 18 cents a pound is good. It's looking like a good year. Cornelius mentions that he needs to sell his girl Jenny, and he points her out, sitting over there on the quilt.

"She the one that don't talk?" Amos McKee asks.

"Well, it's true, she don't. But she *is* learning to work a cotton field." He knows her muteness will be a problem. But she looks so much better, in her new dress. She should bring four hundred.

But Amos McKee's not interested, nor is John Randall or William Jones. And when Pless Halloran walks over, Cornelius stops talking about her. He wouldn't want Jenny to go to the Hallorans' hardscrabble place. But one of the others might yet come through; they hadn't said no, outright.

He goes back to dance once more with Euphonia, and then once with Mary Anna Randall. Then he turns to Ruetta Halloran, whom he'd been watching out of the corner of his eye. Ruetta wears a limp dark frock. Her hair's the same color as her skin, and she has those pale eyes like all the Hallorans. What is there about the way Ruetta walks, the way her hips move? He's glad to see she's walking toward him.

He dances with her, and, slight as she is, she fills his arms in a loose-limbed way that keeps him grasping for her. Her wide mouth is beckoning and he remembers what it's beckoning for.

When the reel is over they slip down a path into the dark woods. They find a place of soft pine-needles and lie down, Cornelius silent, Ruetta giggling. Then Cornelius finds her mouth with his own. He pushes her bodice open and she pulls up her skirt for him. He puts his hand on skin that's smooth as a china cup, and finds the part of her he wants, downy and seamed. Only the strum of the banjos sounds through the trees as they move in rhythm together. It's over in the time it takes the musicians to finish another tune.

He rolls away from her and lies breathing heavily, looking up at the inky sky. After a moment he hikes up his pants and sits up. Ruetta sits up too, fumbling to tie her bodice. Cornelius hops up and stretches out his hand to her.

Poor white though Ruetta is, she's a goodhearted girl, and she's watching him with hungry eyes. She's looked at him that way since the first time, over a year ago now. But try as he might, he can think no more of this with Ruetta than of the horses mating in the field. It's quick and meaningless. He's glad Ruetta giggled. What it means to her, he hasn't the slightest idea, even if she did lie there looking at him a little longer than necessary. Well, he'll send her a present in a few days; something he can buy in the settlement. He'll get Malachi to take it over there.

They go back to the frolic, where he dances once more with Ruetta, knowing her flushed cheeks and wrinkled dress would give them away if the crowd was sober, and ignoring the way she bends her head into his shoulder. Then he turns his attention to other girls. Adelaide Johnson, Mary Anna Randall. Prettier girls than Ruetta, and more proper, too. He sweeps each country girl around, enjoying their different scents and the way they feel in his arms, and ignoring Ruetta's long face as she sits with a glass of whiskey at the edge of the clearing and watches. It wouldn't do to dance too much with Ruetta, anyway. People might talk.

It's nearly dawn when the frolic breaks up. Most of the people drive away in their buggies, calling weary goodbyes as they leave, and others stretch out on blankets on the ground. As the music dwindles, Cornelius hitches the horse to the wagon. Then he looks around for Jenny, who's curled up like a puppy asleep on somebody's old quilt.

"Come on, Jenny!" he calls, but she doesn't stir. "Lord," he mutters as he goes over to where she is. He feels drained, his body weary with dancing and whiskey and sex. He walks over to the sleeping girl and lifts her under the arms, trying to get her to walk, but her knees give way. "Let's go, pigtails," he says, shaking her. Then he lifts her again and walks her awkwardly over to the wagon.

He settles her in the back of the wagon and drives away, slumping as he holds the reins. The frolic is over, faded away with a few spiritless banjo tunes, the girls in their calicos gone home with their families. The horse plods along the road as the sky turns pink in the east. The road takes them through the woods, across the low stream and around the curve toward the cabin.

Here, barely visible in the brightening morning, is the place Cornelius loves best in the world, his own hundred arpents of land and the cabin and the little house he'd built by himself. But there's disappointment here, too. Will Stephanie ever see this place? And behind him in the wagon sleeps his little African, unsold.

He drives up to the cabin and unhitches the horse, then half-carries the stumbling girl through the cabin to her bed on the back porch. He goes inside and sits on the side of his own bed and pulls off his boots; then he lies down and closes his eyes, still thinking about Stephanie, still sad.

CHAPTER NINE

Less than an hour after Cornelius rode away from Carefree, Emile told Stephanie what he'd said to Cornelius. And for a moment he thought she'd strike him, if the years she'd spent at the Elizabeth Girls' School hadn't bred it out of her. Looking at the furious young woman standing before him in the parlor, he wondered where the little girl with the chestnut curls had gone, the one who ran to his lap every time he came home to Natchez, happy as a lark to see her papa. It was hard to see that child now. She was still perfection, though.

For the next week, Stephanie stayed in her room, refusing to speak to Emile or join him in the dining room for meals. Muffled sounds of sobbing alternated with sullen silences from behind her bedroom door, which remained firmly closed.

"Miss Stephanie say she eatin' in her room again today," Esther says mildly on the second morning as she pours Emile's coffee. He sits alone at the head of the long polished table.

"She can suit herself," Emile mutters.

Overhead, the mahogany punkah swings slowly, pulled by little Philip, the son of Charlie the stable-boy, whose simple job it is to swing the punkah to stir the air.

"Philip, you bigger than your little brother?" Emile asks the child.

"Yes sir."

Through the open window comes the duplicitous call of a mockingbird, a bright hollow sound. Emile butters a biscuit. "You not the one's been chasing my chickens 'round the yard, are you?"

"No sir."

"I certainly hope not."

But on the fifth morning, Emile throws his napkin down. "Well, let her live the hermit life!" he says, storming out of the room. "My temper can outlast hers any day!" His coffee raises tendrils of steam to be taken by the punkah's breeze.

He goes down the hall to the room at the back of the house that serves as his office and spends the rest of the morning there with his paperwork. Expenses have to be recorded in the big ledgerbook, orders written to merchants and notations made of discussions with Esther and the male slaves who see to the maintenance of Carefree's grounds and buildings -- the thousand details of running a large city house.

But the house is too quiet. At midday he gets up and walks down the side-hall to Sophronia's room. He wants to ask his sister the questions that nag at him -- questions about Stephanie that perhaps a woman can answer. What to do about a girl who knows so little about the world, who wants to marry her latest infatuation? Should he let Stephanie make a life-changing decision like marriage, she who six months ago could think of no one but John Landerson? And who six months before *that* was giggly over Abel Smith's son, Madison?

But Sophronia is asleep, her face in full sun under the open window and an empty bottle of Cherry Bounce on the table beside her bed. Emile stands for a moment studying the profile of his sister, so different from his own. He, so much the son of their French father, his face narrow and sharp; her features those of their Irish mother, but swollen now with drink, distorted out of prettiness. Her breath whistles. Emile goes back to his paperwork.

The next afternoon he raps on Stephanie's door.

"Go away!" Stephanie snaps.

"You come out here, Missy! What do you mean shutting yourself up like that?"

"I most certainly will not come out! I may just die in here! I don't have a thing to live for anyway."

Emile stands with his hand on the doorknob, but he doesn't turn it. Instead, he storms down the hall and goes to his own bedroom and slams the door.

The next day Charlie brings a letter from the post-office in King's Tavern. Esther takes it in as Emile eats in the dining room, alone except for Philip. Even before he tears the letter open, Emile recognizes the chicken-scratch handwriting of Bernard Ratout, his overseer on the plantation on Bayou Boeuf.

The drought that worried Emile before he left the Boeuf at the end of May still stands unbroken, Ratout wrote, and last week a "farr" swept through the fields of dry cane. The crop is half gone, turned into ashes in one night. Ratout and the slaves were able to save the house and cabins by beating at the fire all night.

Emile sniffs the letter; it smells of smoke. Well, cane was always a gambler's business, he knows that well. Fire or frost can wipe out a crop any year, as every planter knows, but three good years can make a fortune. Emile's had many good years. He planned to stay at Carefree for another month; by then Stephanie would've gotten over her snit and fixed on some other boyfriend. But Ratout's letter means he'd better get back to Rapides Parish to see what's left of the crop. And maybe Stephanie would even miss him.

He spends the rest of the day winding up the household's business, leaving the place in running order for however long he'll be away. The next morning he bids Stephanie *adieu* through her closed bedroom door and looks in on Sophronia who's still sleeping. Then he rides away from Natchez, relieved to be going back to his cane plantation in Rapides Parish, a four-days' ride.

The oldest slave at Carefree is Lucy Ida, who turned ninety-two, or so everyone thought, on the day Emile left. Too old to do any serious work and too restless to sit idle, she sometimes, in her frail birdlike way, helps the younger women with the lighter chores. On her birthday, she decides to help Esther in the big house, so at mid-morning the two women are in the hall dusting the rosewood furniture and polishing the silver candlesticks that sit on French tables along the walls. And Lucy Ida wants to talk.

"I see Miss Stephanie still hidin' herself away," she says. She rubs the candlesticks vigorously with a cloth, her bony shoulder-blades sawing against the damp fabric of her dress. "You ought to do somethin' to help that girl get married."

"*I* ought to do somethin'?" Esther says. "And just what do you expect *me* to do?"

"Well, now, you're good at helpin' young folks find their hearts' desire. Everybody knows it. It do seem to me you taken on those kinds of troubles before."

Esther smiles. "Everybody knows it?"

"Yassum." Lucy Ida replaces the creamy candles and steps back, cocking her head to see if they're standing straight. "You're *known* all over Natchez for it. Look at how you found my girl Sarah her Rob. I nearly give up on that girl ever findin' herself a man. But no, you found Rob, and him from right here in Natchez, so Sarah's still here to help me. Now, I appreciate that, Esther."

"I just put people where they can find each other. Then nature just takes its course."

"And don't forget Charlie. You brung Daisy here to learn lace-makin', and first thing you know, her and Charlie's got three chilrun."

"Four, just almost. Daisy's lyin' in, as of this mornin'. Charlie told me. Aunty Feddoe's with her."

"Now see. You're known for that. You the one the young folks can count on. And Miss Stephanie needs some help right now, I'd say." She sits down hard on a chair.

When Esther doesn't answer, Lucy Ida says, "I always felt sorry for that pore motherless child. When Miss Josephine died, I remember how Master Emile just went wild. Turned the whole house upside down with his grievin'. And he not givin' one thought to findin' a mammy for the child that was left to him. And her not but five years old, not knowin' a thing about what was happenin', or where her mamma was. By the time he give her a thought, she'd done attached herself on to you. It's a good thing you took to the child. And you know Sophronia's just worthless to be left responsible for the girl."

Esther stops dusting and stands with her hand on her hip, staring out the open front door. Match-making comes easy for her, that's true. She hasn't match-made as much lately as in her younger days, but she can be so good at it when she tries. "Well, it's true Miss Stephanie just like my own child," she says. "Don't feel one bit different to me than Theresa or Helene."

"Well, what you think about this man that's been courtin' her?"

"He seem like a fine gentleman."

"'Course, Master Emile don't think so. But you know true love come when it come. It might not run on Master Emile's clock. You gotta let nature take its course."

"Nature can take its course without my help."

"Well, you helped Daisy and you helped Sarah. You surely do the same for Miss Stephanie." She rocks back and forth on the chair with her head bobbing. "No, if Miss Stephanie want to marry this fine gentleman, I don't believe you should just sit by and see the girl denied."

After Lucy Ida goes back to the slave quarters to sleep the rest of the afternoon away, Esther thinks over what the old woman said. When Stephanie's door opens and the girl comes downstairs, Esther sees how the girl's lips are pinched together and how she sighs as she plops down first in the parlor, then on the gallery, then out on the back gallery. Later Stephanie follows Esther out to the kitchen, where she sits at the table and watches Esther cut up a chicken. She puts her elbows on the table and props her chin on her hands as Esther flours the chicken.

Esther's younger daughter Helene is there, bored and getting in the way. Finally Esther sends Helene out to pick blackberries and sits down at the table, her flour-caked hands folded in front of her.

"Now listen, Missy," she says, "we can't have you carryin' on the way you been doin'. Why don't you write a letter to Master Carson? That's what I'd do if I was you. Tell him he can still come visit you. Tell him Master Emile's gone back to the Boeuf, and you're allowed to have callers far as I'm concerned."

"You'll let him come visit me?"

Esther nods. "I can't let you keep mopin' around like you been doin'. I been worried you'd make yourself sick. I know Master Emile wouldn't want that. And what harm can there be in you and Master Cornelius enjoyin' each other's company?"

Stephanie jumps up and throws her arms around Esther. "Thank you! I'll go write him right now!"

"Pull back, Missy, you gonna get yourself covered with batter!"

As Stephanie flies out of the kitchen, Esther goes back to her cooking. Sometimes things go so well that a person can take pure satisfaction in it. Here she's gotten Helene out from underfoot, and made Miss Stephanie happy, and got the kitchen to herself, all in a few minutes' time. She hums an off-key tune as she swings the iron skillet over the fire and carves a wedge of lard into it.

And it's always interesting to see what happens when you put two young people together and let nature take its course. It's been too long since she's done any big matchmaking. Now the world seems like it's going to be put right, and something important's gonna happen.

She drops pieces of chicken into the hot grease and watches bubbles nibble the edges of each piece. When she stops humming, the only sound in the kitchen is the skillet's reassuring sizzle.

CHAPTER TEN

"Come *on,* Jenny," Cornelius says for the third time. "We've got to work this field. You standing here looking at the work won't get it done." The girl stands in the cotton-row staring at the hoe. Nearby, Malachi works along the row. He wipes sweat from his forehead with the rag he wears around his neck.

Cornelius glares at the girl. "If you think you're gonna mutiny, you can think again," he snaps. Jenny's worked more or less willingly in the cotton field up until now, and the cotton has to be finished before they can drain the swamp. But today a revolt is plainly what she has in her dumb little mind.

She holds the hoe upright, balancing the handle delicately between her thumb and forefinger. "Are you going to get back to work?" he asks, putting as much threat into his voice as he can. Really, the only time he can sound angry with Jenny, little as she is, is when he really *is* mad at her, but he's working up to that now. She's been here more than a month, dumb as a stone the whole time, but she should know by now she can't just stop working.

After the frolic they'd taken it easy for a couple of days. But then Cornelius decided they'd have to work longer hours. So yesterday the three of them hoed cotton from first light until dark, and then dropped wearily into bed right after supper. He knows full well that when he's not here to oversee Mal and Jenny, they spend as much time under the oak tree as in the field. And his courtship of Stephanie took him away many days earlier in the summer.

Stephanie. He still hasn't decided what to do about her. For now he can't see her, with Emile still at Carefree. He'll have to wait until September, when cane harvest is starting on the Bayou Boeuf and Emile is sure to be gone from Natchez. Then he'll try to figure something out. His meeting with Emile gave him a new resolve to become a planter.

The cotton has to be hoed four times this summer. But today, Jenny decides to rebel.

"Get back to work, Jenny!" he orders. But she stands without moving, looking sideways down the row of cotton. She holds her hands out to him.

"What is it, splinters? I'll get 'em out, and then you get back to work."

But when he grabs her hands, he sees that the problem isn't splinters but watery blisters which sit like bubbles on her fingers and palms.

"Well, you can't work with your hands like that, that's for sure," he huffs. "Let me see if I can find some gloves in the house." He motions for her to follow him back to the cabin.

Jenny sits on her bed while Cornelius goes inside. Searching through his bureau, he finds an old pair of kid riding gloves, which he takes outside and slips on the girl's hands. But she winces as the stiff leather presses against the ripe blisters.

"Can you work in those?" Cornelius asks. She closes her eyes and grimaces in exaggerated pain, drawing a slow breath through clenched teeth. So he eases the gloves off and tosses them over on the shelf.

"All right, I'll have to pop those blisters," he says. He goes back inside and comes out with a needle. Then he motions for her to sit on the step. He sits on the step below her and reaches for her hand. She draws in her breath again as he holds the needle to the largest blister, but he holds her hand tightly.

"Oh, don't cry. It won't hurt," he says, knowing it won't if he can work quickly. He pops the first one. She tries to pull her hand away, but he holds it tight. Then he gently presses out the fluid.

"Now the other hand," he says. She studies the broken blisters on the one hand as he works on the other. "There. Now they won't hurt as much. I've got to get back to the chopping. You come on back out there and sit yourself down under the tree. That's what you want to do anyway, I reckon. And when those blisters heal up, back you go to the hoe, you understand?"

She trudges back to the field after him. He hands her the hoe and points to the tree.

Cornelius mutters to Malachi, "I guess I better get her some gloves."

"Yessir," Malachi says without looking up.

Cornelius scowls as he hoes. It's not that Jenny sitting out will make much difference, since she's not much of a worker. It's the idea. Too bad John Randall or one of the others hadn't seen fit to buy her. She's just one more obstacle in what seems like a long, long road.

The day drags on. All that day Jenny dawdles in the shade.

In the late afternoon a bank of dark clouds rises above the trees to the west. The men walk back to the cabin in the dusk, carrying their hoes across their shoulders. Cornelius watches with irritation as Jenny trots along ahead of them in a kind of hop-and-skip walk, fresh as a spring colt, while he and Malachi trudge along the furrow, bone-weary from their long day in the field.

It rains hard during the night. At dawn the stream that runs across the road near the cabin is spreading under the trees, a churning curl of brown water fifty feet wide. But by noon the stream's fallen back to normal. Since they can't chop cotton in the mud, and since the sky's clearing, Cornelius decides to make the muddy ride into the settlement to get Jenny some work-gloves.

At the store he finds a pair of simple cotton gloves, just a bit larger than child-size. They look little to him, but he thinks they'll fit Jenny. And he buys some sugar and coffee to save another trip into town.

He stashes his purchases in his saddlebag and is about to mount and ride away when the hotelkeeper swings open the door of the hotel next to the store. "Mister Carson!"

Cornelius walks over. "Yes ma'am?"

"This just came today. I thought you might not be expecting it, so when I saw you passing by..." She hands him a letter.

Cornelius sees immediately that it's from Carefree. And not on cheap paper either, but a proper letter on good white stationery, his name written in Stephanie's looping hand. He pauses for a moment, steeling himself for what he fears the letter might say, before he opens it and begins to read. Then he lets out an Indian whoop, waving the paper over his head triumphantly.

The hotelkeeper grins. "Well, I guess you got good news," she says, her weathered face creasing into a smile. "I got a whole bag of mail this week, and I know for a fact half of it's foreclosure notices or fugitive warrants. It's nice to know somebody got something good."

"Yes, ma'am!"

Cornelius lopes over to the horse and jumps on. He rides away, war-whooping and drawing stares from shoppers on the sidewalk as he gallops past.

When he reaches the cabin he pulls Tearose to a halt in front of the porch. Malachi sits in the rocking chair which he'd set out under the tree in the yard. Jenny dawdles near the porch.

"I got some good news from Natchez, Mal," Cornelius says as he swings down from the saddle.

Jenny watches with the mute alertness that Cornelius has grown used to. Impulsively he grabs the girl's wrists and swings her around.

She stumbles to a halt. He turns to go into the cabin.

"Dance, *dance*," Jenny says, starting to spin with her arms out. She stops suddenly.

"You can talk?" Cornelius asks.

"That girl can talk after all?" Malachi asks.

She wobbles backward.

"Mebbe that's all she know how to say," Malachi says.

"That can't be all," Cornelius says. "It's not a half-way thing. Either you talk or you don't."

"Well, why didn't she talk before now?"

"I don't know. It's good she can, though." Cornelius sits down on the step and unfolds his letter and re-reads it as Malachi stares at Jenny, who drags her toes in the mud to trace a pattern there.

"I knew a mute once, up in Alabama," Malachi says as Cornelius reads. "It was a idiot-boy. Never opened his mouth to say a word. Looked perfectly all right, too, just to look at him. Just couldn't talk. Couldn't do nothin', actually."

"Well, I expect Jenny wouldn't talk until she learned the language. Maybe it took her this long to learn it." He stands up. "I'm going to Natchez tomorrow, Mal." He folds the letter and puts it in his pocket. "Take Tearose down to the stable." He turns to Jenny. "You gonna talk for us again?"

She hunches one shoulder and twists around to look at the horse.

"I hope you do," Cornelius says, patting her head. He goes up the steps into the cabin.

CHAPTER ELEVEN

"My girl Jenny can talk," Cornelius says, sitting with Stephanie on the sofa in the parlor the next day, examining her soft white hands. Each tapered finger ends in a perfectly shaped nail, each nail graced by a white half-moon curving from the soft flesh. Their small-scale perfection fascinates him, the way her fingers lie lightly in his palm, slightly spread. He rubs the back of her hand gently with his own big fingers.

"Well, why shouldn't she talk?" Stephanie asks. "She's -- what did you say, ten? My goodness, Cornelius, any ten-year-old can talk!"

"Well, Jenny couldn't." The breeze moves the lace undercurtains ever so gently against the velvet draperies. What had been a delicious Natchez spring has changed into a sultry Delta summer, and all the doors and windows are open. Stephanie puts her face close to his. He feels her breath on his face. The curve of her breast is against his arm.

Josephine's portrait stares from the wall. This is the same room where he'd met Emile a few weeks ago. Well, what Emile denied him, here in the parlor, he can still take. It's not the gentlemanly thing to do, but then Emile didn't treat him like a gentleman. There comes a time when a man has to take what he wants and ask permission afterward. Stephanie puts her arms around his neck. There's a fragrance of roses about her. It reminds him of his mother's roses that bloomed under his bedroom window back in Georgia, where he grew up.

After Cornelius leaves, Stephanie goes into the bedroom upstairs where Esther is folding pillowcases and dresser-scarves, snapping each one into the air to smooth it and then folding it into a neat square. Pouting, Stephanie flops onto the bed and picks listlessly at the bedspread.

"Esther, I want to marry Cornelius."

"You thought about your papa?" Esther asks quietly.

"Yes. And I can't do anything about what he thinks. But Cornelius and I want to get married. We want to elope."

Esther looks out the window to where sunlight shimmers on the dark waxy leaves of a magnolia tree. After a moment she says, "Well, that could be arranged, I expect."

"Would you help us?"

"I might. I seen how you moped around this house after Master Emile sent Master Cornelius away. I been afraid you'd make yourself sick, and I sure couldn't let that happen."

"Cornelius is coming back next week. Can you help us? Find us a priest who'd do it?"

"If you're sure, I'll help you. And if you won't say one word about me to your papa. And not a word to your Aunt Sophronia neither."

Stephanie sits up on the edge of the bed. "I'm sure, and I won't."

Esther begins to sort the linens into little stacks. The crocheted and tatted scarves would have to go in the bureau until Daisy could get up from her childbed to iron them. But Daisy can't get up yet, and she can't feed her baby neither. That was a worry. They'd had to hire a woman from another house to come over and feed the scrawny little thing.

And oh Lord. Miss Stephanie is so young, but old enough to marry. And she and Master Cornelius had found each other -- with a little help, of course. Esther would be known for her matchmaking all over Natchez. The thought makes her shiver all over. But Stephanie doesn't see it.

That night Esther tosses on her bed, her mind imagining Emile's furious face in the dark outside her window; but the morning light calms her, as it always does. Best to start things moving right away, she decides. Get this wedding over with.

As early as she dares the next morning, she taps on the door of Sophronia's room.

"Come in," calls a bleary voice.

Esther opens the door. Sophronia lies sprawled on the bed, her hair a dark mop on the pillow. She's half covered by a sheet, but one leg sticks out, a skinny white shank. Esther stands just inside the door.

"Miss Sophronia, ma'am, I need to go into town to get some spices for the kitchen. And since I'm goin', I thought I might pick up some calico while I'm there. For the dress Daisy'll be gettin' now that she's had her baby."

"She's had it?"

"Yes 'm. A fine boy. And I know she be most appreciative of a new dress."

A sour silence follows. "How you gonna get it made up?"

"Lucy Ida and me can work on it. Daisy had a hard time with that baby."

"Get me my bag, then," Sophronia says, waving toward the bureau. Esther hands it to her.

Sophronia wriggles herself up against the headboard and fishes out a dollar. "Get the cheapest," she mumbles. "Oh, you want a pass, too."

"Yes, ma'am."

Sophronia waves again toward the bureau, where Esther finds a pencil and a sheet of writing paper in a drawer cluttered with brushes and hairnets. Sophronia writes with the paper propped against her knees, crudely printing the word "Pass" and Esther's name, misspelled "Esta," and then her own long name.

"Thank you, ma'am," Esther says.

"And bring me the receipt," Sophronia snaps as Esther goes out the door. "My brother keeps records, you know."

"Yes ma'am."

Esther hurries out through the back door. The idea of Sophronia saying get the cheapest calico, almost begrudging Daisy the new dress she has coming because of the baby -- Lord, Esther can almost hate that woman.

But walking into town, on a fine day like this, with puffy white clouds flying, it's hard to stay angry. She'll just forget about Sophronia and enjoy her walk into Natchez town, high above the breezy river.

Esther keeps some little secrets. Sophronia never needs to know that she sashays into town whenever the mood strikes her, whether she has a pass or not. Sophronia never comes into the kitchen. How would she know that Esther keeps a good kitchen and never, ever runs low of anything? And even though Esther's always a little nervous when she's out without a pass, well, there's a liberty in these walks into town. She loves them.

There's always so much to see in Natchez. Today, on a side street, some men are pitching pennies. They look like businessmen in their proper suits and ties, but they bend over their pennies as if the gambling is the most important business they'll do all day.

And sitting on that wall behind them, three little boys are smoking cigarettes, blowing fancy smoke-rings. They're new at it. And down a hill in the next block is a fight. A ring of men moves back and forth with the action. There'll be money changing hands on the outcome of that fight, no doubt.

Esther knows to keep her ears as well as her eyes open. And at the dry-goods store two white women she's seen in town before are talking loud like country women do, and Esther overhears.

"Protracted meeting...."

"Saint Catherine's Creek, all this week..."

She moves closer to the women, eavesdropping and fingering bolts of fabric. She tucks what they're saying into a corner of her mind. The day is working out so well.

She finally settles on a blue plaid she knows Daisy will like. And in honor of the perfect day, she decides to get it, even though it's not quite the cheapest. The dollar will pay for it, and yet it's not so fine that Sophronia will think anything of it.

"I know how to get you married," Esther says when she gets back to Carefree and Stephanie comes into the kitchen with an expression that says *Hurry!* It seems Stephanie's face says that a lot lately. "I heard about somethin' in town, and it'll be your chance to elope."

"Well, tell me! For goodness' sakes, don't make me wait and wonder!"

"Well, there's a Methodist camp-meetin' startin' up not too far from here. It's up by the Saint Catherine Creek."

"And someone there could marry us?"

"There's bound to be a preacher."

"Then we'd better do it," Stephanie whispers. "Esther, now wait. I want to be married in the Catholic Church. I always thought I'd be married in the Church. A Methodist wedding? That wouldn't satisfy a priest, would it? And don't you think we ought to get married in Vidalia, or down in Woodville? That's what most people do."

"Law, child, Methodist's a church. One church good as the next, I'd say. And one place's good as another, too. It ain't like your papa's gonna come after you to put a stop to it, 'cause he ain't gonna know about it." The words sound more stern than she intends, but this flighty girl can make her almost angry sometimes.

And why is Stephanie suddenly so worried about getting a priest? No white person at this house ever gave a thought to Judgment Day. Master Emile might call himself a Catholic, but he hadn't been to Mass as long as Esther can remember. As for Sophronia, it'll be her funeral the next time she shows up at church. And this Miss Priss might have religion on her mind now, but only because she's scared of what she's getting herself into. That prie-Dieu at the foot of her bed hasn't been knelt on for years. Esther dusts it every week.

"When Cornelius comes back tomorrow, I'll tell him," Stephanie says, putting her hand to her forehead.

"A Methodist marriage? Of course it counts," Cornelius says, laughing and taking Stephanie into his arms. They're sitting in their favorite place, a corner of the gallery where a big camellia bush hides them from anyone passing on the road.

"I'm not sure," Stephanie says.

"It'll be fine." He's just as glad not to have a Catholic wedding. He considers himself a low-church Anglican like his mother was. When he was a kid she took him to a musty-smelling country church where they sat in a pew together and read from a little prayer-book with yellowed pages. They prayed for the Church. They prayed for President Monroe, calling him "James." And later they prayed for that scoundrel Quincy Adams -- "John" -- who stole the election of 1824 from Colonel Jackson.

But flickering candles and statues of saints aren't for him. And why would the service be in Latin? He figures there's nothing wrong with English, unless the priests are keeping something a secret. They should use a language everyone can understand. There are already too many languages in Louisiana. For every person speaking English, the next one might speak French, and then if you go to the courthouse, like he did when he bought his land, the documents were all in Spanish. Why add Latin to the gumbo?

Other than that, the words spoken don't really matter to him, as long as the whole thing's legal. And he's not particular about the sect. When they buried his mother up in Georgia, they buried most of his religion, too. And it's withered even more since he left Georgia and came down here. When he was a boilerman, the only time he thought about it was sometimes on a Sunday morning if the steamboat happened to pass a town with a church-bell. Then the mellow clang, barely heard over the *whomp-whomp* of the steam engine, might call to mind his boyhood. On the Cocodrie, his cabin is far from any church-bell.

But he'll certainly be able to understand a Methodist parson better than a priest.

The next morning Esther gets Charlie to bring the buggy around to the front gallery and she and Stephanie climb on. Esther drives northeast toward Washington, six miles up the Trace. As they travel through the dappled green woods, jostling against one another on the buggy seat, they pass families with furniture tied on top of wagons, and solitary traders, and merchants with mule-teams pulling covered wagons, all hell-bent for Natchez. Finally they cross the Saint Catherine Creek, and around a turn in the road they come to a clearing.

The encampment looks like a settlement of gypsies to their city eyes. In the trees around the clearing, some people have set up tents, and others are camping in covered wagons. Cooking fires flicker and columns of white smoke rise through the trees.

Children race about, babies are wailing, and clusters of women talk among themselves. Some sit by themselves with Bibles in their laps. Farther off in the woods, blacks have set up their own camps; their tents are made of quilts thrown over ropes between the trees.

In a large brush-arbor in the middle of the clearing, a fiddler is scratching out a hymn.

"First we have to find the preacher-man," Esther says. "The next service 'll be startin' before long." She pulls the horse up in front of a tent where an old couple sits on a log.

"Can you help us, sir?" Esther asks. "We lookin' for the preacher. Is he 'round here?"

The old man seems half asleep, but his wife lifts the pipe from her mouth and points with it toward a covered wagon several yards away.

"Reverend's ova theya," she says, her voice a squeak. Her sunbonnet frames a toothless face with a prominent whiskery chin.

"Thank you, ma'am." Esther drives over to the covered wagon the woman had pointed to. Its flaps are closed.

"This is the place, Miss Stephanie," Esther says. Then she calls, "Reverend! Reverend!"

After a moment, a burly man sticks his head through the wagon-flaps. "Yes, I'm here! I'm here!"

"We lookin' for the reverend here. That be you, sir?"

The rest of his large body emerges through the flaps and he climbs down. "Yes, that be me." His quick eyes go from Esther to Stephanie, who sits with her hands clasped. "George Hudson. What kin I he'p you with?"

Esther glances at Stephanie and then says, "This lady wants to get married to her young gen'a'man, so we lookin' for someone who can do it. Can you do a weddin', sir?"

Esther sees his eyes sweep Stephanie's figure. Well, everybody likes to count the months before a baby comes, but Esther is sure there's no baby here to be counted. Stephanie misses the way the man looks at her, Esther sees. Law, the child has so much to learn.

"I done more weddin's then I kin count," he says, his round face creasing into a smile. "And glad to do 'em, too. Better t' marry than t' burn, like it say in the Good Book. I got my record-book in there," he jerks his thumb back toward the wagon, "where I write 'em down, and it's gettin' prett' near filled up. I did two weddin's last week, up near Tupelo. But whar's yo' man?"

"He ain't with us today," Esther says. "We just come out here to see if you'd do it."

Stephanie speaks for the first time. "It'll have to be Friday."

"All right. This meetin'll still be goin' on then, and on 'til Sunday night. You and your man just come on out. Try to get here before the two o'clock meetin'. We have a meetin' at ten, and then one again at two. And the big one at night. If you can come between 'em, that's best, 'cause most folks is out prayin' in the woods then."

"Yes sir," Stephanie whispers.

"Well, it's set then," Esther says. "Thank you, sir."

He nods and they drive away, rocking to left and right as the buggy labors over the hard-packed ground.

As the buggy rumbles down the steep bank of the creek, Stephanie suddenly turns to Esther. "Oh, Esther, I forgot! How much will we have to pay him? I didn't think to ask!"

"Faugh, Miss Stephanie, don't worry 'bout things that ain't your trouble. Master Cornelius'll pay the preacher. That's the way it works."

"Oh."

As they drive up out of the creek, drops of water spin from the wheels. The fiddler at the meeting far behind them begins to play again, but the bright sound drops an octave and then fades away as they drive back toward Natchez.

CHAPTER TWELVE

"A present come for you, Miss Stephanie," says Charlie, bringing in a box wrapped in white paper and setting it on the parlor table. "It come from Barron Hall. Their stable-man brung it over."

Stephanie sees immediately that it's from John Landerson. Opening the box, she takes out a china cup, fragile as anything, with a green and gilt edging. She sinks onto the sofa and holds the cup up, turning it to admire the delicate artwork.

John Landerson. When he visited Stephanie the last time before he went off to Europe, he broke a cup that was part of the set of Carefree china. Stephanie smiles, remembering the afternoon of horseplay in the parlor that sent the cup crashing to the floor.

Now he's replaced it. It's not a perfect match, but close. The Coqterre china, forty settings of Old Paris Paste, each piece painted with a green band and rimmed in gold, and each piece with a different flower in the center. It was Josephine's wedding china. Sending the cup is a way for John to announce he's back from

France, six months older. John with the straw-colored hair. She remembers.

But it's too late.

She feels she'll burst if she doesn't tell someone about her plans to marry Cornelius! Oh, she must tell it! But who would she tell? She sees so little of her school friends anymore; Patricia and Selma married, Veronica off touring Europe, and Bella moved to New Orleans. The only one left is Elenora Frankle. She'll have to tell Elenora.

That afternoon she drives herself to the house where Elenora lives with her old parents. Elenora is sitting alone on the porch as Stephanie's buggy rolls to a stop in front of the gate.

"I've got some news to tell you!" Stephanie calls out in her high schoolgirl voice. "If I don't tell someone I'll pop!"

Elenora stands up and waves. "Well, don't pop, no matter what you do! Come on up here and let's sit out. It's so hot."

Stephanie runs up the steps and hugs her. Elenora speaks to a house-girl who sticks her head through the door, and a few minutes later the girl brings glasses of lemonade tinkling with precious ice, frosting in the heat.

"Oh, this is heaven," Stephanie says as she sips the lemonade. Ice in July. The Frankles are known to have money, even if it doesn't always show. But it shows in quiet ways.

"And what's your news?" Elenora asks. "Don't keep me in suspense, Steph. I can't wait another minute to hear it."

"Well," Stephanie says, "I'm engaged!"

Elenora puts her hand to her mouth. "Engaged? Are you really?"

"I really am. To Mister Cornelius Carson. We're getting married the day after tomorrow."

Elenora looks confused. "But what about John Landerson?"

"Oh." Stephanie waves her hand to shoo a mosquito. "That's off. But John's back in Natchez, did you know? He sent me a present."

"John's back? For heaven's sake, who's this you're marrying, this Cornelius Car--"

"Carson."

"How am I supposed to keep this straight? First you say you're engaged to this man I've never heard of, and then you tell me John's back. Who is he, this Cornelius Carson?"

"He's a farmer, out in the Cocodrie."

"You're leaving Natchez!"

"Well, I'll be coming back to visit," Stephanie says quickly. "But you've got to promise me you won't say a word about this to anyone."

"Why on earth not?"

"Because it's a secret, silly. We're eloping. We've got it all arranged. Papa doesn't know a thing about it, and neither does anyone else. I'm only telling you because I had to tell somebody."

"Or you'll pop, I know. Don't pop, Stephanie. Marrying's serious business. You're running off and getting married the day after tomorrow?"

"Unless it's raining or something."

Elenora frowns. Stephanie stares out at the yard. Now she's unhappy. She shouldn't have come here. Elenora's stiff as a canestalk, everybody knows it. Every town has a few old maids, and Elenora will probably be one of Natchez's. Stephanie can see it in her friend's plain face.

The next day Stephanie is almost glad that it does rain. It comforts her to hear the raindrops pattering on the soft ground. All day she stays in the cool house, not even thinking about her marriage except when Esther asks her which dress she wants to wear tomorrow.

"Oh, that yellow frock, I suppose," Stephanie says. After all, it might still be raining tomorrow.

But Friday dawns fair. When Stephanie wakes, she thinks the blue sky, cloudless through the tall windows of her bedroom, is rebuking her for this hasty wedding.

Why be in such a hurry to marry Cornelius–or anyone, for that matter? Propped against the bed-pillows, she looks across the room at the mirror above her dressing table. Her pale and hollow-eyed face stares back.

There on the dresser sits the china cup John Landerson sent her. She hasn't seen him, hasn't even returned a note of thanks to him for the thoughtful little gift he sent. Surely he's wondering why she's ignoring him. He sent a gift because he wants to see her again, to pick up where they left off, probably. It's a marriage his parents would welcome. Uniting the two grandest houses in Natchez -- wouldn't that be a plum, now?

Why did she ever want to marry Cornelius? She had such a leisurely, ordinary, easy life before she took it into her head to marry this farmer from the Cocodrie. What came over her to cause her to fight so with her papa, to leave him angry and hurt on the day he left for the Bayou Boeuf? What caused her to forget all about John, when they were good as betrothed, just because Cornelius waltzed into her life?

She must have a nosegay. The thought's a distraction. Every bride must have a bouquet. She jumps out of bed and looks around her room, but aside from a gardenia blossom that wilted during the night in a vase on her dresser, there's nothing here that passes for a nosegay. In fact, she realizes, standing in the middle of the room, she's had none of the pleasures of a proper Natchez wedding -- no parties, no gifts, no friends invited to be bridesmaids. Just a yellow frock she's already worn several times, and a secret wedding at, of all things, a Methodist protracted meeting out in the country. And then to have to face a husband, and the wrath of her papa. What could she have been thinking?

She longs for her mother. I'm an orphan child, she thinks; tears sting her eyes. If Mother were here, she could tell her daughter what to do, what to expect. But Mother is long dead, killed by murderers on the Trace and now existing only as a portrait in the parlor.

She certainly can't ask Esther what to expect with Cornelius. Oh, some slaves had "weddings"; some of the funny dress-up ceremonies were even held right here at Carefree. But slave weddings were about as necessary as a hot wind in summer, and as binding as dried-up glue. In the slave houses, anybody could marry anybody they want to. Dear as Esther is, Stephanie can't ask her one thing about what goes on between a man and a woman in the dark. And she certainly can't ask that stiff Elenora Frankle.

Feeling afraid and very alone, she climbs back into her bed and pulls the covers up over her head.

"It's my own fault, I know it," Esther says as she washes dishes in the kitchen. Lucy Ida sits and watches, her fingers hooked through the handle of a coffee cup and her lower lip bulging with a chaw of tobacco. Either Lucy's chaws are getting bigger all the time or her face is shrinking, Esther thinks. The old woman sits with her bony knees poking up under her apron and drops of the milky coffee dribbling into her lap.

"I ain't raised the girl right," Esther says. "I held her back, not lettin' her go about town like most girls. And Master Emile--" she snorts, "--he always off on the Boeuf, not payin' the girl no mind. No mind a-t'all. How could we expect the girl to have a regular understandin' of things?"

"What don't she understan'?"

"Not one thing, seems to me most days. She's a lot like her mother, seems to me. Miss Josephine, she was a weak lady, too. Just hardly able to get by, whenever Master Emile would take hisself away to the Bayou Boeuf."

"I don't recall he went there much 'til she died."

"Well, that's true, he didn't. But Miss Josephine, she had to have help. Weak, she was. When her baby boy born, she carried on like she the only lady in the world ever had a baby like that, all twisted. Shoo. I told her, you cain't feel so bad about it. You can have mo' babies, I says. But, oh, she took on."

"She did, I remember."

"And now I see Miss Stephanie 'bout to get married, and her not knowin' one thing about how to take care of herself."

"You say she can cook and clean. We ain't seen her do it, though."

"She *can* cook and clean. That not what I mean. What I mean is, she ain't tough. Even a white lady's got to be tough to get along in this world. You can't just crumple at the first wind that blows agin' you. And I think she *will* crumple. She weak, kind of like a baby herself. You know what I mean. You can see it in her eyes. They soft and puppy-like." She looks out the window toward the arbor. "Miss Josephine had that puppy look, too, most of the time."

"Well," Lucy Ida says, "I expect Miss Stephanie jus' got some growin' up to do yet. What young girl ain't? She may's well do it married as not. Sometime havin' a man helps. 'Course, you wouldn't know about that."

"No, I wouldn't, Lucy. I never been married and I never hope to be. You excuse me now. I better go start gettin' her dressed."

Esther goes into the big house and climbs the stairs. She walks into Stephanie's room without knocking.

"Now, Miss Stephanie, there's one thing we need to discuss we ain't said nothin' about yet." Esther stands at the foot of the bed and looks at the mummy-like form lying on the bed swathed in sheets from head to toe.

Stephanie inches the covers down and stares at her with wide eyes.

Esther sighs. She can guess what's troubling Stephanie. No matter what Lucy Ida says, she feels sorry for the motherless child.

"The thing is, I don't dare let you go out to the Cocodrie without Master Emile knowin'. You might gonna be Mrs. Carson today, but you still little Stephanie to him. You come right back here after your weddin'. Then you sit yo'self right down and write your Papa a letter and tell him you married. Then see if he let you move out to the Cocodrie. Married's one thing, but movin's somethin' else. It ain't my place to give you a say-so on that."

A woman would have to be blind not to see the relief flooding the girl's face. Well, Stephanie would figure out what she had to figure out, like every other girl did. If a girl wants to have a man, she has to figure it out.

"And I'm thinkin' you better get up and let's get you ready. Master Cornelius be here before long, and y'all won't want to keep Reverend Hudson waitin'."

"All right," Stephanie says in a tiny voice. She sits on the side of the bed, watching as Esther takes the well-ironed yellow frock from the chiffarobe and lays it across the bed. And the only new thing Stephanie has to wear, a frilly bonnet with a velvet ribbon.

Esther says, "Let me get you some coffee," and bustles away down the hall. In a few minutes she's back. Stephanie sips the coffee, holding the cup with both hands.

"Now I think," Esther says, going back to the chiffarobe, "this pink ribbon would add somethin' pretty to that dress. Seem like a girl should have somethin' extra pretty on her weddin' day, don't it? You put this on, and then you better go on down to the parlor to wait for Master Cornelius. Happy as he looked the last time he left here, I'd be surprised if he ain't here earlier than usual."

Stephanie feels a thousand times better, knowing she'll get to come back here to Carefree, to her own room, her own bed. As soon as Esther leaves, she gets up and lets her nightgown fall to the floor.

Then she stands in front of the mirror and stares at herself. Her nakedness looks like nothing to her, just her own breasts, navel, loins -- the parts of her that are always kept hidden. But this would be what Cornelius wants to see.

Well, a man's blood must beat much hotter than her own. When she's sat with him these last few days on the gallery or in the parlor, with his arm around her -- oh, she liked that. She felt secure, and safe, and protected. And if he expected more, his breath on her face and his lips touching hers, his hands brushing her breasts discreetly, well, that was the price she'd pay for the attention he gives her, his straight-on way of looking at her, and his big knowledge about the world. She likes it more than not.

It scares her, the thought of marrying, but it's exciting, too. It'll be something new, after so many months in this quiet house. Since she'd finished school, the days have dragged along so slowly. Some days, boredom is like a brown cloud that hangs in all the rooms, smudging the very air. And she'll be coming home tonight.

She steps into her petticoats and then drops the yellow frock over her head. As she fastens the buttons she turns again to admire herself in the mirror. She likes this dress with its nipped-in waist and spreading skirt, and the neckline that demurely exposes her shoulders. The dress improves both her figure and her complexion. Let Cornelius look at her all he wanted; she's coming back to Carefree tonight, husband or no.

But her eyes are swollen and she doesn't look like herself. Sleeplessness and tears have pooched out her eyelids and given her blue eyes a little pig look. She pinches her cheeks to raise the color. Then she pins her hair up on top of her head and loops the pink ribbon around her waist.

Opening the door to her bedroom, she looks back one last time at her disheveled bedroom, and sees the cup John sent her. On an impulse she walks over and picks it up. Someone painted this, she thinks, peering closely to see the brush-strokes, tiny ridges of paint just barely visible in the larger designs. Someone in France -- a woman, certainly. The dainty artwork has a woman's touch.

Will she ever see France?

Quickly she sets the cup back on the bureau and runs downstairs to the parlor to wait for Cornelius. She sits on the sofa, tapping her feet and clasping and unclasping her damp hands.

CHAPTER THIRTEEN

Lucy Ida sits on the steps leading down from the back gallery, looking out to where the hill slopes down to a pond. Like a round mirror, the glassy surface of the water reflects the trees. Ducks fly over in the blue sky.

Esther goes out with her mending basket and sits beside her. "What you settin' out here in the hot sun for, aunty? You could take sick, sittin' out in this heat."

"I'm all right," Lucy Ida says. "Gotta die one of these days anyhow. May as well sit out if I feels like it."

Esther looks through the garments in her basket, giving each one a quick pat.

"You look awful restless this morning," Lucy says.

"I am. I need to settle down." Esther looks toward the slave house. "How's Daisy doing this mornin'?"

"Not so good yet, or her baby neither. Pore sickly li'l ole boy baby. Daisy can't get up yet. She's got the milk fever. She may's well take it easy whiles she can, 'cause she get up, they's a stack of ironing waitin'. Only ways a woman can get any rest in this slaves' life is childbed and gettin' old. If she live to get old."

"You did, aunty."

Lucy Ida claps her hands on her knees. "Law, I say I did! Ninety-two this month, and I remember every year I had, since I was about four or five."

Esther threads a needle and holds up Theresa's blouse, which has a side-seam pulled open. She lays the garment in her lap and begins to stitch it up. "Now, what do you remember from four or five? I can't remember anything that far back."

Lucy looks out toward the trees. "I remember my mammy making hoe cakes for me one winter mornin', and the wind just howlin' 'round the door of our old cabin, and me sittin' on the floor waiting for that hoe-cake. I couldn'a been but maybe four."

"And where was that?"

"Up in South Caroline. I only been in Mississippi since I was fifty. In South Caroline before that."

"Well, you earned your reward, after all these years. You can take it easy."

Lucy snorts. "There ain't no reward for bein' a slave."

Esther's big hands rest on her basket. "Well, I been in Mississippi my whole life. Born and raised. And I used to think I could get my freedom some way, but since I been older, I figure slaves is just what we is. Make the best of it and don't let it bother you. Wait for that better world that's comin'."

Lucy Ida glances at her, then looks away. "I never could make the best of it. I used to want my freedom so bad, but I guess I went after it in all the wrong ways. My old master, James Foster, he said he'd give me my freedom someday. That was when I was twenty. That oldest boy of his came visitin' me. Ugliest man for a young man you ever saw." *Tee-hee.* "You'd think that might've give James Foster a reason to give me my freedom, just for a reward, but it didn't. By the time I was thirty I figured James Foster wasn't nothin' but talk, so I decided to go for it another way. I run off twice. Second time I had to wear a iron collar for three months. So then I just went wild. Law. There wasn't nothin' I didn't do."

"I can't imagine you wild, aunty," Esther says as she goes back to her sewing.

"Well, I was. And I had a good reason to be. I used to wish I could just fly away like a goose, and be free. Then when I was fifty, I come down here. My master's son, he sold me to a man comin' down to Mississippi. Seem like the whole state was comin' down here then. So here we come too." Lucy is silent for a moment, listening to the ducks squawking as they settle at the shore of the pond. "My whole life I been tryin' to figure out how to get what old James Foster promised me. Now I'm so old, I think maybe I finally figured it out."

"How?" Esther asks warily. Lucy sometimes puts a barb as sharp as any fishhook in her words.

Lucy spits a stream of tobacco juice onto the black soil next to the step. "Just get old! Then old master gotta take care of you, and he can't make you work. Live long enough, you get back at him."

"You ain't gettin' back at Master James Foster. He be dead by now."

"I gettin' back at who I can."

Esther bites off the end of her thread and folds Theresa's blouse into the basket. Then she stands up.

Lucy Ida speaks up again. "Miss Stephanie's goin' off to get married today?"

Esther nods. "She's in there waitin' for Master Cornelius right now."

"I'm glad you helpin' her out. That girl get married, there won't be nobody here need waitin' on but Sophronia, and you can take it easy."

Some ducks fly over, low, and land at the pond. Lucy turns her small face upward, to look at the sky where they'd passed. "You ought to take it easy as you can," she says. "Don't fret yourself about Miss Stephanie gettin' married. It's just nature takin' its course. And you know what? Old as I am, I still wish I could have that ducks'-eye view."

Stephanie nudges the curtains back to peek out when she hears someone riding up to the house, but she waits in the parlor until Esther brings Cornelius in. Then there he is, handsome and smiling, and he carries a nosegay he's picked somewhere along the road -- wild roses and violets. She takes the flowers and lets him bundle her into his arms.

He wears a black broadcloth coat; the fabric of his shirt is soft over his muscular body. She loves the smell of him.

Of course she'll marry Cornelius. What had she been thinking? She hasn't come this far with him to back out now. She brushes her hands against her eyes. It won't do for a bride to have wet cheeks.

"Shall we go?" he asks formally, releasing her. He motions toward the door.

Esther stands in the doorway. "Now y'all comin' right back here after the marryin'," she says to Cornelius. "I give Miss Stephanie my say-so to get married. After all, I could see she was gonna make herself sick, the way she was moping about, but you know I can't actually give her my say-so to move away from Carefree. That'd have to come from Master Emile."

Cornelius glances at Stephanie. "Esther's right, Cornelius," she says. "I can't move out to the Cocodrie with you 'til Papa gives permission. I'll write him a letter. This very evening." Her voice wavers. She feels weak again.

Emile's name hangs in the air. Stephanie puts her face against Cornelius's sleeve.

A crash in the shrubbery outside the window makes them turn around to look. Esther bustles over and leans out the window. "You girls go on and quit spyin'!" she orders. "Or you gonna get a switchin' sure enough!" They see Helene and Theresa running across the lawn giggling, their skirts swinging as they scamper.

"Y'all best get movin'," Esther says as she turns around. "Before Miss Sophronia overhear something she ain't supposed to hear."

Stephanie and Cornelius hurry out. Cornelius helps Stephanie up into the buggy and then climbs up beside her. He drives eastward out of Natchez. Stephanie turns once to look over her shoulder at the big red brick house receding on its tree-sprinkled hilltop.

See, it isn't such a big thing to get married, Stephanie tells herself. She and Cornelius are travelling the same road she travelled with Esther a few days ago, except now it's muddy and soft instead of dusty and hard. The woods haven't changed. There's the same turn in the road she remembered, and the place where three cabins line up along the road, and the dip to ford Saint Catherine's Creek.

And then they're at the same place she'd been a few days ago, only now the congregation is singing. The two o'clock meeting must be starting. Why, she knows about that, and can name when all the services are! And before hardly any time passes, here's Reverend Hudson again, looking just as he looked before. And he has a little book, which he flips open. He has them stand in front of him, outside the brush arbor.

Cornelius is repeating some words. It's just like the May Cotillion at the Elizabeth Girls' School, when every girl read a part. In a moment she sees the men staring at her, and she knows it's time for her to say her part, too. And she does.

And if Cornelius surprises her by putting a little gold ring on her finger, well, he's always brought her presents, like this nosegay. The ring is a plain gold band, a little too big.

Hudson snaps the book closed. "Now we gotta sign the paper," he says. "Here's the evidence. Spell your names for me." And Cornelius spells both their names, which is just as well. There's a flutter in her throat.

Hudson scribbles the names. "Oh, we need a witness," he says. He motions to another man who stands nearby. "Tom, come witness this here marriage."

"Yessir." Tom marks an "x" on the bottom of the paper Hudson holds out for him.

"Oh, I forgot you cain't write," Hudson says. "Well, that'll do, anyway." He writes "Tom Frazier his mark," on the bottom. Then he signs his own name and hands the paper to Cornelius.

"And I always record weddin's in my book. Here 'tis." He lifts a leather-bound book from atop a trunk and writes their names in it. Stephanie sees that he misspelled her last name, writing "Coqutar," but she doesn't correct him.

Cornelius hands the parson a dollar bill. Hudson shakes Cornelius's hand and then rushes off to his sermon without looking back.

"Let's get out of here before they want us to stay for church," Cornelius says.

They run to the buggy and drive away. Cornelius holds her close to him.

"That was my mammy's ring," he says.

"Oh," Stephanie says. Well, it might be second-hand, but you couldn't tell. It gleams in spite of a patina of tiny nicks and scratches. It makes her hand look strange. They drive down the creek's steep bank. As soon as they drive up out of the creek bed, the road is narrower, and the woods thicker, than she remembers.

Cornelius says, "Let's stop." He turns the buggy onto a side path, the kind of barely-used track that leads to some isolated field tucked away in the deep woods. He pulls the horse to a halt in a little clearing. The trees, freshened by yesterday's rain, are full of birds. Stephanie turns to him. This is not familiar.

He reaches behind her and pulls out a folded blanket. "I brought this in case it might rain," he says, "but I can think of another use for it."

He helps her down. Then he pulls off his coat and lays it on the seat. Stephanie looks around, half-expecting to see someone, but all around are just the leafy woods. Cornelius spreads the blanket on the ground behind a hedge of honeysuckles growing up a dead tree's skeleton. Then he sits down and pulls her down to him and takes her into his arms.

"How's it feel to be married?" he asks, putting little kisses along her throat.

Oh, she starts to say, it's not so different from everything else, but he kisses her again and then fumbles with the buttons of her dress. Sunlight dapples across her breasts, and she feels its warmth and a breeze on her belly. She looks down at her own white body as his hands caress her breasts, her belly, the insides of her thighs. He whispers to her and a warm wave of desire sweeps over her -- that is familiar -- and her hips thrust upward as she reaches for him.

But then he won't stop. Whatever brief moment of desire she's felt for him has gone. And he's propelled by some unstoppable force. His face is next her own, his breathing loud in her ear. And this is different from anything she's ever done.

When he finishes she lies shamed under him, her teeth clenched, her eyes closed so she won't have to see him looking at her.

He rolls away from her and she reaches down for her dress, which is crumpled at her feet, and pulls it up. Then she gets up and pulls her petticoats on and draws the pink ribbon around her waist.

"I want to go home."

He gets to his feet, closing his trousers, and looks at her closely. "Are you all right?"

She fumbles with the ribbon, finally getting it to tie. Where is her nosegay? "Let's go, please!"

He bends over to put his arm around her and his face right in front of hers. "Are you all right?"

But his face is a watery blur. She turns away from him to walk back to the buggy. And her nosegay is a crumpled mess, back there on the blanket.

She rides in silence all the way back to Natchez. When they arrive at Carefree, she stands stiffly on the steps. Cornelius kisses her.

"Stephanie, what is wrong?" he asks. She hears a new sound in his voice, but it's too much to think about. She's had enough new things for one afternoon.

"I'll come back on Saturday," he says finally, staring hard at her.

She nods and continues standing on the steps as he rides away. Then she returns alone to her peach-colored bedroom, her shoes slapping the stairs in time with the ticks of the hall clock. For once Esther and Lucy Ida and Esther's two brats are nowhere around.

She unhooks her wrinkled dress and lets it fall to the floor. Then she steps out of her petticoats, and flops onto her bed.

So that's it, what all the hot rising blood's about. What the girls whispered about at school. Stories, and fantasies, and, she knows now, falsehoods. Now she knows it's more than the hot rush of desire, the feeling that a man absolutely wanted her, and her alone. The rest of it's dirty, and it hurts. And it was shameful, to do it out in the woods. Why couldn't he just wait? She throws her arm over her face.

And the way he'd been when it was over, standing in the woods, putting his shirt inside his pants. She'd been shocked at the intimacy of that moment; it was in a way more intimate even than the embrace itself. No other woman ever saw him that way, she's certain.

Now she wants more than anything to get her sore and dirtied body into a hot bath. She opens her bedroom door and leans out, calling "Esther!" but no one answers. Those lazy bones have probably gone back to their own quarters by now, and her pitcher of water is all she has. But she wants to wash.

She pours the water into the wash-basin. Then, using a tea-towel Esther left folded on the dresser, she washes herself. She puts on her dressing gown and kicks the garments she wore today into the corner. Esther will take care of them.

She unpins her hair and lets it fall loose and then brushes it hard. Then she sits down at her desk and takes out a sheet of writing paper. She has to write her papa. He has to know what she's done. She starts once and crumples the letter up and throws it on the floor in frustration.

Then she starts again, dipping the pen into the inkwell and scratching it across the page. After all, it shouldn't be so hard to write a letter to her papa. She's written him so many letters down through the years, and this one's no different. Her handwriting is the same as ever, same loops and scratches. She'll just tell him what she has to tell him. That's all.

A half-dozen men have gathered under the hill, where Cornelius waits for the ferry. They're talking about a fight in Vidalia. Cornelius can see that they're frantic to be over there. They pace the dock, looking across the river. But the ferry sits unmoving at the Vidalia landing. Cornelius stands apart from them, holding his horse's reins.

He hates leaving Natchez this way, but he doesn't know what else to do. He didn't expect Stephanie to react to him the way she did. The girls he'd had before -- Ruetta Halloran in the Cocodrie and, before her, the fast girls in New Orleans – they'd enjoyed him as much as he'd enjoyed them. And before that, when he worked on boats like this big steamer *John Jay* that was pulling out from the dock, and he'd gone to visit the girls that all the boatmen knew, those girls always seemed to welcome him. Some, he thought, even favored him.

Cornelius thought he knew what pleased a woman. And he tried to please Stephanie. It had been in his favorite way, too, out in the woods, with only the sounds of nature all around them. Nature's bedroom. So why this hurtful reaction from Stephanie? What did he do wrong?

At last the ferry begins to move, torturing the other men on the dock with its slow approach. When it arrives Cornelius waits until the others rush up the plank. Then he leads Tearose onto the ferry.

It'll be good to get home, even though it'll be dark before he gets to the bayou. There's still the cotton waiting to be worked. Malachi and Jenny won't do much if he's not there to see that they work. And the crop's looking so good.

Natchez-Under-the-Hill smelled dank and boozy, but out here on the river the breeze cools his face. But it doesn't feel right to be leaving Stephanie in Natchez.

And what did he do wrong? What?

CHAPTER FOURTEEN

In the morning the letter that took Stephanie an hour to write lies folded on the desk with Emile's address inscribed on the outside. From her deep featherbed, Stephanie watches sunlight draw a rectangle halfway up the bedroom wall, so she knows she's slept later than usual.

Esther, carrying Stephanie's breakfast tray, opens the door. Stephanie sits up on the bed and stares at her. Her body feels sore.

"Lucy Ida died last evening," Esther says. She sets the tray on the table.

"Died?"

"Yessum. Died about six o'clock. Just lay down for her rest, and then after a while she couldn't breathe too good, so she called out to Theresa. So Theresa seen she was bad, and she run and got me. We was all with her when she passed."

Stephanie blinks. Her eyes feel grainy and dim. She can't think of what she should say. "She was ninety-two, after all."

"She was."

"No wonder I didn't see anybody when I came back yesterday."

Esther comes over and takes her hand to look at the ring. "And now you Mrs. Carson," she says. "Ain't that fine."

Stephanie pulls her hand away. "Well, I don't know how fine it is, seeing as it happened on the day Lucy died."

"Master Carson's a fine man."

Stephanie glances at the pile of clothes in the corner. Well, Esther can just think what she wants.

"I need fresh bath water," she says, pointing toward the wash-basin with its gray cold water.

"Yes, ma'am. Now, Lucy Ida is laid out in her room in the quarters. Sarah and me washed her body, and laid her out there. We waked her last night."

Stephanie stares at the older woman, pondering the odd phrase. We waked her; but you can't wake the dead. Lucy Ida didn't waken.

"We buryin' her at twelve o'clock," Esther goes on. "And I knew you'd be there, most surely, seein' Master Emile's not here and Miss Sophronia -- well..."

Stephanie puts her hand to her forehead. Go to a burying? Can't Esther see this is the worst day for it, when she has so much to figure out? But Esther's standing there, looking wise like she is, and she's right, of course: Lucy Ida belonged to Carefree, so it's only proper for a white person from Carefree to be at her funeral. It occurs to Stephanie that in all her life she's never been to the slave burying ground down the hill.

"All right, I'll go," she says.

She looks over at the letter on the desk. Best to get it mailed and out of the house. "I'll need my black dress. Get it for me, will you? And get Charlie to bring the buggy around. I'm going into town this morning."

Esther goes over to the chiffarobe to get the dress. "You comin' to view the body?"

Oh Lord, that too? "All right. When I get back."

After Esther leaves, Stephanie bathes and dresses and brushes her hair. Standing in front of the mirror, she spreads her fingers to study her ring. It still looks strange. She takes it off and sets it on the dresser.

She drives to the King's Tavern and stops the buggy on the street. She climbs down and stands for a moment, smoothing her skirt and patting her hair into place. Looking up, she sees a familiar gray horse cantering down the hill, and its rider with the shock of blond hair can only be John Landerson. She puts her hand up to her mouth. Oh, she can't see John. Not now.

She darts in front of a barouche coming from the other direction and runs into the King's Tavern to mail her letter. Looking out through its smudged small-paned windows, she sees John ride past without slowing.

When she comes out, she squints in the bright sunlight. A group of half-grown boys are sauntering along the sidewalk, catcalling and shoving at each other. One of them calls out something to her. She doesn't catch it, but all the boys hoot in her direction as they prance by.

She blushes as she runs to the buggy and climbs up. What are they laughing at? Is there some oddness about herself she hasn't seen? Can't they tell she's a respectable woman?

She yanks on the reins and drives away. If Cornelius were here, he'd protect her from this riff-raff. As she drives up the street she notices her ringless hand. Already it looks as if she should have the ring on. Maybe there is something to this marriage, after all. Mrs. Stephanie Coqterre Carson. It has a solid sound to it. She'll put the ring back on, as soon as she gets back to Carefree. And whatever Papa says, she'll just handle when the time comes.

And it's odd how having a little wedding ceremony, and wearing a ring, and doing what Cornelius had done yesterday -- so indecently out in the woods like a couple of savages -- could make her think she was so respectable, in town.

But back at Carefree, there's a body waiting for her to view it. She dreads it as she drives up the hill to her home. A body! Has she ever seen a dead person before? Not that she remembers. Why can't Sophronia get up out of her bed and do something, for once? But it's getting on to twelve o'clock. She has to hurry.

She gets down from the buggy and walks through the long central hallway out to the back of the house. At the slave-house, all the slaves of Carefree, and a few from neighboring houses, are standing around the door of Lucy Ida's room. The women are dressed all in white with tignons wrapping their heads. Even Esther's two girls are wearing white dresses. The men wear shabby black coats. The slaves stand back to let her pass.

Oh, she isn't ready for this. They're expecting her to be the mistress of Carefree, and it should be Sophronia! Or Papa should be here! She steps into the low-ceilinged room.

Like all the slave rooms at Carefree, Lucy Ida's room is small and simple, its only furniture a bed and chair and a shelf for her things. And there on the narrow bed is little Lucy Ida, looking like she's asleep, wearing a white dress. An open pine coffin sits at the foot of the bed.

Gray-haired Sarah sits next to her mother's body, but she stands up when Stephanie comes in. Stephanie knows she should do something, but what? She puts her hand on Sarah's arm and says, "I'm sorry, Sarah."

"Thank you, Miss Stephanie." Then Sarah begins to heave long sighs which turn into sobs, then wails. Stephanie stares at the floor, studying the little cracks between the boards where she can just see the light on the ground beneath. How long should she stay? What should she do? She abruptly walks out the door and runs up the steps into the main house.

But it's five minutes to twelve, she sees by the hall clock. And Charlie the stable-boy is standing at the front door, peering down the hall. She walks over to him.

"I brung the buggy for you to ride in, Miss Stephanie," he says. "It's a good ways down to that cemetery, so I knows you want to ride."

Stephanie sighs and walks out across the gallery. Is she not safe anywhere? She climbs up into the buggy and Charlie climbs up in front. He drives around to the back, where the men are carrying the coffin out of Lucy Ida's room. They form a procession, first the men with the coffin, then Sarah, held up by Esther, then Stephanie and Charlie in the buggy. The other slaves have waited for Stephanie to get in line. They follow straggling in a line down the hill past the pond.

They go slowly through the woods and come out onto a clearing hemmed in by a sagging wooden fence. This is the slave burying ground, Stephanie realizes. There are little humps of earth -- old graves, without markers. A hole with a mound of dirt on one side marks the place where Lucy Ida will be buried. Stephanie gets down from the buggy and stands beside Sarah and Esther as the men set the coffin on the ground.

Stephanie looks around. These mounds under the grass -- were they all Carefree slaves, once? She never knew any to die, in her own short life. And some of the graves are so small. Did all these children die at Carefree?

Charlie says a prayer, his voice getting louder and softer and covering up Sarah's sobs. Then Charlie starts to talk, stepping out in front of the others in his dapper small way.

"We here to bury Lucy Ida, who died yestiddy," he begins. "She was ninety-two years old. She belong to Master Emile Coqterre here in Natchez, Mississippi, for more than forty years. Before that, she belong to Master William Foster in South Caroline. And before that, she belong to Master James Foster, Master William's pappy. She come to Mississippi when she was fifty years old, and she had her daughter with her when she come. That's Sarah over there." He points in Sarah's direction. "Now Lucy's free -- free -- of all her burdens, and may the good Lord rest her soul."

Charlie's speech is over. "Amen," Stephanie whispers, making the sign of the cross.

The women move away as the men lower the coffin into the ground. Stephanie touches Esther's arm. "Esther, who are all the ones buried here? I didn't know so many had died."

"They mostly chilrun," Esther says. "Two of 'em's mine -- those two over there by the fence. And the rest belong to the others, or they just older ones that's gone on."

"What on earth did they die of? Yellow fever?"

"Yellow Jack took most of 'em. My two died of malaria, and they not one year old. Two li'l boys."

"I never knew that. Didn't you want markers for their graves?"

Esther walks beside her, looking at the ground. "I couldn't read 'em if they *was* marked. I know the one closest to the fence is Littleton, and the other one is August."

Stephanie climbs up on the buggy and rides back in the procession to the house. She has so much to think about -- her marriage, and what Cornelius did to her, and Esther with two babies buried in the graveyard without markers, and Lucy Ida. Lucy Ida was born ninety-two years ago -- 1741. And even after all this time, someone said the name of the man who was her old master back where she was born. James Foster. Would her own name be told someday, somewhere, at a funeral for Daisy's little just-born baby, when he died? Suppose he lived ninety-two years like Lucy Ida did. That would be 1925. Would some speaker at his funeral say, "He was born at Carefree in Natchez, Mississippi, and he belonged to Mrs. Stephanie Coqterre Carson"? Well, he belongs to Papa, really. But just suppose they said it was her? A person's name might be told anywhere, anytime. Even ninety-two years away. Mister James Foster probably never dreamed his name would be told ninety-two years later, and a long way from where he was, in South Carolina.

Her name might be told too, in some far-off place at some far-off time: Mrs. Stephanie Coqterre Carson. It was a rather thrilling thought.

All that afternoon she stays in her bedroom, propped up against the bed-pillows and staring at the blank wall opposite her bed, thinking. Her wedding ring still sits on the dresser, next to the cup John sent her.

She has to do something about her marriage, she knows. Cornelius will be back tomorrow. He was wounded by the way she treated him; but she'd been wounded, too. Taken by surprise. And much too roughly.

But what can she do? She knows so little -- nothing, really, about what to do, or what could make it better. And how can she ever find the words to tell Cornelius? Words that never passed her lips before -- how can she have the courage to speak them now?

Here she'd hoped and dreamed, and thought about it, and it just wasn't fair for her lovemaking with Cornelius to be just -- like it had been, rough and dirty and out in the open. It could *not* be like that. She wants it sweet and delicious and full of love. It has to be.

She gets out of bed and slips her ring back on her finger. Then she goes downstairs to Sophronia's room. When she was younger, she'd talked to Sophronia many times when Papa was away on the Boeuf, but lately Sophronia's fallen in love with John Barleycorn and almost never comes out of her room. There's no one else she can possibly ask, but praise be stars if Sophronia isn't drunk as a goose by this time of the day. She eases open the door.

"Aunt Sophronia?"

Sophronia looks up. Stephanie swallows hard. "May I talk to you, please?"

Sophronia shifts herself around and puts her pillow up against the carved headboard. "Why, sure, Stephanie. Come on in and have yourself a seat." She pats the edge of the bed for Stephanie to sit beside her.

Stephanie hesitates. Sophronia doesn't seem really drunk. Her voice is a little loud, her speech a little slurry and eager, but she doesn't sound exactly sotted. So Stephanie closes the door and goes over to sit on the side of the bed.

"Now, what's troublin' you?" Sophronia asked. "Somethin' about Lucy Ida's funeral, I bet. I saw y'all comin' up the hill down there, and I was *proud* of how you went down there in place of your papa."

Stephanie purses her lips. *It should have been you.*

She takes a deep breath. "Did you know I got married?" She holds out her hand so Sophronia can see the ring.

"Lands, no, I didn't know it!"

Stephanie cringes. She wants Sophronia to keep her voice down. Sophronia grabs Stephanie's hand. "Well, look at that! A weddin' ring! And when did you do this?"

"Yesterday," Stephanie whispers. Well, Papa would know soon, so everyone else might as well know. "Cornelius and I eloped." In her sober moments Sophronia must have seen Cornelius here at Carefree, sitting in the parlor or on the gallery steps.

"Well, that's just fine!" Sophronia wriggles herself up until she's half-sitting. She smiles, almost coquettishly. She was pretty once; Stephanie can see it now. "Your Papa doesn't know, though, does he? Well, he'll come to accept it, I know."

"Well, um, I need to talk to you about it," Stephanie says, looking down at her hands. "There's nobody else I can talk to, and I -- need to find out some things."

"Well, just ask me any questions you have," Sophronia says. She pats the girl's hands. "I might be able to help. I was married once, you know."

"I didn't know that!"

"Oh, I don't talk about it much, but yes ma'am, I was married for five years. Then Mister Johnson went off to sea and I never saw him again. But I believe I remember what it's like to be just married, and seventeen."

Stephanie swallows again. Well, Sophronia was being friendly today, trying to rise up out of her drink to help. Stephanie looks at the older woman she called "Aunt," although they're really no relation. Her stepfather's sister -- breezy and loud, so different from her Papa.

Why did Sophronia's life take such a fall? Here she is, no more than thirty-five, and all she thinks about are drinking and then sleeping it off. And not being bothered about anything.

For Stephanie, things have to be better. Otherwise, her own life might take a fall, too. She plunges ahead. "Well, Cornelius was -- just too rough, you know? It didn't feel right to me, but he didn't even ask me. He just kept going, and it hurt, and it was like I wasn't even there. And he wouldn't stop. Why would he do that?" Stephanie's eyes brim with tears of embarrassment.

Sophronia smiles, knowingly. "Oh, honey, that's -- just men. My husband Mister Johnson was like that at first. It's up to us women to teach 'em."

"But how can we? He was so strong I couldn't move."

"A man *is* strong. And we just have to tell 'em what we like and what we don't like. That's what I did, and Mister Johnson learned. They can all learn."

"Why don't they just know already? Cornelius knows so much. He's been everywhere, and he can do so much. How could he not know how to treat me? I thought he didn't even love me."

"Does he treat you good otherwise, honey?"

"Well, yes! He brings me things and treats me good. It's just this. And I had no idea!"

"Well, you've got to realize that these men we marry, most of 'em have never been with a decent woman before. How could they? There's no proper women available. So the girls they're with before they marry, they just don't give 'em any idea how to be with a virgin. Or even with a decent woman. It's just quick and pay 'em the money. It ain't real love."

Stephanie swallows hard. "So what can I do?" Her face is burning.

"Well, you've got to tell him what you like. Or show him. He probably wants to rush. They all do. You got to get him to take his time. It's the only way to make it good for you. If he rushes, it won't be good, and it'll hurt."

"I don't know if I can tell him. Or show him."

"One way you can slow him down is, remember, he'd like you to do things for him, too."

"He would?"

"His body's got feelin's too."

Stephanie nods numbly. This hasn't occurred to her. "He's coming back tomorrow."

"Then that's when you start. Just put on your prettiest dressing gown, and make him welcome. Just show him how to take his time, and you do some things for him, and it'll be good for you like it is for him. But you'll have to teach him what to do." Sophronia's voice grows softer. "Child, all this rememberin' Mister Johnson's makin' me sad. You better go on out of here now. I don't like to dwell on the past too much."

Stephanie walks out and closes the door. Then she goes upstairs and lies on her own bed, thinking about what Sophronia said.

Sophronia was right. Well, she'd better make some plans. She has to teach Cornelius what she wants, if she was going to be his wife; and if he was going to be her husband, he has to learn it.

Already today she's done things she'd never thought she could do. She's sent a bold letter to her papa, and comforted Sarah, and stood for Carefree while they put Lucy Ida in the ground. And she'd talked with Sophronia about things she'd never talked about with anyone. She could certainly teach Cornelius. When he comes back tomorrow, she'll begin.

And when Esther comes in, she's going to tell her to put that cup in the hutch with the rest of the china. It's such a close match, by tomorrow nobody will be able to tell it from the rest of the cups.

CHAPTER FIFTEEN

Something unusual is making Cornelius so snappish, Malachi thinks. At breakfast he yelled at Jenny when she dropped her half biscuit for the dog like she always does. And now, working in the field, Cornelius wants them all to work so fast.

Well, Malachi can hoe cotton only so fast and no faster. If Cornelius leaves him behind in the cotton row, that's how it'll have to be. He'd rather work alone than alongside a sour-hearted master any day. He's seen enough of those. And last night when Cornelius kept the whiskey to himself, drinking way too much of it, well, Mal won't talk much to somebody who won't share the jug.

Cornelius has got hisself married, Mal thinks. When he came home last night, he took a paper from his coat pocket and set it on the bureau, smoothing it out. A marrying-document, Malachi would bet. But Cornelius came home by hisself, and he didn't say a word about Miss Stephanie.

He'd talked about this Miss Stephanie for the past few days like she was already here with them. He'd had Mal and Jenny mop the cabin floor and pick up whatever needed picking up inside the cabin. But she ain't here now.

The change in Cornelius rattles Malachi more than Jenny, who steps lightly around it, thinking about her kittens and half-understanding the language. Malachi was surprised, a few weeks back, when Cornelius didn't sell the girl at the frolic; he'd have sworn that was gonna happen. But since then she's become a passable worker, and even learned to talk a little, so maybe Cornelius plans to keep her. Maybe.

In the late afternoon, Malachi sees Jenny sitting on a log by the little house, playing with the kittens. He goes over and sits near her, picking up a short, thick stick from the ground. "You want me to carve you a doll?"

She shrugs. "Yessir."

He snorts. "You don't have to 'yessuh' me. I'm just an old slave," he mutters. "Course, you say that to everybody, 'cause you don't know no different." He takes out his knife and begins to whittle. He talks in a low voice so Cornelius, who's sitting on the porch some yards away, can't hear. "You need to learn some things, though. Bein' a slave ain't good."

She doesn't look at him.

"I was sold away from my mammy when I was twelve years old," Malachi goes on. "Sold away to pay a gamblin' debt of my master's oldest son. And I never seen my mammy from that day to this. If I was free," he says as he gouges eyes in the wood, "the first thing I'd do is, I'd go see my old mammy. 'Course, I don't know if she's alive or dead, but I'd go to Virginny and find out. My brother, too -- I'd like to see him. But I don't reckon I ever will get to."

Jenny's feet tap out a silent tune.

"Now, my first home, that was a big plantation. Tobacky. What I miss the most about the big plantation is the get-togethers and the singing. When I first come here, it was lonesome, with nobody but me and Cornelius for the longest time, and nobody else much coming by to talk to. And then he got you, and at first you wouldn't talk. Me and him both, we thought you was a mute." He looks over at Cornelius. "He think he gonna be rich someday, but I don't know. It look to me like it's a long way between him and those rich planters.

"I was sold three times in my life, but I expect the last time was it. Master Cornelius, he'll probably keep me. You get old, you get hard to sell. I had two wifes, one at the second place I was at, and one at the third. One place was a cane plantation, one was tobacky, and one was cotton. I guess this place counts as cotton, too, but it's the littlest place I ever worked at.

"When slaves is sold – oh, that is a awful sight. The master, he never let you know 'til it happen, 'cause he knows how you gonna act when you find out. If he ain't been cruel, the slaves'll be screamin' and cryin' not to be sold, the men and women both. And cryin' for him not to sell the chilrun. I seen slaves runnin' around like crazy people, so bad the master and the overseer had to round 'em up with horses. Oh, you don't know!" Chips fly off the wooden doll. "So if you ever gonna be sold, just remember, you won't know a thing about it 'til it happen. They always keep it a secret."

Jenny sets her kitten down on the ground.

"Course, they *is* that underground railroad," he goes on. "That freedom road. But I ain't goin' on it. And you for sure ain't. A little old kid like you, you'd be catched by nightfall."

"And *then*," he says dramatically as he turns the figure over to carve its back, "you'd get sold for sure!"

Jenny leans over to pull her wandering kitten back between her feet.

"Sit still, girl. How you expect me to finish this doll with you wigglin' around like that? I might cut my finger. Where you from, anyways?"

Jenny shrugs.

"Well, I knows he got you in Natchez, but you come from Africa, I bet. Where's your mammy?"

Again she shrugs.

"And what's 'Kofi' mean?"

"Hm?"

"We heard you say that one mornin' when you was still asleep. You said 'Kofi' plain as anything. Cornelius asks me what it means. How'm I suppose to know? He looked at me like I was keepin' something a secret."

Jenny's hands draw a shape in the air. "Kofi," she says. "My brother."

"Where's your brother at?"

Her fingers drum against her skirt. She shrugs.

"Well, I don't know where my brother is, neither."

He whittles out indentations for the doll's legs and then hands her the crude figure. "Here's your play-pretty. Now, you go on and let me be."

Jenny turns the doll over in her hands and examines it carefully as her kitten scampers off unnoticed. She gets a scrap of an old rag from the cabin and winds it around the doll, and spends the rest of the evening playing with it, crooning to it and tucking it into her bed.

The girl probably thinks he's just a foolish old story-teller, Mal thinks. She's probably already forgot everything he said. And maybe he's foolish all right, but everything he said to her today is true.

The next morning when Cornelius gets up he smells the odor of a bear on the porch. He sees its spoor around the steps, and the stinging yellow scent burns his nostrils. On the bed not two yards away from the steps, Jenny sleeps on her stomach like she always does, with one arm circling her doll. It's a worry that a bear's come so close. But impatient as he is to get to Natchez, he realizes this is something he has to see about before he leaves.

He leads Tearose over to the little house, calling "Mal!" before he reaches the door. Malachi swings the door open and comes out, his face creased with sleep, his pants sagging on his frame.

"Yessir?"

"A bear's come in the night, Mal," Cornelius says, pointing toward the porch. "It came right up near where Jenny sleeps. You watch out for it 'til I get back."

"Yessir."

"Keep Jenny close by the cabin, will you? Don't let her go out farther than the stable. And if she draws water, you go with her."

Mal rubs his stubbly chin. "You think it'll come back in daylight?"

"Ain't no telling. I'm going to Natchez, and I might not be back 'til late. She's still asleep. If you see that bear, both of you go in the cabin and close the door. Put a chair against the door if you have to."

Cornelius looks at Malachi; Mal's getting old, he thinks. He can see it in the old man's rheumy eyes and sloping shoulders. It's almost like he's melting into the earth. Cornelius has the sudden thought that if he stayed home today he could keep Malachi from getting old and protect Jenny from the bear.

But something else is calling him -- a promise he made to come back to Natchez on Saturday, to resolve what must be resolved. He's responsible for his two people here, but in Natchez a woman who has his name is waiting. Well, go he will. He mounts the horse and rides away. But all through the long ride he remembers the bear's spoor, and it bothers him.

Hours later, when he gets to Carefree, Esther answers the door. Cornelius sees Theresa and Helene peering out from under the stairs, like the spies they are. Esther shoos her girls out the back door, threatening to take a switch to them, and then goes out herself.

The house is quiet except for the ticking of the hall-clock. He walks down the hall, looking into the empty rooms on both sides. The staircase is in front of him, curving upward to the second floor. At the top of the stairs he calls "Stephanie?" The door nearest him opens, and Stephanie is standing there. She wears a gauzy dressing-gown, and she hasn't bothered to tie the ribbon around her waist, so it hangs open from her shoulders. And from behind her the sunlight floods her with a peach-colored glow.

She steps back from the doorway. He walks in and shuts the door. He stands just inside the door and looks at her for a long moment.

"Are you all right?" he asks, as he'd asked her two days earlier. She hadn't answered then.

"I am," she says.

He sits on the chair and pulls off his boots. Then he goes over and kisses her, pushing the dressing gown away from her and leading her over to the soft featherbed. From the hall downstairs the hall-clock chimes the noon-hour, a mellow slow cadence. Then the big house is quiet again during the whole long afternoon, while upstairs two people are quiet, but together.

CHAPTER SIXTEEN

Emile stands at the edge of a charred canefield with Bernard Ratout.

"Nothin' much we can do now, m'sieur," Ratout says, wiping his face with a bandanna. Under his straw hat his hair sticks to his forehead. "Wait for Janyerry and burn off the stubble like we always do. We be gettin' ready for the next crop then, anyways."

"It makes an ugly sight, all this burned," Emile says, motioning toward the blackened field that spreads to the horizon. "I hate to look at it. What we need now 's rain."

"Don't look like much chaince," Ratout says. Both men squint up at the sky.

A rider is raising a cloud of ashy dust along the edge of the field. "Where's Hawthorne been?" Emile asks, recognizing the figure on the horse as his brawny field-hand.

"I sent him into town this mornin' to get some supplies."

Hawthorne rides over to them and swings down from the horse. "Letter come."

"What'd you do, ride straight from town without slowin' down?" Ratout asks.

"Yessir. I knew Master Emile 'd want his letter."

"Every letter I get lately's been bad news." Emile turns his back to them as he rips it open. He knows Stephanie's stationery and her round script.

Sweat inches down the back of his neck as he reads. Then he slaps his leg furiously with his hand and his shoulders slump. The pages flutter to the ground. He snatches them up and stuffs them into his pocket. He storms away across the field.

"Guess I shouldn' a been in such a hurry to bring it," Hawthorne says, patting the roan's quivering flank.

The office that Dr. Herman Brice has on Franklin Street in Natchez has one window, but it's so dirty and lined with bottles that he keeps a lamp burning all day. Especially on a day dark as this one, when rain drums the roof and black clouds swirl over the town. It's been dead quiet all day, no patients wanting to come out into the rain. He's surprised when Emile Coqterre, dripping in a gray cape, opens the door.

"Lands, Emile, you could've waited til the weather got bad." The doctor's eyes twinkle, and he extends his soft hand to Emile's wet one. Emile shakes off his cape and hangs it on the coat-rack. His hair glistens with raindrops and his trousers stick to his legs.

"You should've stayed home 'till the rain passes," Brice says.

"It might not pass," Emile says. He sits down on the wooden chair next to the door. "Actually, I ain't been home yet. I come from the Bayou Boeuf, and the rain caught me in Vidalia."

"Well, you could've waited it out at some hotel."

"I could've, if I chose to," Emile says. "I figured I'd stop in and see you instead."

"What can I help you with?"

"Well."

The doctor sees something in his friend's face. Emile looks much older than when he saw him last. He must be -- what, fifty? Fifty-two? Brice knows this look, when age comes on too soon. He's seen it before, in other men whose death isn't far off. A warning bell rings in his mind.

"I need to show you something," Emile says, standing up and unfastening his pants. He shakes his legs out of his trousers and pulls off his shirt. Then he sits naked on the chair, holding up a leg to the doctor's scrutiny. "I have this." He touches his leg.

The doctor bends over his leg, glancing over Emile's well-developed torso, his chest not sunken, his belly with its thin pad of fat, the dark fringe around his genitals. Just above the knee on Emile's ropy thigh, he touches a soft mass that bulges under the skin. He frowns.

"And I have it here, too," Emile says, touching his lower lip lightly. "That thickened place." The doctor runs his finger along the lip, leaving a salty residue for Emile's tongue.

Then he probes with his fingers over the leg again. Emile says nothing as the doctor touches and ponders and then motions for Emile to put his trousers back on.

He pulls up a chair opposite Emile. "How long you had these places?"

Emile shrugs. "Some months. I didn't pay 'em any mind before, but I think they're growing."

Brice scribbles on a slip of paper.

The rain washes the window. Emile fastens his damp, cold shirt. "What are they?"

"Gumma." The doctor looks up from his notes. "Syphilitic in origin. You knew that, didn't you?"

Emile nods.

"I'd say that maybe when you were young you spent one too many nights under the hill with Mother Celine's girls," Brice says.

"I did," Emile says. "You ain't telling me nothin' new. I guess I figured the disease had left, when the rashes went away. I could've taken the mercury treatment."

"You could've, but you didn't," Brice says. "For a lot of men it does go away, but you had the child that was --"

"Deformed," Emile says. "Terrible, to have that happen to my wife."

The doctor shakes his head. "The disease was still in you, then. There's babies born blind and deaf and deformed all over 'cause of it. It's a present men don't want to bring home to their wives, but they do. And you ain't lucky, Emile. It's still in you. That's what these masses mean."

"What do I do?" Emile asks, standing up. He walks to the window, reaching up to touch a bottle of brown liquid on the sill.

"Do?"

"Is it gonna get worse?"

"I think so."

"My stepdaughter got married," Emile says. "She wrote and told me she's eloped. That's why I come back."

A gnat circles the lamp.

"What I'm most afeared of," Emile says, turning around to face him, "is -- if the wasps of madness start to swarm. What do I do then?"

"Put your affairs in order now, Emile. That's all you can do."

Emile opens his purse and takes out a damp dollar and hands it over.

"Don't go out in the rain," Brice says. "Wait 'til it passes."

"I need to get home," Emile says, shrugging into his wet cape. "It may not pass anytime soon. I gotta talk some sense into Stephanie." He opens the door and steps out.

When he reaches Carefree, he sees that the parlor windows are full of golden light. And he sees the silhouette of his daughter and Carson sitting together on the sofa, their backs to him. Cornelius's arm is around Stephanie's shoulder, and they look proper and at home. Emile dismounts in front of the gallery.

The same golden light gleams through the glass sidelights beside the door. Emile opens the door and goes in, stamping his boots and dripping water on the black-and-white marble floor. Stephanie, followed by Cornelius, rushes into the hallway. Emile sees their young, startled faces.

Stephanie holds out her arms to him, and, wet and weary though he is, he lets her hug him. He looks over her shoulder at Cornelius, taking in the younger man's direct gaze. But he sees that Carson is not gloating, not unkind at his defeat.

"Papa, we're married," Stephanie says, stepping back to stand beside Cornelius. Her shoulder brushes his arm.

"I know." He extends his hand toward Cornelius. "Mister Carson." Cornelius steps forward and, with a kind of graceful half-bow, shakes his hand.

The angry speech Emile had rehearsed in his mind as he rode the empty roads between Rapides Parish and Adams County vanished when the door opened and Stephanie came out to greet him, her skirts bouncing. She had that same little bobble in her walk that Josephine had.

Emile is exhausted and furious at the young couple standing in the hallway -- *his* hallway! – just like it's *their* home and *he's* the guest. It shakes him to his boots.

But looking at Stephanie, he knows he has to be civil to her young man. And even though something bad is growing in him, he has to keep his fear in check.

And he has to do it even though Carson, in his boots and his bumpkin's hunting shirt, acts as if he belongs right here in this big house Emile built for Josephine. And here's Stephanie with her glowing face and her flushed cheeks, the happy bride.

Emile goes upstairs to change his wet clothes. He sits on the side of his bed with his head in his hands. How can this be? Only a few years ago Stephanie would run out to meet him whenever he came back from the Bayou Boeuf. She'd watch for his horse from her bedroom window and then run halfway down the drive, holding her arms up to him. He'd lift her up onto the horse and then, saddle-sore and weary though he was, he'd give her a rollicking ride up to the house, both of them whooping like wild Indians.

He goes back downstairs and pulls up a chair opposite the sofa where Stephanie sits with Cornelius. He can almost see her as a child again, but at the moment she looks quite womanly as she leans against Cornelius.

If Stephanie leaves, Carefree will be an empty house. He remembers how he felt when she shut herself up in her room, determined to marry Carson. Well, he'll see what he can do. He'll try to keep her here as long as he can, right where she belongs, at Carefree. There are tactics to use when defeat is looming. When he fought in the Creek Wars, nearly twenty years ago, those tactics saved his life. Now, as then, he can use the tactics of delay.

"Now," he says, "I've been thinking, Stephanie, it won't do for you to leave Carefree without a proper send-off. So I want you to let me give you a reception. We'll have it right here. This house has been without frivolities too long. And since I wasn't able to give you a wedding dress, and all that, let's get you a fine ball gown, the finest you can find in Natchez. Or we'll order one from New Orleans. And we'll invite all our friends. You stole my chance to give you away to your husband, and that should've been my right."

For the first time she looks just a trifle shamefaced. But the pain in her eyes passes in an instant.

"Then all Natchez will know about our marriage!" she says to Cornelius.

"Daughter, didn't you tell anyone about it beforehand?" Emile asks.

"I only told Elenora Frankle."

"Then all Natchez knows about it already," Emile says. "Do you mind if I ask exactly *how* you got married?"

Stephanie glances at Cornelius. "Well, we -- we found a Methodist camp-meeting, and there was a preacher there, and he married us. Reverend Hudson. It's all legal."

Emile gives her a cold, long look. "Your mother would be heart-broken to think you weren't married in the Church."

But she returns his gaze, unflinching. "We *are* legally married, Papa."

He sighs. "Now, you understand, this reception will take some time to arrange. You'll have to plan it, so you can't move out to the Cocodrie just yet."

Cornelius starts to speak, but Emile continues, "You must do me this honor."

"Of course Papa's right," Stephanie says, turning to Cornelius.

"Well, plan it right away," Cornelius says, shifting on the sofa.

"How about the second Saturday in August? That's over three weeks from now," Stephanie says.

"Long enough," Cornelius says.

"That'll do," Emile says.

As Cornelius rides away, Stephanie and Emile stand on the gallery and watch him go. He waves one last time from the end of the drive.

"Cornelius's been coming to see me every other day since we got married," she says. "He can't stay the night, though, because of his people out on the Cocodrie. He always says he has to go back and see about them."

"Has he told you much about his place?"

"Oh, yes, and it sounds beautiful, really. He's got a cabin, and a house for Malachi. That's his field hand. And there's Jenny, who's ten. And he's built a stable, and he says his cotton looks so good."

"You think you want that life?"

"I want to be with Cornelius. He's gonna be rich someday. He's trying to clear more of his land. He's only got forty arpents cleared so far, but if he can clear his swamp, he'll double his cotton next year."

Emile has some thoughts of his own about the Carson place on the Cocodrie, because he's seen it. On his way back from the Bayou Boeuf, he stopped at the settlement and asked at the hotel. He found the bayou road and rode out there, past cotton fields and thick woods, and across a little stream that ran across the road. When he reached the Carson place he sat on his horse at the bend in the road, tired from his ride and worried about the lumps in his leg.

He'd studied the little place. He could tell Carson wasn't there. Emile saw a black girl on the porch with some kittens, and an old uncle hoeing in the garden. Neither saw him watching.

The place had the look of ambition, he thought, in its well-hoed fields and tidy cabin. And the place was well-kept, not strewn about with trash like so many cabins.

And the cotton. He could see that less than fifty arpents were planted. Three hands could produce twenty-four bales; and it might bring as much as eighteen cents a pound, but cotton prices were falling now.

Now cane, the business he was in. In cane, three years could make a man rich. But it took capital to get into cane, capital in money and land and slaves, and capital is what Carson plainly didn't have. But now he's married rich. And money begats money. Carson's not the first man to think of another way to get rich besides the sweat of his brow.

This farm didn't look like any place for Stephanie, but at the moment it seemed like she was going to have to learn that for herself. He rode away unhappy, and then the rain caught him in Vidalia, so he stopped in to see Herman Brice and hear his latest bad news.

This was all bitter. Gall and wormwood.

Well, time's on his side. In the meantime, he can wage a subtle campaign. With a marriage, the first flush is the hottest; after a few weeks, Stephanie might not think this Carson fellow so wonderful, and she might decide not to give up her good life in Natchez. The longer he can keep her at Carefree, the better.

The next morning at breakfast, after Esther brings in their eggs and sausage and pours the coffee for them, Emile says, "Stephanie, I can't imagine you without a housemaid. How're you gonna manage out there in the country with the cooking and washing and all the rest of it?"

"Oh, I'll manage. Cornelius has a girl, Jenny. I'll get along."

"It's more work than you think, the life of a country wife. You'll wreck your hands."

Stephanie puts her hand flat on the table, her gold wedding ring gleaming in the sunlight. Her hands are soft and white. "I'll be able to manage it."

"I think you need a housemaid."

She sips her coffee. "I'll be fine."

"So I'm thinking of sending Theresa out there with you," he says as if she hadn't spoken.

Stephanie sets her coffee cup down and stares at him. "Oh, Papa, no! Esther would hate to give up her daughter. She's lost two children already. Did you know that? They're buried in the slave graveyard. I'd never take another child away from her."

"Well, I can't have you working like a country woman. I just can't stand the thought of it."

"I couldn't take Theresa. Besides, I don't get along with that girl so well. She's not reliable. I know she's old enough to work, but she's lazy as sin. She'd never work out."

"Well, the other one then. Helene. She's younger, but she could work hard."

"No! She'd be worse. I couldn't stand having her around me. She talks constantly. She'd never do. I won't take either one of those girls!"

"Well, who, then?"

"Cornelius *has* a girl. Jenny. She's a field-hand; at least that's what he's using her for. Why don't I get him to bring Jenny here, and she can stay at Carefree 'til the reception, and Esther can teach her some housework. Cornelius says she's smart."

And Carson'll have his fortune made next year at the latest. "All right. When Carson comes back, why don't you suggest that to him? You're gonna need help. I just don't think you should be out at the Cocodrie without a maid. And we'll have to see how long it takes this girl to learn housework."

"All right, if it's that important to you. But I'd live in a tent with Cornelius if I had to."

Not if I have anything to say about it.

"You think Esther can teach Jenny to be a housemaid?" Cornelius asks. He sits on the side of the bed and leans back to pull on his boots.

Stephanie lies on the bed, stretching like a kitten, her arms over her head.

"She'll have to," Stephanie says, gazing up at the ceiling. "He won't let me live there without a maid. So you bring Jenny next time you come, and Esther'll keep her here 'til the reception. Then we'll take her back to the Cocodrie with us, and she'll be all trained."

Cornelius chuckles. "I can't picture Jenny as a housemaid, but I guess Esther can give it a shot."

"Esther can do anything she sets her mind to, you know."

"I don't doubt that," Cornelius says, leaning over to kiss her.

But later, riding home, he worries about Jenny learning to be a housemaid. Harvest is coming, and the cotton has to be picked. A lot of house-slaves think field-work's beneath them; Jenny might pick up some of that at Carefree. Cornelius and Malachi can do most of the hoeing, but Jenny can't get too housified to help with the picking.

But how much cotton can a girl pick, anyway? A full cotton sack weighs a hundred pounds, and Jenny wouldn't weigh that much herself. She couldn't carry even a half-full sack.

He can't picture her as a housemaid in an apron, folding linens and carrying food-trays and slop-jars. She's been a field-hand all summer. And she's such an inky little shadow of a person, darker than Esther, who's a mahogany color, and darker even than Malachi.

Jenny still wears only one dress, the green-checked one Margaret McKee sent over for her; sometimes she looked at him so thoughtfully, fingering the sides of the dirty dress. Esther would do something about the dress. A housemaid has to make a presentable appearance.

But if Jenny being a house-maid is the only way Emile will let Stephanie come to the Cocodrie, well, maybe that's not such a hard requirement. At Carefree, Jenny will learn more English too.

The next Tuesday he and Jenny walk out to the buggy. “You’re not coming back with me today,” he says. “You’re gonna stay at Carefree for a few days.”

“Stay?” Her voice rises to a squeak. She rocks back on her stick-like legs.

“Just for a few days. Miss Stephanie’s mammy’s gonna teach you how to be a housemaid.” He motions her up on the buggy and Malachi waves them off. Jenny stares straight down the road and doesn’t look back to see him.

CHAPTER SEVENTEEN

Cornelius had thought about riding Tearose to Natchez and popping Jenny up on the old mule Sam, but he figures the plow-mule would look out of place at Carefree, and there isn't any use giving Emile something else to criticize. So he borrows McKee's buggy and he and Jenny drive to Natchez in it.

He likes the way she sits up straight beside him, her dress tucked around her legs. He wants Emile to see that although his Jenny's just a little girl, she can make a good appearance for a housemaid.

"Fine day for a ride, eh, Jenny?"

She shrugs and leans forward and puts her hands under her knees.

"Don't worry about your kitties. That old mamma cat'll take care of 'em. I bet they'll be a lot bigger when you come back. Kitties that young grow awful fast."

He glances at her. Well, a child always enjoys having pets. He knows she won't say much, quiet as she always is. But he's heard her mumbling English words, and he knows she's smart.

In the late morning they reach Vidalia. As they cross the river on the ferry, Cornelius wonders if Jenny remembers the last time they crossed the river, just two months ago.

Esther and Stephanie come out onto the gallery as they drive up to Carefree. Cornelius kisses his wife.

"Here's Jenny," he says. Jenny stands beside the buggy.

Esther puts her arm around the girl's shoulder. "Well, so this is li'l Jenny," she says. "I believe I'll put her in my room with me, if you don't mind, Miss Stephanie. This girl's got a lot to learn, and that way Theresa and Helene won't be able to pick at her."

"Fine," Stephanie says, but she hasn't more than glanced at the girl. She takes Cornelius's arm.

"Thank you, Esther," Cornelius says as they go up the steps.

Esther is intrigued; this is the blackest, stillest child she's ever seen, not a bit like Helene or Theresa. She looks like a statue in her green-checked dress. Esther leads her around to the slave quarters behind the house.

"Now, I live here on the end," Esther says. "Next door, that's my girls Theresa and Helene, where I can keep an eye on 'em. Used to be Lucy Ida's room. The room on the other end down there's Aunty Sarah. Right on top of her is Rob's room. He's our ferrier and the blacksmith both, when he ain't gardening. And then up there in the other two room is Daisy and her four chilrun, in one room, and Charlie in the room next to 'em. He keeps the stable."

Esther's room smells clean and piney. She opens a trunk set against the wall and takes out some quilts. "You can sleep on these," she says, handing them to Jenny. Esther takes the quilts outside and lays them over a bush to air out. When she comes back she says, "Well, I have to learn you all the housework I can in three weeks. But first, you got to have a bath and get this head washed."

She picks at the girl's hair. "I don't believe Master Cornelius had the first idea how to take care of somebody like you. Let's find you somethin' clean to wear. Didn't you bring any more dresses besides that one? Well, let me see what I got that Helene might have. You definitely gonna need more than one dress."

"Yessum."

Esther puts her arm around the girl.

"Now, don't you worry about nothin'," she says. "I'm gonna take care of you just as good as your mammy would've. You different from most li'l girls, I can see that. But I ain't gonna hurt ya. Now let's us go look in Helene's room for a dress."

The room next door still has Lucy Ida's airless scent. The day after Lucy died Esther moved Theresa and Helene in there without saying a word to anyone. She knew Charlie and Daisy could use more space, with all their children, but Esther grabbed the chance to get it for her girls. So now Theresa and Helene sleep together on Lucy Ida's thin feather mattress. This new little visitor will sleep on the floor in Esther's room.

Esther finds two dresses -- one a biscuit-colored muslin, and the other a plain gray calico -- in the bottom drawer of the chest. Her girls had worn these two or three years ago. She snaps the dresses in the air to take some of the wrinkles out.

"The next thing is to get you bathed." Esther takes a cake of soap from the soap box and then leads Jenny to the pump behind the kitchen where a bamboo hedge screens them from the road.

She pours buckets of water over the girl's head and scrubs her down like a colt. Her skinny body gleams in the sunlight.

Esther stands the girl in front of her and brushes her hair back from her face and rolls it into a bun on the back of her head, just up off her neck, and pins it. Then she hands Jenny the gray dress.

"Now come let me show you some things." They go back into Esther's room and Esther takes a looking-glass and holds it up.

"Now, you keep yourself lookin' good," Esther says. "Miss Stephanie ain't gonna want no tattery housemaid 'round her house."

She takes the girl to the kitchen, a room deep and cool, with a brick floor and a big cooking fireplace. Black pots, pans, skillets, spoons and tongs hang on hooks from the ceiling. On a table are baskets of brown eggs, loaves of bread wrapped in towels, a bowl of butter, and loaves of sugar. A row of watermelons sits on the floor along the wall, their yellow sunspots bright as little lamps.

"I was just gettin' ready to make some sweet potato pone when y'all got here. So now you can help me. That's something Miss Stephanie likes, so it'd be a good thing for you to learn," Esther says. She takes some sweet potatoes from a wooden bin and sets them on the table. "Now, we got to peel these and grate 'em." She gets a knife out of a drawer and peels one potato, then gets out a grater and a bowl. "Now, you hold this grater in the bowl," she says. "Then scrape the ole yam right over it. Be careful don't scrape your fingers." A minute went by. "Or maybe you better just watch. " She points Jenny to a stool.

"This is always good," Esther says. "Now, we just put in some vanilla and spices and sugar and milk. And some eggs. You want it soupy, so we'll put in lots of milk." She cracks brown eggs into a bowl and whips them around with a fork, then pours them into the sweet potato mixture.

"Now we have to bake it." Esther bends over the fireplace, stirring the embers into life and adding more wood.

When Esther's back is turned, Jenny sticks her finger into the bowl and tastes it. She puts her finger in again, and yanks it back when Esther smacks her.

"Don't put your fingers in fresh food, child! That's too much like what Helene and Theresa would do. Of course you hungry, and I didn't think. You like corn?"

Esther puts two ears of boiled corn on a plate, along with a dollop of butter, and sits Jenny at the table.

In the afternoon Jenny follows her back to her room and sits on the side of the bed while Esther mends clothes. When they hear sounds outside, they walk around to see Cornelius driving away down the hill. Stephanie stands on the gallery steps. At the turn of the road he looks back and waves.

"He'll be back in a day or two," Esther says. She sees the look on Jenny's face.

But she knows how to deal with unhappy little girls, and she takes Jenny's arm and leads her back to the slave house.

CHAPTER EIGHTEEN

Miss Delores's Shoppe, right here in Natchez, has just the design Stephanie wants for her dress, but the fabric has to be ordered from New Orleans. Get only the finest, Emile says. It's to be a confection of a dress, aqua silk, with a dropped neckline and leg-of-mutton sleeves. Rosettes of pink silk will be tucked into every fold of the full skirt. And when the fabric finally comes, Stephanie drives to Miss Dolores's for a fitting.

"I believe this is the prettiest dress I ever made," Miss Dolores says, pushing a strand of gray hair up under her cap. "'Course, I just hope I can finish it in time for your party." The aqua silk fabric rustles in her fingers. Stephanie thinks she'll faint.

"I don't feel well," Stephanie says the next day as she and Emile have breakfast. She touches her forehead with her handkerchief.

"It's already pretty hot, even this early," Emile says. "It'll be hotter than this out there on the Cocodrie, you know. It's flat, low land over there. They don't get the river breezes."

Stephanie pushes her plate away and goes upstairs to lie down.

"She's got a big case of nerves," Esther says to Emile later. "Girl's got a big party comin' up. That'd be enough to make anybody nervous."

Stephanie, looking pale, comes downstairs a few minutes later. "Let me get y'all something to drink," Esther says. A few minutes later, Jenny walks slowly into the parlor carrying a tray with goblets of water. Esther hovers right behind her.

"Can that girl learn to be a housemaid?" Emile asks.

"Well, I'm teachin' her," Esther says. "She's got a ways to go, Jenny has, but she's learning."

"Not big as a minute, though, is she?"

"Nossir. Ten years old, Master Cornelius say."

"You see to it that she learns what she needs to learn," Emile says. "No matter how long it takes."

"Yessir."

Stephanie sips her tepid water. "She's learned a lot already. Won't Cornelius be surprised?" She giggles as Emile scowls.

"I don't want her leaving here 'til she's fully trained," he says. But when he looks at Stephanie, he sees his own defeat. It's galloping in from the west, from the Cocodrie. His tactics of delay are failing.

And Miss Dolores finishes the dress just in time for the party. Esther, shadowed by Jenny, moves through the house like a general, ordering the other servants about in a tone that invites no backtalk.

The day before the party, Emile goes to Stephanie's bedroom to talk, but he finds her primping and twirling in her dress before her mirror. The gold wedding band gleams on her finger.

He goes downstairs and stands in the open doorway, looking across the lawn. Gardeners are trimming the hedge that lines the drive. He feels unnecessary here in his own house. The reception will happen, Stephanie will leave Carefree, and he can't stop any of it. The gumma on his lip worries his tongue.

"Jenny!" Helene's urgent whisper causes Jenny to turn so suddenly she nearly drops the heavy pot she's lifting from the fireplace. She hefts the pot to the table with a thud, a little of the pot liquor spilling, and then looks in exasperation at Helene. Esther, who's gone to the privy, told Jenny to stir the greens and then take them off the fire. And now comes this nosy Helene to mess things up.

"What?"

Helene motions for her to come to the door.

"It's Theresa!" Helene says in a loud whisper. "You ain't gonna believe this, but she's changed! Rob's put a spell on her, and if you ain't keerful, he'll probably put one on you too!"

Jenny can't believe anything Helene says, because she's been tricked more than once. It's Helene who jostles up against her when she carries the tray in the big house, and it's Helene's foot that jabs out from behind doors to make her fall on the waxed floors. Helene's meanness always happens when Esther's not around. But Theresa's usually there, laughing at her.

But a spell now; that's a big thing. And if Theresa is changed into something else, and if Rob's the one who did it to her, well, Jenny knows Rob. He's a big boy who works in the garden. Just yesterday she heard him scolding Theresa for walking too close to his tomato plants.

Helene, jumping up and down in excitement, motions for her to come outside.

"Miss Esther said for me to stay here," Jenny says, but she steps out into the sunshine anyway.

"Come see what that spell did to Theresa," Helene says. She takes the girl's hand and pulls her over to the slave house. Jenny's never been invited into the room where Theresa and Helene sleep, until now.

Helene cracks open the door with an exaggerated hesitation because of what might be inside. She and Jenny peer through the crack. "Oh, she ain't here," Helene says. "I better go find her. She can't be runnin' `round loose whilst she's in a spell." She dashes around the corner of the slave house.

A moment later she shouts, "Here she come, Jenny! Watch out! Don't let her get too close to you with her spell on!"

A large brown dog lopes around the corner wearing Theresa's polka-dot dress, which drags on the ground; its paws are through the sleeves. The dog, one Jenny hasn't seen before, brushes right past her and leaps onto the bed, circling and biting at the dress it wears. Helene chases into the room after it.

"You see her, Jenny? You seed what Rob done to her? Now how we gonna get him to change her back?"

"What?" A dog wearing Theresa's dress? And where *was* Theresa? Or was this dog her, changed by a spell? And why would Rob do such a mean thing? Any mean thing Theresa did couldn't be bad enough to call for this spell.

Helene has her hands on her hips. "Okay, Jenny, I guess you know how to figger this out. Our mamma think you so smart. Now how you gonna get Theresa back outta this spell?"

At that moment Esther appears behind them in the doorway. Her mouth falls open when she sees the dog.

"What are you girls doin'?" she says in a loud voice. "Jenny, I told you to stay in the kitchen!" She reaches for the dog. "Helene, you will be the death of me yet. Puttin' Theresa's dress on this old dog. Now it's all dirty again. And here I'm tryin' to get everything ready for that big party tomorrow! I tell you --" She slaps Helene.

Jenny steps back into the corner of the room. Helene holds her shoulder where Esther slapped her. Esther raises her arm again, and then stops.

"Why -- did -- you -- do -- this?" she asks. Before Helene can answer, Theresa, wearing her other dress, walks into the room.

Jenny sees now. It wasn't a spell after all, just another trick. She should have known better than to trust Helene about anything. Rob probably can't make spells anyway.

Esther sags. “Theresa, take your dress off’n that ole dog. I knew you girls was feeding that cur in here. I never should’ve let you have your own room. Jenny, get on back to the kitchen. I know you didn’t have nothin’ to do with this.”

Theresa kneels beside the dog and begins to unbutton the dress. Esther turns to go, then stops at the door and looks back at her two sniffling daughters.

“Can’t you girls see I’m tired?” she asks.

Jenny can see it. But tomorrow’s the reception, and after that Esther’s work will be lighter. And she’ll be going home again with Master Cornelius to the Cocodrie, where she won’t have to put up with these two girls who torment her. And where nobody casts any spells.

CHAPTER NINETEEN

Charlie and Rob carry a round-topped trunk into the bedroom and set it in the middle of the room. Esther is right behind them.

"Where on earth did that come from?" Stephanie asks.

"It was your mother's," Esther says, raising the lid. A faint sweet odor rises from the trunk, which is lined with a pale flowered paper. "It's been down in the storeroom all these years 'cause we never had a use for it. But now we can use it to put your things in to take to the Cocodrie."

"Oh."

Stephanie sits on her bed and chews her lip as Esther begins to pack her things away. She wraps a porcelain-faced doll in a cloth and places it in a wooden chest along with a ceramic figurine of a Chinaman in a wide hat, and her inkwell and quill pen and some writing paper from the drawer of her desk. She sets the chest in the corner of the trunk. Then she takes some of Stephanie's seldom-worn dresses out of the chiffarobe and folds their skirts over and lays them in the trunk.

As she watches Esther pack the familiar items, Stephanie feels an egg of dismay growing in her stomach. Tomorrow she'll leave Carefree. The chiffarobe with its doors standing open confirms it. But she's set her course, and it can't be changed. Even thinking of Cornelius doesn't help. When she thinks of him, it's here, on her soft featherbed in the afternoons, not in some unknown place in Louisiana.

"I remember the day your mammy moved into this house," Esther says. "It was a day 'bout like this 'un, too. A warm summer day. Miss Josephine come here with just this old trunk and that old spinnin' wheel that we keeps back in the yeller bedroom. And with you and your cradle, of course. You was just a babe."

As the hall clock strikes six, Jenny comes upstairs to help Esther. Stephanie watches them fold her petticoats, chemises, and nightgowns. Too restless to sit still, she goes downstairs.

She walks to the front door and sees Emile riding down the drive. At the bottom of the hill he turns the horse toward Natchez. She hasn't spent much time with him the past few days; she'd been too busy with party preparations to talk to him, and now when she wants to talk, he's gone off somewhere by himself. She sits on the gallery, half-hidden behind the big crape myrtle bush. In the blue twilight, the insects are beginning to thrum.

A horse comes up the drive. Stephanie peers around the bush to see Landersons' stable-hand, a half-grown boy named Frank.

"Good evenin', Miss Stephanie. I brung you a letter." He hands her the letter; and oh Lord, it's from John Landerson.

"Go on back to the kitchen. Sarah'll give you a sweet."

"Thank you, ma'am."

Mosquitoes dart about, and Stephanie goes inside. She turns up the lamp.

John writes a bold hand; the letters are vertical slashes on the robin's-egg-blue paper. A small folded packet of the same paper inside the letter holds something else. Stephanie sets the packet aside as she reads:

My Dear Stephanie:

Tomorrow is your wedding reception, and all of Natchez, I am sure, will be there to meet your new husband. I shall like to meet him, also.

Three weeks ago, when you ran into the King's Tavern -- did you think I didn't see you? I'd recognize your little walk anywhere. And I know you saw me.

When I heard you had gotten married I understood why you sent me no note to thank me for the token I brought you from France.

So here's another token -- something I took from you the last time we met -- do you remember? I carried it with me to Europe as a keepsake. Perhaps now that you're married you'll want it back. Or perhaps not? I'll see you tomorrow.

John

She unfolds the packet; a small ivory button falls into her palm. She recognizes it immediately; this is the one Esther had to replace on her yellow frock. The one John pulled loose from her bodice one afternoon in the parlor, so many months ago, before she pushed his exploring hand back to where it belonged.

John's so impertinent, returning this to her now. It's his way of teasing her. He must still be thinking about her, to send this over. Oh, he's naughty!

She looks up at the portrait above the mantle; the face of her mother gazes across the room. Oh Mamma, she thinks, why can't you be here with me? And Papa -- her real Papa, the one who created her, not Emile Coqterre -- if her real Papa had lived, surely he wouldn't let her leave Natchez for an unknown life in Louisiana. But she's an orphan child.

She squeezess the button so hard with her fingers that it makes a round pink impression on her thumb.

But after a minute she composes herself. Well, she'll just have to be brave. She didn't foresee how she'd feel on this last afternoon before she left her home. John's letter lies on her lap. She can't keep the letter; it's impertinent of him to send it to a married woman. And it wouldn't do for anyone else's eyes to see it. She raises the chimney of the lamp and lights the corner of the letter. As it glows and catches she takes it to the cold fireplace and drops it in. In a moment it's just a little pile of black ash on the freshly-swept bricks.

She goes upstairs to her room. She certainly won't discard a valuable button. But her room looks so odd now; it's not the sanctuary it's always been. There's the big deep trunk, and Esther and Jenny busy folding and packing her things into it. The chiffarobe is mostly empty; the aqua gown she'll wear tomorrow is the only dress still hanging in it. Everything is changing, and way too quickly. When Esther and Jenny aren't looking, Stephanie flips the ivory button into the open trunk.

Before dawn, Esther has the other slaves sitting at the table in the kitchen, drinking coffee and eating the eggs and bacon that she fried in a black iron skillet. By the time the sun's up over the tops of the trees, she's moving through the downstairs rooms in the big house, dusting and straightening one last time before she joins Daisy, Sarah, and Jenny in preparing the food. As she works her way through the house, she finds odd things -- Emile's boots kicked to one side near the front door, a strange little pile of ashes in the fireplace in the parlor. Well, this big soiree has everyone upset, she figures. Miss Stephanie getting married is one of those changes that life brings along ever so often to keep everybody off-balance. And it's peculiar how things that are supposed to make people happy do just the opposite. Master Emile looked downright miserable yesterday, and Miss Stephanie looked about to cry when they were packing her trunk. But there's no helping it now.

"Mamma! Ma-a-mma!" Helene whispers from the doorway of the dining room. Esther, checking the settings of silver and china on the buffet table, continues counting until she finishes. Then she glares at Helene.

"I told you to get Theresa and go see if Daisy needs help," Esther snaps. "Go on."

"Mamma, I can't *find* Theresa," Helene whines. "I looked and looked. She ain't in the house, and she ain't nowhere else that I can see."

"What you mean, you can't find her?"

"I looked all 'round. Last I seen her, she was walking off with that boy Marcus and they was headed down the hill."

"What boy Marcus?"

"Oh that boy. He came visiting Theresa. You know."

"I don't know. But I know one thing, you girls is gonna be the death of me yet. I need you and her to be helping me today. Jenny already helping. You wait right here."

She stalks down the hall and goes out to the slave house, calling her older daughter's name.

"Oh Lord A-mighty!" She runs to Theresa's room. The girl's extra dress is gone; the nail sticks out on the bare wall. She hurries back into the house, where Helene stands against the wall of the dining room.

"Who is this Marcus boy?" Esther takes her daughter's face between her large hands.

"He just some ole boy, Mamma," Helene says, beginning to blubber. "Theresa wanted me not to tell."

"What you mean, he just some ole boy? I know you girls been sneaking off. Why can't you be good, like Jenny? She don't run off. No ma'am. She do just what she's told. How long's Theresa been gone?"

"She left a while ago, Mamma." Helene draws a shuddering breath. "She gone for good. I know she is!"

For the first time a thread of fear comes into Esther's voice. "Hush, child," she whispers, looking around. The hallway is empty. It wouldn't do for Master Emile to overhear this. That silly Theresa -- what might a headstrong fourteen-year-old take into her mind to do?

"How you gonna get her back, Mamma? What you gonna do if she run off?"

"You be quiet, you hear me? Don't you be saying things like that! You want Master Emile to hear you?"

Helene's eyes are big. "No, Mamma. But --" she begins blubbering again. "But if Theresa's run off --"

"Who is this Marcus?"

"He one of Landersons'. He sweet on Theresa."

"Lord A-mighty." There's more fear than anger in Esther's voice now. Where could Theresa be? With the party coming up this afternoon, nobody would be paying attention to Theresa, so Esther has time on her side. If Theresa planned to run away for good, she certainly won't get far, and then, who knows what can happen? That silly boy will be caught too. At the thought of what could happen then, Esther leans back against the wall. "You go on outside and see if Daisy need help, and don't you say one word about this, you hear me, or I'll --"

She looks up to see Emile walking down the hall, his face twisted as if he has a bad headache.

"You do what I say," she mutters to her daughter. As Helene runs out the back door, Esther composes herself and turns to say, "Good morning, sir."

Stephanie opens her eyes and then closes them again. What strange room is this she's in? Her desk-top catches the sun, the waxed surface looking barren without its scarf. She closes her eyes and drifts back to sleep.

She's had a restless night, listening to the hall-clock chime two, then three, then four o'clock. Only as the sun rose did she fall into a deep, dreamless sleep.

Now she opens her eyes again. Jenny's standing next to her bed. The girl came in so quietly that Stephanie blinks twice to make sure it's not a ghost.

"Good mornin', Miss Steffanneh," the girl says. "Daisy sent me to ask" -- 'ahsk', the girl says -- "if you want your breakfast now."

Stephanie squeezes her eyes shut again. "What time is it?"

"Clock sang ten times."

"What?" Then she realizes Jenny's talking about the chime.

The girl. Cornelius's Jenny. Stephanie hasn't paid her much mind since she'd been here, but now she sees her for the silly little clumsy thing she is. Stephanie's seen her let trays and glasses slip out of her hands more than once. But Cornelius likes Jenny, she could see that; every time he comes to Carefree he brings the girl a treat, peppermint or taffy. Ruining her, probably.

Why is she standing so close to the bed? And with her hand resting on the bedspread. It's presumptive. Stephanie can't have her standing right there and watching her. She didn't even hear the girl come in. A slave sneaking around too quiet is one thing she won't stand for.

"Go on and let me be," she snaps. "I'm still sleepy."

"Yes'm," Jenny says. As soon as the door closes behind the girl, Stephanie sits up and groans. It's all happening too fast -- the wedding, the reception, everything. But the clock keeps chiming; there's no way to slow things down. She covers her face with her hands.

CHAPTER TWENTY

When Cornelius rides up to Carefree just before noon, Esther is waiting at the front door. "Oh, Master Cornelius, welcome! Ain't this a grand day for you and for Miss Stephanie, too!" She takes his satchel. "Now, I'll just get Daisy to press your suit, and I'll bring it right up to you. You can wait upstairs in that bedroom at the back. Miss Stephanie's got Jenny and Helene in her bedroom helpin' her dress. Well, I don't know how much help they is, but they watchin' her dress, anyways."

Cornelius goes upstairs; the door to Stephanie's bedroom is closed, and he hears girls'voices from inside -- Stephanie's, Jenny's.

He grins. Watching Stephanie dress is a nice sight; he could understand why two little girls would want to watch. He walks down the hall to the bedroom at the back of the house.

This is a forgotten bedroom, its only furniture a bed and a bureau and against one wall the old spinning wheel that belonged to Josephine Coqterre. Stephanie had shown it to him once. Thinking of the dark-haired woman whose portrait hangs in the parlor downstairs, Cornelius tries to picture her sitting at this wheel. But the image is overtaken by another: his mother spinning, long ago in Georgia. She'd hated the tedious task; a woman could spin all day and have only enough thread to make a yard of fabric. But now there's fabric for sale in the stores, and most of the old spinning wheels gather dust, as this one does.

When Daisy raps on the door and hands him his pressed suit, he quickly changes into the clothes he's brought for this special occasion -- the dress shirt he wore the first time he met Emile, and the white broadcloth suit he had tailored by a seamstress in the settlement. The price of the suit, $10, seemed extravagant when he paid for it, but it feels well worth the cost today, when he intends to dress the equal of any man in Natchez. He wants to look worthy of Emile Coqterre's stepdaughter. As he brushes down his sleeves and wipes the last specks of dust from his boots, he hears noises from downstairs -- the rumble of buggies. The guests are arriving.

He goes out into the hall. Jenny's just coming out of Stephanie's room, her back to him as she quietly closes the door.

He's seen Esther's improvements on Jenny every time he's come to Natchez in the past few weeks. The grimy green-checked dress is gone; now whenever he sees Jenny she's wearing a clean dress with an apron tied around her waist, and her hair's pulled tight to the back of her head and rolled into a bun.

"Hey, Jenny. You ready to go home today?"

"Yessir."

She half-smiles. That sudden whiteness in her eyes is like a lamp turning up. But it vanishes in a flash. Well, maybe Jenny can turn into a housegirl after all. She seems to have learned some manners. He wonders if she's been practicing words under her breath while she was here.

She goes downstairs and Cornelius stands in the hallway for a moment. He wants to go in and see Stephanie in her room, but Helene's probably still in there with her. Esther comes up the stairs.

"Why don't you go down to the parlor while I see if Miss Stephanie's ready to come down? Then y'all can go in to the reception together."

Cornelius goes downstairs. Guests are already laughing and talking in the parlor, and more are driving up the road. Rob, who's been turned into a butler for the occasion, stands by the door.

Cornelius waits in the hall. He knows he'll be a curiosity today among these guests; all Emile's friends will want to see the man Stephanie married. But Jennie Carson brought him up the equal of anyone, bless her soul; he's comfortable facing this well-dressed company of strangers.

Sophronia stares at the bottle of Madeira wine sitting on the table by her bed. The sunlight streams through it. She loves the warm look of drink in a bottle, and loves it even more in a glass.

She hears the sound of someone hurrying down the stairs, and sighs. She has to get up, has to get dressed, and she's late. She doesn't feel ready for this, even though she's held off drinking all day. Or maybe she needs a drink for this occasion.

Maybe she won't go to this reception; she could just stay in her room and sleep. But now, hearing the chatter of excited voices in the house, a compulsion comes over her: she has to be there. She heaves herself out of bed and peels off her dressing gown.

She studies herself in her mirror. Her hair looks a sight, dry and straw-like. She's not old, just thirty-four, but her form is changing, she sees; her arms and thighs are flabby. Her breasts hang limp. No babe had ever suckled there, and for ten years no man has either. Not since Mister Johnson went away, to sea or Texas, she's never been sure which, just as she's never been sure about the spelling of his name -- Johnson or Jeansonne. On documents he left behind he spelled it both ways. She met him in Mississippi; he was Johnson then. Her own spelling wasn't so good either, but she knew how to spell her own name.

She opens her chiffarobe. Is this all she has to wear? Every dress smells of mothballs, and every one's a dark, dreary garment. Three of the dresses are black, and all are old. Widow's weeds.

Up from the well of her memory comes a vision of herself as she was at sixteen, not yet married, in a dress of green silk, dancing at a ball in New Orleans. That was before her parents died of typhoid, before Obadiah Johnson came into her life. Then so quickly she became an orphan, and then a wife, and then a widow without means, her husband having disappeared at sea. Or gone to Texas.

Her brother Emile came to rescue her. He did her a kindness, bringing her here to Natchez to live at Carefree. She's grateful, really. But after he became a widower, he hid himself away in the Bayou Boeuf, leaving her to take care of this big house and all these slaves and that little Stephanie. It was all too much for a girl of twenty-two. What did she know about running a big household?

Well, the days of the bright silk frocks are gone, that's for sure, and today, for this reception, her choices are she can wear black, or gray, or deep mahogany brown. Not a festive garment in the bunch. She sighs.

Make do, she thinks. She pulls on her petticoats and reaches for a black dress. She wore this crepe ten years ago, so it can't still be fashionable, but it'll have to do.

The dress buttons easily, she's glad to see, and it does emphasize her small waist. And even better is the way her skin, untouched by sun, glows against the black fabric. Probably no other woman at the reception will be wearing dramatic black, she realizes with a thrill. Oh, they'll be there in their pastels and prints, but she, Emile's reclusive sister, in her ebony gown -- well, there's a chance to make an *entrance* there. Didn't she remember something about making entrances, from her New Orleans days?

She buttons the dress all the way to her neck, snapping the little pearl buttons closed until all her white skin is covered. Well, this will never do, she thinks; it's not flattering at all. So she unbuttons the top a third of the way down and lays the wings of the bodice back to expose her throat and chest. There, that's the way she wants to look. She folds the wings inside the bodice and then gets a brooch from the dresser and pins it over the top button. Stepping back from the mirror, she studies her reflection. Then she unpins the brooch and unfastens another button and repins the brooch. Now a line of cleavage peeps out from the deep v-neck.

She brushes her hair, tilting her head to one side and then the other. Then she twists her hair up into a lavish coil. The height of the swirl makes her seem taller. And she pinches her cheeks and bites her lips into a bruised pout.

Her life doesn't have to be over, she tells herself. She's still young. And with Stephanie married and leaving the house, that's one responsibility she'll be free of. And today, men are coming. Who they are, she hardly cares. But she'll be here, waiting. There's some joy in the anticipation of a party; she remembers that from her New Orleans days, before Mister Johnson or Jeansonne came into her life.

Stephanie forces herself to go through the ritual of dressing; even the aqua silk dress with the bodice so well sculpted to her own shape, and the rosettes tucked into the gathers of the skirt, can't cheer her. Whenever she stops primping long enough to think, a tidal wave of dismay comes back. She keeps waiting for it to stop, but it won't.

Does she have to go through with it? Are her days at Carefree really over now? All Natchez society will be here to see her off. Just as when she played the May Queen at the Cotillion at the Elizabeth Girls' School, she'll have to be an actress today.

But *no*! she thinks. I can't, I won't, leave my home. I'll just have to tell Cornelius.

She goes downstairs, glad that no guests are in the hallway. Cornelius is waiting at the door to the drawing room. She takes his arm and he bends to kiss her. She squeezes his arm urgently, and she intends to say, *I want to talk to you*, but the noise of laughter and the commotion in the drawing room catches his attention. He leads her into the big room to greet the guests.

Papa's standing against the far wall. His face is tense, and he wears a black frock coat -- fitting, Stephanie thinks, for a day when he thinks she's leaving. And he looks haggard. But he'll be so happy when she tells him she's staying, after all.

Emile walks over. "Why don't we stand over here?" he suggests, so they form a receiving line near the front windows. Stephanie stands between the two men. Cornelius smiles at her and she thinks again, *I must tell him! I must!* But it will have to wait until after they've greeted the guests, who're surging toward them.

Elenora Frankle's mother passes through the receiving line. Elenora is right behind her in a plain gray dress decorated only by a string of simple pearls. Elenora hugs Stephanie and admires her wedding ring. Stephanie forces herself to smile. She wishes she could talk to Elenora in private. But it's too late to seek advice.

"Well, I wouldn't have thought I'd ever say this about anyone, but your Mister Carson is handsomer than John Landerson," Elenora whispers, glancing over at John, who's standing near the door.

Stephanie didn't even see John come in. But he's already walking across the room toward her; there's no getting away. Her face flames; surely John won't mention the button he sent over.

John shakes Emile's hand and then turns those familiar ice-gray eyes on Stephanie, as he bends to kiss her hand. He straightens and smiles at Stephanie as if their secret is shared by everyone in the room. But Elenora's right. John's features are heavy; Cornelius's are refined. And John in his swallow-tail coat and ruffled shirt can't compare to Cornelius. And Cornelius isn't relying on his father to make him rich; he's doing it himself, like a true gentleman. She sees John's gaze sweep down her figure -- is he looking for a mismatched button? -- and then whatever he says escapes her. Her heart pounds; will he say something scandalous, to embarrass her here in front of everyone? But he steps quickly past her to shake Cornelius's hand. Then he strides across the room, to where some young ladies are gathered near the punch-bowl. As the other guests pass through the receiving line, John flirts with first one girl and then another, and even turns to favor Elenora with a smart remark and that same appraising glance he gave Stephanie a few minutes ago.

She feels a pang as she realizes he's already forgotten all about her; the letter he sent was just a tease. John is like that, about as constant as a tomcat, she can see it now. He could never be a faithful husband.

But if she weren't a married woman, she'd be over there in that laughing group of friends.

From across the room Sophronia flutters her fingers in greeting. So her aunt got out of bed to come to the reception. Here she is, in a dramatic black dress with a decolletage that stops just a bit south of what's proper on a large bosom. Sophronia's hair, which for years has been only a frowzy mop on the pillow, is combed and pinned.

Her aunt must have been a belle once; Stephanie can see it. And Sophronia is smiling! Imagine, Sophronia having a good time. Of course she has her fortification, even here. Stephanie sees her set her empty wine glass down and then take another from the sideboard. When Sophronia comes through the receiving line, still holding her glass, Stephanie kisses her cheek.

"I owe you a debt, Aunt," she whispers.

"I should say you do, and so does your handsome young man," Sophronia says, batting her eyes in Cornelius's direction. "He has such good manners. I always pick up on a gentleman's manners right away, you know." Sophronia's eyes twinkle like the jewels on her earlobes.

She moves away and a minute later Stephanie sees her throw her head back and laugh at some man's remark. She's never heard Sophronia laugh before, a laugh with an edge to it, a bar-girl's cackle.

The musicians begin to play their violins, and the dancing begins. Stephanie and Cornelius dance around the room once, and Stephanie dances the next dance with Emile. When John walks toward her, she takes Cornelius's arm. But John walks past her. Stephanie goes over to the other side of the room to talk with her friends and to think, what am I doing?

From where Cornelius stands, he can see Jenny sitting halfway up the stairs with her face pressed against the banister, watching everything through the slats. Philip sits next to her. Then he hears an unwelcome voice. "Mister Carson, I'm surprised you found time to come courting in Natchez," Jake Turley says, "with your crop needing work."

Cornelius turns around. He smells the liquor on Turley's breath. "Oh, I made time."

Turley takes a drink of whiskey. "Say, I've been meaning to ask you. You still own that girl up there on the stairs?"

"Yep."

"Think you'd want to trade her? My wife wants another house-girl, and my overseer Dubrenne wants to trade a field-hand -- Wonderful, Dolly's boy. He's sixteen. Does that girl know house-work?"

"She's not for trade."

"You could use a field-hand, I bet, taking in that other field you're draining. And Wonderful's a full hand; he's strong and reliable."

"She's not for sale and she's not for trade."

"Wonderful's one of my best workers. It'd be a good deal for you."

"Jenny's my wife's pet," Cornelius lies. He walks away. Halfway across the room it comes to him that it's Turley, not Dubrenne, who seeks out the young girls. He stops in the middle of the room.

"Lord, what next?" he mutters to no one. All the gossips in the Cocodrie have it wrong, welcoming Turley into their company and slandering his overseer. Dubrenne was probably telling the truth, that day at Cedar Breaks, when he said he hadn't seen Jenny. Turley could easily get one of the field-hands to snare her. Any one of them could catch a little runaway and hide her in the house.

Dubrenne would probably move on to a new job before long; overseers always do. But even when Dubrenne moves on, Cedar Breaks will still be a dangerous place for young slave girls.

He can just see Jenny's feet tapping to the music. Once again he feels what a heavy responsibility she can be. He's been lightened of that load while she was here with Esther. But in the Cocodrie, he'll always have to be careful with her.

The room seems darker, as if a cloud has pulled over the sun. He goes over to the corner where Stephanie stands with her friends and takes a glass of brandy. When the music begins again, he takes Stephanie's arm and guides her onto the dance floor.

"You look so stern now," she says as they dance.

"Oh, I am. I've just got a neighbor I don't like."

"Is it Mister Jake Turley?"

"The very one."

"I've always thought he was strange," Stephanie says.

"You don't know the half of it."

When the music stops, Stephanie feels flushed with the heat and the noise of the afternoon. The room spins. Maybe this will all just go away, she thinks; after this reception, she'll go up to her yellow bedroom and lie down, and Cornelius will know she won't go to the Cocodrie. She can't tell him now; he looks so stern, so preoccupied, that she can't find the words.

She slips away and walks down the hall toward the back door. In the pantry, she leans against the cupboard, her hand to her chest and her eyes closed. The music is muffled here, and she's alone. She can think.

She opens her eyes a moment later. John Landerson, with a glass in his hand and the odor of whiskey on his breath, stands before her, grinning.

"Well, little Miss Coqterre," he says, putting his hand under her chin and caressing the smooth skin of her throat. "I saw you run away down the hall. Is something wrong?"

Tears burn behind her eyes. "Oh, John. I don't really want to go to the Cocodrie. I really wish I could stay here--"

"Why don't you?" He steps toward her, putting his hands on her shoulders, and pressing his leg into the gathers of her skirt, between her legs. "You should stay here, not waste yourself out in the country--"

Then all at once he bends down and kisses her, hard, and murmurs into her ear as he fumbles with the buttons on her dress. She tries to push against him. His hand is inside her bodice, squeezing her nipple. "Stay here, where you'll be close to me," he mumbles.

She pushes against him. He steps back but keeps his hand cupped around her breast.

"What's the matter, little tease," he says. He relishes his power over her. She can't move away. "Nobody can see us here. They're all in there having a good time. Everybody's happy for you. You and your farmer. Is he as good a lover as I am?"

She puts her hands out and pushes against his chest, her face burning with anger. "Get away from me! Get away! Get away!"

He steps back suddenly, and she realizes that her bodice is hanging open. She fumbles the buttons closed.

"I thought you wanted to stay here," he says. "We could have a good time together, you and me."

She glares at him and stalks out of the stifling little room. In the hall she stops to catch her breath, smoothing her clothes and patting her hair into place.

Then she walks back to the drawing room and hurries over to Cornelius. He smiles at her and pats her arm.

Now she knows she has to go. John Landerson will talk, sure as anything, will tell what he's done and make up more, and say she was willing, at her own wedding reception. He's no gentleman. She has no choice now but to let the day take her where it will. Whatever speech she'd prepared for Cornelius -- no, she can't say the words. She has to go.

John saunters back into the drawing room. Stephanie turns her back so she won't have to look at him. She sips a cup of punch. The musicians begin another tune. When she looks around again, she's surprised to see that John has chosen Elenora as his dance partner.

Cornelius smiles and asks, "Did you cool your face?"

She nods. After all she's gone through today, her mind in a turmoil, it all comes back to this: Cornelius is so kind. All the long afternoons they'd spent together during the past few weeks have taught her that. And he's standing here next to her, strong and dignified. No coxcomb like John can hold a candle to him.

Kind-hearted Elenora can have John Landerson. Elenora's too good for him, but with her looks she won't have many to choose from. It doesn't matter. Cornelius is the handsomest man in the room.

CHAPTER TWENTY-ONE

The guests dine, and Jenny and Helene carry trays of food in and out. Cornelius watches that neither of the little girls walk near Turley. Esther stands at the doorway, her broad face furrowed with worry. She looks distressed, Cornelius notices, but the whole household has worked hard for this day.

After the meal the music begins again, and the guests return to dance in the drawing room. Cornelius stands at the side of the room and keeps a wary eye on Jake Turley, who looks drunker than ever.

As soon as the last guests leave the dining room, Esther motions for Daisy and Helene and Jenny to clear the table and set out fresh dessert cups. Then she walks outside, past the back gallery and down the hill behind the house. Her apron flaps in the breeze. As she reaches the path to the slave graveyard, past the pond, she sees Theresa coming toward her, alone, out of the woods. Her legs go weak with relief, and she puts her hand over her mouth.

But the surge of relief is quickly replaced by an equal surge of anger. She stops and waits, her hands on her hips. Theresa's usual sashaying walk is now a slow stumble.

When the girl gets closer Esther calls, "Where have you been, girl? I a good mind to --"

But Theresa's face is crumpled and tear-streaked. When the girl gets close, Esther can smell corn-liquor on her breath. "Where has you *been*?" Esther asks. "You get back to your room, and don't you come out. I can't dare let Master see you like this. You been with that boy, ain't ya?"

"Marcus and me," Theresa mumbles, "we went down to the --"

Esther raises her hand. "Girl, don't even *tell* me. And if I ever find you gone again, without a pass and without tellin' me, I'm gonna switch your legs 'til you can't stand up. You understand me?"

"Mamma, he *said* he'd take me to Ohio! Up to the free soil! He *said* it! But he didn't do that. He just wanted to get me down in the woods with him. That's all he wanted. And then after he was done he took off to home, without even waitin' for me."

"Theresa, why would you go believin' any old boy that comes along? Why? Ain't I raised you with more sense than that?"

"Yes, Mamma," Theresa says, crying.

"Hush yourself, and go in your room. And stay in there! You ain't fit to be seen, so you ain't gonna get to say goodbye to Miss Stephanie either. Just go hide yourself where nobody can see you." Reeling a little, Theresa totters to the slave house and goes inside.

Esther still feels shaky as she walks back to the house. Well, it's partly her own fault, the way the girls are. She shouldn't have moved them out of her room. Once they got their own room, there were too many hours she couldn't watch them like a hawk, and they got to thinking they could do what they wanted. But they had know that of all the people in Mississippi they had about the least right of anybody to do what they wanted.

And what might happen to a girl like Theresa if she got caught out without a pass, trying to get to Ohio. Oh, at the thought of it Esther stops just inside the back door, where she can hear the music still playing. She leans against the wall, in case her legs won't hold her up.

"This is the best known cure for a hangover," Emile says, pouring himself a shot of whiskey. He holds the bottle out to his friend Josiah Hargraves, who shakes his head no. The men sit in Emile's dark little office at the back of the house. The curtains are closed to keep out the bright sunlight. An appropriate darkness, Emile thinks, for a day when defeat is on him.

He'd like to see Sy Hargraves more often. Sy is good company. Even though, as a middle-aged bachelor, Sy can't possibly understand what it means to lose a daughter. The chatter of the reception guests is muffled through the closed door.

"I shouldn't have gone down to Under-the-Hill last night," Emile says. "But I had to get away from the house. All this cleaning and fixing, all this talk of dresses. Too much frou-frou." He waves his hand as if to brush the thought away. "I thought I'd see some of my old girlfriends down there. But you know what? Francine, and Lovey, and Delight – they ain't there no more. It's all new girls now." The whiskey begins to warm his veins. He feels soberer. "I'm sorry, Sy. I only talk like a Frenchman when I'm drunk or hung over. I didn't want her to marry this farmer, you know."

The two old friends sit in silence for a few minutes. "Well, Stephanie's found herself an ambitious young man, I'd say," Sy says. "I can see it." He stamps out his cigarette.

"Carson's got nothing and he wants everything."

"Well, she might change her mind after a while, Emile. Sometimes these young girls, they think it's romantic, living in the woods with their young men. But when they see what a hard life it is, they repent their choice."

Emile shifts in his chair and touches his thigh where the alien solid masses are.

"It's easy to repent, but undoing a marriage -- that's hard." He shakes his head, then rolls a cigarette and strikes a match. "You still an abolitionist, Sy?"

"I am. For economic reasons. Not a popular position."

"You ain't surprised about that, are you?"

"No. But I know the South needs industries, not just cotton and cane and rice. The way planters rush to plant those crops, you'd think the Good Lord Himself reserved them for us. And I know you've done well with cane, Emile. But all this emphasis on agriculture is holding the South back. The South needs mills. Factories."

"That's dirty work. Commoners' work. And you know blacks can't do that kind of work." An edge comes into Emile's voice. "That's not our way of life." A white trail of smoke from his cigarette curls into the air. "I wish I could keep Stephanie in Natchez."

"You can't. It'd be useless to try. Society's on their side. Every giggling girl and arch matron and gap-toothed crone will be pulling for 'em. The women'll even give it a romantic twist. You know, star-crossed lovers, and all that. True love triumphing."

"For every triumph there's a defeat hiding somewhere," Emile says. "I learned that in the Creek Wars. You know, I think as soon as all this marriage celebration is over, I'll go to New Orleans for the mercury treatment."

"Why now?"

"Well, up 'til now I haven't wanted to think about it. I figured, just take what come. *A chaque jour suffit sa peine.* But with Stephanie married -- and it's her own doing, she didn't ask my opinion -- nobody needs me here. Herman Brice told me awhile back I should get the mercury, but he says now it might be too late to do any good. Ratout can run my place on the Boeuf 'til I get back. He let half my crop burn up this year, anyway. To hell with the rest of it. I guess I'll come back cured or crazy."

"Let me give you the name of my doctor there," Sy says. The laughter and chatter from across the hall grows louder.

"They're getting ready to leave. I have to go tell Stephanie goodbye," Emile says. He stamps out his cigarette and stands up.

"Does Stephanie know you're going for the mercury?" Sy asks.

"No," Emile says. "Even drunk as I am I know better than that. She didn't ask my opinion about marrying this fellow, and I won't ask hers about this. Besides, I can't talk to my daughter about something like that."

Stephanie, glancing through the tall drawing room windows, sees Charlie bringing Cornelius's borrowed buggy around to the front of the gallery. And the lump of dismay comes back; she'd managed to put it aside for the past hour while she ate Esther's fancy food and laughed with her friends, but her departure is reality now; there's no stopping it.

Seeing Charlie and Rob bringing her trunk downstairs and hauling it out to the gallery, she wants to cry out, "No! No! Let me stay here in my own home!" But John Landerson is over there, looking at her out of the corner of his eye.

Cornelius goes to get his satchel, and Jenny hurries down the hall with a battered little bag of her own, which Esther must have given her.

Papa must be hiding somewhere, since she hasn't seen him for an hour, and even Esther's gone off to heaven knows where. Stephanie feels abandoned.

The guests move toward the door as Cornelius goes out and sets his satchel in the back of the buggy. Stephanie sees that Jenny's already sitting up in the back of the buggy. The guests crowd onto the gallery.

"But where's Papa? Where's Esther?" Stephanie stammers as Cornelius returns to her side. At that moment Emile comes out of the house, squinting as if the afternoon sunlight hurts his eyes. Charlie and Rob hoist Stephanie's trunk onto the back of the buggy.

Stephanie puts her arms around Emile's neck. "Oh Papa, I'm sorry," she whispers, choking back sobs. "I wish I could stay."

"Now, let's have none of that," he says. "Done's done."

She hears the slurring in his words.

"That trunk going to sit there the whole trip without jostling?" he asks, moving away from her to examine the straps that hold the trunk in place.

"It'll sit there fine," Cornelius says.

Esther hurries out the front door and comes down the steps to hug her. Now Stephanie thinks her heart will break for certain, as she says goodbye to the one who's raised her for a dozen years. But Esther, sniffling, turns quickly to look at Jenny. "You remember what I learnt you, Jenny," she calls. The girl nods.

Cornelius shakes hands with Emile, and then he helps Stephanie up onto the seat. As they drive away down the drive Stephanie turns around and waves at the crowd of guests gathered on the gallery.

"Write to me, Papa!" she calls, but she thinks he must not have heard her. He goes up the steps and inside the house without looking around. Some of the younger guests race down the hill after them, hooting and hollering.

CHAPTER TWENTY-TWO

By late afternoon they come to the settlement. Stephanie looks around. There's the hotel, and next to it the general store. A few houses, new looking. A fence around an empty lot. Well, this is a place she'll get to know, for better or worse; she'll learn the look of it.

She'd been quiet for most of the drive out here, not looking at Cornelius. Jenny sits up in back, proper in her nice tan dress, her face up the feel the breeze.

As they leave the settlement Cornelius glances around at the girl. "You glad to be coming home, pigtails?" he asks her.

"Yessir."

He pulls Stephanie over to him. "How about you, Stephanie? Like what you see of Louisiana so far?"

"Well." Stephanie looks all around the low hazy horizon, where trees hem the green fields. "I haven't paid it much attention. I'm just tired, I guess. I do love the smell of the air, though. It smells like the sea."

"Swamp smells," Cornelius says, his arm around her shoulder as he holds the reins loosely with one hand. Tearose trots at an easy pace. "Or maybe it's the smell of fish."

Stephanie makes herself smile, remembering how he'd once bragged to her about his cooking skills. "If you catch us some fish, I'll cook it," she says.

"Mal's the fisherman. Are you as good a cook as I am?"

"What kind of question is that? I'm probably a better cook than you are. Esther taught me. All those years when I didn't have a mammy, she kept me with her. I followed her around the kitchen and learned everything she knew."

"Well, I learned everything my mammy knew, too, 'cause I took over the cooking when she got sick. Malachi and I been eating my food for going on five years now. Jenny, too, just lately. I even cooked a bear one time. Shot it right out here in these woods. Big old black bear. Greasy as hell, but good."

"Surely you didn't eat a whole bear!"

"No, I had the McKees, and they had their relatives, and between us we ate what we could and gave the rest to some Baptists. They had a camp meeting down that other road back there."

Stephanie is silent for a moment. "Do you ever see a priest out here?"

"Sometimes. Once in a while I see Baptists."

She shifts away from him. He pulls her back.

"It looks so mysterious, the way the roads just go off into the woods. And it's so quiet," she says.

"It's been too quiet at my cabin. But now you'll be there, and it'll be perfect." He squeezes her knee. "If you look close, you can see my house through those trees over there."

Stephanie turns to look. "I can't see it," she says.

"Just give it a few minutes, and we'll come into plain view," he says, "if sunset doesn't catch us first."

In a few minutes they drive across a stream and up out of the woods.

"Here we are," Cornelius says as they reach the cabin. "Well, what do you think?"

"I -- like it," she stammers. He helps her down and she turns around to take in the whole place.

Here it is, the place he'd said so much about. She sees a decent cabin made of logs, with a porch across the front, and off to the side a smaller cabin. On one side is a garden.

An old man comes out of the cabin and hurries over.

"This is Malachi," Cornelius says. "Of whom you have heard, of course."

"Oh, hello," Stephanie says.

Malachi stands a respectful distance away and half-bows to the young woman. "How do, Miss Step'nie," he says. "You is so very welcome to be here, so welcome."

"Let me show you the fields," Cornelius says, putting his arm around her shoulder. He leads her over to the fence. Out there are his hundred arpents of land, half-swamp, half-cleared and planted in cotton. Harvest is not far off. She stands close to him, saying nothing. What could she know about cotton? She's hardly ever seen it before it reaches the streets of Natchez, already baled and loaded onto wagons and headed for the steamboats under the hill.

They go back to the cabin, where Malachi lights a lamp and sets it on the mantle.

"That's the bedroom's over there," Cornelius says, pointing to the door at the other end of the room. "And this is my kitchen." He steps back and gestures toward the fireplace. "Except it's yours now. Mal and I are looking forward to tasting your venison. Right, Mal?"

"Yessir."

Stephanie walks over and looks out the back door to the line of trees that circle the horizon on all sides.

"Are you saddle-sore from the long trip?" Cornelius asks.

"I'm tired," she says, turning around. "I could make a cup of tea. Where's your girl gone?"

"Oh, Jenny probably headed down to the stable," Malachi says. "She's got some kitties down there she likes to play with."

"Maybe you better go get her, Mal," Cornelius says. "Miss Stephanie might need some help. I've got to ride over to McKee's and take back the buggy."

"Why don't you let Malachi take it back?" Stephanie asks.

"I want to thank Amos for letting me use it."

"You gonna be able to see to ride back in the dark?" Malachi asks.

"There's a moon, and I've got the lantern if I need it," he says. "Help me with Miss Stephanie's trunk." The two men go outside and heft the trunk out of the buggy and carry it into the cabin and set it at the foot of the bed.

Then Cornelius drives off into the deepening twilight. Stephanie goes back into the cabin.

"They's some potatoes cooked, ma'am, and some cornbread," Malachi says from the doorway. "I made 'em. They in that pot over there. We've got chickens and turkeys, as you probably noticed. And Master Cornelius likes to hunt. Me, I tend the garden, so we got vegetables. Master Cornelius, he do the cooking for us."

"I'll be doing the cooking from now on," Stephanie says. She brushes her hand over her forehead. "I learned how to cook in Natchez."

"Law, from what Master Cornelius told me, I figured you never set foot in a kitchen, you being Master Emile Coqterre's daughter."

"You needn't worry about eating. I'll see to it that y'all eat well."

"Well, that mighty nice," Malachi says. "You know, Master Cornelius, he cooks good, but plain. I reckon that's the Georgia way. Might be nice to have some cooking from somebody that knows how to *season*."

"I season things."

"Thank you, ma'am," Malachi says. "That's a relief in itself. I expect I'll turn in now. I know you and Master Cornelius tired from that long trip. I sleep over there in the little house. You need anything, you let me know."

Stephanie sees him hesitate just a second, as if he expects something else, before he turns to go. She stands in the front room and watches through the open door as he walks across the yard. He's very old, she realizes -- just an old barefooted field-hand.

Lamplight flickers on the smoke-darkened bricks around the fireplace. Stephanie goes over to the fireplace and touches the black crane hanging there. She swings it out and back. It creaks. A pot, scrubbed clean, hangs from it. The dry sink is stocked with sugar and corn meal, and clean cloths hang on nails on the walls. A table and two chairs and a three-legged stool are set in the middle of the room.

She sits at the table and looks through the open door of the cabin, across the porch, and out toward the cotton field. Her head aches and her back is stiff from the long trip. She's quite alone. She folds her hands on the table.

Out there, in the fading twilight, is a vista she doesn't like. Beyond Cornelius's cottonfields are black silhouettes of trees spiking up into the purplish sky. It looks raw and lonely. She looks away.

And her trunk is sitting there in the bedroom at the foot of the bed. She has a sudden vision of Carefree, its wide halls and white-painted doors, its French furniture and hovering servants. Has she chosen right, to come here? A lump is in her stomach, a hard knot of homesickness for Carefree -- for Papa, for Esther, for her bedroom with its soft featherbed.

She swallows hard and puts her elbows on the table and blinks back tears. She'll have to tell Cornelius she loves it here, because that's what he'll expect her to say. *He* loves it; that's clear enough.

But it's so -- wild. And this cabin is as simple as the slave quarters at Carefree. Esther has a better kitchen -- a much better kitchen -- than this one to cook in. And at Carefree, the walls are plastered; here, the walls are rough-chinked logs, and bound to hold dirt.

But she can't go back, not after all she's done to get here. Papa and all her friends have seen her off. She'll have to stick it out. If only that feeling of hopelessness would leave her.

And if she's made a bad bargain, at least it was her own choice. She'd never relinquish that grown-up right, to make her own choices.

If only she can make herself see this place with the eyes of Cornelius's ambition. She has to believe, like he does, that they'll drain and clear more land and plant more cotton. If she can believe that someday -- she won't give a thought to whatever comes in between -- they'll have a fine plantation home, and a family of handsome children, and dozens of slaves, then she can stand to live here. She has to make herself believe they'll be rich someday. Cornelius believes it.

Jenny comes into the cabin, carrying the satchel Esther gave her. She walks out through the back door and pushes the satchel under the edge of her bed. Stephanie, accustomed to the polite ways of Carefree slaves, is a little irritated that the girl comes right through the room without so much as a by-your-leave. The little African was quiet as a mouse the whole long trip out here.

"Jenny!" Stephanie calls, "I need a cup of tea. Bring some water."

"Yes ma'am." Jenny comes back into the room. Stephanie thinks she hears a little of Esther in the girl's accent.

Jenny gets the bucket down from the shelf next to the fireplace. Obviously, the girl's used to drawing water; it must be one of her chores. She goes out across the yard. In a few minutes she's back, the bucket filled.

Stephanie opens her trunk and fishes out her tea-kettle and the tin of tea. She unwraps her china cups from the petticoats they were wrapped in and then sets them in rows on the table. Jenny has slipped out again. Obviously the girl doesn't know how to wait around in case she's needed, like a good house-servant.

A few minutes later Cornelius rides back to the cabin. Stephanie goes out to the porch.

"Would you like some tea?"

"Yes ma'am."

They sit at the table and she pours the tea into her china cups.

"You know, we never had tea before, in this kitchen," Cornelius says. "Just our coffee, in the mornings. Tea's nice." He raises the cup in a half-toast.

"That's why I brought my tea-set. Esther told me not to forget it. She said I might have the only tea-set in the Cocodrie."

"You might."

"The girl drew the water for me," Stephanie says. "Now I don't know where she's gone."

"Jenny? She's probably gone back down to the stable to check on her kitties again."

Stephanie waits for him to say he'd go call her, but he doesn't. "I hope Esther taught her what she needs to know," she says. "I'm going to need some help."

"I'll need her to work with me in the fields until the cotton harvest. Then you can have her as a house-maid."

Stephanie sips her tea. Well, that little housemaid would have to learn to wait on her. Cornelius probably has no idea what a house-servant does. But the girl will learn.

Stephanie looks out to the back porch. "You know, we can't let her keep sleeping on the porch like she's been doing. Look how close it is to us." She points toward the bedroom.

"I've been meaning to build another room on the little house for her. Mal and I'll start on it this week."

Later, Cornelius and Stephanie sit out on the steps of the back porch. Stephanie looks across the moonlit yard at a raccoon shambling along the edge of the fence. Jenny comes through the cabin without saying a word and lies down on her bed and goes to sleep. Stephanie sees Cornelius glance at the little girl as she gets into bed.

When Cornelius and Stephanie go to bed, the rough crispness of the corn-husk mattress and its soft rustle and sweet musty smell are new sensations to Stephanie. Her head is on Cornelius's arm, her lawn nightgown light against the heat. Well, Papa's wrong about one thing; it's really no hotter here than in Natchez – it's the same sticky nighttime heat. Cornelius doesn't have mosquito netting for their bed, but tonight there aren't many mosquitoes. She'll have to see about buying some netting.

She's still mindful that Jenny's sleeping nearby, just outside the window. "Do you realize," she whispers, "that we've never made love in the dark?"

She presses up against him. Lovemaking in the dark was bound to have its joys. When touch was the only sensation, there would have to be little explorations, he using hands and lips to find her, and she him. In Natchez, she'd been giving him sweet lessons. Now she can learn something from him. It's the honey nectar of her life.

If only she can learn to love this place as Cornelius did. If only that sick feeling in her stomach would go away.

"Here's your hoe," Malachi says to Jenny the next morning as they prepare to go to the field. "You ain't forgot what work is while you was gone, did you?"

Jenny makes a face at him as she takes the hoe. "No."

"I think she's got a Natchez accent," Cornelius teases. "She's probably a regular city girl now."

"As long as she don't get too good to hoe cotton," Malachi says.

Jenny walks over to the fence. She'd answer the men if she knew what on earth they were talking about. She learned so many new words in Natchez.

But *why* do they hoe cotton? Nobody's ever told her.

They work all day in the field. In the evening Jenny slips into the cabin and presses herself against the wall, watching Miss Stephanie, who stands at the table wrapping loaves of bread in towels. Miss Stephanie wears a pink checked dress with a row of buttons down the front, and her smooth brown hair is parted in the middle and pinned up in the back with a comb. There's a smudge of flour on her bodice, above her apron. She glances at Jenny and keeps working.

Oh, it's so good to be home, Jenny thinks, even if she has to work in the field. Back where her own bed is, and her kitties. Already Miss Stephanie has the kitchen smelling so good.

Stefanneh. Stefennee. Well, Jenny can't ever hope to say it right, that pretty name, this pretty woman has.

CHAPTER TWENTY-THREE

In September they pick the cotton. And Malachi thinks there ain't nothing about farming that shows how far they've come as a half-picked cotton field. Off to the left, beyond where Jenny is picking, the field is sprinkled with white. Off to the right are the plants that've already been picked. They'll have to be picked again, and again, and again. It might be the new year before they're done.

Cornelius lets Malachi pick a row by himself, at his own pace. Malachi works down one side of a row and then back up the other side, his stiff fingers going as fast as they can. Since he's been here in the Cocodrie, he's started measuring the passage of time by the cycle of planting, hoeing, and picking. This year the harvest came on suddenly, the woody bolls springing open all at once, and there's the soft white fluff of cotton. Some of the cotton hangs down out of the bolls like raccoons' tails, so powerful is the burst. Working in the field now, picking cotton and lugging the familiar weight of the sack that hangs from his neck, Malachi remembers all the harvests of his life.

Nearby, Cornelius and Jenny work fast down a row together, each taking a side. Cornelius walks to the end of the row to empty his sack.

"Up in Alabama," Malachi says one day to Jenny when Cornelius is too far away to hear, "I had a overseer that weighed every basket of cotton every night, and he give out whippings if the basket warn't heavy enough. But if you picked more, you had to pick more the next day, or you'd get a whipping." He squints up at the sun. "I could pick two hundred and twenty pounds a day, back then."

Jenny stands with her hip cocked out. "Why you saying something that ain't so?"

"It is so, girl."

"Well, if he was mean, why didn't you go tell your master?"

"We did, girl. We told him 'bout the beatings, and showed him our backs. But shoo, he didn't care, as long as the cotton came in."

Jenny goes back to her picking. He never knows if she believes what he says, but he needs to tell her some things. This little African don't know much.

"I remember how you saw the cotton when it first turned white." He chuckles. "You clumb up on that fence and stood propped against the top rail, looking at the field like you never seen anything like it.

"And it *is* a right pretty sight. It look just like the snow we had in Virginny when I was a boy. 'Cept this white sprinkle ain't for playin' in. This is the most work of the year, pickin' this cotton."

Cornelius comes back with his empty sack and starts working down the row with Jenny, who glances at Malachi and then starts picking. Malachi works along, falling back because he's slower. Well, let them go on ahead. Every chance he gets, he'll tell Jenny what he knows, whether she'll take it for the truth or not; somebody's gotta tell the girl what slavery is. It'll be easier on her to hear it from him than to find out for herself someday, 'cause that's how you learn it, when you ain't expecting anything.

Ever since he'd been with Master Cornelius, Malachi has slept sound as a babe on his corn-husk mattress, knowing it's as soft a bed as he's likely to get and knowing Cornelius ain't likely to give him anything worse. But as summer changes to fall he finds he has to get up in the night to relieve himself into the ditch behind the stable. He won't bother walking to the privy. This nighttime walk is something he's gotten used to. On this November night, there isn't any moon, just a glittering starry sky. He runs his hand over his gray hair and hurries, fumbling with his pants as he trots. He hates getting up in the cold. Miserable night, he thinks, yearning for his warm bed.

As he stands at the ditch, impatient at the slow splatter of his water, he turns and looks over at the black shape of the cabin. Cornelius wouldn't like him using the ditch. Then something up above catches his eye.

Up there, where in his whole life he's never noticed anything but twinkly stars and the moon, is a shower of stars. He knows what shooting stars are; he's seen them on summer nights, fast streaks across the sky, gone before you can be sure if they're real or not.

But this is different. A stream of streaking, shining lights filling the sky; a hundred, or a thousand, falling stars. Is it the end of the world? He rubs his eyes, then looks again and fumbles his pants closed. Should he tell Master Cornelius? He'd want to see this. And he'd know whether it was the end or not.

He hurries over to the cabin; as his bare feet thump on the wooden porch, he cringes. He wouldn't want to waken Miss Stephanie.

Above his head, stars continue to fall, showering across the sky in silence. He taps on the door and then stands back, craning his neck to look at the amazing sky.

Cornelius comes out, his face creased. "What is it, Mal?"

"Master, look!" Malachi whispers, stepping back and pointing at the sky.

Cornelius walks out to the steps and looks upward. "What on earth -- "

Mal says, half-whispering, "Is it the end of the world?"

Cornelius walks down the steps and out into the yard, craning his neck back to look. Stars fly across the sky in an endless stream.

Malachi waits, but Cornelius doesn't say anything for a few minutes. He looks around, but Malachi has already checked to see that everything's normal. There's the cabin, and the little house, and the stable. The animals take no notice.

"I don't know what it is, but it ain't the end of the world," Cornelius says.

The sky sparks and streaks.

"I never seen anything like it," Cornelius says. "Let me get Stephanie up to see this."

"Yessir," Mal says, sitting down on the steps. "I never seed anything like it neither."

Stephanie comes out wearing a dressing gown, and Cornelius points up at the sky. She gasps. "Oh Lord!" she whimpers. "What is it?"

"Falling stars, I guess," Cornelius says. "Mal saw it first, and he woke me up to see it."

"Oh," she says in a high, whispery voice, "it might be the end."

"It's not the end, I'm sure," Cornelius says, putting his arm around her shoulder. "It's just some -- I don't know, falling stars or something. Let me get Jenny up."

Jenny's hard to wake; even the cold night air won't rouse her. Cornelius walks her stumbling out of the cabin, although at every step she'll looks like she'll tip over and sink to the ground in a heap, asleep. Cornelius holds her upright and gets her to open her eyes.

"Look up, Jenny." He points upward.

She rubs her eyes with her fists, and then comes wide awake. "Oh, what is that?" she asks.

"We don't know," Cornelius says.

Jenny sits on the step below Malachi, looking up. She wraps her arms around her knees and stares at the sky.

Stephanie sits down on the top step beside Cornelius. She puts her arm through his and presses her face against his arm, child-like, as if she'd climb onto his lap if she could.

"I think it must be a meteor shower," Cornelius says. "I've never seen one before."

"Me neither," Mal says. "But I guess that explains it. Whatever that is."

"Something in the heavens," Cornelius says vaguely.

"I don't like it. It makes me feel sick," Stephanie says, closing her eyes and putting her face down into the crook of Cornelius's arm. "It might be the end of the world, for all we know."

Cornelius pats her arm.

For the rest of her life Stephanie remembered how the sky looked that cold night, long white jets sparking across the firmament as if sending a warning. Even sitting close to Cornelius couldn't ease her mind about it, that night or later. In one particularly bright moment, when it seemed the whole sky was in motion, she saw -- she relived it later through many sleepless nights -- the sky actually opened, and a face of a man appeared. Oh, it was huge, and it looked down at the people who sat watching. And what a face it was, the face of a strong young man, darkly bearded, and scowling at her. She'd gasped when it appeared.

That was when she put her face down into Cornelius's arm to hide herself from the vision. When she looked up again, the rift in the heavens was closed, and she knew Cornelius didn't see what she saw. But she couldn't forget it. As dawn came, fading out the stars, and she stood up to wrap her dressing gown tighter against the chill of dawn, it came to her that the vision she saw was of her own real father, so long dead, but come back to rebuke her. Come to tell his daughter of her folly.

He wouldn't have wanted her to live out here on the Cocodrie, and in that place where dead souls live, wherever it is -- Stephanie had only vague ideas about that -- he couldn't rest until he confronted her. Everyone knows the dead watch over the living. She'd never seen a portrait of her father, and no one ever described him to her; but his blood was in her veins, and she recognized him sure enough, with the blood-tie. Her father, killed on the Natchez Trace, and buried in the forest by the Chickasaw Council House, leaving a young wife and baby daughter in Natchez. Surely he'd have wanted his daughter to marry well, to live a safe life in town.

And she'd gotten herself into a marriage he couldn't approve of, and he came to reproach her. And tomorrow night, or the night after that, she might wake up to find him signing to her again through lights in the sky. She dreads how she'll feel then.

"Guess the folks in town'll have somethin' to say about that," Malachi says when the sunrise fades out the stars. "I bet they plenty scared, lots of 'em."

"I bet you're right, Mal," Cornelius says with a chuckle. Stephanie has gone back inside, and Jenny is asleep, curled up on the bottom step. "And I bet when all's said and done, they'll say it's a meteor, or something like that."

Two weeks later Cornelius brings a newspaper from town. He sits on the steps and reads out loud an article about the star-shower they saw; the paper said it was a display from a meteor of the Leo constellation. Astronomers were calling it the Leonid shower. People throughout the South were saying they'd seen visions in the lights; one man in Texas said he saw a whole parade of chariots coming out of the sky, and the ancients holding stars in their hands.

"I don't believe a word of that," Cornelius says, chuckling.

Stephanie, after listening to Cornelius read the article, goes into the cabin and shuts the door. Malachi notices. He saw the sick look on her face that night. He himself is willing to say it was a natural thing, if that's what Cornelius says, but that little woman was scared plenty by something she didn't understand, he could tell.

CHAPTER TWENTY-FOUR

On a September day two years later, Malachi looks up to see Stephanie walking toward them along the edge of the field. She walks with a bounce in her step that flounces her brown skirt.

Miss Stephanie isn't tall, and she's become a thick-waisted little woman in the two years she's been here, eating her own cooking. She usually won't say much to Malachi directly, but ever since the night of the star-shower he thinks he understands her pretty well, just by watching. The way her mouth is pinched tight so much of the time, and the way she snaps at Jenny and him, and sometimes even at Master Cornelius—that must mean something.

Living out here on the Cocodrie must be quite different from what she was raised to expect, he figures. These late-summer days he often sees how her smooth young face looks tired when she serves the meals. And Jenny can't often be spared for housework since they got the swamp drained and cleared and planted this year. Jenny knows some housekeeping -- once in a while Miss Stephanie takes her over and sets her to washing or scrubbing -- but usually the girl's right there with them in the cotton. And no babe has come along to take Miss Stephanie away from the housework or to sap her energy.

"I need to go to the store," Stephanie calls out across the furrows to Cornelius. She wears a straw riding bonnet. "And I want to mail my letters."

Malachi notices that Jenny glances up and begins to hoe more slowly. The girl loves to ride into the settlement. Master Cornelius often takes her with him when he goes, and if he can't take her he'll bring her a piece of peppermint from the store. But Miss Stephanie never asks to take Jenny, and she never brings any candy. Looking at Jenny's open, hopeful face, Mal thinks it's a pity Miss Stephanie won't take more of a shine to the girl.

Cornelius glances over the cotton field for a moment, frowning. Then he says, "Well, all right. Mal, you go with Miss Stephanie."

"Yessir." Malachi empties his sack into the cotton basket at the end of the row. He knows Master Cornelius thinks it's silly, the way Miss Stephanie won't drive into the settlement alone. White women sometimes have that idea, that they can't go anywhere by themselves, but they can end up stuck at home, if no one's around who can go with them.

But Malachi doesn't mind going. It's easier to drive Miss Stephanie into town than to pick cotton down rows that never seem to get any shorter.

As he trudges up to the cabin, Malachi reflects that the place has changed since the cotton picking time two years ago when Miss Stephanie first came here. Besides the banana trees she planted, there's rosebushes along one side of the cabin, where the sun hits them all day. And the chickens that used to run loose in the yard are penned up now. The chickenyard was put up right after Miss Stephanie laid down for a nap one day and woke up to find chickens in the house, pecking in some flour she wanted for a piecrust. Old Leopard still skulks around the porch, but stiffly, like Malachi himself. Cornelius hasn't run hogs for awhile.

The little house has grown by another room, which he and Cornelius built for Jenny right after Miss Stephanie moved here; so now two doors look across the yard at the cabin. And the stable houses not just the horse, but a smart black gig too, bought with the money made from last year's cotton.

"Don't dawdle. I want to get going," Stephanie says without looking over her shoulder.

"Yessum. I'll hitch up the buggy."

Walking over to the stable, Malachi wonders if he's dressed well enough for a drive to the store. He looks down at his pants, frayed at the bottoms. Miss Stephanie doesn't ever seem to think he needs new clothes and wouldn't spend a penny if she could help it. And she didn't spin or sew, either. But Master Cornelius looks out for him, and gives him his hand-me-downs; the pants always have to be folded up at the bottoms. And Cornelius always sees to it that he has a hat, too; a man needs a hat, to work in the fields. Once Cornelius asked him if he wanted shoes, but Malachi hadn't ever worn shoes and doesn't think he could learn to wear them now.

Jenny still has the same dresses she brought back from Natchez, when Master Cornelius and Miss Stephanie got married. Back then, her skirts swept the ground; now the long shanks of her legs are starting to show.

Miss Stephanie still wears the same clothes she came here with, too, but her waists are pulling awful tight now. Some of her dresses, it looks like she'll burst out of them if the seams pull any tighter. Master Cornelius dresses pretty fine, Miss Stephanie sees to that. He has a new shirt every year, and high leather leggings and a wide Spanish hat. Miss Stephanie likes to show him off when they go to the settlement, Malachi figures.

He brushes dirt from his pants legs and then decides his clothes are all right.

As good as he's going to get, anyway.

After Malachi and Stephanie drive away, it seems a little lonely to Cornelius without Mal nearby. Most of the plants are as tall as Cornelius, so he picks the higher branches. Jenny's fast little fingers fly through the lower branches.

Cornelius knows that Stephanie's letters are the main reason she goes into the settlement. She writes more and more letters, sitting at the table in the cabin under the lamplight most nights, frowning in concentration as her quill pen scratches across the paper. The letters go out to her Papa, to Elenora Frankle, to women in Saint Louis and New Orleans she knew from her school-days. Cornelius thinks these letters take the place of the real-life world of the bayou in Stephanie's mind. And in her letters there's no place for him, Malachi, or Jenny. He's never asked to read any of her letters, but she sometimes reads aloud the ones she receives.

Stephanie troubles him with her strange, tight coolness. When did her patience for him begin to fail? Cornelius muses about it as he works. It started soon after he'd brought her here; he noticed it early, but at first he thought it was just learning a new way of life that caused her to turn inward. And then as the months went by he blamed Emile, who didn't answer any of her letters at first, even though she mailed them to both his addresses, at Carefree and on the Bayou Boeuf. For a year the man didn't write her a line; then a letter came, and two months later another -- letters with a tentative, halting tone that sounded nothing like the feisty Frenchman Cornelius remembered. Emile's long silence must have shaken Stephanie's confidence.

Cornelius sees that troubled look she wears so much of the time. And she never says a word to him about the cause. No child has come along, which probably didn't help things. In bed she seems more resigned than eager for him; that giddy joy of their early marriage has faded. And his efforts to get her to take part in the life of the Cocodrie have failed; she holds herself aloof from almost all the people here, and won't go to the frolics or quilting bees which would put her in with the other married women. All she has are her letters, and her trips into the settlement.

And the work. Stephanie scrubs the cabin clean every day, and cooks more food than they really need. But she works so joylessly. She's woven herself an empty life, and Cornelius doesn't know how to fill it.

Jenny's thin fingers are a blur among the cotton branches. The girl's the best picker on the place. She can see the cotton better, since it's more at eye-level for her. She's cute, Cornelius thinks, with her straight posture, her skinny shape and that coal-black skin. Sometimes when he carries his cotton sack to the end of the row, he looks back to see Jenny pause in her picking to wait for him, and she stands so still, looking off to some horizon.

"I'll race you to the end of the row," he says to break the monotony. She straightens up to look at him.

"Not if I don't know the prize," she says, putting one hand on her hip. He likes her smart answers. The girl has a sassiness that no one here tries to curb.

"Piece of peppermint candy."

"You got that candy on you now, sir?"

"I will have, when I next get to the store."

"All right, sir. I'll race."

"No cheatin' now. You've gotta do your half of the bush. No leaving it for me."

"I know I can beat you fair and square." She shakes her head. "I know it. I'm gonna beat."

"The devil you will." They watch each other as their fingers fly. Each refuses to let the other get ahead.

Cornelius hopes to buy another hand with this year's cotton profits. Certainly they *need* another hand, with the land they've taken in. He's got more planted than he can work. But if he buys a young male field-hand -- well, who would Jenny be safe with, besides Mal? Turley's boy Wonderful is still for sale, and for a decent price, but he looks like a boy whose mind is on other things than work. Even a married slave might take a fancy to a budding young girl. Well, choose carefully, Cornelius thinks. Maybe he could buy a woman who could be a field-hand. He'll consider that.

What a strange thing slavery is, he thinks. It brings such odd and unforeseen responsiblities. Put a girl like Jenny in a cotton field to hoe and pick cotton, and then make her kind of pretty, and smart, and life gets full of complications, just like that. Then you have to worry about Jake Turley and his like. It's lucky that Malachi's an old man, and righteous, in his way. Mal would never concern himself with Jenny in an improper way, Cornelius is certain.

And he hopes that as Jenny gets older Stephanie will find some companionship in having her about. For many plantation women slaves are like family. The mistresses of big plantations tend their slaves through childbirths, sicknesses, and funerals. And the best of the slave children become their pets. But Stephanie doesn't like Jenny, scolding her for the slightest slip.

It's because Stephanie grew up without a mother, Cornelius thinks. At Carefree the slaves took care of her, and she probably thought it would always be that way. But any plantation mistress could have told her it was the other way around. Women often said they were the slaves of their slaves. Stephanie would be more content with life on the Cocodrie if she took some satisfaction in Jenny and Malachi.

"I won!" Jenny shouts at the end of the row.

"You don't think I'll remember a little thing like candy when I go to the store, do you?"

"You better not forget," she says, unhooking her sack and flashing that light-up-the-world smile.

He chuckles and shakes his head as he watches her carry her sack to the basket and empty it. Yes, he'll have to be careful when he buys another hand. For an instant there he thought he could see the chrysalis about to emerge into a butterfly.

But beauty in a slave woman is a tricky thing. It calls in attentions both sought and unsought, Cornelius knows. Jenny's his responsibility. When he thinks of her as a grown woman, he pictures her with a husband -- Wonderful didn't look like he'd ever be that -- and surrounded by her children, and having a good life, or at least as good a life as a slave woman could have.

Malachi drives the buggy down the settlement's one main street. Stephanie holds her purse in her lap with both hands.

"I need to go to the hotel first to mail my letters," she says.

"Yessum." He stops the buggy in front of the hotel and Stephanie climbs down and hurries inside.

Malachi knows she'll spend some time shopping in the store next to the hotel after she hands her letters to the hotelkeeper, so he parks the buggy in the shade of a tree.

He looks back to see Stephanie come out of the hotel holding a letter. She walks down the sidewalk, and he can see the pursed lines of her face even from here. She slaps the paper over in her hand to read what's written on the back, and for once she walks without that bounce in her step.

The sun's glare whitens the wooden buildings. The heat makes him drowsy, so he lies down on the buggy's seat, drawing his legs up, since the seat won't fit his whole frame. He pulls his hat over his face to keep the winking sunlight out of his eyes. He knows he should stay awake to watch for Miss Stephanie, but she'll certainly see where he's parked, just a few yards from the store. And sleep is such a powerful need, just now. He dozes.

After awhile he senses that he's sharing his shady spot with someone else, and he moves his hat off his face to look. He sits up, blinking the sleep from his eyes, and finds himself looking into the narrow, pinched face of a white man he's never seen before.

CHAPTER TWENTY-FIVE

In the evening Mal sits on the porch next to the door. Jenny plays with her cat and other than some gnats that fire at them from all around, everything is still. The voices of Stephanie and Cornelius come from inside the cabin. They're sitting at the table, and Mal knows from the rustle of papers that Miss Stephanie has letters spread out in front of her, and she's reading them.

Mal rocks back in the rocking chair, his eyes closed, but he only looks as if he's dozing. By rocking back, his head is close to the door, and the voices are plain. Miss Stephanie sounds excited.

"Well, Elenora says here that a woman up near Tupelo overheard the plot being hatched. The slaves are planning it -- they're gonna rise up and kill the masters. That outlaw Murrell's behind it, of course. He wants to rile up the slaves so they'll kill the whites, and then his men can plunder the plantations. Everyone's scared to death of it."

Cornelius snorts. "Everyone's crazy, Stephanie. This whole country's gone crackbrained. Do you expect me to believe that out there in the woods some outlaws are lurking, and they're going to put the idea into our people's heads to cut our throats?"

"Listen! Elenora says right here that a woman in Mississippi just *happened* to overhear a field-hand talking to her baby's nurse -- her baby's *nurse*! -- about how they were gonna kill all the white people and even the children! The only thing that saved them was the nurse saying she couldn't bear to see the sweet baby harmed. That's all that saved them! So the woman told her husband, and they hanged all the ones that were part of the plot! But Cornelius, it's spreading through the whole country."

"Look. All this craziness started with Nat Turner. That's what's got people so scared. I don't for one minute believe that our people have any harm in their hearts, and I won't even let you say it. For God's sake --"

"Well, in Vicksburg the townspeople were scared enough to go after some gamblers. They hanged five of them, by lynch's law."

"The country's gone stark raving mad, like I said. What would gamblers have to do with an uprising?"

"Well, the gamblers -- well, they're -- they're the undesirable element. And nobody knows who they are, the way they go up and down the river all the time."

"Stephanie, *I* was up and down the river all the time, when I was a boilerman. Hell, if that was the charge, they could've hanged *me*."

"Will you listen to reason?"

"I may be the only person listening to reason in the whole of Concordia Parish."

Malachi hears the scrape of a chair and then the clump of boots as Cornelius leaves the table. He comes outside and sits on the top step. Malachi keeps his eyes almost closed, knowing Cornelius'll let him be if he thinks the old man is asleep.

Cornelius picks up a stick and begins to whittle it. In a few minutes Stephanie comes out and sits beside him.

Looking at the two white people sitting below him on the top step, Malachi thinks about going to freedom. Freedom. He's thought about it his whole life. If he was free, this place would have to run differently, that's for sure, without him here. Miss Stephanie might have to work in the cotton field herself. He has a sudden image of that tight-lipped woman in the cotton field, with a sack around her neck and her hair tied up in a handkerchief, and sweat dripping off her face as she picked cotton down a row that seemed to have no end. He takes his bandanna out of his pocket and wipes his face to hide the chuckle that the thought brings up.

Later, when Cornelius and Stephanie are back inside, Malachi walks over to the little house, where Jenny sits on a wisteria vine she's made into a swing. The vine grows between two trees and one of its big tendrils hangs at the right height for a seat. The sun has dropped behind the trees, casting everything into shadow, but overhead the sky is still a lighted blue.

"There's somethin' I gotta tell you," Malachi says. From the cabin across the way, lamplight glows dimly in the window. He lowers his voice. "Don't tell nobody, though. This is just between you and me."

Jenny stops swinging and waits.

"I saw a man today," Malachi says, leaning against the tree. "He was a white man, and he --," he chokes on the words, "he promised me somepin' more valuable than anything. Freedom." His face is contorted.

"Freedom?" Her voice rises to a squeak. She runs her hands up and down the thick wisteria vine.

"Yessum. He promised me that, just a man I ran into. I was waitin' for Miss Stephanie to come out of the store, and he come and stood by me under the tree, and he says, 'Hey, I want to talk to you.'" Malachi wipes his eyes with his bandanna. "I think maybe it was a angel I saw, right there under the tree, promisin' me freedom."

"Why would he do that?" Jenny asks. "Why would somebody just come along and say 'Here's freedom'? Why would he do that?"

"I don't know why, but he did. He say he was from the north, where they's lots of white folk don't believe in slavery. He says he takes slaves to free soil. Put us on a boat--"

Jenny's eyes are big.

"-- and take us to free soil, turn us loose there. Where we can be free peoples."

"I don't want to go," Jenny says quickly.

Malachi snorts. "Yes, you do, girl. You don't want to be a slave forever, do you? No, you don't. And your chilrun someday, when you big enough to have 'em, you don't want them to be slaves neither. You want to go to freedom."

Jenny scratches the dirt with her toe. "I ain't goin' on a boat," she says in a low voice.

"You'll go if I say go. You got to get on a boat to get to the north. Otherwise you get catched. Don't you know anything? You ain't from 'round here anyways. It'd be just like goin' home. Mebbe you'd see your brother again."

Jenny turns away from him. "Kofi's not up in the north. He's in slavery somewheres, and I ain't going without him. I don't know where he is. If I could find him, I'd take him and we'd walk. There must be a road I could walk."

"There ain't no road but a water road, girl."

Jenny chews her lip. Malachi goes on, "Anyways, this man, he says for me to meet him tomorrow on the bayou, right near the Indian Mound, and he'd give me the word 'bout where to meet the boat. He says to be there at noon. So I'm gonna be there. I'll tell Cornelius I'm sick, and he'll let me go lie down in my bed. He hates anybody bein' sick. And then I'll sneak off through the woods to the bayou. You just don't let on about anything."

"I won't go."

"Yes, you will. You'll go if I say go, girl. You don't know anything. And don't you think for one minute those white folk over there in that cabin care one thing 'bout us 'cept what we cost 'em, and what we can do to make 'em richer, 'cause they don't."

"Well, why don't we just go on the underground railroad, like you told me about? We could just go on up to free soil on that railroad. That's what we oughtta do."

Malachi snorts. "You can't go on no railroad, girl. This man gonna take you and me straight to the north. That's the deal. He's already got the boat ready to go. This is a real chance! To be free for once in our lifes!"

"I ain't goin'."

But Malachi is looking skyward, pure joy etched on his old face. He doesn't know much about any gods, because he's never had a master who thought slaves needed religion, but if there are such gods, he thinks they're up in that blue sky, this warm evening in 1835, and their names are all Freedom.

The next morning, Cornelius decides to go to the settlement to see about buying another mule, and he wants Malachi to go with him.

"Sir, I'm feelin' a little poorly to make that trip. I don't believe I can go."

"The fresh air'll do you good," Cornelius says. "Get Tea and Sam saddled."

"Yessir." On the way to the stable, Malachi stops at the garden, where Jenny's picking beans.

"Listen, girl, Cornelius makin' me go to the settlement with him, so you got to go to the bayou for me. You figure out some way to sneak 'round through the woods and wait for the man. When he show up, you find out the rondy-vu time, and find out where we're s'posed to meet the people who'll take us to the boat. You hear me? You get it right, girl."

"What if I don't want to go?"

"I ain't askin' nothin' hard," Malachi snaps. "It ain't hard to wait in the woods for a man. Hell, every woman I ever had waited in the woods for me, girl. You get this right." He slaps his hat on his head, knowing Cornelius is waiting.

Jenny stands up straight. "I mean to the north? I don't want to go someplace I never been."

"We talked 'bout that already. You want to go. Slavery's no good for you, and when you old enough t' have any sense you'll see it." He clasps his hands together and looks up at the sky. "Oh, freedom!"

He hurries down to the field. Freedom. Whether to go or not isn't even a question for him. He's made his decision, and in it is his mammy he'll never see again, and his brother, and the overseer in Alabama who cut his back with a whip -- Lula smeared his back with lard to help it heal -- and every soft-faced white man who ever traded money for the horny-handed old field-hand. And Lula, the wife he lost when he was sold off from the place in Alabama. Can't Jenny understand what freedom means?

When I'm Free, he thinks, squeezing his fists tight at the delicious thought. When I'm in the free soil, I'll get me a house, and maybe find me a wife. If I get my free papers, I'll go see my mammy again, and my brother, if I can find him. Maybe I'll even go find Lula; I'll buy her out of slavery and we'll go live in the free soil. I might have a farm like this one, and grow the crops for myself. And I'll walk down the street proud, and not have to step aside for anybody. When I'm Free.

He whistles up the horse and mule.

Jenny watches as Cornelius and Malachi ride away, worried about what Malachi wants her to do and jealous that she wasn't asked to go to town, too. Usually Cornelius takes her along, but today he didn't say a word about it. It hurt her feelings.

A moment later Stephanie calls out "Jenny!" and shakes her finger at the dawdling girl.

"Yessum," Jenny mumbles, going back to her work.

In late morning, Stephanie hands Jenny a plate of what she's been cooking, stew and greens and blackberry cobbler. Jenny sits on the step in the sunshine and eats while Stephanie sits inside at the table. Then Jenny hears the bed creak, and she knows that Stephanie's laid down for a nap. The sun isn't yet full up in the sky.

Jenny waits a few minutes to make sure Stephanie's not getting back up to check on her. She sets her tin plate and cup on the step. Leopard can lick those clean.

She folds her hands around her knees, smoothing her skirt over her bony knees. Mal ordered her to go find out about something he called a rondy-vu time: that's a word she doesn't know. Malachi usually won't tell her to do anything; she takes her orders from Master Cornelius and Miss Stephanie. But Malachi looked so strong at her when he told her she'd have to go to the bayou. Maybe she could find out the rondy-vu time, just so she could tell Mal?

Maybe there wouldn't really be a man on the bayou. And even if there is, finding out the rondy-vu time doesn't mean she's leaving.

She walks across the yard past the little house and down the path into the woods, her feet crunching on the pine needles. The Indian Mound is about a half-mile away, a rise in the forest floor next to the bayou, and everybody knows about it. Trees grow over it, and arrowheads silt out. Jenny has a pair of the chipped stones that Cornelius gave her. But all the Indians are gone.

She walks past the Indian Mound and over to the bayou. She figures Malachi was probably dreaming when he thought some man was going to be here. She stands in the shade for a moment where the path comes out at the bayou, and then she turns back. Miss Stephanie might wake up any minute and look for her.

But the next minute she hears a noise on the water. She walks back into the shadows under the trees and waits, remembering the sound of another canoe that once came up another river where she was.

A man turns the pirogue around in the middle of the bayou. He sees her.

"Where's Malachi?" he calls.

"He couldn't come," she says when she finds her voice. "Our master made him go to town today."

"You Jenny?"

She nods, surprised that this stranger uses her name. Malachi must have told him about her.

"Come out here where I can see you," he says. Jenny takes one step forward to place herself in sunlight. He looks her up and down.

"Okay. The meetin' place is right here tomorrow night, just after sunset. We'll be here waitin' for y'all. We'll take you in the pirogue up to where we have a wagon waitin', and we'll carry you over to the river. We have a boat waitin' south of Natchez." He misses the girl's dropped expression. "You'll be safe once we get to the boat. Tomorrow evenin', just after sunset. You understand?"

She wants to say, "Just Malachi's going. Not me." But her throat clenches tight and no words come out.

The stranger paddles away down the bayou, the light sound of the oars fading as he goes around the turn.

Jenny lopes back through the woods, where she takes a bucket to the pump to draw water. Her heart pounds. The man said to be at the Indian Mound, right after sunset tomorrow -- and Malachi could go if he wanted. But she's staying. The sunshine glints on the water in the pan as she washes the dishes and sets them on a towel. Stephanie is still asleep.

Jenny thinks about Cornelius. He probably saw her talking to Mal this morning in the garden. If she stays and Malachi goes, Cornelius is bound to think she knows something, and he'll make her tell. And then he'll go after Mal. If Mal got caught, then what? She knows Master Cornelius wouldn't treat him bad, but the old man might get caught by somebody else. She's heard stories about the things that happen to runaway slaves.

And she knows something herself about what happens when a person leaves home. She had to leave her home once, back when she was just a little child. Mal just doesn't know what it's like, to leave your home. He's thinking it's a good thing, but she knows better.

So she thinks. She knows when the rondy-vu time is, but she won't have to tell Mal. She can tell him wrong. When the idea comes to her, she smiles and presses the towel to her mouth, so pleased.

Mal and Cornelius come back late that night after Jenny's in bed. Mal stands in her doorway and holds his lantern up.

"When's the rondy-vu time?" he asks. "I'm ready to go."

She hesitates just a second, but he doesn't notice. "That man says for you to meet him at the Indian Mound," she says. "He says to be there at sunrise, not tomorrow, but the next day."

"Oh glory be!" Mal swings the lantern and the light jumps all around her room. "Tomorrow I'll be thinkin', move along sun! Don't dawdle in your path today! 'Cause tomorrow I'll be leavin' this slave's life behind!" Looking at his face, Jenny feels bad that she lied to him, and she starts to speak up about it, but her memories are too strong. She lets Mal go to his own room thinking of the wrong rondy-vu time.

The next night, Jenny, lying in her bed with the covers pulled up to her chin, can't hear Malachi snoring in his room like he usually does, so she knows he's not sleeping. He's too excited to sleep, she figures, because he's waiting for dawn.

Well, she knows it's no good to leave home. She did that once, but she'd never do it again. The man in the pirogue would be gone by now, anyway. What she did is best for Mal. He just didn't know it, that's all.

Jenny gets up before the sun rises and slips away from the little house. She doesn't want to be there when Malachi gets up, because she knows he'll try to get her to go with him to the bayou. And she wouldn't want to see his disappointment. So she goes over to the cabin and sits on the steps for awhile, listening to the light snores of Cornelius and Stephanie, and then as the sky lightens in the east she decides to walk down the road.

The sun comes up in a watery cloud-streaked sky and dew sparkles the fields. Here's the half-picked cotton, the rows running straight over to the fence. A rooster crows, then another.

She's sure what's she's done is best for Malachi. There's no reason to leave because there's no place else they can go. It was hard for her, at first, when she came to a strange place. It would be hard for Mal to go to free soil. Where would he live? How would he get his food?

Now here, they can live all right. Oh, the cotton's hard work. But it's not a bad place. Miss Stephanie doesn't like it, but all she knows is Natchez and here.

She walks until the sun is high up in the sky before she turns back to the cabin. Malachi is sitting on the steps eating his breakfast, and Cornelius is sitting behind him in the rocking chair.

"Oh, here's Jenny," Cornelius says. "I was about to send a search party for you."

"I went for a little walk." She feels Malachi's hard eyes on her.

"Good thing you come back," Mal mumbles, spreading molasses across his hotcakes with his knife.

Later, in the cottonfield, Malachi waits until Cornelius goes back to the cabin before mentioning what they're both thinking of.

"I went to the bayou, but nobody come. And where'd you go off to?"

"I told you I wouldn't go. I just went for a little walk down the road. I'm not goin' away."

"Well, I ain't neither, I expect. No man come for me. I guess it was all a trick."

"It must've been." But Jenny feels hurt, looking into Mal's sad eyes. It's not as bad as how afraid she'd feel if she left here, but still it's a shadow, darkening the bright day. She'd played a trick on Malachi, who'd never played any tricks on her. She stares down hard at her work so she won't have to look at him.

As they go back to their picking, Jenny tries to make herself feel better about what she did to Mal, but the bad feeling won't go away. She hadn't seen how she'd feel when this was all over. For the first time she realizes that even when she takes the best choice, as she did when she lied to Malachi, and no matter how sure she is about something, life has a lot of turns in it, and some of them, she can't see coming.

CHAPTER TWENTY-SIX

Stephanie steps onto the porch as Adelaide Halloran rides up to the cabin. Wiping the back of her hand across her forehead, she sighs. There's so much to do today; she's put three pots to simmering over the fire some hours ago, to beat the heat, but on a day like today she won't beat it. Already the steam in the air is bearing down like a blanket. Out in the field, where Cornelius and the two field-hands are, haze hangs like a curtain. Even the birds are quiet.

Adelaide swings down from her horse -- she rides bareback, too poor to have a saddle -- and stands in the slotted shade of the banana tree. Adelaide is thin as a mouse and has a quiet odd manner. All the Hallorans are like that. Sometimes Stephanie wonders if that family eats regularly. If they don't, it's their own fault; they certainly have enough kids to help tend a garden. All those girls, their names ending alike -- Ruetta, Henrietta, Deseretta -- and their rough boys whose names Stephanie doesn't know. Hallorans' land is the soggiest and poorest-looking stretch along the whole bayou.

Adelaide wears a blouse that was probably white once, and a skirt as tattered as any slave's. Stephanie never wants visits from this particular neighbor. But Adelaide is a white woman; there's nothing to do but be cordial. Stephanie forces herself to smile at the woman who wants something, no doubt.

"Oh, Mrs. Halloran, come and sit with me under the tree and cool off," Stephanie says. "You've had a hot ride this morning already. Would you care for some tea? And you can water your horse at the trough over there by the stable."

Does Adelaide know she's being snubbed? For a proper woman, at a proper house, a stable-boy would be called to water the horse. But Malachi is down in the fields with Cornelius and Jenny, and Stephanie is not about to lead Hallorans' nag anywhere.

Adelaide leads the horse to the trough. Stephanie brings a chair from the cabin and sets it next to the rocking chair under the tree, and then she brings out two glasses of tea. Tepid tea; icehouses are a rivertown luxury, not found here.

Adelaide sets her horse to grazing nearby and walks over. Stephanie motions her toward the rocking chair -- she remembers her manners that much, at least -- and takes the straight-backed chair for herself. Adelaide's dirt-darkened toes peep like little secrets from under her skirt as she rocks.

"Is your family well, Mrs. Halloran?"

"Yes ma'am, they well." Adelaide sips the tea, her little finger raising daintily in the air. "I've come to tell ya somethin' for yo' own seffitty." Stephanie catches the accent. Safety, the woman says.

"My safety? Well, what is it?"

"Well, ma'am, it's 'bout Murrell and his men. You've heard of 'em, I s'pose?"

She has indeed; the whole Cocodrie, and, judging by the talk around here, the whole state from Feliciana to the Attakapas, has heard of the band of outlaws who're on a rampage, plundering and stealing and hiding out. And not getting punished either. The governor's relatives are said to be in the gang, so the law won't go after them. Wild old John Murrell, whose daddy was a preacher, likes to quote scripture to a man before shooting him. And his men disembowel the dead and load their bellies with sand and rocks and sink them to the bottom of the nearest bayou. Murrell and his men steal whatever they can -- gold, cattle, slaves.

"So what is it about Murrell? Is he hereabouts?" Stephanie can't help staring at the other woman. Adelaide has the lopsided mouth of a woman losing her teeth.

"Yes ma'am, they say he is. Some say they seen him. They got a white man in the jail in Vidalia right now who they say's part of his gang. He was a stranger who come through here. From where, nobody knows. He's gonna hang."

"What charge have they got him on?"

Adelaide smirked. "Don't need no charge, ma'am. It's lynch's law. They kin whip 'im good, or they kin hang 'im. And if it was me, I'd say hang 'im and be done with it. Whippin' ain't enough for Murrell's men." Her face looks as bitter as if Murrell preyed on her personally. "They say nobody's seff." *Safe,* Stephanie understands. "I know you is here at your place all alone with your slaves some of the time, when Cornelius is gone to town or somepin'." Stephanie is startled to hear Adelaide refer to Cornelius so familiarly, by his first name. "You better watch out. That's what I come to say. Me, I got fambly around all the time, so I don't worry so much."

And you don't own any slaves, Stephanie thinks. She bristles at the other woman's advice. Poor whites are presumptuous and forward. And think themselves the equal of anyone.

"Well, I'll tell Mister Carson, of course, and we'll keep an eye out. But I never see any strangers, out here."

"And keep an eye on your slaves too, ma'am. That's who Murrell goes after. He promises to give 'em they freedom. And 'course they take it up. You know they all ready to run away first chaince they git. Then Murrell sells 'em agin. Which they got comin', of course. But you better watch the ones you got."

I don't want your advice, Stephanie thinks, but she feels unsettled. She'll have to tell Cornelius, and of course he'll think it's all nonsense. And why did Adelaide come all this way to tell her about Murrell? To scare her, no doubt. Some people love to scare other people. And they pick their victims; those they think would scare easiest get the most lurid tales. In Natchez Stephanie heard old women tell new brides tales of childbirth so horrific it was a wonder the young women ever consummated their marriages. Out here in the Cocodrie the men and women both tell stories about winters when rats ate all the corn, or about murderous Indians lurking in the woods, back when there were Indians. Or tales of John Murrell. Oh, storytellers' eyes glitter and their faces come alive, when they tell such tales. For herself, she long ago decided not to believe any story coming from a lively face such as Adelaide's was now.

"By the way," Adelaide says, her crooked mouth widening in a smile to reveal gray teeth, "you got any butter-beans you kin share?"

Just after breakfast a few days later Amos McKee rides by with a sack of peaches. He hands them over to Cornelius as he sits on the porch drinking the last of his coffee.

"I've got a tree that won't stop producing," he says. "Can you use these? Margaret's preserving all she can, but it's getting ahead of her and the girls. I hate to see 'em go to waste."

"Tell me what your fertilizer is, and I'll put some on our trees," Cornelius says, pointing toward the half-grown peach trees that grow a few yards away, their branches green with leaves, and their fruit already taken. He takes the sack. "Give Miss Margaret our thanks. Visit a while?"

"I'd like to, but I'm off to town for the missus. Your first picking done?"

"Not yet. We're more than half done, though."

"Mine's almost done. Say, you heard about what happened at Turley's?"

Cornelius shakes his head.

"Well, this was just yesterday. You know Turley's blacksmith Lafayette?"

"I do. I take him some business on a regular basis. Whenever something breaks, which is pretty often."

"You won't be doing that again. Lafayette's in jail in Vidalia."

"In jail? Why?"

"He went after Turley with a crowbar. Gave him some bad licks, too, on the head. Old Turley, you know he can't hardly fight at all. Dubrenne had to pull Lafayette off of 'im."

"Whatever came into Lafayette? Drinking?"

Amos shakes his head. "No. I don't think he'd been drinkin'. As I heard it, Lafayette says Turley was messin' with his daughter. You know, he's got that girl that's about twelve. Clarissa, her name is. Lafayette says he found Turley bein' improper with the girl."

Cornelius stares at Amos. He knew that what Lafayette said was right. "What're they going to do to him?"

"Hang 'im, most likely. I understand it's what Turley's insistin' on. 'Course, from everything I've ever heard about that place, it's Dubrenne they oughta hang."

It's not Dubrenne, Cornelius thinks.

"Well, I'll be goin'," Amos says. "You comin' to the frolic next week?"

Cornelius stands up. "Oh, my wife don't care much for those," he says. "We'll probably miss it." .

Cornelius takes the peaches into the cabin. Then he paces the porch as Jenny and Malachi get their sacks. He goes with them to the field.

Cornelius worries. Will they ever finish picking cotton? He planted all his arpents in the spring, figuring he and the two field-hands could pick it. But field-hands can plant and hoe more cotton than they can pick. They're all getting tired now.

Lafayette in jail. Cornelius drags the weight of that like a too-heavy cotton sack. He remembers the powerful black man who worked bare-chested in his blacksmith shop at Cedar Breaks, his muscles like gourds under his skin. And always polite, always competent, whenever Cornelius took work to him. Cornelius was always ill at ease, being at Cedar Breaks. But when Lafayette hired out to work he could keep what he earned, especially if Turley didn't know about it. Clarissa he'd seen only once, a girl littler than Jenny, and about as skinny. She hung around her father's shop once or twice when Cornelius was there. What Lafayette says about Turley is true.

It comes to Cornelius that he might be the only one in the Cocodrie who knows the truth about Turley. And Lafayette would surely hang, if Turley gives the word. Attacking a white man means death to a slave.

But even if Cornelius went to the court in Vidalia, how could he help? He's got no firm evidence of Turley's guilt, and bringing a charge against a respected planter is no light thing. It's just that he knows, in his gut, that when Turley offered to buy Jenny that day two years ago at Carefree, he had one thing in mind for her. It was the look in the man's eyes.

All day he picks cotton with the image in his mind of Lafayette's daughter, leaning against the wall of the blacksmith's shop. By mid-afternoon he's decided to let the matter be. Let the law handle it. The cotton has to come in.

But that night he can't sleep, even after Stephanie presses up against him and moves her legs over him. He turns away from her, unable to get Lafayette out of his mind.

In the morning he decides the cotton can wait a day. He'll go to Vidalia. He makes up an excuse about needing to buy some implements, and Stephanie, who was up early to steam the peaches, doesn't seem to care.

"I'll take Mal with me," Cornelius says. He doesn't feel like making the trip alone.

"Good. Jenny can help me with the preserves," Stephanie says. Cornelius knows she wants the girl to work in the cabin more.

Cornelius and Malachi reach Vidalia just after noon, a few minutes too late to see a double hanging. The crowd's beginning to drift away from the large old tree where two slack bodies hang, one black and one white.

"What on earth is that, sir?" Malachi asks when they're some distance away. He leans forward on Sam to see better.

"What it looks like," Cornelius mutters. He recognizes the well-muscled form of Lafayette dangling beneath the moss-draped branch. The other man he doesn't know, a white man of slight build, his features slack in death. Nearby, the horses they'd been stood on a few minutes earlier are tied to a hitching post.

A man rides over and begins to talk, even though Cornelius doesn't know him.

"Well, you missed it. Them two rascals died different, I'll say that." The man wore the rough clothes of the back-country. "That white man, he never said a word. He was one of Murrell's men, they said. But the ole buck now, he yelled and screamed right to the end. End of the rope, that is. Ain't nothin' can yell louder than a scared darky." He chuckles.

Cornelius feels sick. Lafayette was screaming to save his daughter, certainly. The people standing around the tree came out to see a noontime entertainment, but they saw a travesty. From the tree over there hung what used to be Lafayette, polite and competent, and another man caught in the craziness of a slave terror. Both killed by slavery, in a way.

Malachi won't look. He turns the mule around and faces the brown cliff where Natchez sits. Cornelius sees his grim look.

"Let's go home, Mal," Cornelius says, and he spurs Tearose to a trot and they leave the town. Cornelius has a lump of guilt in his belly. If he hadn't waited to come to Vidalia, he might have saved Lafayette. If he'd come yesterday morning, when he first found out about it. He probably couldn't have done anything for the other man, since the whole country was crazy for blood. But Lafayette's daughter might be with Turley right now. He closes his eyes at the thought. What recourse is there? He has no standing before the law in this. It wasn't his slave being bothered.

Slavery dirties us all, he thinks as he and Malachi ride out of town. If there were some other way to get the crops worked, I wouldn't own a single slave. But there's no other way.

In two-and-a-half years Stephanie hadn't been back to Carefree. She let her letters be her only connection with that old, other life she had before she married Cornelius. She exchanged letters with Emile and her friends, but she wasn't sure she'd ever go back to Natchez. During her first year here, when Emile didn't write at all, and when her real father came to her in the star-shower, she was ashamed of her wrong choices. Then gradually something else took over: a joyless determination to make something of the place on the Cocodrie. Even after all this time, her feeling that she'd come down in the world haunted her. So even when tempting invitations came, such as to Elenora's wedding to John Landerson, and then to the house-warming for the house John built for Elenora -- and named for her -- Stephanie declined.

It's hard, this country life, especially when she has so little help from that useless Jenny. Sometimes the girl dawdles so over the simplest chores that it takes a smart smack to get her moving along. But she never slaps Jenny when Cornelius is around; he favors the girl so, and spoils her, too, spending good money on sweets. He'll ruin her for housework, Stephanie thinks, but she never challenges him directly about it. He has such a blind spot there.

But this year at Christmastime, an aching homesickness comes over Stephanie. She feels a pull back to Carefree, to see her Papa, and Esther, and all the others. Christmas is a time when fine Natchez houses fill with relatives and friends and invitations flow to Carefree for the fanciest soirees. But the cotton isn't all picked yet, so she knows she'll miss another Natchez Christmas.

As she cooks Christmas dinner in the Cocodrie, a wild turkey Malachi trapped, Stephanie remembers how at Carefree the windows would be decked with holiday greens, and how her Papa would call all the slaves together and hand each of them a jar of molasses.

She can't admit it, but she's tired of fighting her lonely, inner struggle. Her mind refuses to carry the battle further. The mistakes she made can't be undone. She wants to go home.

In January they finish picking the cotton, and Cornelius takes it to the gin. A few days later he and Stephanie sit at the table with papers in front of them, and calculate the profit.

"I guess I ought to feel rich," Stephanie says with a tight smile.

"Well, as I thought, we didn't produce twenty-four bales, and the cotton didn't bring fifteen cents a pound. We've got more land for cotton than we have hands to bring it in." Cornelius stretches his long legs out and drinks from a half-filled glass of whiskey. "Next year we ought to get another field-hand."

Stephanie studies a paper covered with figures. "Now, what will Mal and Jenny do until it's time to plant again?" she asks. "That's some months off. The animals and that little bit of corn won't take up all their time."

"That's true," Cornelius says. "I thought I'd go deer-hunting. Mal can go with me. We can kill some hogs, too."

"What about the rest of the time? What'll they do?"

"Rest, I guess. They deserve it."

"Well," Stephanie says, "I've been thinking that Jenny could learn to spin. You know, lots of plantations have a spinning house where some of the slaves spin. Those that are sick, or old, or just plain without anything to do, they do all the spinning for the slaves' clothes. You can save lots of money doing that, I'm told. Margaret McKee told me she's thinking of getting a spinning machine. A man in Vidalia's got one for sale for a hundred and thirty dollars."

"You'd have to spin from now 'til Judgment Day to save a hundred and thirty dollars spinning your own clothes."

"Well, the McKees have lots of slaves, so it's worth it to them. But I've been thinking. I already *have* a spinning wheel. It's at Carefree."

"You gonna sell it to Margaret?"

"Cornelius, it was my *mother's.* And I don't know how to spin. But Esther does. She told me so one time. She says she used to spin all the time. Why don't you let me take Jenny to Carefree, and Esther can teach her how to use the wheel. Then we can bring the wheel back out here in the buggy, and she can use her idle time here for something useful. She can spin and she can learn to sew, too. Esther's a good seamstress. That way, Jenny can make all her clothes and Malachi's too."

"You don't want to let her just play around, like a little kid?"

"Well, she's not so little anymore, in case you haven't noticed. She's practically up to my shoulder. She must be about twelve by now. Her dresses are all getting way too short on her, and I don't want to spend good money on calico or muslin for new dresses for that girl. You know what things cost."

"So you want to take her to Natchez? Well, go then. Jenny'd probably like to see Esther again. And while you're there, spinning or not, you can get her some cloth for a new dress. Even if you have to buy it in the store."

Stephanie runs her hand over her hair, smooth and tightly pinned. "All right. We'll take the buggy tomorrow."

Cornelius gets up. "Right now I told Jenny I'd take her fishing." He goes over to the door. Then he stops and looks back at Stephanie. "My mammy used to spin and make clothes, up in Georgia. It's pretty tedious work, as I recall. You don't know what you're getting into. I bet Jenny won't like it."

"She'll like it if I say so," Stephanie snaps.

Cornelius shrugs and goes out across the yard, calling, "Je-e-nny!" Stephanie gets up and goes out to the porch, where she leans against the door, her arms folded. Cornelius and Jenny have their poles and bucket of worms and are walking off into the woods toward the bayou with their poles on their shoulders. The girl walks just a step ahead of him. Jenny looks little compared to the tall man.

"Oh, Cornelius," Stephanie says, bitterly and softly to no one, since no one's around to hear, "you know so many things. And you *think* you know everything. But I swear you don't know who you love."

CHAPTER TWENTY-SEVEN

The cabin could seem so dark in the late afternoon, Stephanie thinks. She turns up the lamp and stirs the fire. Then she sits at the table and stares at the papers lying there. What her efforts have brought her in two years here lies before her -- $1100 -- a year's profits. And not enough, never enough. Especially if they must buy a field-hand, who'll easily cost $800 or more. Never enough.

She takes a sheet of writing paper and dips her pen into the fat-bottomed inkwell, touching the quill to the lip. She poises the pen above the paper for a moment. Then, her lips set into a tight line, she begins to write. After a few moments she stops and re-reads what she's written, then crumples it and feeds it to the fire. She starts again. Again, into the flames.

Finally she has a page written; she reads it several times. Then she folds her hands and looks out through the back door of the cabin, where the horizon is a line of raw-cut trees.

The letter will do, she decides. She'll mail it when she gets to Natchez, not before.

State of Louisiana, Parish of Concordia
January 12th, 1836
My dear Cornelius,

I have chosen to write thoughts which I am unable to express any other way. I am mailing this from Natchez but please know that it has been written in the Cocodrie. It is not my father's pleadings that have moved me.

I write to tell you of a decision which I have made over some months, carefully and deliberately I think, but made quite alone since I have no confidantes. And you, who should have been my confidante, cannot be. I understand that now.

I will not give you in writing all the reasons for my decision, nor do I wish to tell them face to face. Let this letter be the entirety of my message.

I will remain at Carefree. I will not return to the Cocodrie. Pray do not think I can be persuaded otherwise. If you come to Natchez, I will not see you. I loved you once, but no more.

Jenny I have with me here at Carefree, under Esther's supervision. You may come get her whenever you wish. You can get the buggy too.
Stephanie Carson

She looks up to see Cornelius and Jenny returning, Cornelius carrying a string of fish. She slowly folds the letter and, dipping her pen one last time, writes Cornelius's name and address on the outside. Below the address she writes, "Please forward this letter with speed."

Then she seals the letter and tucks it into her purse. As soon as she gets settled at Carefree, she'll take this letter to the King's Tavern and mail it. The smell of catfish is in the cabin as Cornelius carries the catch through the room and out to the back, where he and Jenny will clean them on a table set under a tree.

Stephanie and Jenny drive away to Natchez the next morning, Stephanie clicking the reins hard and Jenny half-turning just once to wave at Cornelius and Malachi, who stand in front of the cabin watching them go.

They pass the settlement without stopping, the buggy straining through the mud, because it's been raining here. The horse churns up the mud, so Stephanie guides the buggy along the firmer ridges in the road. As they travel east it looks as though it's rained harder here; all the fields hold water like saucers. Gray black-rimmed clouds rumble overhead.

The buggy still smells of new leather, and Jenny's proud to be sitting up beside Miss Stephanie, who looks so fine in her black dress, her skirt wide with many petticoats. Jenny's a little ashamed that her tan-colored dress has nothing under it, her bony knees poking up under the skirt.

Stephanie wears a straw bonnet. Jenny, with no bonnet, has smoothed and pinned her own hair with extra attention this morning. She still wears it in the style Esther taught her, brushing it back into a satisfying thick roll and then folding it over on her hand, tucking all the strands in and then pinning it. She once had six hairpins, but two are broken. But she can manage with four. She doesn't have a looking glass, but her fingers can tell her if the pins are holding.

Esther gave her the hairpins the last time she came to Natchez, over two years ago. Esther: who is she? Jenny has just a distant memory of a tall, kind woman. And Carefree -- Miss Stephanie chattered on about it this morning as they prepared to leave. Carefree is so important to Miss Stephanie. Jenny can't remember it very well.

Natchez comes into view, a splendid sight on the bluff across the river, and Jenny quivers with excitement. Two years ago she'd come to Natchez to learn housekeeping, and now she's coming back to learn to spin, Miss Stephanie says. Would spinning be harder to learn than housekeeping?

When they come to the ferry landing in Vidalia, Jenny's knees begin to knock together. She puts her hands on them to hold them still, glad that Miss Stephanie doesn't seem to notice.

"Oh! Miss Stephanie! You come home!" Esther runs down the steps and opens her arms wide, taking both Stephanie and Jenny in her embrace. "Did y'all drive all this way by yourselfs?"

Stephanie smiles. "We certainly did. I'm brave as a pioneer."

"And look how big this Jenny has grown!" Esther exclaims, holding the girl at arm's length. "She's almost as tall as you! Why, if you ain't careful, I believe she'll grow taller than you."

"She might," Stephanie says. She lifts her satchel out of the buggy. "Get Charlie to put the buggy in the back, will you? We're here so you can teach this girl how to spin. You can use that old spinning wheel that's upstairs. Is Papa here?"

"Yessum. He'll be so pleased when he finds you here. But—well, he's 'sleep right now."

"I'll surprise him later. He won't know I'm here, and when he goes to supper, there I'll be!" she says over her shoulder as she goes up the steps.

"Wait --" Esther begins, but then Philip comes around the corner of the house, and she turns to him. "Philip, take care of this horse. Jenny, you remember where to go?"

"I don't think I do," Jenny says. Philip stares at her.

"I'll take you back there in a minute," Esther says, turning toward the house. "Miss Stephanie --"

But Stephanie isn't paying attention to Esther. She walks into the big house, taking in the familiar details and dimensions of the long central hallway, the stairs rising before her. To her left is the doorway into the parlor, to the right the drawing rooms where her wedding reception was held. And it's all so quiet. All during the months she's been gone, she remembered the chatter of guests, the rush of activities leading up to her reception. Now there's just the ticking of the hall clock. And the house seems smaller now.

She goes up the stairs. Here's her peach-colored bedroom with the big four-poster bed, and over there the armoire, and her writing desk. It all looks familiar and strange at once. She turns around so she can see every detail, every angle. She touches her silk counterpane, then lies down on it for a moment, relishing the softness of the featherbed. She wants everything to be familiar again.

And yet --. And yet --. It seems flat, somehow, to see the rooms again, and Cornelius not here. She pushes him out of her mind. She gets up and peels off her dress -- it feels grimy from the trip -- and steps out of her petticoats. She opens her satchel and takes out her dressing gown, a fine one she wore here at Carefree before she ever set foot in the Cocodrie. She hasn't worn it much in the Cocodrie, because she didn't want to ruin it. But it seems fitting to put it on today. She smooths the fabric down and ties the ribbons. It's good to be out of her heavy dress and into something lighter.

She walks down the hall to her father's bedroom. She just wants to peek at him, sleeping; it's been so long since she's seen him. She eases the door open and looks into the room. Theresa and Rob are bending over the bed, and when the door opens they straighten and look up, startled. A stench hits Stephanie's nose and she steps backward.

"Close the door, Miss Stephanie," Rob says, and she sees they're placing towels around the gaunt man on the bed. Is that her Papa? His hair salted with gray and his cheeks sunken below his high cheekbones? Only his sharp profile is unchanged. Esther hurries up the stairs.

"Oh, I was comin' up to tell you," Esther says, taking the young woman's hands and pulling her back into the hall. "We stayin' out of that room since this mornin'. Master Emile -- he's got the cholera. They say it's come up the river again on the steamboats. They say it's in the air. Master Emile is awful sick. Thank goodness you come today."

"Thank goodness?" The stink of the sickroom is thick in the hallway. "You think it's good I brought myself here to where there's cholera?"

"Master Emile – he'll be glad to see you."

"He can't see me, Esther! Is he conscious?" Stephanie waves her hand in front of her face and sinks against the stair-railing, trying to get away from the putrid odor.

"No 'm, he's been 'sleep since about noontime. All mornin' we been givin' him green figs and salt, like the doctor say. But now we can't rouse 'im. I don't know --"

"Cholera." Stephanie presses her hand to her stomach as if she might vomit. A new wave of stench emerges from the bedroom. "I can't go in there."

"No ma'am, don't even try," Esther says, taking her arm. "You can't do one thing for him. You can see that. He's got it bad. If I was you --"

Stephanie stares at her. "I can go home. To the Cocodrie."

"Yes'm. You cain't do no good here, not with him like that. All you can do here is get yourself sick. Why n't you go on back, you and Jenny both? That way, you won't get it, most likely."

"What about you? And the others?"

"Me? I got no other place to go. This my home. If I get the cholera, I get it, that's all. You go on back, an' Mister Emile, if he don't get better, we let you know."

"You mean, if he dies --"

"Yes'm. He might. But you can see we takin' care of him. We cleanin' him up all the time, takin' turns at it. Master Emile always good to us, and now we good to him. But you don't have to stay here with the cholera."

"No, I don't." Stephanie backs away. "I'll go, and then if anything happens, you let me know. Send a rider out to the Cocodrie. I'll go. That's what I'll do. I'll get Jenny. We're gonna head back."

She hurries down the hall to her own room, where she closes the door and then stands with her back against it, tears stinging her eyes. Oh God, her Papa so sick! And unconscious, not even knowing she's here. He looks so little and shrivelled, and there's that awful stink. A person with cholera can be fine at breakfast and dead by dinnertime. She has to go; it'd be insane to stay.

She throws off the dressing gown and stuffs it back into her satchel. Then she pulls on her petticoats and the dress she wore here. She wipes her face dry of tears and smooths her hair.

She leans out the window that faces the slave house. "Jenny!" she calls. If her father should waken, she wouldn't want him to hear. She's determined to leave, whether he's conscious or not. "Jenny!" After she calls the second time, Jenny comes out.

"Get your things. We're going back to the Cocodrie."

"Huh?"

"Home! We're going home! Get ready."

"Home? Now?"

"Yes! I'll meet you at the barn."

Stephanie grabs her satchel and runs out of the room and down the stairs. She pauses at the door to the parlor. Her mother's portrait still hangs there-- the face she so often studied when she was growing up here, of a young woman like herself. The woman in the portrait has the same gaze that she has, and her painted face is smooth, her ivory cheeks tinged with pink. Death, an unannounced caller, took Josephine before she was twenty-three; and death could come for Josephine's daughter, too.

Stephanie opens the front door and runs around the side of the house to the barn. She expects Jenny to be there. Instead there's only Philip, watering the animals.

"Philip, don't make a sound," Stephanie says in a low, urgent voice. "Hitch up my horse, and then bring the buggy to the front of the house. Be quick, but be quiet!"

The boy looks scared. "Yessum."

"Oh, where is Jenny?" Stephanie stamps her foot. "I guess I'll have to go get her."

She runs to the slave house and finds Jenny in Helene's room.

"Helene's sick, Miss Stephanie," Jenny says, standing next to the girl's bed. "She's so hot. You should feel her head."

"Oh, for heaven's sakes, what is wrong with you, Helene?" She puts her hand on the girl's forehead.

Helene looks up pitiably. "I don't know," she rasps. "I just started feelin' sick, and I threw up, too. And now I feel worse."

"Jenny, we've got to leave here this minute," Stephanie says. "Esther can tend to her." She runs back into the main house and calls out to Esther, who's gathering a fresh stack of towels for the sickroom. Esther drops her towels and runs out the back door with her apron flapping.

"What is the matter?" she asks.

"Helene's got fever," Stephanie says. "Go see." She points toward the slave house. "I'm leaving now. Jenny too." She turns to Jenny. "Go get your bag."

She and Jenny throw their bags into the buggy and then drive out the back gate. "Thank goodness we're getting away from there," Stephanie says as they turn onto the street.

"I thought we were gonna stay longer. I was gonna learn to spin, wasn't I?"

"Jenny, will you please be quiet!" Stephanie snaps, cracking the reins. The buggy clatters away down the road.

When they get to the top of Silver Street, they can see dark clouds scudding toward them from the low horizon to the west. Then the horizon vanishes. As they turn onto the long slope down to the river, Jenny asks, "Why does the sky look like that?"

"I don't know."

The river is roiled, white-caps dancing where normally it carries only slow swells and eddies. A sprinkling of raindrops stings their faces. "I hope we get home before the big rain hits," Stephanie says. "If we don't, we might have to make umbrellas out of our petticoats."

"I don't have a petticoat. Maybe we should turn back."

"We're not turning back." Stephanie pulls back on the reins to hold Tearose in check as the horse canters down the slope. "I hope the ferry gets here quick."

Natchez-Under-The-Hill is ending the day as usual, drunk. A man trudges down the sidewalk toward the ferry landing, the wind whipping his coat.

A steamboat and two flatboats are docked at the landing, rocking in the wind. The ferry arrives from Vidalia just as Stephanie and Jenny reach the foot of Silver Street. The last passenger is slow in leaving the boat.

"Hurry up, there, straggler!" the ferryman shouts. "I got passengers who want to cross! Move along, damn you!"

The man shuffles off the ferry. Then the ferryman gives the signal to board and Stephanie drives the buggy up the ramp. She sets the brake and ties the reins to the railing. Jenny gets down from the buggy and holds onto a pole. Out here on the river the wind seems to come from all directions. The ferry rises and sinks in the swells. Only a few passengers are making the crossing.

Stephanie makes her way closer to Jenny.

"I'm glad to leave that place behind!" Stephanie shouts over the roar of the wind as the ferry ploughs out into the river. "I'd never stay where there's cholera! Never!"

"But what about your Papa? What about Helene?"

"My Papa -- well, it's not your concern. There was nothing we could do for him. Or Helene." She hangs on to the railing as the wind whips her skirt.

The ferryman calls out from the pilot-house, "Y'all travelling far today, or just to Vidalia?"

"All the way to the Cocodrie," Stephanie shouts. "And we don't appreciate your language, sir, as we heard it a few minutes ago!"

The ferryman, a dark Creole, yells, "You may not like my methods, missy, but I've gotta get as many people across as I can. I might not get t' make any more trips this evenin'."

"You think the storm'll get bad?"

"I'd say so. I seen this before, these white caps. You only see 'em when there's a bad storm. If I was you, I'd take a room in Vidalia for the night. You kin go home tomorrow."

Stephanie faces the chopping water again. "No, thank you. They'll overcharge and it'll be a shabby room. We'll be home in a few hours."

"Not likely in this weather," the boatman shouts. "Storm's comin' from the west. It'll be blowing in on us in an hour, I betcha."

"Bet me all you want," Stephanie retorts. "But we're going home today."

"Suit yourself, missy," the ferryman mutters. "I only charge for the trip. The advice is free."

When the ferry docks at Vidalia, Stephanie and Jenny climb back into the buggy and Stephanie drives down the ramp. She gives the horse its full lead as they head west through the town. Behind them the wind lifts a steamboat docked across the river at Natchez; the big craft slides sideways until it crunches into the dock, splintering the wooden jetty. The gust passes and the steamer slowly rights itself as crewmen scurry around the decks.

As Stephanie and Jenny drive west, the wind stills, then shifts. A biting rain begins.

"Miss Stephanie, let's stop and put the top up!" Jenny says.

"Oh, all right. Stop complaining." Stephanie pulls the buggy to a stop. The rain stings their faces as they struggle with the heavy leather top; finally they have it raised and tied. Stephanie shakes the reins and Tearose trudges with his head down. In the stiff wind, the top doesn't really protect them from the cold rain.

"Why don't we stop 'til it passes?" Jenny asks.

"No! I'm not stopping 'til I reach the Cocodrie!"

When they get to the settlement, curtains of rain are sweeping the deserted streets. The buggy's wheels creak through the mud. After they leave the settlement the road gets worse. Twice they have to get down and push the buggy out of the mud while rivulets of brown water slosh over their feet.

"Let's go back to the settlement!" Jenny pleads. "We could get out of the weather there."

"It's too far to go back! We're almost home," Stephanie shouts. Rain glistens on their faces.

Big trees heave in the wind, and the road is soft as pudding. Just as it seems the horse won't be able to go forward, the rain slackens.

"See, we're almost there," Stephanie says. "It's lightening up."

The rain begins again as they reach the place where the stream crosses the road. Normally the stream is only a couple of yards wide, a dog-ford; now it's a hundred yards wide. Water swirls around trees which a few hours earlier had stood on dry ground.

"We can't drive across that stream!" Jenny yells into the wind.

"We can make it. This stream's never that deep," Stephanie mutters, cracking the reins. "The only way we're gonna get out of this weather is to get home." The buggy rolls into the water but a few feet further it lurches and then stops hard. The horse stands up to her belly in the roiling water.

Stephanie cracks the reins again, and Tearose leans forward to pull, but the wheels are stuck solid.

"Let's unhitch her and leave the buggy. We're soaked anyway. We'll ride over to the other side."

"We won't make it," Jenny says. But Stephanie has already jumped down and Jenny has to follow. She feels the current reach for her thin skirt and lash it to her thighs. Stephanie wades up to unhitch the horse and then tries to mount her. But her sopping petticoats pull her down. The horse stumbles around in the swirling water. Stephanie shouts, "Let's wade her across!"

They leave the buggy where it's stuck, with water cascading through the spokes of the wheels, and they pull the horse farther into the stream. Jenny feels herself being lifted from the stream-bottom, and she grabs the reins to keep her balance.

Stephanie shouts something, but her words are strangled out by the roar of the creek. They can see the road rising from the water a few yards in front of them.

Suddenly a surge of water hits them, throwing Jenny into the horse's side. She grabs for the reins and realizes that the horse is swimming. She looks for Stephanie, but all she can see is the horse's straining head. Strange things, some warm and soft, some cold and stickery, scrape her legs as the brown water curls away from her. Tearose half-drags her out on the other side, and she's alone.

She drops the reins. Then she runs up and down the edge of the stream, stumbling and slipping in the mud. Out in the water, the overturned buggy bobs.

The squall eases in a few minutes. Jenny calls Stephanie's name until her voice gives out, then she starts to wail. She can't go back into the water to search for Stephanie; the current would wash her away like a leaf.

So she pulls the horse up the road toward home. She tries to hurry, but her feet slip and sink in the mud, and she's too tired to get herself up on the saddleless horse.

CHAPTER TWENTY-EIGHT

Cornelius is sitting in front of the fire in the cabin when he hears Jenny's shout. He comes out onto the porch as she stumbles out of the spitting rain.

"Where's Stephanie?"

"Back there where we were tryin' to cross the stream." Jenny's teeth are chattering.

Cornelius lopes down the road the half-mile to the crossing. His hopes fail when he sees the buggy tilted on its side in the stream. He wades out as far as he can, grabbing a limb of a downed tree so he can stay upright. He can't see Stephanie.

Malachi comes out of his room when he hears Jenny crying. As soon as he understands what she's saying and he sees Cornelius running down the road, he gets the mule and rides through the field to McKee's place to get help. Within the hour other neighbors and their slaves come to the stream crossing to help; even Dubrenne brings over some strong men to help with the search. Turley himself shows up to help, his forehead streaked with several healing scars from the blows Lafayette gave him. By the time the last of the searchers fan out into the swamp, it's dark.

Women come to the cabin, and Margaret McKee oversees them as they cook for the searchers and keep a fire going. Jenny, her dress drying slowly, sits on the floor in front of the fire all night; after several hours she curls up and sleeps.

All night the men tramp the swamp, their lanterns flickering against the trees; the stream is narrower now, but still roiling.

Sometime in the night the rain stops for good. In the gray morning light the searchers still stomp through the mud where the stream churned, their grim purpose mocked by birds which call brightly from the trees. It's a mild day for January, almost springlike.

Pless Halloran spots the body a mile downstream. Jake Turley and his men Wonderful and Pete slog through the mud to pull it out.

She hadn't died gently. Her petticoats are tangled around her legs, and her chestnut hair is unpinned and strands of it are plastered across her face like seaweed. Her eyes are half-open, and her face is smeared with mud.

Halloran looks around and whistles softly. "The others must've come right near here last night. There's their footprints right over there." He points toward a mud-bank nearby. "I guess it was that black dress that hid her."

"We'll never get a wagon in here with all this mud," Turley says. "We'll have to carry her out to where the land's firmer. Pete, you go get the wagon and spread the word that she's found."

"Yessir."

As Pete slogs away through the swamp, Turley bends over to lift the stiffened body, with one hand under her waist and the other under her neck. Suddenly he yanks his hand back in horror. A writhing brown furry animal hangs from his hand; its needle-like teeth hold him. Pless Halloran sees the possum's unhealthy red-streaked eyes and its foaming mouth. The animal dangles from Turley's frenzied hand.

Turley shrieks.

The big rat-like animal drops free and hits the mud nearby and scurries away right over the woman's body that's still sprawled on the ground.

Turley gapes at his bloodied hand; the possum has left a raw wound across the fleshy area above his thumb.

"Goddamn it!" he roars. Blood runs in rivulets over his hand and drips from his fingers.

Pless takes out his bandanna. "Wrap it wit' this," he says. Turley is shaking. He stands like a hurt child as Pless ties the grimy bandanna around the wound. In a moment blood has soaked the thin fabric.

"You better wash that hand when you can," Pless says, although they both know Turley has more than just the wound to worry about; the froth on the possum's mouth could mean only rabies. But looking at Turley's gasping parchment face, Pless chooses not to feed his fears.

"Let's take her on back," he says, but first he takes a stick and pokes the body to make sure no more animals are denning there. Then he and Wonderful lift the heavy body and lug it out of the swamp to where voices can be heard, shouting the news.

Turley doesn't stay to watch them load the body onto the wagon. He rides away with Halloran's bandanna still wrapped around his bleeding hand. Pless lets him go with it, knowing that Turley now has something more serious to worry about than a borrowed bandanna.

"Here they come," Margaret says. Jenny goes with the women out to the porch to watch as Pless drives the wagon up to the cabin. They can see the hump of a body in the back, covered with a blanket. Right behind the wagon Amos McKee drives the buggy which he'd managed to pull from the stream-bed. Cornelius and the other men trudge behind the buggy.

Amos and Wonderful carry the body into the cabin and lay it on the table. Then the men leave the room. Cornelius lingers, awkward in the presence of the women. Once he puts out his hand and touches Stephanie's forehead. Margaret puts her arm around him and says something in such a soft voice that Jenny can't hear. Cornelius nods and walks out to the porch where the other men are.

Jenny wants to go outside with Cornelius and Malachi, to share her anguish with theirs, but she knows she's expected to stay inside with the women, although they don't need her help. She stands against the wall and watches as the women unfasten Stephanie's dress and petticoats and then wash the body and dress it in the damp peach-colored dressing gown they take out of her satchel.

Several hours later Cornelius and Malachi carry a plain pine coffin into the cabin and set it on the floor. After they place her in it, Cornelius signals Malachi to nail the lid on the coffin.

"She's not beautiful anymore," he says in a strained voice, as if to explain it to Margaret, who looks as if she would take Cornelius's sorrow for her own if she could. Then other women bring cedar boughs, still dripping, from the woods and arrange the greenery around the coffin, and take candles from Stephanie's candle-box and set them at either end of the bier.

Cornelius sits in the rocking chair for hours, staring at the coffin. Jenny and Malachi sit on the porch. From time to time Cornelius walks out and sits near them with his head in his hands. Neighbors come and go.

After they found the body, Cornelius asked Amos to make the trip to Natchez to tell Emile Coqterre. Late in the day Emile comes to the cabin in a large barouche pulled by two horses. The carriage's wheels are caked in mud, and the horses are winded. Emile looks gaunt and wasted, his hair unkempt and his cheeks so sunken his face looks like that of another corpse. He can't walk without support, so Rob and Charlie hold him up. Even half-dead as Emile seems to be, he manages to clump up the steps and into the cabin. Cornelius stands up.

When he sees the pine coffin, Emile seems to sag even more, and Rob and Charlie shift their grip.

"I want her buried in Natchez," Emile rasps.

Cornelius looks surprised. "I have a plot in a field Malachi and I've been clearing. There's an arpent that makes a suitable cemetery."

"I won't have my daughter buried in a swampy field." Emile's words are bitter. "She'll have a proper burying place in Natchez, where she belongs."

"This is our home."

"Her home's at Carefree, in Natchez. If you ain't took her away from there, she'd still be alive." He lurches out to the porch. "You!" he shouts at Malachi. "Help my boys load the coffin onto this barouche."

Malachi glances at Cornelius.

"Sir --" Cornelius says, but Charlie and Rob are already lifting Emile onto the front seat of the buggy. Then they go back into the cabin and each take one end of the coffin. Seeing how the coffin tilts as they struggle to lift it, Cornelius motions for Malachi to help them load it into the back.

"I've set the funeral for Saint Mary's Church at three o'clock tomorrow," Emile says, staring straight ahead. "Burial in Natchez Cemetery." Then Charlie shakes the reins and with Rob sitting in back to hold the coffin steady, they drive away down the muddy road.

Jenny stands on the porch twisting her apron in the cool evening air. In the past few hours she's learned how heavy sorrow feels. After the barouche goes around the turn in the road, Jenny goes down to her room and sits on the side of her bed.

Why didn't she stop Miss Stephanie from taking the horse into the water? She should have refused -- just said she wouldn't go into the stream. But she'd never told Miss Stephanie an outright "No" to anything. She knew, she could *see,* that the water wouldn't let them through, and she should have said "No! No! No!" Because if she had, all this pain wouldn't be hurting them now. Miss Stephanie wouldn't be dead and Master Cornelius wouldn't be sitting with his head in his hands. When Kofi'd been snatched away from her, she'd been left with a kernel of guilt about him that flowered out at odd moments. Now she has a blossom of guilt as big as a sunflower, about Miss Stephanie.

An hour later Cornelius walks down to the little house, stony-faced.

"Mal! Jenny!" he calls. When they come out he says, "I'm going to Natchez tomorrow. Jenny, you'll come with me. I think you should be at the funeral for her. Mal, you stay here to take care of the animals. We'll take the buggy. I guess Tearose can make the trip."

"Yessir," Malachi says. Jenny looks at the ground. Then she goes back inside and falls into a hard sleep. She wakes the next morning shivering with cold and with swollen, grainy eyes.

Cornelius prepares a breakfast of hotcakes, which they all pick at in silence. Then Jenny takes Stephanie's ruined black dress and her once-white petticoats and scrubs them in the washtub. It wouldn't be right to leave Miss Stephanie's clothes dirty. She hangs them on the fence to dry.

At midmorning Cornelius puts on his frock coat and gets his white Spanish hat. Malachi hitches the horse to the buggy, and

Jenny goes down to the little house and puts on the only thing she has that's clean and dry, a gray dress, plain except for a row of buttons down the front. Then she and Cornelius ride away to Natchez, leaving Malachi alone on the porch.

CHAPTER TWENTY-NINE

Esther watches as the barouche turns onto the drive. It's only a moment before it reaches the house and breaks her heart.

"Oh, it's true, ain't it? Ain't it?" She twists her apron as the carriage rolls to a stop and Charlie and Rob help Mister Emile down. "What that man said! Miss Stephanie all drownt, all drownt, ain't she, jus' like that man said!" She beats the air with her fists.

The men wrestle the coffin from the back seat and struggle with it up the steps and into the house.

"Put it over there," Emile barks, and the men carry the coffin into the dark parlor and set it on the floor in front of the windows. Then they wait to see if Emile wants them to do anything else. But he has nothing to say. He sinks onto a chair, his head down.

After a long silence, he looks up and says, "Charlie, go to the carpenter and get a coffin. She can't be buried like this. Get the finest coffin he has. And Rob, you go to Saint Mary's and get the priest. Bring him here."

They leave Emile sitting alone in the dark room with the pine coffin.

Esther's apron is wet from repeated wipings. She waits for Emile to say something, but after a few minutes she goes out to the slave house, where she shares the sad details with all the slave women.

Later in the day, when she goes back into the house and stands at the parlor door, Emile is still sitting with his head down and his hands hanging between his knees. Hearing the sob that snags in Esther's throat, he looks up.

"I didn't even get to see her," he says. "I sent for the new coffin and went upstairs to change my clothes. But when I came downstairs, this new coffin was already here, and sealed up. The coffin-maker says I can't open it. But she *is* dead, they say. She's dead."

Esther looks at the coffin sitting in front of the windows, where velvet draperies and wide-slatted shutters keep out the afternoon light. The plain pine coffin has been replaced by a shiny black lacquer one with fine copper handles set on a velvet-draped bier. Candles in candelabra flicker at each end.

The sight brings up a memory that raises the hairs on Esther's neck. As Miss Stephanie's coffin is now, so Miss Josephine's casket sat in the exact spot, under the same windows, fifteen years ago. Buried with her own five-weeks babe in her arms.

And Master Emile is sitting here alone, the same way he sat so many years ago, when it was Josephine who died. Esther has such a strong feeling that she's seen this before that she runs back out to the kitchen.

Daisy and Theresa are in the kitchen. The girls have put on their white mourning clothes, Daisy sits at the table, and a new baby -- her sixth -- nurses in her arms.

Esther stares at the familiar faces. Yes, there's Daisy, and Theresa, and Helene lying sick in her room, but improving. Neither of her girls were born yet when Miss Josephine died. So she hasn't lost her senses after all.

Because good things happen and bad things happen -- bad things more often – but her mind hasn't betrayed her. Time is on some kind of track, after all, and it can't go backwards.

A dozen black buggies are parked in front of Saint Mary's Church. Cornelius leaves his buggy at the corner. Then he and Jenny walk up to the church and climb the steps.

The vestibule smells of candle wax. Cornelius looks down at the polished floor, which is streaked with mud. Other people entering the church move past him, but he doesn't look up; he doesn't want to hear any more condolences. Jenny stands beside him.

He realizes all at once that the black skirts and kid slippers of the mourners have been replaced by starched white skirts and wide bare feet. The slaves of Carefree have arrived.

Esther touches his arm. "We had the cholera here in Natchez, sir," she whispers. "Else more woulda been here for Miss Stephanie."

"Has anyone died?"

"Not at Carefree they hasn't. I believe they all goin' to get well. Helene's still down with it. And Master Emile's weak. He had it bad." She puts her arm around Jenny's shoulder and starts to lead the girl into the church. Then she turns back to Cornelius. "I hurt so bad for Miss Stephanie. I can't believe she's gone."

"Neither can I," Cornelius says. He looks away to avoid her grief. Then he follows her into the church.

He feels out of place. This funeral is all Emile's doing, and he's come to it like a stranger, although it's his own wife that died. Up in front of the altar is a fine lacquered coffin; that's Emile's doing. Cornelius wonders what's become of the pine coffin Malachi labored over; by now it's probably been broken up for kindling in the fireplaces of Carefree. Remembering Stephanie's bruised and desperate face, he's relieved that Emile has the coffin closed. Cornelius wouldn't want her face open to anyone's view.

The church is half-filled. Cornelius walks toward the front of the church and finds a place in the first pew. On the other side of the aisle is Emile, with Charlie and Rob on either side to catch him if he sinks. The man looks like a ghost himself. And Sophronia's over there, too, kneeling and clutching a prayer-book. Cornelius recognizes her Irish profile under the black veil she wears, but she's changed since he last saw her, at the wedding reception. Her face is florid and swollen. Pickled with booze.

He looks around. Back a dozen rows Jenny stands next to Esther, looking proper and scared. He knows what the girl's feeling. He saw it on her face during the drive to Natchez, and more than once he wanted to say to her, *It wasn't your fault!* But he can take care of only his own grief.

What Cornelius feels, besides a deep raw grief, is hopelessness. He'd not felt that -- not *exactly* that -- when his mother died; Jennie Carson's long illness made her last breath something she longed for, and she told him so many times. But even so, her dying ripped his heart.

But this is different. All during the long sad trip to Natchez, as Tearose struggled along the puddled roads and Jenny sat silent beside him, he thought about his loss. Stephanie's death darkened every bright prospect he could contemplate.

Did he give her the life he'd promised? They never achieved anything like the plantation life she coveted. Had he been right to take her away from her home in Natchez and bring her out to the Cocodrie? What he brought her to, as it turned out, was an early death. The choices he made for her tormented him now.

Elenora and her husband John Landerson are sitting behind Emile, Elenora big in pregnancy. And the others, older men and women kneeling here and there or sitting in the pews -- Emile's friends. Cornelius should remember them from the wedding reception two years ago, but their names and faces escape him. At the back of the church the slave-women of Carefree sit in their white dresses, a checkerboard of grief.

The priest begins the service. Cornelius glances at Emile, who holds a prayer-book and lists as he kneels.

The voices in the church rise like a drumbeat. Cornelius can only listen; he doesn't understand a word of it. He closes his eyes and lets the Latin phrases wash over him.

When the service is over, the pallbearers, whom Cornelius doesn't know, carry the coffin out to a black-draped hearse. And at the front of the procession, Emile has the place of honor, behind the hearse.

And oh God, Cornelius thinks, he'll never see his Stephanie again. The buggy's reins blur before his eyes.

At the cemetery Cornelius stands with his hat in his hand. The headstones are set around the hillside in even rows, except for two graves at the bottom of the hill. Their plain headstones rest against the fence and their feet face up the hill, just opposite the other graves. These were murderers, no doubt, buried in disgrace that way, head to foot, so that everyone can see their sins, even in death.

Another prayer is said, the final goodbye. The coffin is lowered into the ground.

Esther stands right behind him. When the prayer ends, she whispers, "That's Miss Josephine's grave, sir." She points to the grave next to Stephanie's. "Her babe's buried there with her."

Cornelius stares. Josephine's grave has no real headstone, only a small flat stone disfigured with moss. The stone reads "August 1, 1821."

Why isn't there a proper headstone for Emile's wife and son? Surely Emile will do more for Stephanie.

The mourners begin to drift away. Suddenly Emile speaks.

"Stephanie, you not dead! Ya'll know she's not! Josephine went out to visit her mamma, and Stephanie went out to the Cocodrie.

She'll be back at Carefree befo' we know it. When she come back -- when she come back --"

Rob and Charlie grab his arms. He struggles but can't get free. He sinks to the ground, sobbing and shouting in a garble of words, his forehead pressed to the muddy earth. All the mourners move back from the spectacle.

But Emile's grief, Cornelius understands.

Esther notices Jenny's too-short skirt. And the sight prompts her to ask Cornelius if Jenny could stay at Carefree for awhile. She didn't think of it ahead of time; it just comes to her when they're all at the graveyard. She can see neglect in the girl's dress, and yet she can see that Jenny hasn't forgotten what Esther taught her two years ago about keeping herself clean and her hair pinned. The girl doesn't show many signs of growing up yet, her chest just barely beginning to swell under the bodice of her plain dress, but it can't be long now before she starts growing a bosom and turning into a woman. She's getting tall, almost up to Esther's shoulder.

And she's gonna be a right pretty girl, Esther can see. Jenny has a long neck and full lips which purse in a prim expression, and there's that coal-black skin. The shanks of her legs that show below her skirt are narrow as sticks, but Esther knows well enough that skinny little girls turn into high-hipped, full-breasted beauties in just a couple years' time.

Since yesterday, when Emile came back to Carefree with the body, Esther has cried many bitter tears for Miss Stephanie. If she can keep little Jenny here in Natchez where she can take care of the child, it might help heal the heartache. When Theresa and Helene were born it eased the pain she felt when August and Littleton died, though there isn't a day goes by she doesn't think about those babies.

Master Cornelius is a fine man, but he wouldn't know the first thing about taking care of a young girl. It's wrong to let Jenny go about in a dress that shows her legs. And Miss Stephanie wouldn't have allowed it.

At Carefree, the slave girls are always swapping clothes; Esther's sure she can find the right size dress for Jenny. Slave children swap around too; right now Daisy's boy Walter is living with his grandmammy on the other side of Natchez to give Daisy a rest. So Master Emile probably won't mind if another girl stays here.

After Emile is led away, Esther walks over to Cornelius.

"I know Jenny thought losin' Miss Stephanie was just like losin' her own mammy," Esther begins, and then her tears well up again. She blurts, "I want Jenny to stay here with me, sir! Miss Stephanie -- well, she wanted Jenny to stay here so I could teach her how to spin. She told me so herself. And if you let li'l Jenny stay, I can still teach her to do that."

Cornelius stares at Esther. It seems as though he's off somewhere in his own thoughts. Later that evening, as Esther makes a bed for Jenny on the floor next to her own bed, she reflects that Master Cornelius probably wasn't thinking straight, with Master Emile upsetting everyone so, and Miss Stephanie in the ground not six feet away.

But he'd nodded his agreement and motioned for Jenny to go over to Esther, and Esther put her arm around the girl and led her away.

"He'll come back and get you before long," she said to Jenny, who looked back over her shoulder as Cornelius got on his buggy and drove out of the cemetery without looking back.

Carefree quieted quickly after the funeral. Neighbor women sent housemaids over with food, but there is no funeral meal; this is still a house of cholera. So Esther shows Jenny where she'll sleep and gets the girl settled in, and then tends Helene, who's still sick. That takes the rest of the day.

Helene's getting better, the diarrhea abating, but the girl's face is pinched and her eyes look too big for her face. When Esther lies down to sleep that night her head spins with relief and weariness and grief. She stares at the ceiling for an hour as she listens to Jenny's low rhythmic breathing. The girl sleeps soundly, which Esther is glad of; sleep can help a child get through grief.

Esther always organizes her days at night, thinking through what the next day will bring. Now she thinks: the pallet on the floor won't do for a permanent bed for Jenny, big as the girl is now, so she'll have to get Charlie and Rob to build her a real bed. If she pushes her own bed over to one wall, there'll just be room for another bed. She could put Jenny in with Helene and Theresa, but there's no sense crowding them. Theresa's a big help to her now, especially when it comes to keeping an eye on Helene. Theresa's changed so much since that one wild time she ran off with Marcus. She's become cautious and quiet and grown-uppish – all because of that one time when Marcus took her out in the woods, promising her something better than what she got. Theresa's getting grown up, wide-hipped and sturdy, and she looks at the world with knowing eyes.

Helene now, that's another story. That girl's Reynard Fanner's own child, if there ever was one; anybody could see it. Reynard's there in Helene's restless round face and in the way her skirts flip around her ankles when she walks, ready to tempt anyone who looks her way. Just like Reynard. Esther has only a vague memory of the springtime fifteen years ago when *she*'d been tempted by Reynard, and yielded. And Helene is unreliable just like Reynard. Maybe having sober little Jenny here will help settle her. Finally Esther has thought through all she needs to, and she sleeps.

The next morning she climbs the stairs to Emile's bedroom. He didn't come down for breakfast. He showed such awful grief at the graveyard yesterday, and him still weak from his sickness. All Natchez will be talking about it for a long time. She taps on the door to his bedroom, then taps again, but there's no answer. She pushes the door open an inch and sees his tangled, empty bed.

Who knows what that man might do? She walks out to the barn where Charlie is nailing a board over a gash in the wall. A heavy limb struck the barn during the storm.

"Did you see Master Emile go out of here this morning?"

Charlie nods. "He left just after sun-up. Got up on Dover -- I didn't hardly think he'd make it, weak as he's been -- and off he galloped."

"You don't know where he went?"

"He didn't say a word to me."

Esther twists her apron. "The way he acted at the cemetery, I'm worried 'bout where he'll go. And him just gettin' over being sick, too. But maybe gettin' away is his way of grievin'. There's too many memories here for all of us."

"There's too many memories for that li'l ole Jenny, I can tell you that. She come out here just now to see if Master Cornelius come back to get her yet. I tell you, she walkin' 'round like somebody asleep, that girl is."

"Now, why would she think Master Carson comin' right back to get her?"

"I dunno. I guess he didn't tell her how long she'd be stayin' here."

"I guess he didn't. Well, it's Master Emile I'm more worried 'bout now. Maybe he went back to the Bayou Boeuf. At least he'll keep busy over there. That's the best thing. Try to put all this trouble out of his mind."

As she turns to go back to the house, she has a memory of Stephanie running down the lawn to greet Master Emile when he came back from the Boeuf -- Stephanie about six years old, her chestnut curls bouncing. Oh, she'd always dressed the child so pretty, in little frocks sewn up by a seamstress down on Bee Street, with the sweetest embroidery and the nicest ribboned bonnets to match. No child in Natchez had been so well cared for, so loved.

Feeling that tears are coming and knowing they'll sting her eyes, she goes back into the house and takes Jenny's dress to a tub behind the slave house, where she can pound it. She's already put the girl in one of Helene's dresses that's of a decent length on her.

Then she goes in to see about Helene, who's sitting up in bed talking to Theresa and Daisy. Jenny, skittish as a rabbit, has scurried off to work in the kitchen with Sarah.

Esther, used to running the house for long periods of time while Emile's away, can see to it that life at Carefree continues much as it always has. Right now the main house is silent, its one occupant sleeping away her days; she's no trouble. Whenever Emile's away, the center of life shifts to the slave house, where babies squall, teenage girls squabble and primp, and strong-bodied men and women are in charge. Master Emile might show up again any time, so with the help of Daisy and Sarah and the girls, Esther keeps the main house dusted and waxed and the linens fresh in Emile's bedroom, always ready for the day when he comes back.

CHAPTER THIRTY

"Jake Turley's sick. He's awful low, I hear," the hotelkeeper says as she flips through the stack of mail. Cornelius stands in front of the counter; she knows he's got no letters today, but she looks through the stack anyway, for his sake. He's a somber young man since his wife died. So few letters come for him nowadays. It's not like it was, when his wife was alive; then, letters came and went all the time.

"Sick with what?"

"Hydrophobia." She straightens the stack of letters on the counter. "Bit by a possum, somebody said. He mayn't live out the day, is the last I heard."

Mister Carson looks uncomfortable at the news. "Well."

She knows he won't say more than that; she's told half a dozen people this morning about Jake Turley, and most hadn't done more than grunted. Hard to imagine a man could die and leave so little regard behind, but that seems to be the case with Turley. Well, the news has to be told, regardless; and who better to tell it than herself?

Mister Carson seems so sad, standing there with no mail come for him. It's been six weeks since his wife drowned. A person might want to reach out to him, to comfort that young man, but there's something in his manner that's stiff and cool now. He doesn't look like he'd welcome comforting.

Helene can't believe that Jenny doesn't know when her birthday is, especially since she herself counts every birthday so precious. It's just one more puzzling thing about the girl who arrived so suddenly while she was in her sick-bed, and who shares a room next door with Mamma. Helene can hardly remember the time when Jenny visited here before, almost three years ago, and she's been trying to figure the girl out ever since she felt well enough to get out of bed.

"Well, if you don't know when your birt'day is, how old are you, then?" she asks Jenny as they sit in the kitchen, shucking corn at the table. It's a job Esther gave them after dinner. The papery husks are piled on the floor, and sometimes as they shuck a kernel breaks open; the sweet musty aroma fills the room.

"I don't know. I think I'm --" Jenny says, but she doesn't get to finish.

Helene looks at her. Another thing about this girl is she has an accent like none Helene's ever heard. "You got to know how old you are!"

Jenny's pile of corn almost overflows her bowl. Helene drums her fingers on the table. "Well, I'm gonna give you a birthday, and I'm gonna figure you a age, too. March 20. That's today. And you be -- ten."

Jenny looks up indignantly. "I ain't ten! Miss Stephanie thought I was twelve."

"Well, you wearin' that dress that I wore a long time ago. I'm a lot bigger than you."

"How old are you?"

"Fourteen."

"I think I'm twelve."

"All right, you be twelve." Helene gets up and walks to the doorway. "Mamma must be in the big house. If this is your birt'day, there ain't no reason we should work. Nobody works on they birt'day."

"They don't?"

"Sure don't. Let's go see our friends. That's what I always do on my birt'day." She unties her apron and tosses it over a chair.

Jenny stands up and pushes back from the table. "Your mamma might not like us goin' out."

But Helene is already brushing out her hair with her fingers and putting hairpins in her mouth, so she can't speak. When she finishes her hair she walks over to the door. "My mamma'll understand. She know nobody work on they birt'day."

She stands outside the kitchen and beckons. "You ain't been nowhere else in Natchez since you come here, have you?" Helene asks.

"No. And I don't wanna go anywhere."

"Girl, you gotta get out of this place! You gotta meet some other *people*!" She takes Jenny's arm and half-drags her down the steps. "And quit lookin' so worried. We'll be back before my mamma even notices we gone. Or that snoopin' Theresa, neither. I can't *stand* the way that girl always spyin' on me and then tattlin' to Mamma!"

"Don't we need a pass?"

"We not goin' anywhere where we need one. Will you quit worryin'?"

"But Master Cornelius might come back for me. He wouldn't know where I was."

"Lissen. You been here since wintertime. I don't expect it too likely he comin' back this very day."

They walk through Natchez along back alleys, coming to a vacant lot where a half-dozen young people are lounging on the grass under a big tree. All at once Helene thinks maybe it's not a good idea to bring this new girl here. Jenny has a pretty way about her that boys might like. But they're too close now; they've already been seen. Well, she'll keep the visit short. This is just a little twelve-year-old, after all.

"This is it," Helene says. One older man, so small he might be a dwarf, leans against the tree-trunk smoking a cigarette. Laughter bubbles above the group in little bursts.

"Who's that Miss Bashful you got wit' you, H'lene?" The question comes from one of the older boys.

"This is Jenny," Helene says. "She stayin' up at Carefree. Don't ask me why."

The boy calls to Jenny, "Where you from, girl?"

"Bayou Cocodrie."

"Who your master?"

"Master Cornelius Carson."

"Who that? I never heard of him 'round this whole town." The boy looks around. "That's a good long trip, out to the Cocodrie. I went out to the Cocodrie once. Rode my horse."

"You did not!" Helene snaps. "You makin' that up!"

"I did. Rode clear out there and come back the same day. My horse Feather run the whole way. Got back to Natchez just as the sun was goin' down. And he wasn't hardly even winded."

"He was dead, more 'n likely," another boy says. They all laugh.

"Naw, he wasn't even close to dead. Feather can ride further'n that and not even feel it."

"Feather's just a old farm nag and you know it. Besides, that Old Frog you work for would never let you go that far away. Not mean as Old Frog is." He turns to Jenny. "This boy work for the meanest master in all of Adams County, 'cept for me. Me and him, we is two un-lucky boys."

"Old Frog's a mean 'un, that's true enough," the other boy says. "I just rode away and he didn't even know it. He was down with the flu."

"I don't believe that for one minute," the other boy says.

Some others walk over. "I'm Shell," says a plump girl, "and this is Laura. The boys are Tom, and Frank, and Israel. That little man's Walker Jackson."

"I'm runnin' off one day, me and Tom here," Israel says, stepping close to the new girl.

"You better talk quiet," Laura says. "Somebody hear you, your back'll get it."

"I am, though," Israel says. "Tom and me'll be gone one day, and you'll know it when you come out here and we ain't around. We gonna find that Underground Railroad and go up norse. Up to the free soil."

"You gonna leave your mammy just like that, never see her again?" Shell asks.

"I'll come back and get her."

"You come back, Old Frog have you whipped 'til you can't stand up," Tom says.

Jenny stares at them. That freedom talk. She hears it everywhere. Field hands sing it in the fields, Malachi lectures her about it. Everyone says it's gonna to be the best thing in the world, when they get to free soil.

"So, who else is out there in the Cocodric besides you?" Laura asks Jenny.

"Cornelius, me, and Malachi."

"Malachi a slave too?"

Jenny nods.

"Your master can't be too rich, if he only got two slaves to his name," Laura says. "I guess that means you get to do all the work, right? So where your mammy?"

"I don't know."

"You a orphan then," Shell says. "Laura here's a orphan too. Her mammy died in childbed."

"My grandma died of yellow jack," Tom says.

"I heard they don't have yellow jack in the norse," Israel says.

"You heard lots of things," Shell says. "Most of 'em ain't true."

"Girl, you gonna come out here one day and I'll be gone. You'll know where I'm at," Israel says. "Or maybe I'll just buy my freedom, like Walker did."

They look at the little man who has his back to the tree trunk and one foot propped on it. Little curls of smoke rise from his cigarette. Tom says to Jenny, "Walker, now, he a free man. He don't belong to nobody, so he don't have to run off. He can stay right here in Mississippi if he wants to, or go to the free soil if he wants to. Or do anything he wants."

"Tell us how you got free, Walker," Israel says.

Walker looks at Israel. He's old, Jenny thinks; his little face is a network of lines.

"Well, I ain't never run off from my master, if that's what you're wonderin'. I only got sold one time, and then I was bought by a lady who said I could buy my freedom if I wanted to. So I said, `Yes, ma'am, I sure do want,' and that's what I did. Took me five years to do it."

"Yes, you just up and bought your own freedom," Tom says, nodding vigorously.

"Paid for myself, you might say," Walker says. "I didn't need to run off. My mammy named me Walker after my daddy, 'cause he was always runnin' off. And then when I was free, I needed a last name, so I named myself Jackson. After Andy Jackson the colonel."

"And tell us how you stay free," Tom says.

"I show my papers when I'm stopped," Walker says, patting the vest pocket of his coat. "And of course, I try to stay out of the country areas, 'cuz I might be kidnapped and sold. I only go where there's lots of people around."

"And we could all get our freedom, couldn't we?" Israel asks.

"Well, now, I wouldn't just say so," Walker replies, dropping the stub of his cigarette and grinding it out with his shoe. "First, your master's got to agree to it, and then you got to find ways to make some money on the side. Makin' the money's the easy part. There's always work."

He ignores the eager faces around him. After a few minutes he lies down on the ground with his arm crooked under his head. "I'm gonna sleep now."

Jenny stares at him. He's so little, but he's old. His face is almost as black as her own. Could she ever be free, like this Walker Jackson? Would Master Cornelius let her buy her own freedom?

"I might do that some day, what Walker did," Israel says, to break the silence.

"I thought you was runnin' off," Tom says.

"Here come Old Frog," Shell says quietly. "Y'all better mind yourselfs." They all stare at the ground as a white-haired man walks toward them, tapping a cane.

"I am runnin' off someday," Israel says in a low voice. "Old Frog wouldn't let nobody buy they own freedom."

The white man stops at the edge of the lot. "Get over here, Israel!"

Israel lopes over to the old man, his long legs flexing as if the joints are hinged. Jenny understands why the young people don't want to look at Old Frog. They want Israel to have some dignity left, so Old Frog wouldn't be the complete master of him in their eyes. The skin on the back of her neck prickled when she saw how Israel changed when Old Frog called his name; he turned right into a slave again.

"Let's go home, Jenny," Helene says. "You met 'em now."

Jenny and Helene walk across the lot. When they reach the alley, she stops and looks back. The young people are drifting away. The little heap of Walker Jackson hasn't moved.

Slavery and freedom. She hears that talk everywhere. And what slavery means to Walker Jackson isn't the same thing it means to her, because he bought himself out. It took him five years.

Maybe she could get out too. She could ask Master Cornelius if he'd let her buy her way out. The next time she sees him, she'll ask. He might see it her way. Right now she's glad Helene's headed down the street back the way they came. Jenny doesn't really want to be out somewhere with this silly Helene, and maybe missing Master Cornelius, who might come back any time to get her. She has something important to ask him when he does.

At the frolic Ruetta Halloran has a new print dress, and she swings her skirt like she wants everyone to notice. Dancing a reel with Euphonia McKee, Cornelius can't help but keep one eye on Ruetta. It's a warm April night, filled with gnats and with smoke from the fires in the clearing. The women's dresses are a kaleidoscope of colors, and the men talk politics. The Whigs won't have a chance in the fall election, all agree; that little fox Van Buren will take the White House. And they talk falling cotton prices. Laughter bursts up as the fiddlers start another tune.

But for Cornelius the laughter seems empty. He shouldn't have come to the frolic; it was only Margaret McKee's prodding that got him here at all. Stephanie'd been dead only a few months, and now that he's here he realizes he should've stayed home.

But then Ruetta comes over to him, arms open, and he takes her thin frame into his arms to dance.

"We been missin' you at these sociables, Cornelius," she says.

"Cotton takes work," he mumbles, but he likes the feel of her body as she moves in his arms. The fiddles hum a sweet bright tune on the night air. "You been comin' out to all of these?"

"Haven't missed a one," she says, putting her sharp-featured face close to his shoulder. "Missed you, though."

Her pointed breasts swell against his chest, and he moves his hand around the small of her back. Stephanie wouldn't come to these frolics, but he remembers Ruetta from frolics before he got married.

The music winds down. Ruetta seems as reluctant to move away from him as he is to have her leave. He bends toward her, putting his face in her hair, which smells of tobacco. She's probably taken up a pipe, he figures; her mother smokes one.

He takes her hand and leads her away through the trees; their feet crunch softly on the pine needles. In a moment the music begins again, much softer, and the sky looks light through the tops of the trees.

He pulls her down onto a bed of pine needles. Ever since Stephanie's death, his nights have been lonely.

He seizes her.

With only a few quick caresses he takes her, ignoring her simpering protests that he's hurrying too much. Then he lies panting with his head on her hard chest.

She feels like nothing to him. Her thin form is frail as paper in his arms, nothing like Stephanie's heavy, warm fullness. And Ruetta's crass eagerness, her giggling willingness to lie down with any man who asks for it -- the thought makes him roll away from her and sit up.

"You in a hurry tonight," she says.

"Yeah," he mutters. He turns away from her as he buttons his shirt and closes his trousers. She stands up and smooths her skirt. He knew he should say something about her new dress.

"Your dress is pretty," he says, stuffing his shirttail inside his pants. He stands a few feet away from her.

She looks at him curiously, her head cocked to one side, as she presses her hair back into place. Then she turns and flounces back through the woods to the frolic, where another reel is winding to a close.

At the edge of the lighted dance area she pauses and waits for him, but he turns away from her and walks quickly over to where Malachi waits.

He's turning away from all of them. The frolic seems pointless to him, and Ruetta was worth only the time he'd given her.

So he motions for Malachi and they drive home to the cabin. With a mumbled "G'night," Malachi goes off to the little house.

Cornelius sits on the porch for a while, watching the moon slip an inch down the sky. He pours himself a glass of whiskey and listens to the night-sounds.

Alone. He thinks about the star-shower, nearly three years ago. The Leonid Shower. The people who saw it that night put their own thoughts into it. The star-shower flew away to some mysterious part of the universe, and left only the usual sky. But the people who saw the star-shower still remember it, and wonder. How big is the universe? When he looks out at the dimmest stars up there, how far away is he looking?

The Leonid Shower seems so long ago, now. All the people he loved then were gathered around him on these very steps where he now sits alone. He hadn't even known how rich he was to have them around, then: Stephanie and Jenny and Malachi. It's hard to believe these steps had once been crowded. Now it's just him and Malachi. And Mal wearies more easily now, and goes to bed when the sun's barely gone down.

How can life take such a turn? He can't get Jenny; she's at Carefree, and he wouldn't want to face Emile, so he stays away from there. There's not much need for her to be here anyway. He manages pretty well with Wonderful hired for day-work from Alice Turley. Everyone talks about how Alice took Cedar Breaks in hand after Jake died; she runs the big plantation tighter than old Jake ever did, everyone says. She acts like a regular country woman, riding right out into the fields to talk to her new overseer Louis Ferison whenever she needs something. Or to tongue-lash him if he's not doing things the way she wants. Dubrenne has drifted off somewhere, to some other overseeing job, probably. Ferison doesn't mind hiring out field hands, so Wonderful will probably work for Cornelius all summer.

But just as Cornelius didn't appreciate the wealth he had back when he and his people watched the star-shower together, he didn't foresee the sharp stab of loneliness he'd feel when it was only him on the steps.

He gets up and goes inside the cabin and turns up the lamp. He has a sad task facing him. Earlier today Wonderful brought over, of all things, Stephanie's purse. He and another man found it in the swamp when they were out hunting, and Wonderful rode over with it just before Cornelius left for the frolic.

The bag, crusted with dried mud, lies on the table. Its clasp is missing and it's deformed like a sea-creature whose spine's been ruptured.

"This is all they was," Wonderful said. "It was just like this, and it was layin' there on the ground in the swamp. I guess the ole flood dropt it there."

Cornelius took the bag and set it on the table, not wanting to examine it just then. Now he gingerly lifts it. Its once-soft tapestry sides are stiff.

Inside is what's left of Stephanie's existence -- her tortoise-shell comb, some hairpins, a few dollars and Spanish bits. A folded paper, partially turned into pulp by the water.

He pulls everything out and arranges the items in front of him. What will he do with all this? The purse, now ruined, he can burn. The money he'll put in his wallet. The tortoise-shell comb and hairpins go into her trunk, which sits against the wall and holds all her dresses.

The paper was a letter, he sees. He unfolds the crackling paper, but the bottom of it is a pulpy mass, and the ink's been washed away. Whatever was written there is unreadable. He turns the paper over and sees his own name and what looks like a phrase, "with speed." His name, written in Stephanie's looping hand.

He carefully tears the pulp from the bottom of the sheet, and then folds the part with his name written on it. He won't go down that well of sorrow again, but he'll have this keepsake. Someday, when his wounds aren't so new, maybe he can look at it again. He puts the folded paper in the top drawer of his chest.

A year later Emile returns to Natchez by the Woodville Road. He bought a ticket on the steamer *Franklin* in New Orleans, intending to travel on it all the way to Natchez, but he got off, on impulse, in Baton Rouge and resolved to ride a horse the rest of the way.

The river was a riot, swarming with commerce and not quiet at all. So many boats ply the river now. Even the flatboats riding the current downstream were no longer the quiet vessels he remembered. Back then, the flatboatmen lounged on the low-riding vessels and watched the passing woods for hours on end. But now, every time the *Franklin* passed a flatboat, the flatboatmen leapt up and danced a jig. Making fun.

Emile's nerves were frazzled. By Baton Rouge, he'd had enough, so he let himself be jostled down the gangplank with the other passengers. Within the hour he owned a blaze-faced mare named Peg, for which he paid $10.06 -- that was too much -- and a saddle, including saddlebags, for $18.50 more, and he was off, up the Bayou Sara road. He rode out over the flats north of town, past moss-draped trees with trunks as thick as rooms, and then up into the stately long hills. He liked knowing that somewhere to the west, near or far depending on how the river snaked, the *Franklin* with its noisy passengers and belching stokestacks was plowing upstream without him.

This horse Peg suits him well enough. She's a big dun-colored horse with good markings of white over her face and an easy temperament -- gentler than Dover, the horse he sold in New Orleans -- and she has the size and strength to make a long trip.

He's glad he's coming to Natchez by horseback; it suits a changed man. He could have paid to stay at a house or hotel somewhere along the way, but he wanted to come home the way he first came to Natchez twenty-five years ago, sleeping under trees in the open air. Every night he ties the horse at a stream where she can graze and water, and he stretches out on pine needles.

He eats the food he brought from New Orleans. Hardtack bread and dried beef. He doesn't need much now, since the mercury treatment. He's light again, like he was a quarter-century ago when he bought and sold a plantation in that part of Louisiana called Feliciana. As he passes near Saint Francisville he thinks of riding out to see the land he owned, so long ago, but he knows gone is gone. No use looking for that long-ago cotton-tract.

When he came to Natchez a rich young man in 1809, looking for ways to spend his money, he thought he was a grand adventurer in a raw frontier town. He found Josephine, and Stephanie, and Carefree, and his place on the Bayou Boeuf. His life gleamed before him, bright and full of hope, but that candle blew out pretty quick. For so many years now, there was a lot of money -- a man couldn't *not* make money in cane -- but the hope died when Josephine did.

And yet, as he rides through the long hills south of Natchez, he finds he's hurrying just a little, to get home. His instincts are calling him to Carefree -- he needs to see the big brick house, his only true home.

He probably won't go back to the Bayou Boeuf again, he figures. He'll let Ratout run the place as long as it works out, and then he'll sell the place. He's been roaming for a year, in the north and south. But he's weak. The mercury treatment sapped his strength; the gumma on his leg and lips are still there, unimproved.

The road goes north, then turns west in a long breezy bend as it drops to the river at Natchez. But Emile stays northward -- he doesn't need to see the river -- and then he comes up the hill to Carefree.

Home. Sophronia's here, and Esther and Charlie and Rob, and old Sarah and Daisy and all those children whose names he can't remember.

He's changed. Shrunken up, and old, and weakened by the mercury. Esther and the others are bound to see it. But if there's one place on earth where he'll be taken care of, and where he can still hold his head high, it's here. He's still himself, on a new horse, like he was when he was a young man, come to Natchez to make a life for himself.

In the kitchen Daisy tells Esther she has another baby coming. The announcement makes Esther and Sarah both turn around and look at her.

"That's awful quick, ain't it?" Esther asks. Daisy's breasts are still full of milk, her baby boy not yet a year old.

"It's too quick, I reckon," Daisy says with a shrug.

"You gonna be old before your time," Sarah says.

Esther shakes her head and goes back to stirring the pot of collard greens she'd put on the fire earlier. She looks out through the window. What she sees makes her start. She drops her spoon with a clatter and runs to the kitchen door, shouting, "Charlie! Master Emile's back! Come out to the gallery!"

Then she hurries to the front of the house and waits with the stable-boy outside the tall doors. She mutters to Charlie, "Oh Lord, he's gone crazy, I can see it for sure."

The man riding up the drive is certainly Emile, but changed: his once deeply creased but clean-shaven face now wears a straggly black beard which reaches to the middle of his chest, and his clothes are tattered. He who was once meticulous, who ordered his clothes tailor-made from New Orleans.

The breeze blows his beard, and she can see that his hair's not been combed for days; it hangs down his back like a hermit's. His eyes still have the crazed look they had on the day Stephanie was buried. As he dismounts in front of the gallery, she hesitates, remembering the awful day when Emile was carried away from the graveside ranting.

She finds her voice. "Oh, Master," she says, going over to the horse, "Welcome back! I'll tell Theresa you're here. Did you bring a bag? Or clothes I need to wash? I'll take 'em into the house for you."

"Get away from there, woman!" Emile says, his voice a hoarse rasp. "It ain't your business what's in those saddlebags! Get away!" He steps toward her.

Esther backs away. Emile unhooks the saddlebags and carries them into the house and up the stairs.

"Oh, Charlie, what's goin' to happen to us with this wild-lookin' man?" she asks.

"I dunno. It beat all I ever seed."

Emile is snoring noisily when Esther and Helene tiptoe to his bedroom an hour later. They peer through the half-open door. He lies sprawled on the bed, his boots muddying the white counterpane.

"Look how he's changed," Esther whispers. "And how're we supposed to keep the room clean, with him trackin' his muddy boots in and puttin' 'em right up on the bed like that?"

"That man's cracked, I'd say," Helene says. "But I'm not surprised. I always knew he was crazy."

CHAPTER THIRTY-ONE

At sunrise on an August morning six months later, Daisy's baby is born, and by noon of the same day Esther and Sarah and the midwife Aunty Feddoe can see that the undersized boy will die. Esther carries the news into the main house with the chicken pie she made for dinner.

When she comes back an hour later to clear the table, she sees that the prospect of losing the child has upset the whole household; even Miss Sophronia has gotten out of bed and now sits alone in the parlor, and she doesn't have her wine glass with her, for once.

And Master Emile is in front of the house trying to get on his horse so he can ride into town. Esther stands on the gallery and watches as he swings his leg up to the stirrup and then sits slumped over the saddlehorn. Charlie holds the horse steady.

Well, there's no way to keep Master Emile home, even though it *is* embarrassing for him to be seen, the way he is. In the half-year since he's been back at Carefree, he's ridden Peg up and down Commerce Street many times. Maybe people won't give him a second glance, after all this time. He's not the only raggedy-looking man prowling the streets of Natchez; the Trace brings them in all the time.

Emile rides down the hill, swaying from side to side.

"Hope he don't fall off," Charlie mutters, shaking his head.

Esther goes back into the house as Jenny and Helene come down the stairs. Each girl carries a quilt.

"Aunty Feddoe sent us to get some blankets," Helene says. "Daisy needs 'em. Aunty says to get as many as we could."

"Well, she'll need 'em," Esther says, but she regrets saying it when she sees how Jenny's expression changes. So she says quickly, "Daisy's takin' it hard, ain't she? I feel sorry for that one. This the first child she lost."

"It ain't lost yet," Jenny says, looking at the floor.

Esther sighs. Young girls never want to admit that a baby could die, even when it was doing just that. Daisy'd had two babies just since Jenny came here. Jenny was just a little child herself back then, barely up to Esther's shoulder. But now she's grown tall, passing Esther up. The girl's bosom bounces and her skirts swing around her coltish legs. And her face is a perfect oval, and black as anything. Anyone can see she's of a different blood than Helene. Or anybody else at Carefree, for that matter.

"It's sad the way Daisy's babies come so fast," Esther says. "It ain't good when babies come too close together. Let me take those quilts. You two go back upstairs and clean up Master Emile's room."

"Mamma --" Helene whines, but Esther looks stern. She knows how to get teenage girls away from a sickroom when a crisis looms.

As the girls trudge upstairs, Esther carries the quilts toward the back door. She hears Daisy's hopeless wail from the slave house; looking over her shoulder at the stairs where the girls went up, she suddenly sees her own ghosts, Littleton and August. Their shadowy shapes sometimes walk the rooms at Carefree, usually when Helene and Theresa are working there. All at once there they'd be, big and husky, two grown boys in place of two grown girls, laughing their big laughs.

Sometimes they say "Come on, Mamma! Let's go eat some of that *good* cornbread!" or some such nonsense, and then she has to shoo them out, laughing at their boyish ways. But if she blinks twice, they're gone. And there'd be Helene and Theresa, looking at their mammy strangely. Right now, as Daisy's cry fades, there those boys are, leaning over the bannister and grinning at her. Esther blinks.

Jenny smooths the spread on Master Emile's bed while Helene stands by the window and watches.

"I don't like bein' in this room," Helene says, while Jenny tugs at one corner of the spread to straighten it. "I *told* Mamma that. That man too crazy for me."

"He don't bite," Jenny says, picking up a shirt from the floor. She sniffs it and wrinkles her nose. "He sure ain't clean, though."

"Let's hurry and get this finished," Helene says.

"Why? 'Cause Israel's waitin'?"

Helene gives her a wicked sassy look. "You just jealous."

"No, I ain't jealous."

"You keepin' an eye out, though, ain't ya?"

"Yes, I got my eye out," Jenny says. "Anybody come along I like, I'll let you know."

"Maybe I'll find you somebody," Helene says.

"Oh, no, you ain't."

"Well, you know, my mammy, she's a match-maker from way back. She helped all kinds of people finds their hearts' desire. She could help you."

"I'll do my own pickin'," Jenny says. "If you don't mind."

"I don't mind. I guess I could help Theresa. I don't think that girl's ever gonna find anybody."

Jenny shakes her head, then folds Emile's shirt and puts it on top of the bureau where he can find it. Then the girls go downstairs.

Jenny takes her sewing bag from the closet next to the door. But on the back gallery the girls wait, and listen. Daisy's quiet now; they both want to go to her room to see about the baby, but they aren't wanted there. All morning Daisy's room's been crowded with Sarah and Esther and Aunty Feddoe hovering around the bed.

"Let's go find Israel," Helene says.

They walk down the path behind the stable to the cane-hedge. Israel sits where he usually does, his knees drawn up and his back against the sweet-gum tree. Helene sits down next to him, her shoulder pressed against his, and shakes open her sewing bag. Jenny plops down a few feet away. She threads a needle and begins to stitch through fabric that was once the skirt of an old dress. She's making Israel a shirt.

"How come it so quiet over here?" Israel asks.

"Daisy's babe's sick," Helene says.

"Well, Old Frog's took a turn, too. The doctor come this mornin'. Old Frog said somethin' about goin' home to Saint Francisville, to be buried by his ole Pappy, but shoo, Saint Francisville's a long way off, somebody said. He cain't be toted clear down there, sick as he is. Jenny, you know where Saint Francisville is?"

Israel always wants to hear about places that are far away, Jenny notices. He, who's never been more than a few miles from Natchez. She's told him how she came to Natchez, back when she was a little child.

"I don't remember no place called Saint Francisville," Jenny says. She holds out the shirt she's making; she's already stitched up the sides.

"Where that city you went through?" Israel asks.

"I don't know."

"Well, how far away was it? More than a day?"

"More than a day, I know that. Maybe it was a week away. Or three or four, more likely. We walked and walked."

"Y'all slept in the nighttime?"

"Well, '*course* we slept in the nighttime. When you think we slept?"

"Well, is there places a person could sleep in the daytime?"

"Plenty of woods out there. Quit talkin'." But she smiles at him, to soften her words. She likes Israel. Ever since the first day she met him under the tree, he's full of freedom talk. She's caught it too, but her plan's different. If she ever sees Master Cornelius again she'll tell him she wants to buy herself out. She's made a little money sewing, and the coins are in a cloth purse she keeps in her sewing bag. Mrs. Landerson pays her twenty-five cents for a baby dress, a nickel for an apron.

She pulls the thread up to make gathers for the sleeve. Helene and Israel look at each other.

Jenny gets to her feet and brushes leaves from the back of her skirt. "I'm gonna go see about that babe."

She walks toward the corner of the stable, where she stops and looks back at Israel. "You still plannin' on runnin' off, ain't you? I hope you around to use this shirt when I get it finished."

He looks sheepish for a minute. Then he grins. "I'll use it."

"If you gone, I'll sell it to Tom," she says. Then she goes around the corner.

It's quiet in the shade. A breeze moves in the cane-hedge. Helene plucks at some blades of grass as she leans against Israel. "Is that right, what she says? Are you runnin' off?" she asks.

He grins again and puts his hand under her skirt, squeezing her leg. "I might. I might not. Don't trouble yourself on it."

"I ain't troublin' myself on it. I just hope you ain't that crazy."

He laughs a short laugh, then sits up and reaches out to fumble with the buttons on her blouse. The buttons are hidden under dainty bows that run down to her waist. Jenny had sewed the bows on for her.

"Get away. Somebody see us here," Helene protests, looking toward the cane hedge; beyond it, chimneys rise toward the sky.

"They ain't gonna see us," he says. "Nobody comes down that old side path anymore. They stay on the road."

"You a foolish boy, Israel," she says, but she lies down and lets him open her dress; she looks up into the sweet-gum tree as he finishes what he started. Every leaf is star-shaped, a tough late-summer green. There's no use trying to stop him, she figures; she just takes it for what it is, an easy comfort. He's running away one of these days; Jenny knows it, and now Helene sees it too. He's good as gone.

As December begins the wind is icy and the fireplace can hardly keep the rooms warm. Jenny puts her feet on a warming brick and covers herself with two quilts when she goes to bed, but now someone's come to get her out of her warm bed and into the frosty room. The pounding on the door rouses Esther, who gets up and lumbers to the door. Jenny sits up in bed, pulling the quilts over her shoulders. Esther swings the door open to let Frank in. He mumbles something before he slips back out.

"Oh my Lord, Israel's run away," Esther says. "Gone up the Trace so's he can get to the free soil." She wraps a shawl around her shoulders and rushes out.

Jenny gets up and goes to the door and looks out. It's still dark. She pulls on her dress and wraps the blanket around her shoulder. Then she runs to the kitchen. Most of the slaves are there.

The fire in the fireplace flickers low in the dark kitchen. Esther lights a lantern and sets it on the table.

Jenny sits down beside Theresa, who's crying.

"I know Israel's been catched, I just feels it in my bones," Theresa whimpers, shaking her head. "There ain't nothin' else could bring Frank out on such a night but that. Pore Israel. Pore, pore boy."

"Will you hush up that blubberin'?" Helene snaps. "You don't know if he's been catched. Could be he's got clean away. He might be clean on up to -- Port Gibson by now."

Jenny presses close to Theresa, her hands holding the ends of her old woolen blanket; it once belonged to Miss Sophronia, and it has her close boozy smell. But it's warm in spite of the two big holes that moths ate in it some winter past.

"Israel probably did run off," Jenny says. She remembers how he always liked to hear about far-off places. "There wasn't no stoppin' him. I tried to talk him out of it."

"Lord, the boy's askin' for it," Charlie says. "I knew a man run away once. They caught him and made him wear bells. Just bells, on a iron collar round his neck, and with all these branches stickin' out, and on the end of every branch was a bell. They jingled ever'where he went. Jingled so you'd hear him comin' a quarter-mile away. Lord. I thought that man'd go plumb crazy, to hear hisself jingle all the time."

"*Did* he go crazy?" Helene asks, her eyes big.

"Hard to tell," Charlie says. "He a sight, though. You'd see him in town, and there he'd be, with that jinglin' collar." He goes to the door and eases it open, craning his head toward the main house. "Ain't nobody up," he says.

"Israel's crazy to run off," Jenny says. "He didn't even have a coat. He had a shirt I made for him, but this cold weather, that won't keep him warm. He should a knew better than that."

"He *might* make it," Theresa says. "Israel's smart. He'd figger out what roads not t' take."

"I always thought Israel was just boastin', the way he talked," Helene says. "He said he'd sleep in the daytime and run at night."

"Law, I hate to think what Old Frog'll do if he catch him. Might sell 'im, I expect," Esther says.

"Don't say that," Theresa says. "Don't even say it."

"I don't think Frank's comin' back," Charlie says. "He'd a been back by now, if he was comin'. We may's well all go back to bed. Frank might 'a made the story up anyways. Or maybe Old Frog won't go after 'im."

"He'd send the 'thorities," Rob says.

"I hope I live to see the day we ain't *slaves* no more," Sarah says. "When that day comes, glory-be!"

"Hush you' mouths, all of you," Esther snaps. "We *is* slaves, so that's all. That kind of talk's what got Israel in this trouble he's in right now."

"Maybe he ain't in trouble," Rob says. "Maybe he's gonna make it--"

"Hope they don't get the dogs after him," Charlie says. "They got dogs can sniff a man a mile away. And Israel can't run no faster than a red-bone hound."

The men stand up and shuffle around as the fire sputters almost out.

"Israel's smart," Charlie says. "He might out-fox 'em. Let's go back to bed. We can't do nothin' here. But I got a feelin' we ain't gonna see him again. He's gone to the Free Soil."

Jenny looks around at the others. The women sit at the table, the whites of their eyes flashing like silver coins. She pulls at the moth-holes of her shawl, winding the threads around the tip of her finger and rubbing little knots there.

She wonders: how easy can it be for Israel to get to the free soil? Where is it, and how far? Slavery's such a big thing, and they're all caught in it.

Theresa begins to wail, a long moan that goes up to the corners of the room against the ceiling where the cob-webs are.

The door opens and Frank steps into the room and closes the door.

"They got 'im." Even in the dim-light, they can see a black spray on his homespun pants.

"Is that blood on your pants?" Esther whispers.

Frank heaves down onto the bench beside the table. All the women stand up and move back.

"It's blood, sure 'nough. They got Israel. Got him right outside of town, headed for Ohio. He was just off the road, hidin' in the woods. Master Barser and his posse got 'im and brought 'im back. And then Master Landerson called us all to go over to the Old Frog's place. All the men gotta to see what happens when you run off, he says. And Old Frog's boy, Master Jules, he told Barser to go get the axe, and Barser did. And Master Barser, he *lamed* Israel, and made us all watch."

Helene touches Frank's trouser-leg. "This is Israel's blood," she says in a whisper. "Is he dead?"

"He ain't dead but he wishes he was," Frank says. "He's got no right foot, now. Barser chopped it off."

Jenny thinks the fire leaps up in the fireplace, and a gust swirls around the room. But it might be just the caught breaths of all of them who're here, hearing Frank's words. She threads her fingers together and puts her forehead down on the table.

We can't stay slaves, she thinks. *They're gonna kill us inch by inch.*

The thought's so wicked, so powerful, that she can't sit there any longer. She gets up and goes over to the door, looking out. But in one direction is only a cold reddening dawn, and in the other the looming square shape of the big house, where, as she looks, a light comes up in one back window. Sophronia must've turned up her lamp to find her way to the chamber-pot.

Sarah's right, Jenny thinks. *Old as she is, she knows. There's gotta come a day when we ain't slaves no more.*

Frank pushes up behind her and she steps outside, to let the boy pass. Then she stands in the cold and watches as he lopes down the hill, past the pond where the ducks are setting up a racket. Then he disappears into the trees.

CHAPTER THIRTY-TWO

"Wonderful ain't for hire this year, Mister Carson," Alice Turley says on a gray morning in 1839, without waiting to be asked. "It'll take all my hands to get this cotton planted, especially since four of my men's been sick for a week and Lathan's still laid up with a snakebite he got last summer. It's festered up again. You better plan on buying your workers from now on."

In the middle of the field she sits astride her horse like a man. Under her straw hat her gray hair is coming loose, long strands floating around her face like feathers. Nearby, Louis Ferison supervises slaves who're planting cotton, shouting at their mules as they wrestle plows down furrows that run straight for a half-mile.

"Zupine! Get that mule movin'!" Ferison shouts at a sweating black man, who curses at his animal; the mule lurches forward. Zupine holds the plow to the ridge of the furrow, where it throws back a seam for the cottonseeds. A boy trudging behind the plow drops seeds from a homespun bag around his neck.

"The way prices are falling, the only way to come out is to plant more acres, and that's what I'm doing," Alice says. "And I need all my hands to do it." Cornelius nods and rides away, considering his predicament.

With eighty arpents waiting to be planted, he needs at least one more hand. And once planted, the cotton has to be hoed again and again, and then picked between September and January. Field hands who pick cotton have to be able to work a long day, get a short night's sleep and then go to the fields the next day and work just as hard all over again. There's no point planting cotton without enough hands. But he has only himself and Malachi.

For three years he'd hired Wonderful for half a dollar a day. Ever since Wonderful married Lucinda, one of Alice's house-girls, he'd turned into something Cornelius never thought he'd be, a steady worker. Lucinda has a fat six-month-old baby that looks exactly like Wonderful must've looked as a baby.

Three years ago, after Stephanie died, Cornelius had deadened a section of low-lying woods near the bayou. He girdled the trees with his axe, leaving an inch-wide seam around each trunk. It was a morning's work, but by April the trees were skeletons. Then he and Mal and Wonderful planted cotton in the open spaces around the dead trunks. And they made a bigger crop -- twenty-four bales -- than any Cornelius had produced before. Last year cotton brought twelve-and-a-half cents a pound at Vidalia, and, Cornelius heard later, thirteen cents at New Orleans. Cornelius made over fourteen hundred dollars, paid in government paper money. He used to get his money in notes drawn on banks -- the Bank of Vidalia or the Planters' Bank in Natchez -- but government money's what people carry now. It'll spend, he figures, but he still liked the solid weight of gold dollars.

He rides back to his cabin through the fields. Alice's fields look wider every time he sees them; for months her sweating slave squads have been busy felling, clearing, burning stumps. All winter the swamps and low places of the Cocodrie have hung with smoke, a white sweet smell.

As Cornelius rides up to the cabin, a cold rain begins. Mal is sitting on the porch whittling a pine stick.

"I figgered it'd rain today," Mal says. "Bad luck for the plantin', I guess."

"Bad enough." Cornelius dismounts and slaps the horse's rump; it trots off to the stable. He shakes his arms and stamps his boots. "What're you carving?"

"Duck. I seen one sittin' in the store window last week, and I figgered I'd try it. Can't do nothin' else in this weather, except sleep, and can't sleep all the time."

"Nope." Cornelius goes inside and pulls off his wet shirt. He stands in front of the fire and rubs his arms. After he changes into a dry shirt and spreads the wet shirt over a chair in front of the fire, he goes out to the porch, where he folds his arms and leans against the wall to watch the rain. It pounds the yard; under the drooping banana trees, water gathers in brown puddles which burst into rivulets that snake across the yard. Mal continues carving, hunching over his work as the chips fly.

Cornelius goes back inside and takes a book from the shelf beside the fireplace: *Moll Flanders,* which he's already read twice. It's hard to read in the gray light, and he's out of books. He's already finished both books he borrowed from Euphonia McKee last week.

Euphonia likes to read, and now he likes it too. Raunchy old Moll Flanders; when Cornelius first read the novel, he chuckled at Euphonia's taste. Rawboned Phony, with her long face and slackening jawline, easing into spinsterhood. Prim as a pincushion. Now that she's thirty-six, as she told him last month -- eight years older than he was -- maybe she figures an old maid might find in books what she didn't expect to find in real life. But he appreciates Phony; not many people in the Cocodrie *could* read, and even fewer cared to. This connection between him and Phony pleases Amos and Margaret McKee in the bargain. And Phony expects nothing in return, which suits him.

He can't make his eyes move beyond the novel's first few sentences, which he knows by heart. The pages feel limp and damp, and mildew is sure to follow. Phony will understand, but it's a shame to think the crisp pages are doomed to yellow and speckle. Nothing stays fresh and new forever -- not Phony's books, and not Phony herself.

He'll return frisky old Moll to Euphonia when the rain stops, and with luck she'll loan him another bold book. He sits for a few minutes, looking around the cabin. Grittiness has settled on the furniture and the floor. Some of his unwashed clothes hang on the antler rack and some are thrown into the corner.

"How long's it been since we mopped the floor?" he calls to Mal.

"I don't recall."

"Too long, I'd say."

"I'd say that's right."

"We might have to do something about it. But not while it's raining."

"Nossir."

The steady rain makes everything dreary. And he's hungry. After Stephanie died, Mal took over a lot of the cooking, although Cornelius still fixed breakfast. And it was Cornelius who still ran hogs and hunted deer and did the butchering. But for four years he's eaten Malachi's peppery-tasting stews, fricassees, and other viddles. Most of it was edible, if flavored with peculiar seasonings. When Cornelius said he wouldn't mind cooking again, Malachi protested. So he let the old man continue his experiments.

Mal comes inside and sets his carving on the shelf. "You want something to eat?"

"I'm not hungry."

Lately, Mal's cooking has slipped a notch, in Cornelius's opinion. At dinner yesterday when he tried to eat what Mal cooked, he let it dribble from his spoon back into the bowl.

"Mind if I ask what this is?"

"Well, it started out this mornin' to be squirrel pie," Malachi said. "But I'm not sure it ended up that way."

"I'm damn sure it didn't end up that way. It's underdone."

"It's somethin', sure enough." Malachi continued to eat. "I was havin' some trouble gettin' that wet wood to burn."

Cornelius picks up the duck Mal carved. "You know, Mal, I used to think we could run this place all right, but now I'm not so sure," he says.

"I ain't been sure for a while now, but I didn't want to say anything."

"We kept ourselves going back in the early days, remember? When it was just you and me here?"

"I remember. 'Course, we was younger then."

"Maybe that's what's different now." Cornelius looks around the messy room.

"Or maybe we just didn't mind so much."

"Maybe."

But Mal's cooking isn't Cornelius's only worry. He sets the book down and walks over to the door. Across the yard the two doors of the little house are closed, both spattered with mud thrown up by the pelting rain. Leaves are piled against the door on the left.

"Wonderful ain't for hire this year," Cornelius says. "I guess I'll have to go get Jenny."

Malachi looks up quickly. "That might be a good idea. She could help us with the cotton, if they kin spare her in Natchez. It'd be nice to see li'l Jenny again. Law. I figured you must 'a forgot about her after all this time."

Cornelius folds his arms and leans against the door, looking out across the yard. He hadn't thought much about this, but it would be a change.

Is Emile Coqterre at Carefree? Cornelius wouldn't want to run into him. But this time of year Emile's probably on the Bayou

Boeuf. Even if Emile's at Carefree, Cornelius might be able to get Jenny by driving around by the back way, straight to the slave house, without going up to the main house. He might even visit Stephanie's grave while he was in Natchez.

The old guilt he feels over Stephanie's death has faded over the years, but sometimes it still nags at him, especially during rains when the stream springs out of its banks.

"It's possible Jenny's learnt somethin' since she been in Natchez," Malachi says late that afternoon after the rain stops. "I believe I'll let her room air out, 'cause when she get here, she won't want it all mustied-up."

Malachi picks his way across the muddy yard to the little house and opens the door to Jenny's room. Inside, Cornelius knows, are Jenny's old things: the doll Malachi carved for her, a penny in a jar, a pair of broken hairpins on the shelf. Hanging from a nail is a dress that Jenny wore, and outgrew, before she went to Natchez. And in the middle of the floor is Stephanie's trunk, with her dresses neatly folded inside. Cornelius and Malachi carried the trunk there last summer, after Cornelius decided he couldn't have it crowd the cabin any longer.

"When you gonna get her?" Malachi asks two days later as they plant corn. The sun is baking the air dry.

"When the road's dry enough." Cornelius knows he'll have to get Jenny soon. Mal will give him no peace about it until he does.

A week later Cornelius drives to Natchez. He comes up to Carefree the back way, past the slave cemetery, scattering some ducks as he drives around the pond. He leaves the buggy in a clearing halfway down the hill, where there's grass for the horse, and walks the rest of the way.

The stately house rises serenely above the old trees at the top of the hill, forming a familiar skyline. But as he walks up the hill, he senses how quiet the place is. It seems asleep; the chirping of birds in the well-clipped shrubbery and the glossy leaves alight with sunshine make the place seem welcoming, but all the doors and windows in the main house are closed, even on this hot day. Only the kitchen door stands half-open.

Daisy and her babies must be somewhere else, he thinks; she always had two or three noisy kids toddling around, and a lap baby as well. And maybe Rob's hoeing in the garden behind the cane-hedge, and Charlie gone into town on some errand.

He walks to the kitchen and goes into the dark cool room. Esther, stirring a pot at the fireplace, has her back turned. Theresa, kneading dough at the table, looks up at him with a surprised half-smile.

"Where's everyone, Esther?" Cornelius asks. The pungent smell of food makes his mouth water.

"Oh my Lord, it's Master Cornelius!" Esther exclaims. She drops the spoon and it clatters into the pot. "Oh, I guess you come to get Jenny, didn't you?" She puts her hand to her chest. "I always knew I'd have to let her go when the time come, but it pains me to think it's come today."

Cornelius steps back. He hadn't thought to cause hurt by coming here, but of course in three years' time Esther would've grown attached to his little field-hand.

She dabs at her eyes with the corner of her apron. "Oh Lord, I nearly forgot myself. Theresa, go get Jenny. Tell her to pack her things. Master Cornelius is here to get her."

"Yes'm." Theresa covers the dough with a cloth. She goes out the door.

"Come have somethin' to eat, sir," Esther says. "We got more than enough stew. Let me fix you a plate." She sniffles as she pokes at the pot to retrieve the spoon and then sets a plate before him.

"You know, I almost didn't recognize you when I saw you standin' there in that doorway. I believe you got skinnier since the last time I seen you," Esther says, pouring him a cup of buttermilk. She spoons up a bowl of stew.

Cornelius nods as he starts to eat.

"You dressin' different these days, too," Esther says. Embarrassed, Cornelius looks down at his frayed cuffs. "'Course, if we knew you was comin' today, we could 'a had everything all ready for her to go." She sets a plate of biscuits on the table. "She'll want to take her sewin' bag, and all her other things. She's a right good seamstress now. That's what I learnt her how to do. I couldn't teach her how to spin, even though that's what Miss Stephanie wanted; it just takes too long. And there ain't no need to spin; there's plenty cloth in the stores. So li'l ole Jenny and me, we just decided to forget about that, and learn her somethin' else. So I showed her a needle and thread, and wouldn't you know, she took right to it."

A young man comes to the door and leans his hoe against the side of the building.

"This here's Helene's husband, Israel," Esther says, motioning the young man in. Israel walks into the kitchen with a stiff hobbling gait. Cornelius sees the reason for Israel's limp: half of his bare right foot is missing, sliced off cleanly an inch above where his toes should be. The wound is raw and pink, newly healed. Cornelius feels a chill. Israel must have run away, and been caught, not too long ago. Cornelius looks away from the grotesque foot. It contrasts with the young man's open, friendly face.

Cornelius stands up. "That was the best meal I've had in a long time. I'd appreciate it if you wouldn't say anything to Master Emile about me coming here. Just whatever you have to tell him about Jenny leaving. He -- well, you remember how it was."

Esther nods. "Yes sir, I remember. But, well, Master Emile, he not like he used to be." Her face creases into deep furrows. "Right after Miss Stephanie's funeral, he went off, and didn't come back 'til the next wintertime. And ever since then, well, he just wanders 'round town like a wild man, and his hair down to here." She marks the length with her hand on her arm. "All his old friends, they just forgot about 'im. And we all scared of 'im. Daisy and Sarah's gone to stay with Daisy's mother on the other side of Natchez. The rest of us, we just tryin' to stay out of his way. He says crazy things. He always talkin' about Miss Stephanie and Miss Josephine." She twists her hands together. "And he never go back to the Bayou Boeuf anymore."

Israel takes one of Esther's biscuits from the pan. "Master Emile, he always right here in Natchez now," he says.

CHAPTER THIRTY-THREE

"He's come for me?"

"He right back there in the kitchen with Mamma," Theresa says, pointing toward the kitchen. "And close your mouth. A bug might fly in it."

Jenny stares at her. Master Cornelius Carson? It's been so long since she's seen him, he's become almost unreal in her mind. Her image of him is like a shadow.

Theresa sits down beside her. "You gonna be all right, ain't ya, Jenny? This is the best thing, for him to come get you now. I think you lucky to be leavin' this crazy house. With that man in there," -- she jerks her finger toward the big house -- "you should be glad you gettin' away from here."

Jenny's facc crumples.

"He brought his buggy for you to ride in," Theresa says. "It's a good thing you goin', seem to me. You don't belong to Master Emile no how. So I say just calm yourself and get yourself packed. Master Cornelius is waitin' for you. Pack quick. He want you to hurry." She drags the satchel out from under the bed.

Jenny looks around the room. Carefree is her home. Her friends are here, Esther and Theresa and Helene; and old Sarah, and Daisy and her babies. These are the people she belongs with.

She hardly remembers the place on the Cocodrie. It's not real to her any more. She can't remember how to hoe cotton.

But her master's here to get her; she has to be ready. Because he wants his slave girl back. He's taking her to a place where she'll be turned into a sweating field-hand, where she'll never get herself free.

When Theresa comes back in with a good dress, Jenny's surprised. "My mamma says to give you this one," she says.

Jenny puts on the dress, which is one she sewed for Helene last year. "I need to take my sewing things," she says.

"I already put 'em in the satchel. I'll carry it for you."

At the doorway Jenny stops and looks around one last time. She was never supposed to be here this long; the room plainly shows it. Her bed's pushed against the wall but it still crowds Esther's bed. After she leaves here, nothing will tell that she's been here. All her things are packed into the satchel Theresa carries. Esther always knew she'd be leaving one day.

Today.

Yanked around again, she thinks. *Slave girl.*

She steps outside the door.

I hate this slave's life.

Cornelius, hearing voices, goes over to the door and looks out. Jenny walks toward the kitchen with Theresa. She wears a dark red plaid dress with a cape.

He suddenly realizes how much time has passed, the three years since Stephanie died, the years of planting and harvesting with Malachi and Wonderful. Is *that* Jenny? Instead of the little girl he expected, here's this tall grown-up-looking girl, and she seems like a stranger to him.

"Hello, Jenny."

She puts her hand up over her mouth to hide a sound like a hiccup.

He stares at her. Well, it certainly *is* Jenny. He recognizes her skinny shape and high shoulders and that inky black skin. She's much taller, of course, but what surprises him most is her sober grownup expression. She doesn't look like a little girl at all.

"You ready to go?" he asks.

"Yessir."

"We'll be off, then," he says. "I don't want to stick around any longer than I have to."

Helene and Theresa come over and hug her. Israel limps over, and, glancing at Helene, kisses Jenny lightly on the cheek. Then Esther wraps her in a swaying bear-hug. Esther sniffles; then she composes herself and dabs at her eyes with her apron.

"You'll bring her back to visit, won't you, sir?" Esther asks. "She like one of my own, after all this time."

"I'll let her visit when I can."

He and Jenny walk down the hill to the buggy. Jenny sets her satchel in the back and climbs up on the buggy.

Cornelius gets up and clicks the reins. The horse trots down the road to the bottom of the hill, around a stand of spindly pine trees and then through a grove of elms, their leaves a limey spring green. The sun licks through the trees.

They drive through the business district and then down Silver Street to the ferry landing. Cornelius glances at Jenny from time to time. She stares down at her clasped hands. It's not easy for her to make this change, he figures, but she'll get over it. For three years she's been leading a different life than she knew in the Cocodrie; she must be about fifteen now, and she has a polished city look. Remembering how he used to bring her peppermints and taffy candy from the store in the settlement, he wonders if she still has a sweet tooth.

On the ferry she gets down from the buggy and stands near the center of the deck, holding onto a pole as the ferry bobs across the wake of a flatboat.

Later, as they drive down the road toward the settlement, Cornelius says, "Malachi and I need help in the cottonfields, Jenny. And maybe in the cabin, too. Mal's not much of a cook, and I don't have the time, especially with the cotton."

"Yessir."

Another mile passes.

"You know, I'm not much of a cook," Jenny says suddenly. "I *am* a seamstress, though. I can stitch up anything."

"Well, we need some mending. But mostly it's the cotton where you'll be working. I have eighty arpents taken in now, and it's all got to be planted."

She's silent again for awhile. "I like to sew, sir. In Natchez I even hired out to make some things. Mrs. Landerson paid me a dollar to make clothes for her baby. I can sew --"

"You're not gonna have much time for sewing," Cornelius says shortly. "It's the cotton that needs work."

"Yessir."

A moment later he says, "I bet you're a better cook than Malachi is."

"No sir, I couldn't be."

After a few more moments pass, she asks, "Is Malachi all right?"

"He's old as the hills, but he's all right."

She begins to look happier. "Do you still have the kitties?"

"Well, we still have the big old tomcat. The old mamma cat's gone off somewhere else. There's some other strays that live out at the stable."

Jenny nods. Her skin's so black; Cornelius remembers that too, her black-as-midnight complexion. He thinks of the star-shower again, when they all sat on the cabin steps together.

"It'll be good to have you back, Jenny," he says, looking straight ahead.

"Thank you, sir."

Malachi stares when Jenny gets down from the buggy, and he grins bashfully when she takes his hand in her both her own and pumps it enthusiastically. But when she carries her satchel to her room in the little house, he walks out to the back porch where Cornelius is pulling off his boots.

"That girl ain't gonna want to work in the cotton," Mal says in a low voice. "She's a house worker, I can see it."

"She may be, but cotton's what I need her for," Cornelius says. "Tomorrow, the three of us better get started. The season's getting away from us."

"Yes sir."

In the evening it rains again. They all sit at the table and eat what Malachi had cooked earlier in the day, something he calls "quail pone." Cornelius sees Jenny take the spoon from her lips with a puzzled look; she wrinkles up her nose. He chuckles; his little African might find she wants to cook after all.

Later Cornelius sits on the porch with Malachi, both men waiting for Jenny's company, but she keeps herself hidden in her room.

"I expect she's tidyin' it," Malachi says.

In the morning, Jenny walks over to the cabin wearing a well-made blue dress and a white apron.

Cornelius stands on the porch. He ignores her cautious smile. "Jenny, we have to plant cotton today," he snaps. "I told you that. Those ain't cotton-planting clothes. Don't you have an old dress?"

"Yessir," she mumbles. She goes down to the little house and comes back wearing a faded green dress that hangs loosely on her form. The apron is gone. But her face is sullen.

Later, as he waits with Jenny in the shade of a tree for Malachi to come down to the field, Cornelius says, "Over there's a section I deadened awhile back." He points across the field to a place where tree trunks rise like toothpicks against the green wall of swamp. "Don't go over there when the wind's up. A tree could fall on you."

"I never been scared of a wind, sir."

He glances at her. She doesn't want to work in the cottonfields, he's certain of it. Well, sulking or not, the cotton can't wait. "Well, just stay away from there, all right?"

"Yes sir."

"Remember when I bought you some gloves?" he asks. "After your hands got blistered from hoeing?"

"Yes sir."

"You were just a little thing, then. Think you'll get blisters when we start to hoe this year?"

"If I do, I can make my own gloves," she says. "I'm a seamstress."

He's forgotten that almost-sassiness. Well, she has to work in the cotton, like it or no; but he hopes she'll take to it. He doesn't want to confront her or anyone else. For years he's lived a pretty solitary life, for the most part; he's come to think it suited him.

Malachi comes out a few minutes later. Cornelius takes a sack of seeds from the wagon.

"Put this around your neck," he says to Jenny. "We've already done the back-furrowing. I'll run the plow along the top of the ridge, and you drop the seed in. Malachi'll come up behind."

She takes the bag. All day they plant cotton, stopping at noon to eat yesterday's cornbread and some bacon Mal cooked this morning.

The next day Jenny wears a sunbonnet when they go to the fields; studying it as he walks along behind her, Cornelius recognizes the light print fabric as one of his own old shirts, long ago handed down to Malachi. That must have been why the lamp burned so late in Jenny's window last night; he saw it as he sat on the step far into the night, watching the stars. She must've been stitching the sunbonnet. But the cotton has to be planted. Sewing can wait.

Jenny turns up her lamp and sits slumped on the side of her bed. She feels sweaty and tired and achy.

Every evening after she finishes working in the cottonfield, she takes out her bag of scraps and her needle and thread. For the first few days after she came here the work seemed so hard, especially with that bag of seeds she has to carry around her neck. Now it's just a matter of getting through every day of working out in the bright sun, in the steamy heat.

This evening she spreads her scraps of fabric on the mattress. This odd-shaped piece of organdy from Helene's cap; a big scrap of red plaid from her best dress; a strip of faded green print she made into a shirt for Israel -- all can be put to good use; she'll make a light quilt. She might even try to sell it.

Master Cornelius will have to take her to the store to get some muslin, for a sheet. She has to have bedcoverings; he can't expect her to keep sleeping on this plain old ticking, even though it's what she slept on when she was younger. She's not a child anymore, and she has to have things better than she had back then.

Her room in the little house is smaller than she remembered, just a little square log room with a window that looks out into some deep woods, and a deerskin -- she didn't remember that -- for a curtain. Miss Stephanie's old trunk was in the room when she first came here, but she asked the men to move it, and now it sits out in the stable. She runs her hand along her mattress; it feels gritty.

At Carefree she'd slept under a woolen quilt that smelled clean. She thinks of Esther and sighs; Esther's room in the slave house will seem much bigger now, with only one person living in it. Then she scolds herself for remembering.

Sewing helps. When she sews, she concentrates only on the line of stitches before her, and all other thoughts float away. She loves the feel of a thimble on her finger. She likes the way a row of stitches can fashion useful things out of the sorriest cloth. Nothing goes to waste: thread can be pulled from hems and re-used, old garments cut down and pieced for something else. An old dress can become part of a quilt, or an apron, or a sunbonnet. Buttons probably never wear out in a whole lifetime.

She still has trouble believing she's really here. When Master Cornelius came for her at Carefree, it didn't seem possible that one minute she was spending her days peacefully in the slave house, and the next minute she was packing her bag to leave. The long buggy ride out here seemed like a dark dream.

Mal is so much older than she remembered; that's the biggest change she notices. And it's quieter here without Miss Stephanie. She wondered, as she rode out here with Master Cornelius, if it would seem like Miss Stephanie was still here in the cabin, but it didn't. It was just an untidy cabin with gritty floors, and a yard with overgrown banana trees and wild-looking rosebushes along one side.

And Cornelius was right: Malachi can't cook. She might have to take on some of the cooking here. Working in the cotton makes her tired and hungry every day.

As for Master Cornelius, when she saw him standing there at Carefree she realized that she did remember him after all. That face was so familiar. But such a storm was in her mind, as she tried to make herself believe that he'd really come back for her, that she didn't notice how he'd changed; but she notices it now. He looks older, and sterner, than she remembers. And he's quieter now.

She didn't have anything but a few scraps to sew when she got here, so without saying anything she brought a couple of the men's shirts here to her room where she could mend them. Their clothes are clean, at least; not like Master Emile's clothes. Emile shouted Esther away every time she wanted to wash his shirts. When Jenny mended his garments – once or twice she took his shirts when he wasn't around – they were sticky and stinky.

Here in the Cocodrie, she fully intends to make herself another dress, as soon as she gets all this mending done and the quilt made. Master Cornelius is bound to take her to town one day soon, and she'll look for some fabric in the store.

She's been eying her old shift hanging from a nail on the wall; it might make a child's dress. On a nail next to it, a doll dangles. Malachi carved it for her a long time ago; it reminds her of her brother for some reason, probably because it's a child's toy. Her brother off in slavery somewhere.

Kofi shouldn't be in slavery any more than I should. Maybe he'll buy his way out too.

When she gets brave enough, she's going to talk to Cornelius about buying her freedom. She'd have brought it up already except for fear he'd say no. He seems reasonable enough, but she better not trust him, just yet. As they work in the fields, or eat their meals, she studies him, trying to read him: Will he say yes, or no?

And she can't remember Kofi so clearly anymore.

A summons to jury duty comes for Cornelius in the mail. "It's inconvenient as hell," he mutters to Malachi as the men drink whiskey on the porch one evening a week later, after Cornelius has been to the settlement and gotten his mail. Jenny sits on the step not sewing for once, her hands propped under her chin, pouting because Cornelius wouldn't buy her the cloth she wanted at the store, a crisp white muslin. "I'll have to be gone for a week or more, and it's come at the worse time."

"Do you even know what th' charge is on th' fella, sir?"

Cornelius shakes his head. "Some man named Joe Montegue, is what I heard in town. Charged with murder, they say. And another man charged with horse-stealing. I don't know which one I'll get."

The first charge wasn't as simple as murder, but Cornelius couldn't say so to Malachi. Montegue is charged with killing a slave. Montegue's neighbor went for the law after the body was found.

"I hate to go," Cornelius says. "But I can't get out of it; my name was in the pot, and the clerk pulled out my name. I have to be at the courthouse day after tomorrow."

"I'll be at the hotel in Vidalia," he says to Mal before he rides away late the next morning. Mal is stacking some light'ard on the porch; he likes to keep a pile of it handy to the fireplace. "You and Jenny finish planting the garden. We've got a few days 'til the cotton's up."

"Maybe we better plant more peas and corn this year since Jenny's here now."

"Don't make it too big or we'll never be able to tend it."

Cornelius rides over to the well, where Jenny is pumping water. "I guess I'll try to get you that muslin when I come back through the settlement."

She continues to pump. The water splashes into the bucket. "Three yards."

"All right."

Sulky little thing, but he figures he owes her something. The meals are better since she's been back; without being asked, she's taken on more of the cooking than he intends, and he doesn't miss Mal's peculiar-tasting stews and sauces. And rends and rips in his clothes have suddenly been repaired, which he finds comforting after years when his clothes seemed to be always coming apart.

CHAPTER THIRTY-FOUR

The hotel in Vidalia gets lots of jurors, Cornelius thinks as he rides up to the shabby building; its long front porch gives a view of the river and the bluff where Natchez sits. And Natchez is where most travelers would stay for the night.

But jurors have to report at eight o'clock in the morning to the courthouse just down the street, so Cornelius pays what he thinks is too much -- 75 cents -- for a room, and after he stables his horse at the livery next door he goes upstairs. A sagging iron bedstead sits in the center of the drab room. Gloomy surroundings probably make for quick verdicts, he thinks. He goes back downstairs and sits on the porch, where he can watch his fellow jurors arriving one by one.

A mixed group, he sees. Some of the men stomp across the porch in muddy boots, straw hats pulled low over their weather-beaten faces. A few, better bred, pull off their wide hats when they enter the lobby. One man arrives in a fancy gig; his slave follows him into the lobby carrying two gleaming leather valises. Every man's face says his life's been disrupted by this inconvenient summons to Vidalia this late-April week in 1838. And in the hotel, everyone's equal; all the men get rooms along the one dusty hallway upstairs.

As it gets dark one last buggy pulls up. A solid-looking man gets down and holds up his hand to a young woman with wheat-colored hair. This juror's brought his young wife, Cornelius thinks.

He gets up and walks toward a tavern he noticed on his way into town. He pays ten cents for a plate dinner of beans and bread, which tastes good. As he finishes his meal, the man and blond woman he'd noticed earlier come into the tavern.

"You recommend somethin'?" asks the man, sitting down next to Cornelius. He's a big man with a square jaw and a steady gaze.

"Beans and bread," Cornelius says, motioning toward his own empty plate. "The whiskey tastes like what they make around here."

"I'll try it. You here for the jury?"

"I am. And yourself?"

"The same." The man scrapes his chair back and stands up. He extends his hand. "Dan'l Vane, from Slocum." He motions toward the woman. "My daughter Hattie."

Cornelius shakes Vane's hand and nods toward the woman. "Cornelius Carson."

Hattie Vane is a big-boned girl in a checked gingham dress, her hair plaited into a thick braid that hangs over her shoulder. She wears a lace cap.

Hattie speaks to the tavern keeper. "We'll have the same as what he had," she says. Cornelius notices the back-country drawl in her husky voice.

Cornelius finishes his whiskey. "I reckon I'll see you in the morning," he says, getting up to leave.

"Yessir. Eight o'clock's what they say. You know what case you're on?"

"No sir."

"It'll be Montegue or Bartell. Bartell's the horse-thief."

"One or the other, I guess," Cornelius says, holding his hat. "Good night." He turns to walk away.

But Vane speaks again. "My daughter come along fer th' excitement of the trip." His cheeks are full of bread which he'd sopped in the bean sauce. "I told her I couldn't afford the extry room, but she kep' after me 'til I give in."

"I never been to Vidalia before," Hattie says. She has a bashful smile, but her eyes are locked on Cornelius's. "And I never seen Natchez neither. Just what you see from the outside here. That big hill over there."

"Well, seein' it from this side's all you gonna git to do, daughter," Vane snaps. "I ain't got the money nor the time to go over there."

"I'll see you in the morning," Cornelius says. Other patrons have come in to the tavern. Lamps stuck in the mud-chinked walls flicker.

Cornelius goes back to the hotel and sits again on the porch. The lights of Natchez wink at him from the bluff across the river. Over there are homes, schools, churches -- a genteel town. Chandeliers are ablaze in the great dining rooms, and important people are sitting at their dinners. At Carefree, which is too far east for its lights to be seen from here, Emile Coqterre will probably be sitting in the parlor with a glass of whiskey, staring at the cold fireplace, lost in some delusional vision, perhaps. And Esther would already have lit the lamps in the hall.

A buggy comes down Silver Street; its lantern twinkles against the black hillside. The light merges with the lights under the hill, a constellation rippling on the water.

Some flatboats have docked at the foot of Silver Street; in the dark they can't make their way between fallen trees -- snaggers and sawyers, the river-captains call them -- that are always a danger. But steamers can travel on clear nights, and tonight there's not a hint of fog. The two big steamers docked at Natchez will probably cast off soon, Cornelius thinks.

Off to his left, he hears a rhythmic *whomp-whomp*, almost too soft to hear at first, but then louder, and it sounds so good: the sound of a well-tended boiler, powering a big boat. He looks for the shower of sparks from the twin fan-topped smokestacks, and then there it is, big as anything, a steamboat coming around the black hump of the shoreline curve. He knew it would be a splendid sight; if he could see it in daytime, it would be almost blinding white. He showed Stephanie a steamer docking at Natchez, once. Such a spectacle. Now he can just make out the dark figures of the crew scurrying about the deck as they throw the mooring lines and bring the big craft in. He leans forward and rests his arms on his knees.

The steamers he worked on during his years as a boilerman had grand salons as fine as any Natchez drawing room. In those salons the pianos tinkled and the waiters poured whiskey from crystal decanters. At night, as the big boats churned their noisy, smoky way down the black river, the cabin-passengers would retire to their private rooms, and the deck-passengers would stretch out on the decks like gypsies, country next to city, black cheek-by-jowl with white.

Back then he'd been as free and unhindered as the river itself. Would he ever have those days again?

He's twenty-seven years old, and responsible for two people and for his land. He'd never thought he'd be shackled as he is.

A lantern bobs down the street toward him. A moment later he sees it's Daniel Vane, coming back from the tavern with his daughter. Vane nods toward him; Hattie smiles. Cornelius says "Good night," and watches them go into the lobby, Hattie's skirt switching about her hips. A few minutes later, after he watches one of the steamers cast off, he goes up to his room.

But in the morning as the jurors wait in the courtroom, a door opens and the bailiff, not the judge, comes in. The bailiff is young, but bald as a billiard; some ailment must have cost the man his hair, Cornelius thinks -- Saint Vitus' Dance.

"Judge's got the ague," the bailiff says. "He cain't get up out of his bed today. These trials 're put off for a day. All jurors stay close around, in case he gets better." Then he goes out, latching the door behind him.

Cornelius whiles away the first hours of morning reading an old copy of the New Orleans *True Delta* on the porch. He pulls the bench out from the wall and sits with his back to the sun and the river, his boots propped against the wall. At ten o'clock Hattie Vane comes out onto the porch. Cornelius folds his paper and moves the bench back to where it belongs. Hattie sits down beside him.

"You like what you've seen of the big city so far?" he asks.

"This is a pretty sight," she says, her big hand gesturing toward the open expanse of river. "But I'd *still* like to see Natchez over they-er." Again he catches her back-country drawl.

"Maybe your daddy'll take you. The ferry-boat runs back and forth."

"He won't wanna come up wit' the fare. He's tight."

"You came all the way from Slocum? How far is that?"

"Hit's a all-day trip."

In front of them the river, a chalky gray-brown color, glints in the sunlight.

"You live close around here?" Hattie asks.

"About a dozen miles from here. Bayou Cocodrie."

"I never been they-er neither."

"Who else lives out in Slocum besides you and your daddy?"

"They's others livin' at Slocum, but just us two lives at home now, since my mammy died. You leave your wife at home?"

"My wife died."

"Oh." A flatboat comes down the river; the flatboatmen pole it toward the dock at Silver Street, eager as billy goats for what they'll find in Under-the-Hill, Cornelius knows.

Hattie circles her knees with her hands. "That's a surprise. I thought you looked like you was married. I kin usually tell 'bout that."

"How do you tell?"

She shrugs. "Oh, hit's jus' things I kin see. I know some spells and things, too. My mammy taught 'em to me."

"Do your spells work?"

"Oh, yes sir, they do. My mammy tol' me her spells could cure the sick and keep the bad things away too. She said her spells was the only reason we all got to Slocum safe, when we come down the Trace from Ohio. She said 'em ever' night, to keep the Injuns off. An' they *worked.* 'Course, I don' remember nothin' 'bout comin' down the Trace myself, bein' so young. I was jus' two when we come."

"I came from Georgia myself, a long time ago. Then to New Orleans, then here."

"All by yourself?"

"Yep."

"I don't hardly ever get t' go nowhere by myself," Hattie says, squinting toward Natchez. "I'm the youngest in the fambly, and I got so many sisters 'n' brothers. They always watching what I do."

"How many are there?"

"Thirteen. An' all livin'. Eight sisters and five brothers. My brother Primus Vane lives over by the Black River. You know him?"

Cornelius shakes his head.

"My other brothers are Secondus, Tertius, Quatrus, and Quintus. I don't reckon you'd know them."

"Those are Latin names."

"They prob'ly is. My mammy went to school some."

"Well, what about your sisters? Do they have Latin names too?"

"Oh -- they's Sayra and Mary and Liz'beth and Nancy." She looks at him. When he says nothing she went on, "And then comes Mattie, Toshy, Nett, Lil, and me."

Your mammy ran out of proper names before she got to you, Cornelius thinks.

Hattie stares at him. "You know, you a nice *lookin'* man, Mister Carson," she says in a soft, dreamlike voice.

"Van Buren'll get re-elected in '40, mark my words," says Gilmer Ford in a loud voice as he stands at the edge of a race-track the men set up. Cornelius met his fellow juror only an hour ago, but the man has so much bluster he'll make Whigs of them all, he thinks. They stand a few yards from the riverbank, watching a horse race.

"The Whigs have a chaince," says a man named Riddle as a sorrel defeats a bay mare; both riders whoop and holler as their mounts clatter to the finish.

Under his straw hat, Riddle's face is sunburned and pock-marked. He spits a stream of tobacco-juice on the ground. "I blame Van Buren for the way things is. Seems t' me if the banks hadn't called in their loans, many a good farmer'd still have his land."

"Goddamn Whigs'll ruin the country," Ford sputters as he walks away.

The jurors had passed an hour pitching pennies in the street until someone thought of racing all their horses. So a track was marked off on the riverbank, and the men put wagers on their own horses or anybody else's that looked good. Hattie, flushed and bright-eyed in a pink dress, holds the bets. The men ride their own horses, except for Ford; he has his slave boy do it. The men nicknamed the boy "Light Leonard," for his complexion and his build, and he rode the Opelousas stallion to victory in every race. Cornelius rides Tearose in three races, and she looked pretty good, he thought, coming in second every time to the Opelousas.

Light Leonard has a ready smile, but the ivory-suited Ford's a sour winner, Cornelius notices. He doesn't even congratulate Cornelius on races well run; he just collects his winnings from Hattie without a word. They come to two and a half dollars, because some men came over from Natchez in a skiff to see the races. Later in the afternoon some of the jurors take the ferry over to Natchez. Cornelius curries Tearose and takes her back to the stable.

After sunset Hattie joins him on the hotel's porch. "I still ain't got over t' Natchez," she says, flopping down beside him.

Cornelius chuckles. "Well, I certainly couldn't take you over there. Mister Dan'l probably come after me with a gun if I did something like that."

"He's just got his jaw all stiff about it," Hattie huffs. "He ain't about to give in to me now, 'cause he told me yestiddy I couldn't go over."

Hattie's a pretty girl, even when she pouts. And she has an easy, unpretentious way about her that Cornelius likes; she sits with her knees apart under her pink skirt as she rests her chin in her hand.

"Want to walk down the river a ways?" Cornelius asks. "We might get a better view of Natchez from there."

"Sure."

They pick their way along the strip of bare earth where the river laps. At one place where a stream has washed out their path, they have to jump it, and Hattie puts her hand out for Cornelius; then he holds her hand as they walk. When they reach a place where their path is blocked by a fallen tree, he pulls her to him and kisses her.

The next day the judge is still sick, so Cornelius spends most of the day with Hattie. When they walk along the river that evening, stopping at the swamp, he kisses her again. This time she takes his hand and guides it inside her dress to her breast. She raises her face to the sky as he presses his lips to her open bodice.

"Let's go back to the hotel," she murmurs.

When they get there she surprises him again, leading him around behind the building to the outside stairs. She giggles as they hurry down the hall to his room, where he takes her out of her dress and has her lie naked on the bed while he undresses. He buries his face in her hair which she unbraided for him; it smells sweet. She giggles beneath him, a welcoming, clean-smelling country girl.

When she rolls over and sits up, he feels cold and alone, in spite of the night's sticky heat. He reaches for her again.

"I've got to go 'fore my daddy gets back," she says, pulling on her dress. As she closes the door and goes out into the hall, Cornelius looks around. The room seems empty. He wants to have her back with him, her head on his arm and her blond hair spread on the pillow. For the first time in a long time he feels a yearning for the warmth and closeness of a woman.

The next morning the judge shows up. The little man looks positively malarial, Cornelius thinks, with his sunken eyes and pallid face. But he raps the gavel sharply on the large oak table that serves as his bench. Cornelius is called for the Montegue jury.

Looking at the slick lawyer who speaks for the defense, Cornelius figures the trial's bound to take longer than it needs to. No sooner is the Montegue case called than the lawyer, a dandy in a frock coat, huddles with the judge to settle some legal ins and outs. Half-sick or not, the judge listens patiently to the man's arguments while the jury fidgets in the hot room and the man who Cornelius thinks must be Montegue sits nervously in the back of the courtroom. Hattie is sitting back there too, Cornelius is pleased to see. The corners of her mouth turn up when he catches her eye. *Hattie likes a secret,* Cornelius thinks.

Just before noon, Montegue is put on the stand. "It was self-defense," he says, turning to face the jury as if they would surely see that it was. "That Joseph was a trouble-maker. Never should 'a took him from that trader, I guess. He was always talkin' back, and that day he was worse 'n usual, right there by the side of the wood-shed. And what could I do? Cain't expect a man t' lissen to a slave sassin' 'im."

But the next witness is Montegue's neighbor, a white-haired old man. His voice is a whispery rasp.

"Alton Montegue's been my neighbor for five or six years," he says, "and it's never good to give testimony against a neighbor. But it was my market man that found the body, and found the hammer too, or what was left of it. I understand the handle was broken off, and it was lying in Montegue's trash-pile, half-burned. And I know Alton liked to beat Joseph on the slightest cause.

"Now I know all darkies need discipline, don't mistake me. But I know cruelty when I see it, and I seen it at Montegue's place too often. And Joseph he picked on more 'n the others. I can rightly believe he killed him."

The doctor who saw Joseph's body also took the stand. "I saw broken bones," he says, his voice filling the courtroom. "Joseph's arm was bent like a chicken wing, and he had broken ribs, too. When I pressed on them, the body gave in like a watermelon that's set in the sun too long. He hadn't been dead but an hour."

"That ain't so," Montegue mutters from the back of the room, but the judge bangs the gavel for quiet.

By one o'clock the jury has the case to consider. As they file out to the jury-room, Cornelius hears the judge call for the Bartell jury.

The jury-room is furnished with only a long table and some rough chairs.

"We need a foreman," Riddle says as soon as the men take their seats. "Let's name one and get this over with."

"I'm fer Master Carson," says Daniel Vane. "All in favor?"

Before Cornelius can object, he's been chosen by a chorus of "aye's."

"Let's see where we stand." Cornelius takes a piece of paper and tears it into squares and passes one to each juror. "Write your yea or nay on it. Yea if you think he's guilty."

The first ballot turns up eight guilties, one not guilty, and three blanks.

"We got to do better 'n that," Daniel Vane says.

Gilmer Ford sits at the other end of the long table, facing Cornelius. "Now, I've got slaves," he says. "And I think I can say what happened wasn't Montegue's fault. You get a riled-up black, what you gonna do? Can't let him strike you--"

"Montegue never said there was a threat of that," Cornelius says.

"And you can't let him think he runs the place neither," Ford says, putting his hands flat on the table. "That's why Montegue's innocent. Ain't a one of us had to face what he musta had to face, with that Joseph."

"He used too much force, I'd say," says Riddle. He traces his finger in a circle on the table. "I can't write, so I couldn't mark my guilty, like you said to do, Mister Carson. But I'll vote my guilty out loud. I don't think he had to do that to Joseph. If it was all that bad, he could've brought the sheriff in on it, and let him take the man and lock him up. Could 've even sold him down the river. I say he didn't need to go so far with Joseph."

"Well, only a slaveholder would understand," says Ford, leaning back in his chair and folding his hands over his watch-fob.

Glancing around the table, Cornelius realizes how Ford's miscalculated; all the other men have sullen faces. Ford's made himself a minority of one, but these men will never make him an authority.

The discussion goes on for another hour.

"Well, we've all got to agree, whether we own slaves or not, so let's vote again," Cornelius says. "Those that can't write, put a straight line for guilty, and a cross for not guilty. And we've all gotta agree, or we'll be a hung jury."

"There's been plenty a trials where they should a hung the jury," says Riddle, and the men all laugh.

"Let's not us be one of them," Cornelius says. "Let's vote again."

"Well, there's no disputin' the fact that Joseph's dead," says Riddle.

"Dead, but why, that's the question." This from Daniel Vane.

"Because Montegue used too much force," says Riddle. "He should 've called the sheriff."

"And don't forget, Montegue did try to cover it up," says Vane.

"What'll people think?" Ford asks, scowling.

"They'll think you can't kill somebody? I'll vote to let 'em think that," says Riddle.

"You ain't a abolitionist, is ya?" Ford speaks in a slow sarcastic drawl.

"No, I ain't. But I know wrong's wrong, and dead's dead," Riddle says.

"What happens to Montegue if we convict 'im?" asks a timid man named Wilson, one of those who couldn't write.

"Jail," says Riddle. "But his wife 'll be taken care of. She's got grown sons who can take over. I know somebody who knows the family. It ain't like anybody'd be left destitute from it."

"All right. Let's vote again," Cornelius says.

And so a vote is taken and this time there are eight guilties, written, and three straight lines; and one not guilty.

"We still don't agree," Cornelius says as he spreads the papers in front of him on the table.

"I ain't never gonna say he's guilty," Ford says. He takes out a pocket-knife and whittles a "v" out of the edge of the table.

"Well, it's late," Cornelius says. He thinks of Hattie, who might be waiting at the hotel. "Let's tell the judge we'll try again tomorrow." He goes to the door and signals to the bailiff.

That evening he and Hattie walk so far down the riverbank that the lights of Vidalia are hidden. She puts her head up against his shoulder as they sit on a grassy spit of land and listen to the little slap of the river a few feet in front of them. Cornelius kisses her, his tongue tracing little nibbles on her salty face and down to her strong chin. Then they walk back toward town. When they pass the tavern Cornelius peers through the door and sees Daniel Vane sitting at a table in the crowded, smoky room, a nearly-full glass of whiskey in his hand.

Cornelius takes Hattie to his room again. Again he feels the comfort of having her with him in a strange bed, in a strange hotel room. But she does something new this time, moving her legs over him and then swinging up to sit astride him as he holds her breasts. It's almost midnight when she leaves his room.

The next day the jury reconvenes, the men looking hungover and tired. As soon as the jurors take their places around the table, Cornelius asks for another ballot, but the results are the same as the day before, still eleven to one.

Again the men argue with Ford, who sits at the end of the table whittling first one notch and then another. By midmorning the men have stopped talking. As the hours pass, Ford chips down to raw wood, and the voting stays the same.

Finally Cornelius calls the bailiff, who escorts him into the courtroom.

"We can't reach a verdict," Cornelius says to the judge. "It's been eleven-to-one since yesterday, and I don't think there's any hope of changing the one vote, or the eleven, either."

The judge glares at him. "Go on back and try again. I ain't acceptin' a hung jury."

"Yes sir." Cornelius goes back to face the sullen jurors.

All that afternoon the deadlock holds. The men are angry at Ford, glaring at him whenever he looks up at them; but most of the time he ignores them. The chips fly from the table.

But late in the afternoon, Riddle slaps his hands on his legs and turns to Cornelius. "We're hung, and we can't be un-hung, no matter what the judge says, Mister Carson. I believe you'll have to go tell him so."

"Any reason to ballot again?" Cornelius asks. But he can tell by the men's faces that there's not. Ford beams.

The judge, angry, has no choice but to let them go.

It's getting dark when Cornelius gets back to the hotel. Daniel Vane won't be leaving tonight, Cornelius thinks; it's a long way to Slocum. And Vane's a pretty good talker, the sort of man who never meets a stranger. He'll want to hash and rehash the Montegue case at the tavern.

And there'll be plenty to say about the other case, too. The other jury found Bartell guilty after only a few minutes' deliberation. He got seven years, the value of a horse being greater than the value of a black man, Cornelius thinks; even if they'd convicted Montegue, he probably would've served just a few months in jail. But Cornelius has other things on his mind.

Hattie stays past midnight in Cornelius's room. This time, he takes her the way he wants to, tasting the slightly salty sweat of her arms and breasts, burying his face in her hair. He feels free with her, this woman he'll never see again; he takes her with an abandon he hasn't known in years. She tires before he did, lying sweating and panting under him, but still willing, when he mounts her yet again.

In the morning she leaves with her father, her face red and her eyes brimming as she says a prim goodbye to Cornelius. Cornelius promises to write to her, and he waves goodbye as the buggy disappears down the road.

In the settlement Cornelius stops at the store and buys the three yards of muslin that Jenny wants, and a piece of horehound candy. As he rides toward his cabin, he sees Alice Turley watering her horse at the stream. Cornelius rides up beside her, hoping she's changed her mind about Wonderful, although it seems unlikely.

"Mister Carson, I've come to buy your land," Alice says abruptly as he rides up.

"It's not for sale," he says just as quickly, turning his horse away.

"Oh, of course it is. Everything is, for a price. And I've got the right price."

"Listen, it's not."

"Well, I own all the land over that way. Randall sold all his arpents to me last week, so that only leaves this little place, and then I'll own all this stretch down to the bayou. So let's make a price that suits us both."

"I'm not selling," Cornelius says. But the thought begins to dart at him, like a bee.

Alice catches the change in his tone. "Well, it's not easy to make a living with the arpents you've got. I know that from my own experience. When you have enough land, you can get by, even with cotton prices falling like they've been. But it's hard to make money on cotton without enough land."

"Yes, ma'am."

"I'll take your arpents for five dollars each," she says. "That'll include your buildings there, and your cabin. I can use it for a cotton-house. And I need another house-girl. Your girl Jenny --"

"She's not for sale."

"Well, think about it. Now Malachi, I couldn't take him. I've got too many old ones to take care of already. But your girl --"

"No, ma'am."

"You sleep on it. Any deal's better on a full stomach and a full night's sleep, I always say. If you decide it's worth it to sell out while the price is high, the offer's good through the weekend. A bird in a hand and all that. You might decide it's a good offer. " She rides away.

That night he makes a fire; a chill's come in. He sits in front of the fire, thinking over the past week. Jenny sits on the rocking chair nearby, her sewing in her lap. She's abandoned her room for once, maybe because it's cold and she likes the fire, or maybe because she's pleased with the muslin and the candy. Malachi's already gone down to the little house to sleep.

Alice put an idea in Cornelius's head, and it hums there now. Sell his land? His one hundred arpents, now mostly cleared, have to be worth more than when he bought them five years ago. He's built a cabin and the little house, a privy and stable and shed. Fenced his fields. And last summer he planted eighty arpents. And Alice offered five dollars an arpent.

Something else is calling him. During the days he spent in Vidalia, he saw the freewheeling life of the river, and it called him back. The boilermen's life, their freedom to carouse and drink and think about life along the passing shore, their only responsibilities the sizzling boiler and the big smokestack -- he feels a strong pull back to that life. He's tried farming; it rewards him at the end of every season, when he takes his cotton to the ginhouse. Then, good money passes into his hands. But the cotton takes so much work.

And he feels a pull to Hattie Vane, but not so much for herself, that country woman who welcomed him in his own bed; any woman would do. That comfort was easy enough to find on the river.

He's not inclined to write Hattie a letter.

From time to time Cornelius stretches his legs and looks over at Jenny. Her head is down and she frowns as she works at her sewing. She's making an apron, and she's already measured and hemmed it, and now she's sewing on a pocket. It's interesting to watch how she holds the white fabric up before her face now and then, studying what she's done so far, and then continues with her quick little stitches.

There's a stillness about Jenny, a quality she's always had. Sometimes in the morning, before they go to the field, she waits in the yard; and she's like a statue, unmoving, one foot in front of the other. She has that quietness about her when she sews, too. She was unhappy when she first came here; he sensed it. But over the past few weeks she's gotten used to being here. And he'd gotten used to having her here. He likes buying her the candy she likes and the fabric she wants, and she's become the steady person he remembered. Something of her calm has rubbed off on him, he thinks.

After a while he says, "Better put your sewing down, Jenny. It's late."

"I need to take just a few more stitches, sir." She throws him a sidelong glance, and he shrugs. She finishes the pocket and then bends over to bite off the thread. After she folds the garment in her sewing bag, she hops up. "Goodnight, sir."

Jenny never seems to fear walking off alone into the dark, but he follows her to the door and holds up the lantern for her anyway. He admires her courage; he's seen glimpses of it on more than one occasion.

She hesitates on the step, and he sees that it's pelting rain. Then she runs toward the little house on tiptoe.

Jenny, now. He'd never sell her to Alice Turley; he feels too keenly how he hadn't saved Lafayette at that place. And even though Jake Turley's dead, Alice is a stern taskmistress; he's seen how she swears and shouts at her workers, and he wouldn't want that for Jenny. He can't imagine handing her over to Louis Ferison's hard-edged supervision.

Malachi's old, and he can't be sold; if he was, he'd likely be mistreated and overworked. He's always been a slave, and old as he is, he's probably found his last master, in Cornelius.

But Jenny has her long life ahead of her, and she deserves something else. She really doesn't have to be a slave. If Cornelius wants to be free to go back to the river, Jenny can -- what? But it's only a half-formed thought, and goes to no conclusion.

Three months later, a letter comes for Cornelius; he's surprised and glad when he gets it at the hotel. But when he opens it, he sees that it's a sad crumpled letter, hard to make out, but with a startling message. As he reads it he almost drops it on the sidewalk, and the first thing he does when he gets back to his cabin is feed it to the fire. Even though neither Mal nor Jenny can read, he wouldn't want it lying about. And he has some thinking to do.

Whatever his situation up until now, he has something new to consider, with this letter from Hattie Vane.

"Im in a fambly way," she wrote in an awkward hand. He hadn't thought to wonder, when he was with her, if she could write. But her father couldn't; he remembered that from the polling in the jury room. "And there's no dout hit is yourn, since you the only one I been with." The paper is speckled, as if it's been rained on. Still, the message is clear enough.

"The only one I been with" -- well, that's possible enough, although he didn't notice any bashfulness when he had her in the hotel in Vidalia. If she led the backwoods life he supposed, she might not have been around many men.

Still, this is something to contemplate. He knows his duty; if the babe's his, so be it. He could run; men were known to head to Texas over this kind of news, but that didn't feel right. And it's not something he can do, anyway: to leave his land, to abandon his two people. No, that's not something he could do.

He'll go to Slocum, he decides. Meet with Hattie, and with Daniel Vane. See what the situation is. That's the only thing to do. He leaves the next morning, after he tells Malachi and Jenny to start hoeing the fields.

All his daughters married off early and pretty well, Daniel Vane thinks as he stands on the step in front of his cabin and watches Cornelius Carson driving away with Hattie. She got herself in trouble, but she wasn't the first of his girls to do it; and he knows the cure. That's why Carson came here, and why they had a quick "I do" before a Baptist circuit-riding preacher.

Carson looks more promising than the men his other daughters married. Daniel hadn't had to get the shotgun or the sheriff to get Hattie wed. Carson came in decently, unthreatened, and he gave a sensible account of himself. He owned a house set close to a bayou, a couple slaves to help with the work, and a hundred arpents in cotton. He won't be a bad husband for a big-featured woman with a short temper and a head full of back-country superstitions.

It's Daniel's last child that was leaving, and the most spoiled. It's a shame Flory can't be here to see it, he thinks. Her marker's a wooden cross in the Slocum cemetery. But knowing how Flory always loved to dwell on the bygone days, Daniel takes a moment to reflect on Hattie's marriage; it's plainly the end of something in his life. He's been in Slocum more than fifteen years, and the cabin he built is starting to sag to one side, now. Maybe it's time to sell out and move on.

Watching the buggy as it rolls around the blackberry bramble that marks the boundary of his land, Daniel remembers how little Hattie, the baby, came down the Trace sitting atop a mattress on the wagon while he and Flory and the older children kept a sharp eye on the woods, looking out for murderous Indians and robbers. Later, Flory would swear she didn't sleep at all during the whole two months they'd travelled, she was so afraid.

Over the years she told all the children about the spells and superstitions that kept them safe on that long journey. Daniel didn't hold with superstitions, but he couldn't fault Flory for hanging on to them. So many dangers lurked for ordinary folk like them, who came from Ohio to the Southwest in search of something better than what they had, and who ended up pretty much the way they were before, hardscrabble farmers but in a place where the winters were warm.

CHAPTER THIRTY-FIVE

On a scorching day in July, 1839, Jenny and Malachi chop their way down a row of cotton. Heat shimmers in the air around them.

"You ever goin' to learn to stay out of that woman's way?" Malachi asks.

Jenny straightens up and puts her hand to her back, which burns as if a fire has been set in her muscles. She pulls the bandanna from her head and wipes perspiration off her glistening face. Malachi stands up, too, and together they look toward an oak tree at the edge of the field. Its cool green shade beckons.

"Out of Hattie's way? I do stay 'way from that crazy woman, if you notice."

"I notice you a nettle to her most ever' day. She whackt you again yesterday, didn't she, at the smokehouse?"

Jenny pulls up her sleeve and touches her arm lightly. "This whole arm's sore from it. She come after me 'cause she thought I was dawdlin'. And I wasn't."

"Why don't Master Cornelius stop her from hittin'?"

"'Cause he don't know she does it, that's why. She never does it when he's around." She purses her lips as she looks at the horizon. In the wide field it looks as though they're in a bowl of trees; the woods in every direction are a low green rim around the blue sky. "She's a thief, too. I had a necklace I got in Ferriday; the innkeeper's wife gave it to me after I told her it was pretty. And I kept it on the shelf by my bed. And yesterday I come in from the fields and it was gone." She begins to hoe again, grim-faced.

"Where you think it be?"

"I bet if I looked in Hattie's dresser, I'd find it."

Malachi begins, "You got t' understand --"

"Don't tell me what I got t' understand!" Jenny hacks at the brown earth. "She's a thief, that's all."

Malachi always wants to say it, the cause of their misery. But she understands the old man only spoke to brand a woman like Hattie, who steals things and hits people.

"Did I ever tell you," Mal says, working slowly, "about a place I used to be at, up in Alabama?"

"Yes, you told me."

But Malachi goes on, "The ole master up there, he had this big horn, and every night at nine o'clock he blow the horn, and we all supposed to be in our own cabin when that horn blow. 'Cause he'd send the overseer by to check up on us. But he had this boy, young Master Edwin, and Edwin, he was a mess. The death of his ole mammy, I do believe. And some nights Edwin decide to blow that horn just like his daddy, and it mightn't even be dark yet. So he blow and he blow, and we all had to go to our own cabin. Law. They some sad faces those nights, Lula and me sittin' in our cabin big as anything, and the sun warn't hardly down."

Jenny continues working. She tries to picture a much younger Malachi, with a wife. It's hard to see how he ever was young.

And Malachi always has his speeches ready, and always about slavery.

"If your skin's black," he'd say, "you a slave and that's it." She could see that he was saying it as much to himself as to her. It bothers him that he's a slave. His mind won't turn it loose. He even wanted to run away from Master Cornelius one time. He never talks about the day when his one chance passed him by, when he went to the bayou with his satchel and waited for a pirogue that never came. A little bolt of guilt flashes in Jenny's mind, but she hacks at the weeds harder, and brushes it away.

Even a person who's always been a slave wants to run away. Malachi does, and Israel did too.

For herself, she knows she didn't start out as a slave; she just got caught in its net, somehow, and that makes her different from Malachi and Esther and everybody else. But she's saving her money; it's hidden in a place Hattie'll never find it. Someday she'll talk to Master Cornelius about buying her freedom. She's still trying to decide when and how to bring it up.

She says, "Go rest. I'll tell Master Cornelius you over by the tree. This sun's too hot for you."

"You can't chop this cotton by yourself, girl. Lord, these rows are long." He looks down the row behind them. "I never would've figured Master Cornelius for a coward. If you ask me, he's plumb scared of that woman he's married to."

"If he's got good sense he'll stay scared of her. Here he come now. You go on and rest. I'll finish this row."

Malachi hesitates for a moment, then walks toward the tree, tamping his hoe down the row like a cane. Jenny notices how his shoulders are stooped now and how he throws his legs out stiffly with each step. In the shade, a water jug waits.

From the end of the garden, Hattie hears the thin wail of her son in the cabin, but she ignores it. She's come out here to pick vegetables, and she means to do just that. A half-dozen blood-red tomatoes are already cradled in her apron. As she walks over to where she left her basket, she spies two watermelons she didn't notice earlier, hiding under a tangle of leaves in the next row. Holding her apron to one side, she stoops over to thump each melon hard. The deep hollow sounds tell her they're ripe enough.

She straightens up and looks out to the field, where Cornelius is walking along a cotton row toward Jenny. Hattie watches as they talk for a moment and then begin the rhythmic motions of chopping the cotton, their hoes swinging almost in unison. The slave-girl has a strong, high-shouldered build, but she looks dainty from this distance next to Cornelius.

Malachi's not with them. He's resting, no doubt, as he does so often these days, an old man whiling away his hours in the shade while the rest of them work. Hattie fumes.

All year she's watched that slave girl, and the old man too. They're useless, both of them. Before she came here she dreamed of what it would be like to have someone wait on her, but Jenny's nothing like what she pictured. The slave girl turned out to be almost her own age, which was a startle, and the blackest thing she ever saw. And Jenny'd been with Cornelius a long time; Hattie can see how comfortable he is with her.

While Jenny secretly glories in her fit young body -- Hattie can see it in the way the girl walks, her skirts switching about her high hips -- Hattie had to lumber through a miserable pregnancy followed by a two-days' labor, and then had to face taking care of the red-haired boy she delivered the last day of January.

She can't stand to have Jenny in the cabin. The black girl's not humble at all, and Hattie's not about to let her rise so high as to be a house-girl. When Thomas was born, Jenny brought him two gowns she sewed, and Hattie took them even though she didn't really want to. And even as fast as the boy grows, and as many clothes as he wets, she won't put him in the gowns Jenny made.

And then having to cook for Malachi and Jenny: that's another insult. At least she sees to it that they never share the table even if it's raining. The two slaves eat outside and if it rains they take their plates to the little house.

Hattie wants to sleep all morning and have an easy life like she had when her mother was living. Sometimes when she's dog-tired she sits at the table and nurses the baby; and closing her eyes she can see Flory's wide form standing at the fire at home in Slocum, stirring something good to eat. It's not fair that her mother died when she was only fourteen, and then hardly any time after that, she got this squalling babe. And no one warned her off it.

She'll never have another one, she's decided. Most nights she sleeps with her back to Cornelius, and when he touches her she refuses him. The price of that old passion's too high; a woman knows what can come of it. Cornelius brought her to this new life; she never in her wildest dreams thought she'd have to work so hard, dawn to dusk, and then have to coddle a fretful young'un all night. So Cornelius can just wait, she's decided, until after he visits the apothecary in Vidalia, to get something so there won't be more babies. He says he'll go there, but he ain't made the trip yet.

Hattie sees how Cornelius is with Jenny. Always favoring her, taking up for her. Who could say he's not dipping his wick there, too?

Inside the cabin, Thomas is working himself up to a full scream. Hattie walks back to the porch with the basket. Malachi can bring up the melons later. She'll see about the baby, but let him squall for a few minutes. It'll clear out his lungs. Meantime she wants to take a look at Jenny's room. She knows the girl earned two dimes last week for sewing a pinaforc for Margaret McKee's granddaughter. If Hattie looks, she'll find 'em. And see what else Jenny might have in there, too.

As she walks out of the little house a few minutes later, she hears someone coming. Adelaide Halloran is riding her horse up the road. Hattie smiles and waves.

In the afternoon Cornelius sits with Hattie in the yard while she knits stockings. She works fast, her needles a blur. Two coins weight her apron pocket.

"How do I know she ain't hexed the baby?" Hattie asks Cornelius. "They can do that, you know -- hex the baby, and then it comes out wrong."

Cornelius stares at his wife. "Jenny ain't hexed the baby, for hell's sake. You can think of the craziest things."

"Well, I've heard of it before. Adelaide told me about it. In Rapides Settlement there was a woman whose slave-girl hexed her, and her babe was born with the cord 'round its neck, and when it was born it was holding a devil's foot in its hand, and hit died."

Of course, Cornelius thinks, the tale comes from Adelaide Halloran, and of course Hattie swallows it whole. Too many times he's come up from the fields to find Adelaide gossiping on the porch, and Hattie hanging on every word.

"Nobody can hex another person," he says.

"I think Jenny could."

"Well, I've had her for six years, and she hasn't hexed anyone that I've noticed."

Hattie's needles clack. "Maybe she hexed Stephanie, and that's why she died."

"That wasn't Jenny's doing."

"How kin you be sure?"

Cornelius swears under this breath. "Hattie -- "

"Well, she did die, didn't she?"

"Lots of folks died in that storm. Hell, it wrecked the whole delta."

"I didn't like Jenny from the first day I come here. She's surly, that girl is. I kin tell what she's thinkin'."

Cornelius has heard Hattie's views on Jenny too many times. This war started the day Hattie got here.

Thomas wails. Hattie drops her knitting onto her lap. "A baby that cries all the time," she mutters, "has got somethin' wrong with it. Some hex is put on it."

"You could get Jenny to help with him."

Hattie tosses the knitting aside. "I just as soon keep her 'way from him, if you don't mind."

"I don't mind. I need her in the field."

"I want you to sell 'er. Take the money and buy a girl I kin stand to have around me. Some gal who can he'p me in the house and take Thomas off'n my hands." She gets up and stalks toward the cabin, then stops as she reaches the steps. "Prices of slaves been goin' up, you know. A strong girl like Jenny'd bring a good price in New Orleans." She pauses a moment longer for his answer. He says nothing, so she goes into the cabin and closes the door.

Cornelius stares at the cabin. Hattie's hard attitude toward Jenny is a turn he hadn't expected. He has to resolve it, but how, he doesn't know, exactly.

A moment later Hattie comes back out onto the porch, holding Thomas and swaying to quiet the infant. "Adelaide says --"

Cornelius curses and stands up.

"Adelaide told me --" Hattie raises her voice, over the baby's cry, "-- that a strong girl can bring eight hundred dollars in New Orleans. She says Alice Turley got that much for one of her girls. Lucinda, it was."

"What?" Cornelius asks. Alice sold Lucinda?

"Adelaide says Alice is sellin' every hand she has that can't do field-work."

Cornelius turns quickly and walks toward the cotton field. If Lucinda was sold -- and he has no reason to doubt that it's so -- what does that mean to Wonderful? And did Alice sell the baby, too? Wonderful's pride, that baby was. Cornelius feels sick. This is what slavery always comes to, he thinks. Sooner or later it poisons everything.

But he'll never sell Malachi or Jenny. That's an old resolve he made going back to the time when it was just him and Jenny and Malachi on the place. Malachi was an old man, getting weaker by the month, and Jenny a young coltish girl. He can't turn either one of them out into the dangerous world.

For the rest of the day, he works alongside the slaves in the fields. At evening they come back up to the yard and sit on the ground under the oak tree at the far side of the yard. Jenny brings a bucket of water from the well, and they pass around the gourd-dipper and pour big draughts of the cool water into their mouths, letting it run out and down their necks, cooling them inside their clothes. Malachi pours the water over his head. Drops sparkle on his gray hair.

They pull their legs up under them, resting their arms on their knees. When Cornelius looks across the yard, he sees Hattie standing on the porch with the baby, watching them.

He looks over at Jenny. Perspiration glistens on her smooth face, and she looks tired.

I'll never sell you, Jenny, Cornelius thinks, studying her profile. *But something's got to change.*

She closes her eyes and puts her palm flat against her forehead.

I'll take you back to Esther, at Carefree. And Hattie can think I've sold you. When the idea comes to him he leans back against the tree-trunk and grins.

The next evening as they clean some fish Jenny stumbles against a barrel of brine that Hattie wants to soak the fish in. The brine splatters across the floor. Hattie leaps up from the table and slaps Jenny hard, across the face.

Cornelius crosses the cabin in two steps and seizes Hattie's wrist. Hattie shakes her arm free and glares at him. Thomas begins to scream.

"You get her out of here," Hattie hisses. But Jenny, crying, has already run to the little house.

"Take her next Friday," Hattie says in a low voice as she sits with Cornelius the next evening in the cabin. Leopard slouches with his head flat on the floor next to Thomas, who lies on a blanket flailing his arms and legs.

Cornelius sips his whiskey and watches as Thomas begins to work himself up into a scream. "Why next Friday?"

"'Cause we need the money and we need it quick. The sooner the better. And the poster I seen in the settlement says there's a auction at the slave house that evenin'. You kin get a good price for Jenny and Malachi -- "

"I won't sell Malachi. He's too old."

"Well, he can't hardly do any work."

"That's true, he can't."

"An' if we buy another one with the money from Jenny, he's jus' a extry mouth to feed."

"I realize that."

"He still has to be fed."

"Yes."

Hattie scoops Thomas up roughly and unbuttons her dress, pressing her nipple into the baby's mouth. Cornelius looks at her swollen white breast for a moment, then looks away. He scrapes his chair back and stands up.

"I said I'd take Jenny. That's all I'm doing." He snaps his fingers for the dog and leaves the fuming woman alone with the baby.

The next day, as a storm threatens, Hattie goes out to the stable looking for a place to put the baby's outgrown clothes. Thomas is growing so, he has a pile of gowns that don't fit him, and the bureau drawers are full of his diapers and blankets. She thinks that out in the stable there might be a bin or chest she could use. In one corner of a slat-sided stall, she sees a round-topped trunk, its metal top half-rusted. She pulls the pin from the hasp and raises the top.

When Cornelius returns to the cabin a few minutes later, his work-day cut short by lightning and churning clouds, he's startled to see Stephanie's dresses piled in a heap on the table.

"What are these?" Hattie asks.

He stands just inside the door and looks at the pile of clothes. "They were Stephanie's."

Hattie picks up an aqua-colored dress with rosettes sewn into the folds of the skirt. As she bends over, her flax-colored hair falls into her eyes, and she brushes it back. She never braids her hair anymore, he's noticed, just brushes it quickly of a morning and then pushes it back from her face the rest of the day.

Her big fingers handle the fabric gingerly. "Well, I never seen anything like these." She turns the fabric inside out to study the construction, picking at the tiny stitches that hold each rosette in place. "I could'a been wearin' these frocks."

"They won't fit you. She wasn't as -- tall as you." Hattie holds up a black crepe, the dress Stephanie wore when she drowned. Jenny had washed it after Emile took Stephanie's body back to Natchez, and when Cornelius returned alone to the Cocodrie he put it in the trunk with the others.

"This is the prettiest stuff I ever seen," she says. "Look at this crepe. I bet this is silk, or somepin'. I should'a been wearin' this."

"It won't fit, I told you," he says, not looking. He stares at the cold fireplace. "You're taller."

"I kin make Jenny let the hem down for me." Hattie paws through the pile. "And there's petticoats, too, and nightgowns." She picks up a tortoise-shell comb and pushes it into her tangled hair.

Cornelius walks over to the table and puts his hand on the pile of clothes. "Why don't you give Jenny one of these dresses? I'm taking her to Natchez on Friday. She needs a good dress to wear."

He sees that Hattie instantly understands; a girl in a proper dress will make a better appearance at the market, will bring a higher price.

"She kin have this one," Hattie says, reaching to the bottom of the pile and bringing out a wrinkled yellow frock with a pink ribbon looped around the waist. She hands it to Cornelius.

Thunder growls across the sky. Jenny, sitting on the side of her bed, her head down as she works at her sewing, looks up through her open door. Cornelius is coming toward the cabin.

"Jenny," he calls.

She puts her sewing down and walks to the door. Cornelius stands next to the wisteria swing. "Listen," he says in a low voice, ignoring Malachi, who comes out of his own room to hear. "I'm taking you back to Carefree on Friday. You can stay with Esther from now on. Emile Coqterre's gone crazy, but you can stay out of his way. Don't say anything about it to Miss Hattie, all right? She thinks I'm taking you to -- someplace else." He hands her the yellow dress. "Here's a dress for you to wear when we go. And get all your things packed Thursday night. We'll leave early Friday morning."

She runs her hand across the wrinkled fabric. "I'm leaving?"

"Yes."

"Is Malachi goin' too?"

"No, he'll stay. But with you here -- and Miss Hattie -- well, all this trouble has to stop."

"It ain't my doin', sir."

He raises his hand in exasperation and turns away.

As he walks toward the cabin, Jenny looks over at Malachi. She holds up the dress.

"Slave girl gettin' moved around again, Mal," she says in a low voice. Then she goes into her room and kneels by the side of her bed and raises the mattress an inch. She touches a cloth bag. At least her money's safe.

"I had a dream last night," Jenny says the next day as she and Cornelius hoe the cotton. They move their hoes together, one row apart. She wears her old green dress, a sunbonnet shading her face. "I dreamt I was on a river, but I didn't know which river it was. It warn't the Bayou Cocodrie, though, I know that for sure."

"Maybe it was the muddy Mississippi."

"No sir, it wasn't that one either. I don't know where it was. But my brother Kofi was with me. And it seem like we was playin', 'cause we was on the ground, and scrapin' up the dirt with little sticks. Makin' a town, like. I could see it clear as anything. Even the way the sun was shinin' through the leaves."

"Sometimes I have a dream," Cornelius says. "Usually I can't remember it in the morning."

"No sir."

A few yards away Malachi sits in the shade watching them work. The water jug rests at his knees.

Jenny goes on, "I wonder if I'll ever see Kofi again. I used to think I'd see him just any time -- maybe he'd be in Natchez, I'd think, and he'd come up to Carefree, or maybe he'd be passin' through the settlement, and he'd come in the store when I was there -- but now I don't know."

"I hope you do see him someday."

"He's off in slavery somewheres. He could be 'round Natchez, I guess, but it ain't likely."

"I expect not." He whacks at the ground. Then he straightens and taps his hoe on the ground.

"Jenny, I wish you could stay here."

That afternoon Amos and Margaret McKee pay a visit; Cornelius is always glad when they visit, and lately Margaret's taken an interest in Hattie. This is the third time this month she's come over with cobblers and cakes and motherly advice about the baby. And today Thomas is quiet, asleep in the middle of the bed. The women are talking inside the cabin while the men sit on the steps.

But then Amos tells Cornelius his news.

"They found him run off yesterday mornin'," Amos says. "So Louis Ferison and some other men went after him. They found him in the woods, clear over by the river. He'd got that far. And Ferison said Wonderful had a gun, and that's why he shot him."

Cornelius stands up, shocked. "I can't believe Wonderful's dead."

"It don't seem like --" Amos says, then looks over at the pump where Malachi is drawing some water. He lowers his voice. "Well, it seems to me Alice Turley ain't had the best o' luck over at her place. First, what with Jake and all. And then this trouble with Wonderful. And now Ferison says he's leavin', and I don't know what she'll do the rest of the season. She'll have to find herself a overseer quick as anything, I reckon. She could use Lathan for a driver. He'd do about as good a job as anybody she could hire."

Cornelius walks a little distance away and stands next to the buggy, looking toward the woods behind the little house. "Wonderful probably ran off to look for his wife and baby," he says without looking back at Amos. "Alice sold them."

"I didn't know that. Now, I wish Alice wouldn't a done that. Darkies set such a store by family. Now me, I even made a special trip to Woodville to buy my Cassie's husband back for her. She kept after me so 'til I did it. And really, they work better if they together with they family."

Cornelius nods, remembering Wonderful.

"Out of all this, the way I see it, the tradin's the bad part," Amos says. "Slave mongerin'. Otherwise, it's the best for both races. But a master has a obligation to keep the slaves he's got, long as he can. Now *you've* still got the same two you had years ago."

"Jenny and Malachi."

"Ain't it hard to work all this cotton with just two hands?"

"It ain't easy."

"But you ain't bought any more, since you got Jenny."

"No." Cornelius looks out at his fields. "Amos, if I had it to do over again, I'd never own a single one," he says as Margaret comes out of the cabin with Hattie, her arm around the young wife.

CHAPTER THIRTY-SIX

In the early morning Cornelius goes out to the stable, his lantern light swallowed by a light fog that hangs over the grass and curls around the trees. He can see red streaks across the sky in the east; the fog should lift early.

As he steps into the stable, he hears little movements. Mice are running in the corners; all the cats have wandered off somewhere else. Even Jenny's tomcat disappeared one day to some neighbor's place where the milk was creamier. The stable smells of old hay, a fragrance made sweeter by the morning dampness.

Cornelius never intended to make a secret of the place where he keeps his money; Hattie has a right to whatever's his, and she knows that last year's cotton profits are sitting in the Bank of Vidalia right now. But she hasn't yet come upon the strongbox he keeps on a shelf, right here in plain view in the stable. There's a leather bag inside with eleven hundred dollars in gold coins. He doesn't consider it his money alone, but it's the profit from when Stephanie lived here, when he still distrusted banks, and Hattie knows nothing about it.

Loosening the drawstring, he counts out eighty coins which he drops into a smaller pouch. Then he tucks the pouch into his saddlebag and buckles the flap.

This money will be what he gets for Jenny, as far as Hattie knows. When he gets back from Natchez he'll show her these coins and carry out this little deceit.

As he walks back to the porch, he sees Jenny standing on the steps with Hattie.

"I finally got Thomas back to sleep, and here she come disturbin' me," Hattie says. "She says Malachi's sick."

"Mal's sick? I'll go see about him." Cornelius turns to walk toward the little house.

"He got the yella jack," Jenny says.

"How do you know?" Hattie says. "You ain't no doctor, can't diagnose nobody."

"His eyes are turnin' yella, Miss Hattie. He been sick the whole night. You got some soup or somethin' he could have?"

Hattie runs her hand through her hair. "I'll see what I got. Come back after 'while. And you be quiet and don't wake that baby."

"Yessum." Jenny runs to catch up with Cornelius. "Can you go for the doctor?"

"Not today. We're going to Natchez."

"We need to put that off a day 'til Mal's better."

"Oh no, you ain't," Hattie calls from the porch. "You goin' this very day."

Jenny scowls.

"Now, what is the matter, Mal?" Cornelius asks as he steps into the dark little room. Mal lies in bed with the quilt pulled up under his chin. The old man's face is wet with sweat.

"Sir, I got it, I'm afeared."

"Got what?"

"Bronze John. He must 'a come round and touched me in the night when I wasn't lookin'." His breath comes in fast deep rales.

"Yellow Jack?"

"Hisself." He shivers. "I'm cold."

Cornelius goes to the fireplace and stirs the fire.

"Can't we get the doctor?" Jenny asks.

"Not today. I'll go for the doctor tomorrow if he's not better."

"Why can't we put off this travelin' to Natchez for one day?"

"Well -- we can't, that's all. Get ready to go."

Cornelius gets the fire burning well, then helps Malachi sit up so he can drink some water from a cup. When he goes outside a few minutes later Jenny is standing by the wisteria swing.

"He'll be all right," Cornelius says. "I'll get Miss Hattie to come down and check on him during the day."

"Yessir." Jenny folds her arms and looks at the ground.

Emile turns Peg south, away from Natchez, trotting the horse down the dusty street. His black suit feels too hot on this warm day. In this part of town the streets are lined with shotgun cottages and noisy children play in the streets. But at the end of the street a foot-path trails right over to the edge of the bluff.

A broken slingshot and a mound of pebbles lie on the path at the edge of the bluff. Some bad boy must've hidden here, to pelt the travelers below. And over there, the grass is pressed flat. Secret lovers must've lain here on some starry night.

Below him, Silver Street curves down to the river.

From here he has a panorama of sky and the green swamps of Louisiana stretching to the west, and the river itself. For a week now he's been studying that curling mysterious surface, and it's beginning to beckon, so far below.

From the bluff, he notices details of the river he's not seen before: how it's made of some milky mixture, neither gray nor brown exactly; and how it seems to swell in its own channel, the swirls and threads of its surface probing this way and that, cut up by the wakes of steamers and flatboats. The solid-looking surface intrigues him; what's its bottom like, or its slick sloping sides?

A horse like Peg could never make the jump, but he could go for it himself. If Stephanie and Josephine and Sophronia have all gone away, he can go too. Stephanie he's not sure of, though. Hers was the only body he didn't see. The coffinmaker sealed up the coffin when he was upstairs at Carefree, and when he came downstairs, there it was, nailed shut. Who knows if she was really in there?

From this high point over the river a man can almost think himself a bird, and fly through the air. Float like a hawk on wide-spread wings, and overshoot Under-the-Hill, and land on the river.

Be a bird, and then a fish. Anything.

A buggy driven by a man in a frock coat rolls up Silver Street. On the seat beside him is a black girl in a yellow dress.

Emile dismounts. He suddenly recognizes that dress, pink ribbon and all; he's seen that before. And the girl, black as ink: he knows her.

He leaves Peg tied to a tree and creeps along the bluff to a big cedar bush, where he crouches to get a good look. Yes, that's Stephanie's dress. And way too fine a dress for a black girl. And that man, too; Emile knows him.

He's always suspected Stephanie's alive, somewhere across the river. And here below him, coming up from Under-the-Hill, is her girl, wearing her yellow dress.

Emile is so lonely now; he hasn't seen Stephanie for so long. But he can ride over to Louisiana and find her. Surely she'll welcome her old Papa; surely she'll be glad to see him.

And he won't have to be bird or a fish. Not today.

Jenny sulks the whole long trip, her arms folded across her lap forming a dark "x" on the butter-yellow skirt.

As they drive up Silver Street, Cornelius asks, "Have you thought about what it'll be like, working at Carefree again? Esther's getting old. You'll probably have to work harder now than you did before."

"I know hard work, sir."

"Master Emile might have opinions about how things have to be."

Jenny holds up her hand, her fingers spread. "Sir, if I can please him, I please him. If not, well—" She shrugs. "I have noticed that some people ain't pleased with anything for too long."

That used to be true for this man, Cornelius thinks. But his ambitions have shrunk in the years since Stephanie died.

Later, as they drive up the road toward Carefree, he asks, "Have you thought about what you'll say to Master Emile? He might have some questions for you. You're not just some little old kid hanging around like when you were here before."

She looks at him. "What kinds of questions, sir? Master Emile probably won't talk to me at all. He probably won't even know I'm there."

"Well, he might notice. You're a lot older now. What if he wants to know how old you are? You have an answer for him?"

"He wouldn't care about that."'

"He might. You can never tell with a Frenchman. They're a peculiar breed."

A slow smile comes over her face. She puts her hands up to cover her mouth. "I don't know how old I am," she says, laughing and leaning away from him.

"Better take a guess." He grins and clicks the reins harder, pleased that he's brought her out of her gloom. They're both hiccupping laughter as they drive up the hill to Carefree.

He drives around the back to the slave house, but the place looks deserted.

"Where would everyone be?" Cornelius asks.

They walk around to the front of the house. The place looks abandoned, with shutters hanging half off their hinges and empty flowerpots scattered across the gallery.

No one answers his knock. He nudges the door open. The house is silent.

"I guess we're trespassers, Jenny," Cornelius says. "Hello? Anyone home?"

His words echo hollowly. Even the hall-clock is still. The silver string of a cobweb, lit by the gleam from the open door, swings from the chandelier.

Cornelius walks down the hall and looks into each dark room. In the parlor the velvet curtains are pulled across the windows, but even in the darkness Cornelius can see that the curtains are shredded across the bottom. And the sofa where he and Stephanie used to sit has gone ragged; its stuffing is partly pulled out.

He stands, puzzled, in the hall. Hadn't this place once been full of life? It smells of death, now.

He hears a sudden noise upstairs, and the low grate of hinges opening. He walks to the foot of the stairs. "Hello?" he calls again.

A goat trots down the stairs, the stuffing of a horsehair mattress hanging from its bearded mouth.

"All this trouble started right after Miss Sophronia died, sir," Esther says. They'd found her in the kitchen, the only person on the place. She's sitting in frail dignity on a spindly chair beside the table, her hands clasped together in her lap.

"Sophronia died?"

"Yes sir. She been dead 'bout half a year now. I went in to see about her one mornin', and there she was dead, layin' on her bed. Drinked herself to death, I s'pose."

Cornelius blinks. Sophronia was a belle at his wedding reception; for the second time in a week he feels a tightening in his chest, for someone who died unexpectedly. But he remembers how swollen Sophronia looked at Stephanie's funeral. John Barleycorn had her in his tight embrace, even then.

"Master Emile, he put the body in a fine, fine coffin, and says he was takin' it to New Orleans, so Miss Sophronia could be buried next her husband Mister Johnson. But I told him Miss Sophronia always said Mister Johnson warn't dead, he just run off to sea. But Master Emile says never mind, he'd find the body if he had to go through every cemetery in New Orleans. Bodies in New Orleans ain't hard to find, he says; they bury 'em up out of the ground in boxes, is what he said, if you can believe such a thing. So he took the body on the steamboat, and stayed gone a month or more. I dunno if he ever fount Mister Johnson, though."

"Where's Mister Emile now?"

"Oh, he back in Natchez, now. He still ridin' up and down the streets. Sometime he come home at night, sometime he don't. I think he sleeps in the woods." She looks out the door. "But since he come back from New Orleans, he says he don't need no big household, with all his people gone. And he keeps talkin' about Miss Josephine and Miss Stephanie and Miss Sophronia. He says he is all alone in the world now, he gonna stay that way. So--," she sighs, "he said he was gonna get rid of ever'body here but me. And he did." Her voice changes. "He sold Theresa and Helene to some ole lady in Louisiana. I don't even know where my girls is, sir. That's the worse part. And he took Sarah and Daisy and her babies -- her youngest warn't but three -- and took 'em to that *place.* I can't even make m'self say the name of it. That place over by the Forks of the Road --"

Franklin and Armfields.

"-- an' he sold 'em off. Israel's workin' in some rice field somewheres, sold to a rice planter. And Rob and Charlie was sent down the river. Charlie so sad 'bout losing Daisy and his babies, he couldn't hardly walk when they took him down to the boat. Rob had to hold him up. And it's just me here now, sir. Master Emile, he say he just need one slave-woman to run the place, and that be me. He say he gonna turn the house over to the goats. And he did. They go in and out, eatin' the stuffin' out o' the sofas and the curtains off the windows."

Cornelius walks to the door and looks out at the big, dark house. Inside are the rooms where he sat with Emile and discussed his marriage, and where important people came to congratulate him and Stephanie.

Esther continues, "If you leave Jenny here, Master Emile'll sell her off. I know he will. He'll get her some papers, and then she'll go to the slave market."

"Jenny won't ever go to the slave market."

"The thing is, you just don't know. I'm gonna be at that slave market someday. I know I am. If Master Emile was to die, who'd keep me? Somebody buy this place, they'd sell off an old woman like me. I know it."

Jenny sags against the wall. Esther speaks again. "The only way you can save li'l Jenny from the slave market is if you take her to the free soil and free 'er yourself. Then she be free, and saved."

"I can't do that," Cornelius says.

"Better that than the slave market," Esther says.

"I can't send Jenny away, young as she is. She can't be put out on her own like that. The reason I brought her here was because I thought you'd take care of her."

"I can't take care of her, you kin see that. But she have her whole life ahead of her. She's a seamstress. She can make her own way."

Cornelius looks at Jenny. Her face is turned away from him, her forehead against the wall. She's a grown young woman wearing Stephanie's wedding dress. It doesn't hang on her as it would have a year ago; she fills it. She's no longer a child. But to free her?

Well, there are free blacks right here in Natchez. Some, bright as any penny, work as janitors or carpenters or laborers; most of these, some old master fathered and then set free to work their whole lives away. Those born with darker skins have it worse. But the master gets a clear conscience and goes to his maker thinking well of himself.

But attitudes are hardening in Natchez; Cornelius senses it. The hated word *abolition* is in the air. And a paper called the *Liberator* is full of ideas that scare everyone. There are already laws on the books. Free blacks have to report to the police to prove their good behavior, or they can be shipped out of the state. An inquisition might be coming for Natchez's free blacks. And Jenny would be alone, a young girl, and without a bright skin.

"Jenny, we'll go back home," Cornelius says.

Esther watches from the kitchen door as Cornelius and Jenny walk around the side of the house and out into the sunlight. Then she goes over to the big house, mincing as if every step will shatter her bones. Ignoring a goat which stands on one side of the door, she goes inside and climbs the stairs to the second floor. In the upstairs hall, she walks past Emile's room and Stephanie's room, both open to the goats. Her feet make little whispery sounds on the floor, and balls of dust dance alongside her skirt.

In an empty bedroom at the back of the house, she sits on the side of the high bed, her feet not reaching the floor. She spends most of every day in this room, ignoring the goat-stench; she keeps the door closed to keep the animals out. Dust coats the cream-painted baseboards and lines the curve of the spinning wheel that sits in one corner. Sometimes, in the quietness, Esther thinks she can almost hear the old jenny sing, a sound she remembers from her childhood.

Her ghosts Littleton and August are here. She's lost her girls, but her boys hover around all the time.

"Now Mamma, you need to get some *rest*," August says. "Let's pull this cover up and keep you warm."

Esther lies down on the bed. The silk counterpane smells old and dusty.

"It was *cool* last night," Littleton says.

Esther breathes deeply. The fragrance of the room reminds her of Miss Josephine.

Littleton and August will watch over her while she sleeps. When Theresa and Helene were here, she shooed those boys away whenever they appeared. But she needs her boys now. They're a comfort to her.

In the afternoon Hattie walks out of the cabin onto the porch, puffing on her pipe and cradling Thomas. A sound along the road catches her attention. But no one is coming.

She sits on the rocking chair and opens the bodice of the aqua-colored dress she put on in the morning. After Thomas finishes nursing, she puts him down in his basket under the tree and goes on with her washing, hanging each dripping dress from the line and smoothing the wide skirts.

These are wonderful fabrics -- such a tight, heavy weave on the black dress, such a lightness in the skirt she now wears, with a little rosette sewn tightly into every gather. Brushing her fingers across the fabrics, she feels a thrill of ambition; she can see herself looking elegant in these dresses, gone to town of a weekday. Adelaide Halloran and her bony girls, and the town ladies in their sunbonnets: won't they think she's fine, now? That lazy Jenny didn't take the time to lower the hems, so she'll have to do it herself, now that the black girl is gone.

After she finishes hanging the dresses Thomas cries again, and she picks him up. Some new rustle comes through the woods, along the road. She walks out to the porch and looks. No one there. She carries the baby out to the back porch and sits there while he nurses again. When he's finished she tamps her pipe down and carries him into the cabin, where a man in a black suit is waiting.

CHAPTER THIRTY-SEVEN

The steamboat *Friendship* lies low in the water at Natchez-Under-The-Hill, her white hull gleaming. Passengers straggle aboard as threads of smoke rise from her twin smokestacks. The flat ferryboat slips away from the dock next to the steamer and moves out into the river toward Vidalia.

"There it goes," Cornelius says as he drives the buggy down to the bottom of Silver Street. "We missed it."

"It'll come back." Jenny fans herself with one hand: the afternoon sun beats down out of a cloudless sky. Beads of perspiration stand on her forehead.

"Be a wait, though." Cornelius glances at her. "Let's get something to drink."

He stops in the shade of a tree near the landing and they climb down. He takes off his coat and loosens his tie. He walks with Jenny over to a well nearby and they drink from the bucket there, taking turns with the gourd-dipper. Then they go back to the shade. Jenny sits down and leans back against the tree trunk, her knees pulled up.

She stares at the river.

"You couldn't stay with Esther," he says, thinking of the sad scene they left at Carefree.

"No sir."

A loud, shrill whistle sounds from the *Friendship*. A last woman passenger stops at the ticket booth, then dashes up the gangplank before the deckhands pull it up.

A moment later the steamer begins to move away from the dock as the sidewheels churn the water. The boat glides into the stream, straightening in the channel and heading downriver.

"I wish I was going with it," Cornelius says.

"Where's it goin'?"

"New Orleans. The last time I was in New Orleans I counted seventeen steamboats, just like that one, all docked right there at the foot of Canal Street."

"These steamboats ever go north?"

"They all go north, sooner or later."

Jenny wipes perspiration from her lip with her finger. "Israel wanted to go north, but he got his foot chopped off for wantin' it."

"What?"

"I believe I'll get another drink of water." She gets up and walks to the well.

He watches her walk away, dark in the bright yellow dress. Would she always be a little mystery to him, his Jenny?

"Why the hell'd you say that?" he asks. But she's too far away to hear him.

The intruder, as tattered a tramp as Hattie has ever seen, stands in the middle of the room. Even from here she can smell the whiskey on his breath. Well, she'll give him a bowl of cornbread, like she would to any tramp, but he'll have to sit on the back steps to eat it, and then be on his way.

"Stephanie. Look at you," he says, holding out his hand. "You just the way I knew you'd be if you married him. And you did, and it all came out the worse, just like I knew it would."

Hattie is angry that this stranger's come so bold into her house. A woman has to watch out for tramps, even way out here. And this one's more forward than most, but she'll stand up to him.

"Who are you, and what is it you want?" Her pipe bobs in her mouth.

His eyes are earnest and sad. "The last time I saw you in that dress, you were so pretty. *Tres belle.* The dress with the rosettes, ordered from New Orleans. And look at it now." He has a hoarse, accented voice. "And you have a babe, too, Stephanie?"

Hattie steps backward, looking out through the door to see if Malachi is getting up to chase away this wild man. But the door of the little house is closed; he's probably still sleeping off his fever.

"You get on out of here," she says. "My name ain't Stephanie, it's Hattie, and I don't know fer a dime who you are."

"Don't you think I'd know my own daughter? You know your old Papa. Let me see your hands. Tell me Carson ain't ruined your beautiful hands." He lurches at her and seizes her arms.

"You ain't my Papa! You get on out of here." She steps back against the wall.

"Don't say that, girl."

"Is you Stephanie's Papa? Stephanie's dead, don't you know that?" A pulsing red fear comes into Hattie's brain; the man's too close. He presses her against the pine boards.

"*Mais non,* you ain't dead. You come on back to Natchez wit' me."

Hattie pushes back at him. "I ain't goin' nowhere," she says, her voice wobbling. If only she could scream for Malachi, get the stupid slave up to help her. He's her only help. Except for Malachi, she's alone. And her voice is failing her.

The baby, crushed between them, begins to scream. The man's face is right next her own.

"Esther told me you came back to Natchez to see me," he says, his gaze sweeping her face as if studying it. "She didn't want to tell me, but I kept asking her, and finally she did. How you came back, and left the same day. How you wouldn't stay, with the cholera there. You couldn't even wait to see to your old Papa, Esther said." His voice cracks. "And on the way back, the storm hit. Oh, it was bad, all right. The wind knocked the cupola right off the Elenora house. One minute they had a cupola, the next minute they didn't." He laughs.

The baby begins to slip from Hattie's grip, and her pipe clatters to the floor.

"But the more I thought about it, I knew you wasn't really dead. You couldn't be. You came back to Carefree to see me. It wasn't you we buried. I knew it. It was somebody else got caught in the flood. 'Twasn't you."

"It was Stephanie that drownt in the flood," Hattie squawks. "She's dead, and now Cornelius is married to me." She tries to stand tall against the wall. "See. This here is our baby, name of Thomas. You see how he looks like Cornelius, with his hair and all. See how long he is. Looks like me, too, some." Her voice comes back, but she sees the flatness in the man's eyes. "I ain't Stephanie. I'm Hattie. Stephanie's dead and buried."

She lowers Thomas to the floor as gently as she can, fearing the man's bulk will crush the baby's soft head.

But he puts his face close to hers. "No! Not dead! That's why I come out here, to take you back to Carefree. Where you'll be safe."

"I can't go and leave my baby," she whimpers.

All at once Emile releases his grip. She wants to run, but the wild man is so close to the baby lying on the floor; who knows what he might do?

"Look at you," he says in a soft voice. "He's turned you into a black-tooth country woman. He's made you hard. He's changed you." He stands back.

"Oh, I'm changed all right," she says, moving an inch along the wall toward the door. If only she dared to reach down and pick Thomas up off the floor. "Changed fer good."

He grabs her again, stepping right over the wailing baby. "Not for good! I'll take you back! I'll make you like you were before. You'll be my *tres belle* Stephanie again." He twists her arm behind her; pain shoots to her shoulder and makes her stumble through the door.

"No, wait, don't take me away! My baby!"

"Leave the brat."

"Malachi," she calls, hopelessly, as her voice fails her again.

Malachi wakes with water running down his face, and his first thought is that he'll get his bed wet. In Alabama, his bed was a pine board, and he had another board for a pillow. The rain came in on him and Lula like this, washing their faces when it began without warning in the night. And Lula would jump up, whimpering because their precious sleep was broken, when they had to be at the fields so early.

But here Master Cornelius gave him a cotton pillow. Where's Lula now?

His head swims with a thousand images. He thinks Lula is in the room with him, watching. "You a sick man," she's saying, her face winking in and out behind his closed yellow eyes. "You like to die, Malachi." Her voice is the sound of a whipporwill.

He doesn't want to die. He swings himself up, saying "Lula--", and then tries not to put his foot into the mess he made on the floor. He opens the door. He'll get help. Maybe Lula's over there, in the cabin, but is he in Alabama?

Or is he in Louisiana? Master Cornelius will help him.

But in the doorway he stops, hanging onto the wall for support. And over there in front of the cabin is a man with Miss Hattie.

And there's a kind of dance between them, as they pull this way and that.

But his gorge rises, black on the ground, and he turns and goes back to his bed. The room spins. He has to lie down.

He closes his eyes as Lula's kind face appears again. She's good to him, that woman. He's content to lie here now, in his misery, and take comfort in Lula's face.

Emile pushes Hattie across the yard and pins her against the horse while he fumbles in his saddlebag. Over his shoulder she sees the door to the little house open, then close again.

She wants to push against him, but he holds her arm twisted behind her. Forced to press her face to the horse's side, she can smell its alien aroma, hear its heavy breathing, feel the saddle creasing into her cheek.

The man has a gun. Its black metallic snout is aimed at her as she twists, ignoring the agony of her arm, and she breaks it to be free of that strong grip. She runs for the cabin, her legs tangling in her skirt. Something is coming for her, whiter than her fears, and its sound is louder than Thomas's screams. The ground comes up to touch her face, and she smells the fragrance of the grass, and the rich decent aroma of earth. Her own heartbeat is in her ears, an irregular drumming that slows, flutters up again, then stills. The last thing she hears is the baby's high-pitched wail, a screech louder than what has been up until now the beating of her own heart.

CHAPTER THIRTY-EIGHT

"Where'd you come from, Jenny?"
"What?"

The road passes between straggly blackberry bushes. Once in awhile they can see cabins nestled up against the woods. Tearose's easy gait lulls them, and the sun has gone under a rising bank of clouds. The reins rest loosely in Cornelius's hands.

"Where'd you come from, before I got you?"

"I don't know."

"How'd you lose your brother, Kofi? Was he with you?"

"Yes sir. He got lost from me right after we got off the boat." Jenny looks straight ahead.

"He got lost?"

"Well, somebody took him."

"Where -- what place was that?"

"I don't know, sir. Some place."

Cornelius lets the horse pull the buggy at its own gait.

"When they took us off the ship, we couldn't stand up." Jenny stares straight ahead. "None of us could. Everybody was staggerin' around, even puttin' their hands down on the ground like three-legged dogs. It was night, dark as anything, and some men had torchlights. They laughed at us. We thought it was some crazy place they brought us to, where the ground jumped." Her fingers punch wells in the smooth yellow fabric of her skirt. "Kofi was whimperin' about that when they took him away."

"Did you know you were coming to Mississippi?"

Jenny glances at him. "Yessir. I knew pretty quick. I heard them say it when they carried me over and put a collar on me." She reaches up and touches the old scar. "I heard 'em say 'Mississippi,' so I knew where I was goin'."

"And then that's where they took you."

"Yessir." She stares straight ahead, chewing on her lip.

In a dreary brown twilight they come to the settlement. The buildings are dark in the dusk. A group of men and women are standing on the sidewalk in front of the hotel.

Cornelius pulls the horse to a stop when he recognizes Amos and Margaret McKee. When Margaret sees him she puts her hand over her mouth and runs toward his buggy with a baby bouncing on her hip. "Cornelius! Cornelius Carson!"

"Well, Margaret! What on earth?" He looks curiously at the fretting baby she carries. "Is that Thomas? Oh, it is. Here, I'll take him. Where's Hattie?" The other men and women move closer to them.

Margaret hands him the baby and puts her hand to her chest, panting. "Oh, Cornelius, what's happened – it's awful!"

His house has seen too much grieving for such a small cabin, Cornelius thinks as he watches Daniel Vane hoist one end of the pine coffin that holds Hattie's body, and Pless Halloran takes the other end. They set it on the wagon to carry it to a little square of earth that's been dug to receive it, just out of sight of the cabin.

A preacher's come from Slocum to read the words over Hattie, and while he's at it he puts in a call for vengeance against the murderer as well.

Looking around at the sad little group that stands at the graveside, Cornelius feels something shift, in his soul. Hattie's gone, taken away from these people; it's a change that breaks hearts, but all life is, is changes. Cornelius can see it everywhere. Daniel Vane doesn't seem like the hard-drinking backwoodsman Cornelius had thought he was. He must've turned to religion after Hattie got married and moved away. In his black frock coat and hat he looks as sober a Methodist as one might find in these woods. But his face is so pulled down with sorrow that Cornelius tries not to look at him. Hattie's brothers and sisters are there, except for one who happens to be lying in childbed this very day. Sayra, that is. Another change.

Amos and Margaret McKee are here, and Euphonia. Margaret holds Thomas, who sleeps soundly. Next to Margaret stands Jenny, wearing the black crepe dress she took off the clothesline last night; it doesn't fit well and it's too hot for this humid day, but she said the color was right for a funeral. Malachi, still feverish, lies in his bed in the little house.

Pless Halloran and all the Halloran women are here; the bony shabby girls are only younger versions of Adelaide. Ruetta wears a secret smirk that Cornelius ignores. Behind her stands Alice Turley, looking old.

By the time the prayers are finished, the coffin sounds with the thump of raindrops; heavy clouds have hung over the Cocodrie all morning, and now the air smells of rain. Hattie's brothers Primus and Tertius shovel dirt onto the coffin, coal-black spots of rain speckling the shoulders of their coats before they have the hole filled.

Later Cornelius stands on his porch with the other mourners. Margaret McKee holds the baby to her chest, his legs splayed out frog-like, her arms circling his back and bottom. She tells again how she found the baby.

"I come over at three o'clock to see about gettin' some eggs, and soon as I got in the yard I seen poor Hattie, crumpled up right over there." Next to her, Hattie's sisters Nett and June stand in silence. Together they look toward the place in the yard where Hattie had lain.

"And I could see there weren't nothing I could do for her, but I ran over here to the cabin, and I found Thomas lyin' on the floor all by hisself, mosquito-bitten, dirty as a pig, and screamin' his head off. The only person on the place was Malachi, and he was sleepin' so hard I thought I'd never wake him. He said he'd been sick. So then I rode home fast as I could, and got Mister McKee."

There's a kind of ceremony telling what happened, Cornelius knows; Margaret had a big part in the drama. But all she wanted was to be a friend to Hattie.

"Can you keep Thomas for awhile?" Cornelius asks Margaret.

"Oh, sure I can." She puts her cheek down on the baby's red head. "Euphonia and me are enjoyin' him. And my girl Mildred's got a new baby, so she don't mind feedin' Thomas too. Two's no more trouble than one. I know she'll be pleased to keep on doin' it, especially if you'll pay her for it."

As the mourners begin to drift away to leave, Amos says in a low voice, "Cornelius, did you hear about Emile Coqterre?"

Cornelius is startled to hear the name. "What about him?"

"They found him floating in the river south of Natchez. Jumped from the cliff, somebody said. Been dead a whole day."

A year later, when summer changed to fall, crisp clean days that smelled of smoke, and that in turn wound down to winter days as gray as Malachi's head, Cornelius still has a sense of change coming. Malachi grows quieter and quieter as he sits with Cornelius in the evenings, sipping whiskey. And Thomas is a red-haired stranger Cornelius visits on Sundays; the boy toddles about the McKees' wide gallery and looks curiously at the tall man who brings him sweets and bounces him on his knee.

On a mild, breezy day in January, Cornelius and Jenny drive the cotton-wagon to the gin with the last of the year's cotton crop. As the gin master counts out the money into Cornelius's hand, he says genially, "Mister Carson, you've done right well this last season."

"Yes sir."

This last season, Cornelius's mind repeats. There seems to be a symmetry about the thought; it doesn't sadden him. He has a sense of time being right for change, and of himself ripe for it, too.

The next week Cornelius, Jenny and Malachi drive over to see Thomas, and take him for a ride in the buggy, which the boy, who loves horses, enjoys. As they pass by the settlement they notice a new business that's gone up alongside the road, next to the little store and the merchant's house. A sign over the door says "Photographer."

Daguerrotypes are tacked onto the front of the building and in the windows.

"Let's go have a look," Cornelius says to Malachi while Jenny changes Thomas's sopping diaper. The two men walk over to study the images of country people. There are portraits of husbands and wives, family groups, blurry-faced babies who can't sit still, an old soldier in his uniform from the War of 1812. The faces stare unblinking from each frame. In a few minutes Jenny comes over with Thomas on her hip.

Studying the plain faces, Cornelius realizes that although portraits of Emile Coqterre and Josephine hang on the walls at Carefree, where the goats can't reach them, he owns no likeness of Stephanie, or of Hattie either. Thomas will never know his own mother's face. A daguerrotype could hold time still, in a world of change.

"Let's get our picture made," Cornelius says. "It's cheap enough, twenty-five cents each."

"All right, sir," Mal mumbles.

"Not me," Jenny says, hefting Thomas to her shoulder. "This look like witchery to me, the way the pictures just stay put. No sir. I don't want t' do that."

"It'll be something new to try."

"Not me, sir. I ain't doin' it."

But you're brave, Cornelius thinks, watching her settle Thomas into the crook of her arm. *You just don't know it yet.*

That night he sits drinking whiskey on the porch steps with Malachi. Jenny works nearby, washing the big pot where she'd boiled some crabs. She wears her yellow dress and her back curves under the fabric as she swings the tub over to let it drain.

The two banana trees Stephanie planted -- so long ago, it seemed – are now spindly and yellow, and sagging against the fence. Beyond the banana trees, at a corner of the woods where some palmettos grow, is an unpainted picket fence. Hattie's grave.

"I think I'll go live in Natchez," Cornelius says to Malachi, but speaking loudly enough for Jenny to hear.

She straightens and looks at him. "In *Natchez*?"

"I believe we'd do just as well there," Cornelius says.

"Yes sir, I believe we might," Malachi answers. His answer is meaningless, Cornelius knows; he agrees to anything now.

"I need to get Thomas back from the McKee's before he starts thinking he belongs to them, and before they start thinking it too. He already thinks Margaret's his mother."

"Yes sir," Mal mumbles.

"He's old enough to be weaned. Jenny can look after him while I hire out to work."

Malachi is quiet for a minute. Then he says, "Awright. I never had no chilrun of my own, and never been around chilrun, that much. But I reckon Jenny can learn to raise Thomas. Hell, it can't be that hard to raise a young'un. Any old mammy can do it. Jenny can learn it."

Looking over at Jenny, who laughs, Cornelius laughs too.

That night the men sit on the steps while Jenny sits alone under the elm tree, her sewing in her lap. Cornelius brings a table out and sets the lantern on it.

"What kind of work you gonna do in Natchez?" Malachi asks.

"I've been a boilerman and I've planted cotton. There's always something a strong back can do."

"Long as it stays strong," Malachi says, looking down at the horny light-colored palms of his hands.

Cornelius feels a swell of sympathy for the old man. "I'll take care of you, Mal," he says.

The next week Cornelius drives to Slocum in the early morning; he'd promised Nett he'd bring Hattie's things over, so her sisters can divide them. When he passes through the settlement in the late afternoon, he suddenly remembers the daguerrotypes he'd had made the week before.

He pays the photographer seventy-five cents and carries the pictures outside. The image of himself is a shock; he normally sees his face only in the looking glass when he shaves each morning. But the camera sees more; the angles of his face, the stern set of his jaw, his square chin. The sun has put crows' feet around his eyes; even though he stares straight at the camera, the sunburst of lines remains. *Well, I'm getting older,* he thinks. And the picture of Malachi is a shock too; it looks nothing like the old man. The other picture is of Jenny, wary of the photographer, and Thomas, a little blurry because he wouldn't sit still. He tucks the three pictures into his saddlebag, thinking that Jenny and Malachi will be as interested in the pictures as he is.

As he rides up to his cabin he sees that Amos McKee's buggy is parked in front of the porch. He dismounts as Amos and Margaret stride over from the little house, with Malachi following.

"Cornelius, I've got bad news to tell you." Amos's expression is grim. "It's about Jenny--"

"What is it?"

Amos glances back at Malachi. His voice is low. "She -- well, she got into a fight with Adelaide Halloran. Jenny beat her with her fists, Adelaide swears. Adelaide's got a black eye and some yanked-out hair, and her nose is broke. And Jenny's got a busted lip. Pless and Adelaide went and got the sheriff, and he came and took Jenny to the jail in Vidalia."

"To jail?" Cornelius repeats. "Why would Jenny--"

"She says when she came up from the fields Adelaide was in her room." Amos gestures toward the little house, where Jenny's door stands open, which is uncommon. "She says she had some money saved from her sewing, and Adelaide was in her room, pawing through her things, and stole her money. So Jenny went at her." Amos kicks at a clod of dirt. "She could hang for it," he says. "I'm sorry, Cornelius."

Margaret wipes her eyes with a handkerchief. "Now, why would Jenny do that?"

Cornelius turns away. He goes into Jenny's room. The bed is pushed out of place, Jenny's sewing bag lying open in the middle of the room, and her dresses thrown in a heap on the floor. "It's been ramsacked," Cornelius says.

"She might hang," Amos says, "especially, the way things are now."

"I'm going over to Vidalia," Cornelius says. "I've got to take care of this."

"You want me to go with you?"

Cornelius shakes his head.

Amos climbs up onto his buggy. "I'm sorry," he says, shaking the reins. Then he drives away.

Cornelius strides toward the barn, scattering chickens as he walks.

She might hang. Amos's words ring in his ears. He remembers another trip to the Vidalia jail, and Lafayette's body, swinging from a tree. He forces the image from his mind.

"Master Cornelius?" Malachi's voice is quavery. Turning around, Cornelius can see the worry in the old man's furrowed face. Since his illness, Malachi has gotten much feebler, his frame shrunken. "They ain't really gonna hang li'l Jenny, is they?"

"No. You go on back and rest."

"Yes sir." The old man shuffles away, his shoulders slumped.

Cornelius goes to the back of the barn, where he keeps his strongbox. A blanket covers it. He yanks off the cloth and raises the lid. He reaches in to grab a leather bag filled with paper money.

Bribery is a possibility. He'll save Jenny with this money if he can. He goes back to his horse and opens the saddle-bag. He takes the daguerrotypes out and drops the money-bag into the pouch. Then he goes into the cabin, where he tosses the pictures onto the bed and takes his small pistol from the chest of drawers. He sticks it into his belt.

He swings up on Tearose and gallops down the road. The horse splashes across the curling stream, sending a mist of silver drops hanging for an instant in the still air.

She might hang. Amos's words have the sound of inevitability, and they ring in Cornelius's mind. *The way things are now.*

No. He touches the pistol tucked under his coat.

Clouds scud across a blue-on-lavender sky that's turning to ink. Cornelius, squinting to make out the direction of the road, spurs the tired horse. Its hooves sound like drumbeats.

It's long after midnight when he sees a sprinkle of lights through the limbs of willows, and on the far bank the lights of Natchez melting on the water.

The jail in Vidalia is a log building about ten feet square, behind a live oak tree on the edge of town. A low lamp glimmers from the front porch of the jail. Cornelius stops a little ways off and ties Tearose to a tree. He can see the jailer sitting on a chair tipped back against the wall. The man's head is down on his chest, and a rifle lies across his knees.

In the darkness Cornelius lopes toward the building, where a low light shines through a barred window. He creeps toward the window, cursing under his breath as a branch crackles under his boots.

He peers through the window. Jenny is sitting on a narrow wooden bench against the wall, her hands folded in her lap. She stares straight ahead at the closed door. A lantern flickers light across the room. A thick rope is looped around her neck and fastened to an iron ring chinked into the wall. She has to sit upright or choke herself.

On the porch the jailer snorts, whistles, and begins to breathe more heavily. Taking one tortuous step at a time, Cornelius inches around the side of the building.

Standing just outside the circle of light thrown by the jailer's lantern, Cornelius takes the gun from his belt, then reconsiders and replaces it. The man snores in slow deep breaths. His mouth hangs half-open; shifting in the chair, he throws his head back against the wall without opening his eyes.

Crossing the porch in two long strides, Cornelius reaches down and seizes the man's gun. There's a crash as the jailer wakens instantly and lunges forward, his chair rattling out from under him.

"Wha--a--at?"

Then his eyes grow wide as he finds himself staring up the barrel of his own gun.

"Don't make a sound." Cornelius's voice is low. Slowly the jailor's hands go up.

"Open it." Cornelius jerks his head toward the door.

"Yes sir. Yes sir." The jailer stumbles to his feet and reaches to his belt for his jangling ring of keys.

His hands shake as he tries to cram the key into the lock. On the third try he makes it. Then he swings the door open.

Cornelius aims the gun at the man's belly and motions him into the room. As the door bursts open, Jenny's eyes flash white.

"Untie her," Cornelius says.

"Yessir."

Cornelius keeps the gun levelled. He's prepared to leave the man incarcerated or dead. He has no other options in mind.

The jailer reaches behind Jenny to unfasten the heavy rope.

"Hurry up," Cornelius snaps.

"I am hurryin'."

As the rope falls loose Jenny jumps up and runs through the open door. The jailer looks at Cornelius in consternation.

"Why you freein' her? She your nigger? She beat up a white woman. She--"

"You say one more word it'll be your last. Sit down."

The jailer sinks heavily onto the bench.

"I'm gonna leave you quiet," Cornelius says, backing toward the door. He aims the rifle level at the man. "I can leave you locked up and quiet, or I can leave you dead and quiet."

"Yessir, yessir," the jailer whispers. "I'll be quiet."

"I don't want to hear a single noise while I'm in hearing range and that's longer than you think," Cornelius says. "Or I'll come back."

"Yessir."

Cornelius blows out the lantern and closes the door on the man's round frightened face. He locks the door and puts the key in his pocket. The lantern on the porch hisses; he blows it out too.

As his eyes adjust to the darkness he sees Jenny a little distance away. He runs toward her.

"Let's go," he says, taking her by the elbow and propelling her toward the horse. He swings up onto the horse and pulls her up behind him.

A half-mile outside of Vidalia Cornelius guides the horse onto a narrow path he can just make out in the darkness. By the skeleton of a large dead tree, he stops. They both jump down and he ties the horse.

This is a low boggy area. "Go over to the river," Cornelius says. "Run." He carries the rifle.

They splatter down the path across some low puddles. After they push through the reeds, they come suddenly to the water's edge. Across the river, a steamer is docked at Natchez-Under-The-Hill.

The river laps along the bank. At a distance down the bank on this side they can see a campfire flickering.

Cornelius stops suddenly and hands her the rifle. "Wait here."

He walks quickly toward the campfire. "Hello!" he calls from some distance away.

The camper stands up as Cornelius comes out of the darkness toward him.

"'Mornin', stranger," the man says.

Cornelius nods his greeting. "I need to get across the river. How much to rent your boat?" He points to the skiff the man has pulled up onto the riverbank.

"Well, I weren't plannin' to hire it out, least ways not this morning--"

"Five dollars if you let me rent it for two hours, and if you don't say a word to anybody who asks. You can pick it up on the other side."

Cornelius sees that this Louisiana man understands the needs of a fugitive.

He stares at Cornelius. "Seven dollars and you can rent her, and my mouth is shut tight."

Cornelius hands him the money and then pushes the boat out into the river. He leans hard into each stroke as he rows along the shoreline. Jenny is waiting a dozen yards away.

"Let's go," he says. She clambers in and sits down facing him, her knees up under her chin. She lays the gun in the bottom of the boat. Cornelius pulls on the oars, leaning into each stroke.

"Where are we goin'?" she asks.

"See that steamboat over there?" In the darkness the big steamer looks like a white ghost; smoke streams from its twin smokestacks. Suddenly a shrill blast comes from its whistle. We've got fifteen minutes, Cornelius thinks. On the boat the boilerman will be furiously feeding logs into the firebox. The heat from the box would be sheening his face with sweat.

When they reach the center of the river, he says, "Throw that gun over." Jenny picks up the rifle and upends it into the water. He pulls the jailhouse key from his pocket and flips it in on the other side.

He rows hard, pulling against the current. The night is mild and still; dawn is still an hour away. It seems almost peaceful out here on the river. For a minute, as the wind stirs against his face, he blinks, thinking the woman in the yellow gown is Stephanie, in her wedding dress, and he can save her; and then she's Hattie. But then he remembers: Jenny.

"What did Adelaide steal from you?"

"All my money I got from sewing."

"Well, how much was it?"

"Thirty-two dollars."

"That's a lot. But not enough to get hanged over."

"I was saving it up to buy my freedom."

"That's not enough to buy your freedom."

"I know, but I figured if I saved long enough, you'd let me go even if I didn't have enough."

"You know what they were going to do with you?"

"Yessir. They told me."

"Weren't you afraid?"

"Not if I had to be a slave forever. Might as well die."

Jenny's face was a dark oval. The brown cliff looms behind her. The steamboat hoots again. *Ten minutes,* Cornelius thinks.

Behind him dogs bark. The jailer must have shouted an alarm.

They scrape up onto the riverbank under the bluff. Cornelius ties the skiff to a log and Jenny scrambles out, holding her skirt up as she wades through the shallow water.

"Where are we goin'?" she asks as they scramble along the base of the hill.

"I'm not going anywhere. If we can catch that steamer, I'm putting you on it, headed for free soil."

She stumbles, falling headfirst across a vine that knotted the path. "The free soil," she says, scrambling to her feet.

The steamer hoots again. Five minutes.

"Unless we miss the boat."

Jenny runs toward the lights of Under-The-Hill, which peep in and out of view. Another hoot.

In Under-The-Hill a piano tinkles. The big boat pulls at its tow lines like a straining bull in a harness.

At the edge of the town Jenny sinks, holding her side. "I can't run no more."

"You've got to," Cornelius says. Up ahead, at the ticket booth, the ticketmaster is just lowering the flap on his window. Cornelius sprints over.

"One deck-passenger for Cincinnati," he says, panting.

The man hands over the ticket. "You nearly missed it," he says as Cornelius hands him a ten-dollar bill.

"Nearly."

Jenny, holding her side, limps over to him. "Here's your ticket," he says. Bending over as she tries to catch her breath, she takes the small green stub.

"Now let me give you your freedom."

"What?"

"Your emancipation." He slaps his pocket. "But I don't have anything to write on." He raps on the window of the ticket booth. The man inside raises the flap a few inches. "You got a piece of paper I could have?" After a moment -- it seems an eternity to Cornelius, who's watching the boat's smokestack belch darker streams of smoke now; three minutes, he thinks – the ticketmaster hands out a pencil and an old half-sheet of yellowed ledger paper.

Cornelius slaps the paper over in his hand and scribbles.

"Document of Emancipation. Be it known by these presents that Jenny--"

He stops. "You need a last name."

"What?"

"A free person's gotta have a last name. Hurry. Think of something. I've got to write it on here."

She looks toward the boat, then back to him. She shakes her head. "I don't know."

"Jenny Cornelius," he says. The deckhands are starting to untie some of the ropes that tether the big steamer. He writes, "Be it known by these presents that Jenny Cornelius is a free person. Now and Forevermore. /s/ Cornelius Carson."

The deckhands are moving toward the gangplank.

"Run," he says. "Don't get off 'til Cincinnati. Remember that. Can you say it?"

They run to the bottom of the gangplank. "Cincinnati," he says.

"Cin-cin-nati," she repeats.

"That's free soil. Don't get off 'til you get there, no matter what. And if anybody asks you, show 'em this paper. But don't turn it loose."

"Yessir." She takes the paper and looks at it. "I can't read."

"I couldn't teach you everything. But this paper says you're free. Do not lose it. And here's some money. You got someplace you can keep it?"

"Yes sir." She takes the money and her eyes flash as she sees how many bills he hands her.

"This'll get you started. Three hundred dollars. You can find work as a seamstress up there," he says.

She stuffs the money into the bodice of her dress and runs up the gangplank. The deckhands are waiting.

"Remember, Cincinnati!" he shouts from the bank below.

She stops on the gangplank and looks back. "Goodbye!" she calls. The deckhands look on curiously. Their hands are on the rope.

"Cincinnati!" he shouts. Then lower so no one can hear, he says, "Don't cry, Jenny girl. Nothing to be afraid of."

"Let's go, girl!" one of the deckhands shouts. She turns and runs up the gangplank, holding her wet skirts. A free woman.

The deckhands haul the gangplank up until it points straight up to the sky. The whistle hoots and the big craft moves away from the dock and out into the stream. It's the *John Jay*, Cornelius notices for the first time.

Jenny stands at the railing. The wind moves her skirt and her yellow dress is a beacon in the night.

The *John Jay*, her twin smokestacks billowing, her boiler vibrating the air with its powerful *whomp-whomp*, moves to the middle of the river. The water behind the wheels boils into bits of silver that melt into the current. Then the big boat rights its course and moves upriver stately as a dowager. The banks are dark except for a few dim lights over at Vidalia on the left and the lights of Natchez-Under-The-Hill on the right. Cornelius stands on the bank and watches until the steamer vanishes around the bend in the river and the billows of smoke have blown away into the darkness.

At mid-day Cornelius returns to the Cocodrie. The cabin is dark, and Malachi's door is closed, although the door to Jenny's room still stands wide open.

He raps on Malachi's door. Malachi opens it, bleary-eyed.

"Let's go, Mal," Cornelius says. "I'm a hunted man, and we're heading for Texas. Get your things."

Mal blinks and says "Yes sir." He shuffles back into his room. Cornelius goes to the stable and retrieves the bag of gold coins, the rest of his money. He throws what belongings he can into the big trunk, which he and Mal wrestle onto the back of the buggy.

"Is Jenny comin' back?" Mal asks.

"No."

As he closes the door to the cabin for the last time, Cornelius is surprised that he feels no sadness at giving up his farm; he has a peacefulness about it. A January frost whitens the ground, and the time is right for going.

He drives to the McKee's place to get Thomas. He tells them he's decided to head out to Texas. He doesn't tell them the particulars, knowing they're better off not knowing what happened in Vidalia. The women quickly gather up Thomas's clothes and fold them into a bag. Euphonia kisses the boy goodbye, and Margaret dabs at tears, although Cornelius thinks Amos looks relieved to be handing over the toddler. Thomas shrieks and wriggles, but Malachi holds him tight.

"I'll write when I get to Texas. I'm gonna deed you my acreage," Cornelius says to Amos. "It'll be payment for keeping Thomas.

And go get my mule out of the field. You can have old Leopard as lagniappe. And take the cow and calf."

"I'll go get 'em later today," Phony says.

Cornelius pictures the long-faced spinster driving the animals home. She'd herd them down the road as naturally as if it were her everyday work.

He climbs up into the buggy. At the last minute, Phony says "Wait!" and runs into the house. When she comes out she hands Cornelius a book, Fielding's *Tom Jones,* as a parting gift.

On an impulse, he leans down from the buggy and kisses her on the lips, cupping his hand beneath her chin. "Marry me, Phony," he says, softly, smiling.

"*No,* I will not marry you, Cornelius Carson," she says, but he sees the glow that spreads over her face.

He holds up his finger. "Now, you've been asked," he says, grinning. "I'll write to you from Texas to see if you've changed your mind."

He clicks the reins while Malachi struggles to hold on to Thomas, and they drive away down the road.

They go west along familiar roads, through woods and then along lanes lined with blackberry bushes, between wide fields waiting for the new year's cotton seeds.

"Come on, now, Thomas, you a good boy, ain't you?" Malachi says time and again to soothe the boy, who whimpers and wriggles to get free. Mal holds Thomas's dress to keep the boy from lunging over the side of the buggy.

Change has come, Cornelius thinks. It can't be stopped, and there's no point thinking it could. The old man beside him, his shoulders slumping as he struggles with the boy, he'll be fading out of the scene before too many years go by. But Thomas'll be here, strong and feisty, and he'll outlast them all. Thomas might see the turn of the century.

After an hour they stop to rest and let the horse water at a stream.

Later, as they drive along between cotton fields, the baby yields to a light sleep, and Malachi settles him across his lap. Relief and fatigue are in the old man's eyes.

Thomas and Malachi must be the people who are meant to live with him, Cornelius thinks, for some reason he doesn't know. But he'll free Malachi when he gets settled in Texas; not in the rushed and desperate way he freed Jenny -- he thinks of her now, on her way to Cincinnati, headed for a life as a free woman -- but with Malachi, he'll do it proper, go to the lawyer's office and fill out the documents.

Malachi won't go anywhere, he thinks; at least not right off. But he might leave someday, knowing he's free; Cornelius will face that when he has to.

He hopes he never keeps another slave. In Vidalia he'd have sacrificed himself rather than keep Jenny in slavery, realizing how it endangered her. He'd had a conceit, that he was protecting Mal and Jenny, keeping them away from cruel hands. But he sees more clearly now: there's no protection in slavery. Not for them, and not for him, either.

He's almost thirty years old, and he's given up an old ambition, to grow rich in the Cocodrie country. That was a young man's dream, and Stephanie, whom he loved, and Hattie, whom he didn't, both had a part in it. He'd been made a widower twice over, and fathered a child, and kept and freed slaves. And now he's a fugitive.

In Texas he'll get a place to live and hire himself out to work. He has money -- nearly two thousand dollars in his pocket, profits from the cotton crop this year and in years past. The money will be a cushion until he gets set up. He'll write to Euphonia, tell her how he's doing. And for all he knows, he might get a letter back from her, saying she changed her mind.

He shakes the reins and Tearose trots faster. Beyond the willows up ahead is the Black River; a small settlement marks the ferry landing. He can see the ferry just pulling away from the dock on the other side. It'll be waiting to take them across when they get to the landing, and they're almost there.

THE END

Made in the USA
Columbia, SC
27 June 2025